Darragh

Natasha Murray

To Jill
Best Wishes
Natasha Murray
Dec 2022
♡

Prologue

"My tiny heart bleeds, brother, and it will not stop until I find you. I hear you call out in the night. I taste your salty tears as you cry for those you have lost. My spirit flies through the fields of Waterfall and skims the lakes and treetops beyond as I search for you. I will not rest until I find you. Be strong, Darragh, like the oak tree that gave us life. We are one; and when our souls reunite, we will laugh, dance, and sing again."

Chapter One

Two weeks early, Juliet Hearn had slid out of the womb and would have hit the bathroom floor had her Dad, Seth Hearn, not been there to catch her. She came into the world kicking and screaming at one minute past midnight, just as the year rolled over from 2020 to 2021. A whirlwind of snow hit the Waterfall West Estate, and the countryside around groaned and gritted its teeth. Another harsh winter had arrived.

Seth had wrapped Juliet in a clean towel and could not believe how his wee baby could yell so loudly. He had called for an ambulance, not wanting to cut the cord himself. The ambulance had taken a long time to arrive because of the snow. Juliet, despite her crying, was deemed fit and ready to take on the world. Jules, not wanting to go out into the snow, had refused to go to the hospital, and she had continued with her day as if nothing had happened.

Seth was amazed by Jules's strength and surprised that giving birth did not seem to slow her down. He adored her and admired her ability to cope with everything thrown at her. Their relationship was better than ever, and their love for each other deepened with each day that passed. Together they were invincible; no matter what it took, they would find their wee boy and bring him home.

DARRAGH

Darragh had been missing for nine months. They were both heartbroken. With sadness, Seth remembered holding Darragh for the first time, and he had to stop a tear from escaping; the pain of separation was too much to bear. Darragh would be walking and perhaps saying his first words by now. April 19, 2021 flashed in neon lights ahead - his second birthday, and it was a deadline in both their minds. If he wasn't found by then, all hope would be lost.

On the day of his abduction, Seth had rung his Granny in desperation to see what the spirit world had to say about the matter. Much to his horror, his eccentric grandparent had sighed and said that the spirits were confused and would get back to her as soon as they had a connection. All they could pass on to her was that Darragh was still alive and that he had been hidden somewhere in Cork. She muttered something about white noise and interference as if the spirit world were behind an old television set and their whispers muddled. Seth was thankful that their son was alive. The past nine months had been agony. In any spare moment, he and Jules drove around Cork, hoping they would see him. Every pram they saw containing a dark-haired boy with big brown eyes was carefully scrutinised, and the pain in their hearts increased as their search came to nothing.

Detective Inspector Lucy O'Leary, Seth's half-sister, assured them that the police were doing their very best to find Darragh. The day after he had been abducted, the police had told them the news that the white van used to take Darragh did not belong to travellers as they had first thought. The number plates had been copied. The traveller's van had been involved in a traffic accident a few days earlier and had been in a garage on the day of the kidnapping. The money bag in the car park was all new notes and sterile; no fingerprints had been left on the plastic packaging.

However, one ginger hair had been found within the bag, and this fragment of evidence was still being analysed. Because of Covid, all investigations had been slowed down to a snail's pace. Seth was desperate to think of a way to find his wee boy. He had promised Jules that Darragh would be home before his birthday and intended to keep his promise.

Having a feisty newborn to deal with was helping dull the pain of losing Darragh. Her beautiful blue eyes were a wonder when Juliet was still, which wasn't very often. For those brief moments, Jules thought that they might be bonding. For the most part, though, no matter how hard Jules tried to comfort and calm her, Juliet refused to comply, screamed, binge fed, and barely slept. Jules was exhausted and prayed to have just one good night's sleep.

Juliet was now eight weeks old, and Jules felt bad that she did not love her baby as she should. She never let her out of sight and had breast fed her constantly, hoping they might bond. *Perhaps one day, Juliet will love me when she walks and talks, and I can explain to her that I didn't mean to take the abortion pill. Perhaps she will forgive me. I just need to sleep for one night, and then I can think clearly again.*

The pregnancy had been difficult, and Jules had bled a lot. The excitement of being pregnant had vaporised and replaced with revolving anxiety in her mind that she would never see Darragh again. She had forgiven Seth for promising to find their boy the next day after he had been snatched. She didn't say anything to Seth, but she could see that this promise was tearing him apart. There was no getting away from it. Darragh had been taken because she had been careless. *If only I had stayed in the flat and not believed that Tom Stone would take us for a drive. I am a terrible mother.*

DARRAGH

Seth had rung the midwife for advice, desperate to find a solution to help Juliet settle. He had asked if it was normal for a newborn to cry so much. He was told their baby was missing being in the womb, and they should wrap Juliet up and ensure she was winded properly. Nothing seemed to work, and when Juliet, exhausted by her efforts to bring the roof down, finally fell asleep, it was a euphoric moment. The sound of silence was a beautiful thing but short-lived. Both Seth and Jules found themselves sleeping in their clothes, too exhausted to change, wash or eat properly. Their lives at the Old Barn had been changed beyond recognition.

***

Seth struggled to open his eyes. He could hear Juliet stirring in her new cot next to Darragh's. *She is going to cry. I know she is. I just have a few minutes before she does.* Jules was fast asleep next to him, and her head was under the covers. Just the top of her fine, curly, blonde hair was showing. This way of sleeping was new; he guessed she was doing her best to hide from the world. Lost beneath the covers, she was safe from the brutal world outside - she had been through a lot. He wanted her to sleep but knew she would have to wake to feed Juliet. Jules had decided to breastfeed her rather than bottle-feed. Seth missed giving Darragh his bottle. He sighed and looked at his phone; it was just before six. *I will take her into the front room and try to get her back to sleep. I swear, Jules was up at least five times in the night feeding our wee girl. This baby needs to give her a break. Surely she can't be hungry again? If only she could tell us what we need to do to make her happy.*

5

Seth got out of bed and went over to the cot. Juliet was rubbing her face with her mitten-covered hands. He could see that she was waking and was aware that her milk supply was in the room. *Can babies smell breast milk?* Gently, Seth picked her up. She was perfect, and when her eyes opened, he saw Jules's beautiful blue eyes looking back at him. There was something bewitching about Juliet, and he knew he would always be there for her. The last nine months had been a worrying time. Somehow, by some miracle, Juliet had hung on and refused to give up. *If only the toad Tom Stone had not given Jules those pills, then I am sure that we would have had a happy child.* A vision of Darragh's smiling face filled his mind, and he tried his best to shake this memory away, not wanting to remember. *I should remember him. How will I get him back if I don't remember what he looks like? I don't understand why Granny can't tell me where to look. The spirits helped me find him before. I will ring her today and see if she has seen anything more. Nine months is way too long to be missing.*

Seth sat on the sofa and looked around for Barney, their white cat. Usually, he would ask for food as soon as anyone was up. Since Juliet had arrived, he was spending all his time outside and was probably looking for mice in one of the barns. He didn't blame him. The sound of a newborn crying was disturbing. Seth held her close in the crook of his arm and ensured the blanket around her was tightly wrapped around her. The swaddling technique was making a difference and did seem to comfort her. He watched her face, wanting her to settle but could see she was agitated as now and again she would frown, and her face would crumple up. He rocked her gently and thought about singing to her. Singing had always calmed Darragh. Singing with Jules had helped their troubled souls too. In fact, it had probably saved them from going completely mad. Their number one hit, Waterfall Way, had been the making of them and now they didn't have to worry about money.

Seth looked out the window at the dark morning and thought about his plans to farm the land again this year. Despite little rain in 2020, the land around them had produced decent crops. Despite Covid, they had managed to get local labour in from neighbouring farms, and between them all, the harvest had been picked the old way - by hand. After paying for the help, Seth and Jules had set up a stall in Cork on the weekends and were selling the vegetables they had grown. The weather had recently been too bad to trade, so they had pickled all they could and stored potatoes in a barn to sow in the spring. Growing the crops had been the easy part, but selling was not so easy. However, they had plenty of food in the freezer to see them through 2021.

From beneath the covers, Jules' eyes opened wide, and she gasped. The room was too quiet and felt empty. She flung back the covers and ran to Juliet's cot. She was gone. *Where is she? Has someone taken her? Where's Seth? Please, please, let her be with him.* She picked up her dressing gown from the chair, ran to the living area, and found Seth sitting on the sofa, holding their baby. She sighed with relief and came over to them and sat down. "I was so frightened that she had been taken. You should have told me that you had taken her. I was so scared."

Seth, seeing her anxious face, smiled weakly at her. "I just wanted you to sleep a bit longer. Look, she is doing ok, and she is sleeping."

Juliet started to make an odd noise, not quite a cry and not quite a moan. "She can smell you. You go back to bed and sleep some more. I am sure she doesn't need any more milk from you. You were up all through the night, weren't you? Perhaps I could give her a bottle of formula in the night so you get some rest. I don't know if that would hurt her stomach mixing different milks."

"We will ask the midwife," Jules said, putting her arms out to take her from Seth. "I will feed her now and then see if we can get through an hour before feeding her again. I don't think I will be able to go back to sleep knowing that she wants to be fed. When Darragh was at the hospital, pre-terms were only fed eight times daily. Darragh was such an easy baby to look after. Oh, Seth. Do you think our Darragh will remember us when he comes home?"

"Of course, he will. He is blood. He will never forget us. I am going to ring Granny today and see if she has any news. I…"

They heard a key go into the lock, and the front door opened. Sinead, using a crutch, limped into the kitchen area, sat down heavily on a chair, and smiled at them both. Her pink hair lit up in the morning light and looked almost like a halo around her head.

"There, I made it. I am walking a little further every day. You two look so tired. Do you want me to look after Juliet for a bit so you can rest?"

"Aww, that is really kind of you, but despite appearances, we are feeling much better today. I think Juliet is a little happier. You can have a cuddle and wind her if you like. When she has had her breakfast, of course." Juliet was latched onto a swollen breast and was sucking away as if her life depended on it.

Seth stood up and put the kettle on. "I will go and tend to the horses in a bit. Do you want a coffee? You know what you are like if you don't have one first thing."

"I had one before I went out. Can't you tell?"

"I should have realised. You haven't sworn once," he said, laughing.

"Am I really that bad?"

"You're like a bear with a sore head. It's funny."

"Seth, you make me sound like a monster. I bet you can't wait for me to move out."

"No, that's not true. We are both going to miss you. Later, we can finish painting the piggery. Have you sanded everything we put down on the list?"

"Almost. That's where I've been. I just have the bedroom windowsill to do…"

Seth's phone began to ring. He picked it up and looked at the caller on the screen. "It's Granny. I hope she has some news about Darragh. We could do with a bit of good luck." *Please let it be good news. Why is she ringing us so early? Is something wrong?*

Chapter Two

"Granny, this is early for you. I didn't think you got up before nine. Is everything ok? Is Bridie well?"

"There's nothing wrong with me that a little sherry wouldn't cure. I am on the first bus out of Dingle. I am coming to stay with you. I have my instructions."

"Instructions? Really? You are coming over to see us? Hold on, Granny, let me put you on loudspeaker. Jules and Sinead are here, and our Juliet, so you will have to watch your language. What do you mean you have your instructions? Have the spirits told you something."

"You cheeky boy! I don't swear. Well, not as much as I used to. I know you are busy, but I'd like to stay in the Manor House if that is alright with you. Christ, this bus is taking its time. Jackie, will you put your foot down and get your arse out of this God-forsaken place. I've got a great-grandson to find, and you mithering over masks isn't making my job any easier."

"Have you got your mask on? You can't travel if you haven't got one."

"I don't need one. There's nothing wrong with me. All this fuss over a little bit of flu."

"You can easily catch Covid on the bus, and it is not good to get sick at your age. Please wear one. I don't want to lose you."

"Don't you worry about me. A little flu isn't going to hurt me. I've faced worse. There, I've put one on, Jackie. Are you satisfied now? If I start to choke, then that will be down to you. What are you all looking at? I have my mask on!

"So, my sweet boy, will you pick me up from Cork when I get there? I know this is short notice, but you need my help. The police are floundering and are as good as a chocolate teapot. Do you have room at the house for me? I want the same room as Bridie and I had when we came to your wedding."

"The house is all shut up. We haven't had guests for a while," Jules called out. "You can stay with us up at the Old Barn. How long will you be staying?"

"As long as it takes. I haven't told Bridie that I have gone. She will be glad to see the back of me. I keep telling her that she should take more interest in Seth, but she doesn't listen. I am sorry for that. She has not been a good mother to you, has she?"

Seth felt a bit awkward. The day he discovered that Bridie was his birth mother had never really sunk in, and he felt guilty for not wanting to get to know her better. "That's ok, Granny. I think you have always been more of a mother to me. Jules is right. You can't stay at the Manor House. It is cold and damp and will be the death of you."

"Granny, you can have my room at the Old Barn," Sinead announced. "I am going to move into the piggery, so that room will be free."

"That's very kind of you, dear, but I will have to have access to the house. The spirits want me to find something in the house to help them connect with Darragh. There is so much interference going on. I have a whisper in my ear from a young girl who passed recently. She has a connection to you, Seth."

Jules looked at Seth's startled face and knew that his Granny was referring to Gemma Day.

"Do you remember a lost soul by the name of Gemma? I knew it was her. She didn't have to tell me her name. I saw her picture in the paper along with that scoundrel Tom Stone. Have they put him away yet?"

Jules held her breath for a moment as her heart pounded in her chest. In April, she would have to go to court and face him once again. She trembled a little at the thought of seeing him. Every day, he had become more demon than human in her mind. She now feared him and could not forgive him for tearing her family apart.

Concerned that Jules was going to cry, Seth answered for her. "The trial starts in April, Granny. It's ok, Jules, don't think about it. I'll be there with you. We will be there for each other."

"I'm sorry, Jules. I didn't mean to upset you, dear. He will get what he deserves. I will make sure of that," Granny whispered loudly.

"Granny, you sound like a character out of The Godfather!"

"I'm just saying... Hello, dear, how are you today? Bridie told me about your husband. You come and sit with me and tell me all about him. I heard the ambulance go by? Seth, I've got to go now. I will ring you when I get to Cork."

"Ok, Granny, see you later."

Granny hadn't ended the call, and they could hear her talking to Penny Dear and smiled as they heard her ask her about her husband's haemorrhoids. Seth cancelled the call.

"I don't think we need to know anymore. Why would you call an ambulance? Jules, you've gone white and look so tired, my sweet girl. You go back to bed. Sinead, would you mind looking after Juliet for an hour while I go and tend to the horses?"

"No, I don't mind. I like being the nanny. She can watch me pack."

"Are you sure you are ok to move down to the piggery?" Seth asked. "Do you mind the smell of new paint?"

"The smell soon goes away, and I am actually looking forward to moving in. I think I am ready to live on my own now. You have to promise you will come down and see me, though."

"Of course, we will. We are going to miss you."

"I feel so drained," Jules said, passing Juliet to Sinead. "I don't know what is wrong with me. The thought of going to court and having to leave Juliet all day is making me anxious. Are you sure you will be ok with her? If she cries, then call me."

"I will rock her in the pram until she sleeps. She might cry a little, but she will be ok. You really need to rest, Jules. You will feel so much stronger and clear-headed after a sleep."

"You are right, but you must promise me you won't leave her by herself. I am just so frightened that someone will take her."

Seth hugged Jules. "My poor, sweet dote, nobody is going to take her. Not like…"

Jules sighed and looked into his big brown eyes and felt reassured. "It's going to be ok. We are going to find Darragh soon, aren't we?"

"To be sure! Granny will help us find him, although I am unsure what Gemma has to do with all this. Do you believe in ghosts, Jules?" Seth asked. "I'm not sure I do,"
"No, not really, but I would accept help from the Devil himself if it means we get our boy back."

Chapter Three

Detective Lucy O'Leary threw down a huge pile of files on her desk. She caught the handle of her coffee cup, sending the contents flying. The black liquid spread across the table and then dripped down onto her seat. Cursing, she ran across the room to the kitchenette, looking for a cloth. The paper towel dispenser was empty. All she could find was a tea towel that needed washing and was splattered with a brown substance. Feeling a little guilty for using the department's one and only tea towel, she ran back to her desk and started to wipe up the coffee. A smell of curry began to fill the air, and her stomach turned as she remembered throwing up the night before.

Lucy stopped wiping up the liquid and gazed out the window as she tried to remember her night out. To celebrate a murder case that led to an arrest and a successful prosecution, they had gone to the Chief Inspector's house for a round of drinks and an Indian takeaway. It had been a very strange celebration, and she remembered drinking a huge glass of vodka, Coke and ice in the back garden with her fellow officers. After two hours of drinking and eating, she had been feeling cold and had decided to walk home. It was only a twenty-minute walk back to her flat, but she couldn't remember any of it. All she could remember was standing up and saying goodbye. She wondered if walking in the fresh March air had caused this amnesia.

She had woken the next morning naked, and with the worst headache she had ever had, and much to her dismay, had found a post-it note on the pillow next to her with the message to call someone called Stephan. He had left her his mobile number. She had winced at the thought of sleeping with someone she didn't know and had sighed with relief when she realised that the tampon she had inserted before going out was still in place. She realised that she really shouldn't have drunk so much and opened herself up to becoming an easy target for men to prey on her. She hoped that Stephan had just been a kind soul that had helped her home, undressed her and gotten her into bed. She prayed that she hadn't told him she was a police officer. She didn't like to tell potential boyfriends that she was a DI, as they seemed intimidated by this revelation. Lucy shuddered again. It was freaking her out, not knowing what had happened to her, and she wondered if she should ring Stephan to find out.

Her single status was wagging its finger at her and mocking her for not having a boyfriend. Lockdown had put dating on hold, and the anxiety of being alone forever was sometimes too hard to bear. Her mother kept telling her that she should settle down and start a family before she was too old. She was starting to think she would never meet the right person and wondered if it was too late to start a family at the age of thirty-five.

Lucy rinsed the t-towel out in the sink and laid it on the draining board to dry. She thought of the post-it note on her desk beside her pen pot. She was curious to see who Stephan was and thought she might ring him later to thank him for getting her home. Just to thank him and nothing more. But it wouldn't hurt to see if he was single.

Not liking the look of the stained tea towel, Lucy scooped it up and dropped it into the bin with the plan to buy some more at lunchtime. She walked back and looked at the huge pile of files on her desk, and sighed. These cold cases were taunting her. The Darragh Hearn case was proving to be more difficult than she could ever have imagined. Seth and Jules had done numerous interviews and appeals on TV, and she had followed every lead she had been given and was nowhere nearer to finding their boy. Seth had spoken to her daily for an update, and she had tried to give him hope each time. He usually rang her in the mornings, and it was good to hear her half-brother's voice and see how he was doing. Today was going to be extra hard to speak to him as she had nothing new to report. One day soon, she would have to be blunt with him. The chances of finding Darragh alive were slim. A tear escaped and rolled down her cheek. How could she tell him that?

The sky was grey, and the wind blew hard on the trees outside her window. For a moment a little sunshine shone in long God fingers down on the roof tops, giving her a little hope. It would be good to walk along the river Lee and try to clear her head. Not allowing herself to talk herself out of going out, she grabbed her coat and bag and walked quickly down Anglesea Street, hoping that she wouldn't bump into anyone. She kept her mask on and knew she was using it to hide from other humans. She craved company but also feared the human race too. Covid had a lot to answer for. When she got to the river, she would take her mask off, breathe in the cool river air, and try to calm her breathing. She could read the signs and knew she was heading for a full-blown panic attack if she didn't watch herself.

The streets were empty, and she felt a little guilty for being out when most were at home continuing with the lockdown programme, waiting their turn to be vaccinated. She shuddered as she thought about getting hers. The last time she had seen a needle, she had passed out, much to the surprise of all those around her.

As Lucy approached the river, she could see a man sitting on a bench feeding some pigeons. She immediately recognised him as Aiden, a well-known alcoholic in Cork. He was always unshaven, and his nose was red from drinking too much whisky. Despite his dishevelled appearance, he always wore a clean white shirt and silk tie beneath a very old, tattered coat. He smiled as he saw Lucy pass by and wished her good morning. Lucy returned the greeting and stopped short, his voice and greetings triggering a small vision in her head. She turned around quickly to look at him and try to make sense of her thoughts. The bench was empty, and she scanned the area looking for him, but he was nowhere to be seen. The pigeons had gone too.

Trying to understand what had happened, she walked back to the bench and sat on it to see if it was still warm. The bench was damp and cold, and the floor was void of crumbs. She shook her head, thinking she might be going mad and then saw a small pink object floating in the river. She stood up to get a better look and realised it was a naked doll with dark brown hair. It was being pulled along by the current. The doll got caught in some rubbish and branches near the bank's edge. It was very odd to see such a thing, and instinctively she knew that this doll was important and somehow connected to her vision a moment ago. She needed to retrieve the doll from the river and hold it in her hands. Lucy got down on her knees, held the wet branch's end, used it like a net and drew the trapped doll to her. The river tugged at the doll, eager to pull her back.

Feeling a little creeped out, Lucy swiped the doll up and wiped the doll's hair from its face. The doll's eyes were brown like her own, and she could feel such sadness flooding from the toy that it took her breath away. For a moment, Lucy could see the doll in the hands of a child. A young girl with long brown hair and brown eyes. The child was sitting in a wheelchair holding this doll. She saw Aiden sitting on the bench, waving to the little girl. He was smiling and knew her well. He was greeting the parents, too, asking them if they were having a good day. The sun was shining, and it was hot. A hot August day, not like today. She couldn't see the father's face, but she saw a ginger-haired lady shaking her head. She was sad for some reason. So sad. She could hear her telling Aiden that her daughter was a little better today, but the ginger-haired woman's eyes were cold. For a moment, she could see Darragh. He was in a cot in a dark room, alone and cold but alive.

Lucy's phone began to ring, bringing her out of her daydream. Lucy put the doll on the floor next to her and took her phone out of her pocket. It was Seth. "Oh, Seth," she said, almost crying. "I think I have a new lead. I just need to find Aiden. Seth, Darragh is in Cork; he is alive and... He is alive."

"I never doubted that he wasn't."

"I don't want to get your hopes up. I've just found a doll in the river, and she's told me that he is alive. If I find Aiden, then he will know more. I am not going crazy, I promise. I know this is not a conventional way to find a missing child, but any vision I have has been pretty accurate." She hoped Seth wasn't going to be cross with her. She fingered a button on her coat anxiously as she waited for him to reply to her.

"Are you sure, Lucy? I don't know how these things work. Do the spirits talk to you like they do with Granny?"

"No, not like that. They just send me clues. Perhaps they think I will understand better that way because I am a detective."

DARRAGH

"I think you should meet Granny. She is on her way here. I have faith in you both. How can I not believe after the spirits helped me find Jules and Darragh before? Are you able to come over for dinner tonight? Perhaps we can work out how we can find... Did you say Aiden? Does he know where Darragh is?"

"He's a local man who likes to sit by the river and feed the pigeons. He knows everyone in Cork and everyone's business. I am pretty sure he will know where the woman that bought the doll lives. Seth, the woman, had ginger hair, and I am sure she fits the description Sinead gave." She didn't mention that Aiden was an alcoholic. "I haven't seen him for a while, though, not since lockdown. I am sure I can track him down. I am free tonight to come over. I am curious to see what Granny is like. What time should I get to you?"

Seth laughed. "Come around eight. Is that too late for you? We have to work meal times around Juliet. I hope you don't mind nibbling on bits of cheese until we can get to the cooker."

"No, I don't mind. How is the wee darling doing?"

"She is keeping us on our toes. We are getting there slowly."

"Seth, when I see Aiden, don't get your hopes up. He is kind and sweet but likes the sauce a bit too much, and he may have no idea who I am talking about."

"I won't, but I am a little excited. I have a good feeling about this vision. I don't want to jinx us, but I think that our luck is about to change."

19

Chapter Four

Seth put his foot down on the accelerator, doing his best not to worry Jules. He didn't want to keep Granny waiting at the Cork bus station. Jules gave him a quick glance, narrowed her eyes, and then looked at the bus timetable on her phone.

"You can slow down. It's ok. We've got plenty of time. There's no need to go crazy. The bus is due at half past five, so we have fifteen minutes to get to Cork."

Seth eased his foot off the pedal and smiled. "That's good. I'll enjoy the ride then. Isn't this car quiet? It feels like we are cutting through the air like a knife. I have no regrets spending all that money on this electric beauty. I do miss the purr of May's jaguar, though."

"That old car was a gas guzzler. We should sell it. I hope Sinead won't mind. She inherited half that old car from May too. I'd like to get rid of it as soon as we can. Every time I see it, it makes me shiver and brings back bad memories. When we get home, I'll ask Sinead. I'm sure she won't mind."

"Sinead says that car gives her the creeps too. The police went over it with a fine toothcomb and it is covered in white dust. Stone's fingerprints were all over it. One of her friends wants to buy it." Seth quickly looked at Jules' worried face and knew she was thinking about going to court. Tom Stone was due to appear in court in a month. It was going to be a harrowing time for them both. He squeezed her hand to reassure her. "My poor wee dote, please don't think about it. When we go to court, I will be with you. That Tom Stone is going to get the book thrown at him."

"How did you know I was thinking about that?"

"I just know that look. You promise me that if you are feeling at all worried, then you will tell me. We are in this together."

"I try not to think about it… I am not looking forward to seeing his pathetic face and hearing what he has to say. I still can't believe he is saying he is not guilty and playing his diminished responsibility card. What the Hell is all that about?"

"God knows! He is not mad. Well, he is. He is a dangerous nutter. At least you can go on video and not see him face to face."

"Actually... I would rather see him in court. I want to see the lawyers tear him apart. That will bring me closure."

"Are you sure? I know that you are one tough cookie, but I worry. I don't want you to get hurt. I'd rather you didn't."

"That's not going to happen, Seth. I can face him head-on with you by my side. You won't leave my side, will you?"

"No, never. I like being with you twenty-four-seven. Do you realise this is the first time we have been together on our own in months? We should go out for a meal together one night. I'd like that. Have a date night. Now we have a steady income from our records, we can afford to treat ourselves now and then. We need to have a little fun once in a while."

"I will go on a date night with you soon. When this Covid business is over, and Darragh is home."

"Yes, when Darragh comes home. Then we can learn to live a little. I know I keep saying it, but it won't be long before he is back with us. I was going to tell you. Lucy rang me this morning and has got a warm lead. We will ask her about it when she comes over for dinner. Oh crap, I forgot to say. I asked her over for dinner. She will be over to ours in half an hour. We will have to order a takeaway. Will that be ok? She is family."

"That's fine, Seth," Jules said, smiling. "A warm lead, you say? Will she tell us what she knows, or is it private police business?"

"She had a vision, so I guess she won't log that on the records. She needs to meet Granny, and they can work out what is going on."

Jules sighed and looked a little sad. "Just a vision? That is not really a lead, is it? I was hoping for something more concrete."

"She thinks a man in Cork saw one of Darragh's kidnappers. She just has to get in contact with Aiden and see if he knows the ginger-haired woman."

"At least it's something. Not exactly a warm lead, though." Jules shut her eyes, trying to imagine her toddler's big brown eyes looking up at her, trusting her to find him." *Stay strong, my sweet boy, and we will find you.* A little chill ran through her as she imagined someone creeping into the house and stealing Juliet. The thought was unbearable. "Seth, I am feeling a bit freaked out. You do think Juliet will be ok with Sinead? Don't you? She promised me that she wouldn't let her out of her sight. It feels really odd not being with her."

"She will be fine with Sinead this morning, and you left her a bottle if she should go mad while we are out. She needs to learn how to be independent. I saw my sisters struggle with their newborns. It will get better. I promise."

"I know, but it's hard to leave her. I think I have separation anxiety... Seth! I can see Granny up ahead. What is she wheeling behind her? It's the biggest suitcase I've ever seen. It's as big as she is. She must have been on an earlier bus. Pull over. She must be exhausted."

Seth pulled up next to Granny, jumped out of the car, and ran over to her. Jules got out, too and then got the biggest smile from her.

"Well, look who it is! I got an earlier bus. I was going to call you, but my old phone died on me. To be honest, I am not sure what happened to it. I was talking away to Bridie, and then she went quiet. When I looked at the screen, it was black."

"You just need to charge it up. I'll do it for you when we get home," Seth said, taking the handle of her suitcase. "I'm glad you told Bridie that you are staying with us. How did she take the news?"

"She was beside herself with worry. I don't know why but she thinks I am too old to be gallivanting around Ireland. I think she was a bit jealous too. I might look old, but I am still young on the inside. Like you, I have the desire to travel and go where I please."

Seth laughed. "I've done my travelling. Are you planning on staying with us long, Granny? That is quite the biggest suitcase I've seen. I hope it will fit in the boot."

"I am used to travelling light. Everything I own is in this suitcase. I don't mind walking to yours if there is not enough room in the car. It's good to be free and out in the countryside again."

A cool wind blew as she spoke, and she shivered a little. "There's going to be snow by morning. You can taste it in the air. My bones are chilling."

"Snow isn't predicted, but you are right. The wind is icy. It is too cold to walk home. It's good to see you," Jules said, hugging her.

"You are not looking yourself. I had to come despite there being a bit of flu about. I know the powers that be are not keen on us leaving our homes, but these are exceptional circumstances, and I know you need my help. Jules, your aura is not shining as brightly as it used to. It is to be expected, I suppose."

"I don't feel too bright. It's been a hard few years."

"I know, dear. We will get you both through this and get balance restored."

Seth squeezed the suitcase into the boot and shut the lid on it. Feeling triumphant for achieving what he thought would be impossible, he opened the rear door so Granny could get in the car. Seth had no idea how old she was. He guessed she was in her late seventies. Her eyes met his, and for a moment he saw a young mischievous twinkle in her eyes. Her small frame slid into the seat gracefully, and she smiled. "This car smells new. You have done well for yourself. Your cousin Nathan says you are pop stars. I knew you would be before you, of course," she chuckled. "The cards told me."

"Did they now! What do the cards say about us now," Seth asked as he started the car up.

"That would be telling. Hmm... I don't know how to tell you this, but I think it is best to come clean. The cards haven't been favourable. You mustn't worry, though. I think the spirits need me to be at Waterfall West in order for them to give me a clear picture. I have had such a complicated time trying to work out the future for you both. I think it has to do with all the deaths that have landed at your feet."

"That makes me a little anxious, Granny. You don't think anyone else will die, do you?" Jules asked as she gave Seth a quick glance to see his reaction.

"I haven't had any Grim Reaper cards come up, so don't worry yourselves. I will work out what's going on when I am in the Manor House and see Juliet."

"Our Juliet?" Jules asked.

"Yes, she has something to tell me too."

"You will have to wait a while. Juliet isn't speaking yet." Jules frowned.

Granny laughed. "Babies don't need to speak. They have a way of sharing news with you. You'll see."

"I was going to tell you. We've invited Lucy O'Leary over to have dinner with us tonight. She is Seth's half-sister and the police officer helping us to find Darragh."

"For the love of God! Was there no end to that man's spawning? Your Dad should be ashamed of himself. It is a good job he is dead. So Lucy is your half-sister. Now that's interesting. I drew a card this morning showing an angel with one foot in the water and one foot on the land. That will be her, then. You say she is a Hearn? I will know if she is when I see her."

"She has long dark hair and big brown eyes. Lucy looks like Charlene," Jules added. "Lucy is nice. You will like her. She looks sad sometimes, though. I think she is lonely."

"That is an angel's plight. They look after everybody and never find love for themselves," Granny said as she did her seatbelt up.

"We are going to order a takeaway. Will you be ok with Chinese?" Seth asked.

"I'll have cheese on toast, I have never had Chinese, and I have no desire to try foreign food now. Not at my age."

"I am sure I can find something a bit more wholesome than cheese on toast. I have a homemade vegetable lasagne in the freezer. Would you like that?" Jules asked.

"No, dear, I am quite happy with cheese on toast."

"If you are sure."

"I'm sure," Granny said, shutting her eyes.

25

Jules looked at the time on the dashboard. It was nearly eight o'clock, and she felt odd being away from Juliet for so long. She wondered what Juliet was going to tell Granny. *It is just crazy talk. What on earth could a newborn possibly tell her?* She looked over her shoulder, relieved that Granny was fast asleep. *This is going to be a very trying few weeks. I hope Granny doesn't stay long.*

Chapter Five

Lucy drove her old Smart car along the gravel drive, and as she passed Waterfall West Manor House, she shivered and checked the car doors to ensure they were locked. The house was shrouded in darkness, and she was glad of that. She knew that the moment she stepped into that house, all the spirits that lingered there would make themselves known. Her mother called it a gift. The reality was quite different. Lucy had lost friends because of her so-called gift. She remembered visiting a friend's house for a coffee. She had only stayed for a few minutes as she had the distinct feeling that she would find a man with his throat cut in the bathroom. She had left, saying she had a migraine and had to get home. Her friend never invited her back for coffee or spoke to her again.

Lucy didn't even have to step foot into Waterfall West to know that a malignant presence was lurking in the darkest shadows, calling out to her and then choking, his mouth full of water. Feeling a little scared, she turned on the radio and smiled. Seth's song, Waterfall Way, was playing. Although the song was no longer number one, it was still played regularly on Irish Country Radio. She sang along to the chorus, enjoying the tune. She liked the song so much that she had made it her ringtone on her phone. She had always loved singing and wondered if other Hearns were musical too. It was interesting finding out about all her relatives. She was surprised to learn she had so many brothers, sisters, nephews and nieces. She wished she had known them when she was young and not been a lonely, only child.

The day Waterfall Way got to number one was also the day when Darragh was taken. She prayed and hoped that Darragh had not been sold to paedophiles. If that were the case, it was very unlikely that he would be alive.

Lucy thought back to when she had first interviewed Tom Stone from the garden of the Manor House to keep her distance during the lockdown. She could still remember seeing his shifty, rat-like eyes staring at her as he gave her and Rufus Parvel details about his whereabouts the night Gemma Day was killed. He had cried like a baby when he heard that she had died. She knew that was just a sickening theatrical stunt. He was guilty as sin but proving this was going to be a monumental task. She wondered if this was why she disliked the Manor House so much. Lucy put her foot down on the accelerator and sped up the drive towards the Waterfall Riding Centre.

Her car bumped along on the cobbles of the stable yard; for a moment, she wasn't sure where to go. She had been to the Old Barn many times, but tonight, because there was no moon, the way was covered in darkness. Much to her relief, she saw a light appear ahead, and hoping that this was the way, she was pleased to find that she was on the track that led down to the barn. She was a little early, so she pulled into a passing point and decided to wait ten minutes before going down to see them.

Lucy thought about what would happen when she knocked on Seth and Jules' door. They would greet her, and after a few awkward moments, they would ask if she had any news about Darragh. She was not looking forward to this moment as she had nothing new to tell. She had asked the spirits many times for their help and guidance, but so far, all she had been given was a sodden doll with hair like her own. She wondered if Darragh had been drowned. She shuddered as she imagined someone with ginger hair holding his head underwater. She thought back to the moment Darragh had been abducted. When the white van had raced away, she had seen for a split second the anxious face of a woman. She couldn't understand why she hadn't remembered this before. Lucy sighed, as this was the same woman she had seen in her vision earlier that day. When she got to work the next day, she would put a photo-fit together of her face and see if she was wanted for any child-related crime.

Seth and Jules would also be keen to know if Aiden had been found. Her search for him had been fruitless. Aiden did not have a contact number. Lucy had visited his council flat, and with her thigh muscles aching, she had climbed six flights of stairs which smelt of cat pee, only to find that he was not in. This was a little frustrating as really he should not be out unless he was shopping or going for a walk. She suspected he might be with other alcoholics in a flat somewhere in Cork or down by the river under a bridge drinking himself to oblivion. The alcoholics who drank there thought that they were invisible to the authorities. To a certain extent, this was true. The police turned a blind eye, not having enough manpower to evict them from their spot on an hourly basis.

Feeling cold, Lucy had gone back to the river. She had found the spot under the bridge where Aiden and other alcoholics liked to sit and drink together. Aiden was not there, so she asked his drinking partners if they had seen him and promised them he wasn't in trouble. Most were too wasted to answer, but one old man, with barely any teeth, had just laughed and said he was probably feeding the pigeons somewhere. Knowing they were being cautious, she pretended she was a relative and was desperate to find him. They ignored her, knowing that she was the police. She could have arrested them all for congregating and not following Covid guidelines, but that would have given her hours of paperwork and would not have helped her find Aiden. Feeling despondent, she had returned to the office.

After hugging a hot cup of coffee, a new action plan surfaced. In her vision, she had seen the young girl in a wheelchair. Lucy had spent the afternoon searching for disability groups and then contacted them to see if they had a young girl on their records that looked a bit like her. It was hard work following all the cases by herself, and she hoped she would get a new partner soon. She was glad she didn't have to work with Rufus Parvel anymore. Rufus did not like how she worked. He would have been making sarcastic comments about her unstructured approach to solving cases and about how women should not be detective inspectors and should be at home bringing up children. Her complaint against him was to be heard soon, and she hoped he would be asked to leave. Fortunately, it suited Rufus to work in an office at the far end of the building, and she could keep contact with him to a minimum.

Lucy noticed headlights in her rear-view mirror and wondered who it might be. The car drew up next to her, and she saw Jules wind the window down. Lucy wound hers down, too, so they could talk.

"Are you lost? Everyone gets confused when they get to the yard. Everything looks so different in the dark."

"Yes, a little. I see a light down there. Is that your house?" she lied, not wanting to admit that she was waiting until the last moment to visit them.

"Follow us down, and you can park next to us."

"Hold on, Seth, I want to go over and talk to Lucy. You two go on ahead," Granny announced.

"We are nearly home," Seth replied.

"No, I need a quiet word with Lucy. She can drive me down," Granny said as she got out of the car.

Lucy was about to wind up the window when she saw a small, grey-haired woman walking over to her. She guessed that this must be Seth's granny. She was her granny too, but from the look on her face, she didn't seem too pleased to see her. Granny got into the car without asking, and her face softened a little.

"Will you give your granny a lift down the hill? I have waited a long time to meet you."

"You have? Yes, of course."

"This is a very small car. Are you sure this car isn't meant for children? I don't think I've seen one like this before in Dingle."

Lucy laughed. "It is for adults. My nephew sold it to me," Lucy said as she followed the car ahead. She noticed that Granny hadn't done her seat belt up, but she didn't say anything.

"Is your nephew a Hearn too?"

"No, I don't think so. Although he does look a bit like Seth. I hadn't thought about that before."

"He is sure to be. Your real father should have had his cock cut off at birth!"

"Oh my! Did you know him well?"

"Well enough not to trust him. I knew him as a child, man, and the scoundrel he became. My cousin has passed now, and I am thankful. However, he keeps trying to contact me, and I keep blocking him. I want nothing more to do with him. But you knew that, didn't you?"

Lucy went quiet for a moment. "There is a warrant for his arrest. Margaret Hearn says that he killed Ivy Brown and escaped to Ireland. We haven't been able to trace him."

"Well, you haven't bothered to look, have you? You knew he was dead, didn't you? How long have you had the gift?"

"I don't know what you mean."

"I would say you had it from birth and never really understood what it was."

Lucy shook her head. "I don't know what you mean. I have the occasional vision, but I wouldn't call it a gift. More of a curse. It confuses things. In my line of work, you should follow a case using factual evidence, not wild dreams."

"I bet your second sight has helped you solve a few cases. I can help you see better."

"I don't know if that would be a good thing. A medium's evidence would not stand up in court. I wish I could see what has happened to Darragh, but instead, I get a patchwork of images that don't make any sense. Take today, for example. I had the craziest visions about a disabled girl in a wheelchair being pushed along by a ginger-haired woman. The same woman snatched Darragh, yet my vision was focused on the girl who looked like me and not the kidnapper."

Granny went silent for a moment.

"Are you alright?"

"I know why you think you saw yourself. You saw another Hearn, to be sure. Perhaps we need to speak to your father, Jethro Hearn, after all. I am sure he has something to say on the matter."

Lucy scowled. "I am not sure I want to. Seth has told me a little about him, and he doesn't sound like he would want to help. He is a murderer. He's missing anyway."

"You know that isn't the truth. He is close by but in spirit form. As I said, he has passed and keeps bugging me."

"We haven't found a body. Are you sure he is dead?"

"I am more than sure. He is making a nuisance of himself, and I wouldn't give him the time of day if it wasn't for Darragh. The spirits are not forthcoming, which might be because Jethro is blocking them from helping us. There is another here too… Gemma wants us to go to the Manor House and share something with us. Perhaps Jethro has put her up to it. I don't know."

"You mean Gemma Day, the girl that Tom Stone murdered?"

"The very same."

"I don't think I want to go into the house. It gives me the creeps. It oozes malevolence."

"I will be there with you. I won't let your father hurt you. I promise. He says he wants to help, but we shall see. He is evil through and through."

"I want to find Darragh. It is tearing me apart that he is still missing. Have you told Seth and Jules any of this?" Lucy asked.

"No, I'd rather not say anything yet. We must wait for the next pink moon, which appears on April 26."

"I don't think Seth and Jules will be able to wait that long. Seth keeps telling me that he needs to find Darragh by his birthday on the nineteenth. They are distraught, and with each day that passes… well, there is less chance of finding him. Why do we have to wait for the pink moon?"

"Many channels are open that night, and sucker fish return to spawn. In my book, spring starts then. So many good things happen when the moon is full and pink, and evil is blinded by its light for a moment. We will have a chance to find Darragh. A slim chance but a chance nonetheless."

Seth waited for Lucy and Granny to arrive and wondered what had taken them so long. They had stopped half way down the track, and he guessed they had been talking. He wondered what Lucy thought of Granny, and he was dying to ask her. Jules was feeding Juliet in the bedroom, and Sinead was looking through the takeaway leaflets, trying to decide what they should order.

"Do you think Granny will eat Chinese or Indian?"

"Neither. She is going to have cheese on toast. She doesn't like takeaways." Seth opened the door and let Lucy and Granny in and then saw Lucy smile at him and knew that she had found their grandparent to be amusing.

"Granny, we are going to order in. Are you sure you wouldn't like to try a Chinese or an Indian takeaway?" Sinead asked.

"You young people go ahead and order in. I am not going to take any chances. I am happy with biscuits and cheese. You do have cheese, don't you?"

"Of course we do. Can I get you a little Biriyani to try?" Seth said, smiling.

"Do you mind if we get Chinese, I don't think I can face a curry tonight? I had a dodgy one the other night," Lucy asked.

"There you see, these foreign foods are not good for you," Granny stated, hanging up her coat.

"Yes, sure. Here, Lucy, have a look," Sinead replied as she handed her the menu. "The Moon House makes a mean house special fried rice."

"It's Sinead, isn't it? I think you had a different coloured hair the last time I saw you. I love that colour pink. It really suits you."

"Thanks. This time it came out great. Usually, I end up looking like a freak."

Jules appeared with Juliet on her shoulder and was rubbing her back, trying her best to wind her. "So we're going to have Chinese then? Will you try some, Granny?"

"No, thank you, dear. Now let me see this baby of yours," Granny said, walking across to her and putting her arms out to take her latest grandchild.

"She might throw up on you. I've only just fed her."

"I don't care. I just want to hold my grandchild and smell her. Don't you think new babies smell so sweet?"

"I am not sure Juliet does. She mostly smells of old milk and, well, you know the other."

"Come here, my little darling, and let your old Granny give you a cuddle," Granny took Juliet from Jules, cradled her in her arms, and stroked her cheek. "You are a windy baby, and you have those bright blue eyes and that golden glow telling me that you are angelic but are going to be trouble. You look so angry and want to tell your old granny much. Let me get that wind up for you, and you will feel a whole better. Then we'll talk."

Seth smiled as he watched Granny take charge of Juliet and was thankful that she had come to stay. His attention turned to a phone ringing, and he realised it was Lucy's phone. He smiled when he realised that her ringtone was Waterfall Way.

"I'm sorry, I will have to take this. It is a work call." Lucy opened the front door and disappeared outside into the darkness.

"Granny, can I get you a cup of tea?" Seth asked.

"Now you are talking. Let me sit down and sort this child out. Your mother was just like Juliet. I spent hours trying to get her wind up."

"Perhaps windy babies run in the family." Seth wasn't sure if she was referring to her daughter Margaret that had brought him up, or her sister Bridie, his birth mother. Just thinking about them made him feel uncomfortable. He had disowned both.

"Bridie was a beautiful child but needed so much attention. You mustn't fall into that trap and mother Juliet day and night. When she is fed and winded, you just need to wrap her up tight and let her cry herself to sleep; otherwise, you won't be able to look after all the others."

"That is easier said than done. I don't like to hear her cry. I don't have any other children to worry about at the moment. She keeps us busy and keeps my mind from thinking about Darragh," Jules said tearfully.

"Don't listen to me. I should be shot for being so blunt. We will find your wee boy, I promise."

Lucy opened the door, and her face was ashen white. "I've got to go. The remains of a body have been found at the recycling facility. A child…" She wished she hadn't told them.

"You don't think it's Darragh?" Jules blurted out.

"I shouldn't have said anything, but I couldn't help myself. Forgive me, I need to go. I am so sorry. Please don't panic. Bodies turn up every week in Cork."

"But surely not the bodies of children."

"No, not children. Usually drug addicts and suicide victims. Granny?" Lucy asked. "You don't think it's…."

Granny frowned. "No, it is not him. Darragh is still in this world, but you need to go and see, dear. There is something wrong, and you will understand when you see the child. Just remains, you say? I just see a pile of tiny bones."

"Lucy, promise me you will tell us straight away if it is Darragh," Seth asked. He looked over at Jules, watched the colour rush out of her face, and knew she was going to faint. He ran over to her and caught her as she collapsed. "It will be ok, my sweet girl. It is not Darragh. Be strong."

Chapter Six

Sunlight streamed through the small hole at the top of the closed curtains and told Darragh that it was day and he should be awake. He smiled and waited patiently for the shaft of light to hit the top of his cot. When this happened, he would be brought something to eat. On good days he got toast, an egg and a beaker of warm milk. On bad days he was thrown a rusk and a carton of juice. When he first got the juice box, he wondered what the small plastic tube was for. Biting into the top of the carton and squeezing it had brought the cool liquid that smelt sweet and sickly to the top, and he had managed to suck it until it had gone. He had called out for more, but nobody heard his cries.

Some days were so dark that he was unsure if he should be asleep or awake. His clothes did not keep him warm, and his trousers' waistband hurt his stomach. He looked down at his tattered clothes and pulled at the elastic in his trousers to stop them from hurting. Peeing usually helped ease his stomach, so he pulled down his trousers and looked for the bucket left out for him on the floor next to his cot to pee into. He had learnt to push the brown lumps that came out of him into the bucket too. He didn't like the way his hands smelt afterwards.

The highlight of his day was to see the woman that brought him food and emptied his bucket. He knew that she was not family. She never made eye contact or said anything, but he liked seeing her all the same. Sometimes when she got to the door, she would stop, sigh and then leave. It was then that he knew he had connected with her. That sigh meant that she had seen him and felt something for him. He cried if she didn't pause at the door for that one brief moment.

He was not sure how his cot had got into this dark room and he remembered his bed being in another house. He remembered seeing his parents sitting on the bed next to his cot and smiling and laughing. In that room, he had been loved. He longed to feel warm arms around him again, reassuring him that he was wanted.

Today was going to be a good day. Darragh stood up and waited until the stream of sunshine made its way along the cot rail and highlighted flakes of white paint he had been peeling away. Eager to continue with his work and doing his best to ignore his rumbling stomach, Darragh picked up his blanket to hug and soothe himself. He then scraped the paint with his long nails, pulled away a large flake, and then dropped it down onto the carpet like a snowflake. More flakes followed, and mesmerised, he watched them flutter down to the stained carpet.

The sound of the door opening and the bright light coming from the room outside stopped his work, and he waited to see his only friend. He smiled when she entered the room. Her long curly ginger hair hid her face, and she kept her head down so he couldn't see her properly. As always, he called out to her as loudly as he could, willing her to reply. Without replying, she dropped a bag of food and drink into his cot and picked up the rubbish. She replaced the bucket with a new one and then stopped and smelt the contents. He had not seen her do that before. He called out some words he had learnt the night before. He had heard her and another shouting at each other outside of his door. He had been frightened because he sometimes heard her crying and didn't want that. He didn't like to hear people cry. When she cried, he cried too. "FUCK OFF," he called. Her green eyes caught his and seeing her surprised face, he said the same two words, pleased that he had gotten her to respond. She gasped, and then backing away from him, she turned, ran and slammed the door behind her. Upset that he made her go so quickly, he cried out the words again and then lay his head down on the edge of the cot, disappointed that she had gone. Tears rolled down his cheeks, and he bawled out, lost and lonely.

***

Jules pushed Juliet in her pram towards Sinead's new home. The piggery renovation was complete, and Sinead had invited her down to see her new home. The pram bounced along, and Juliet appeared to be awake, looking at the clouds floating above. It had been a few days since Granny had come to stay with them, and it was a relief to have a break from her. Although she had been no trouble, the thought of having her to stay indefinitely was disturbing. She had cooked and cleaned for them and helped them in every way she could, but Jules missed having time alone with Seth. *I don't know if I can stand her being with us for much longer. She makes me feel like I am failing as a mother. Perhaps I am.*

Juliet started to cry. "Oh, my poor girl, please let me get to Sinead's before you go crazy on me. Don't you like being in the pram, then? You can see the sky, the birdies and the clouds. Surely, that must be much better than being in my arms."

Juliet continued to scream. Finding the noise intolerable, Jules picked her up and continued on her way to the piggery, doing her best to push the pram with one hand. When Jules reached

Sinead's cottage, the arm holding Jules was aching. Juliet was quiet, at least. *What am I going to do with you?*

Sinead opened the front door and beamed. "Come on in. You do realise that you are my first visitor. I have the kettle on, and I've made cakes. I think they are fairy cakes."

"Think?"

Sinead laughed. "I didn't have self-raising flour, so I used plain and baking powder. They look a bit flat."

"I am sure they will be lovely. Oh, Sinead, I should have bought you a housewarming present."

"No, silly, you are here, and both you and Seth helped me renovate this place, so that is more than enough. It is quiet here, though. I do miss you both."

"We miss you too. It's not going to be quiet for much longer. This little one is about to blow. I don't understand why she is such a cry baby. She is fed, winded, and her nappy has been changed. What else can I do to make her happy? Granny keeps giving me the evils when I try to stop Juliet crying. I swear I am going to explode one of these days. She means well, but she is really getting on my nerves."

"You poor thing. You look exhausted. If you make the tea, I will hold your beautiful girl and try to work my magic with her. I think she just likes being held tight. Some babies are like that. She is just a needy baby, and you mustn't let Granny get to you."

"You are right. I will try my best to ignore her. Here you go," Jules said, handing her over to her and then stopped. "Do you want to sit down first? I see you are not using your crutch."

"I am much better. I have been doing all the physiotherapy exercises they gave me, and I think I've turned a corner this week.

I have thrown the crutch into the cupboard. Next week I should be riding again," she announced with a triumphant look.

"No, Sinead, that is too soon."

"I know. I was just kidding. I do miss riding so much," she said, taking Juliet. She hobbled over to the sofa, and Jules followed her in. "At least I will be able to help Seth look after all the horses again. We will start lessons in a few weeks, and some of the horses will need a bit of schooling. Where is Seth, by the way?"

"He is driving Granny into Cork to meet an old friend. Apparently, she is one of her best followers on TikTok. I think she is going to give her a private Tarot card reading. They are going to meet in the park as this lady is scared to let her in the house in case she gets Covid."

"I wonder what people in the park will think when Granny gets her pack of cards out."

"I don't think they will notice."

"I think that people might. She gets very animated when she is on TikTok. Have you seen her doing her readings? I don't mean to be rude, but she is hilarious and looks like she is conducting an orchestra."

Jules laughed. "No, I haven't had a chance to watch her yet. I love Seth's Granny, but she is driving me nuts. I have never met anyone that can talk so much. I shouldn't be mean because she has helped us so much."

"She has a lot of energy for someone so old. I hope I am as energetic as she is when I am her age."

"Sinead, she is nuts. Seth has got his hopes up that she will get guidance from the spirits to help us find Darragh. Do you think she will be able to help us find Darragh?"

"She helped Seth and I find you both before. I would keep an open mind. She was right about that poor kid found at the recycling centre. All they found were bones stripped of flesh. Who would do such a terrible thing?"

"I was so scared it was Darragh. They could tell it was a girl, but nobody has reported her missing. How sad is that?"

"There are a lot of sick people on this planet! Granny thinks Darragh is alive. I believe her."

"She has been here a week and all she keeps saying is that there is a connection problem and she is waiting for a sign. Seth said that Lucy had a vision too. The Hearns are one unusual family."

"Does Lucy have any more concrete leads?"

Jules sighed. "No, not really. She saw the girl in the van you saw when you got run over. That's something, I suppose. Oh, Sinead, I think I am going crazy and want to do something more to find Darragh. Seth and I are doing a song a week on TikTok, and some of them have gone viral, but our fans have got tired of looking for Darragh."

"Why don't you release another single about Darragh, and if it gets to number one, then the world will look for him."

"That's a brilliant idea. I will get Seth to write a song tonight. I know he is going crazy with all this waiting, and it will give us something positive to do."

"What will you call the song? 'Looking for Darragh'?"

"Mmm… No, it needs to be something that will get noticed."

"How about 'Darragh, Don't Cry'," Sinead said, rocking Juliet gently in her arms.

"Seth will know what to write. He is good at thinking up catchy titles. Sinead, you have the magic touch. Juliet is asleep.

I'll put the kettle on, and we'll try one of your interesting scones," Jules said, inspecting the cakes on a plate near the kettle. "Do you have any jam?"

Chapter Seven

Sinead had made Jules laugh and relax, and they had chatted about music, Waterfall West, and anything that came into their heads. The walk back home had gone well, and Juliet had not woken up when she put her in her pram. This was a little unnerving, and as she reached the front door, Jules realised that Juliet had slept for two whole hours. *I hope she isn't ill. She never sleeps that long during the day.* As Jules backed the pram in through the front door, she saw Seth pull into the driveway. The thrill of seeing his handsome face smiling at her had not worn off. She longed to be in his arms and breathe in the scent of his body. If Granny wasn't there, then she would have easily persuaded Seth to lie with her for a while. Her body was aching for him to make love to her, but she needed to sleep too.

It was nearly six o'clock, and both she and Seth liked to watch the news to see if there were any reports about Darragh. *I doubt there will be any news about him, but there might be something about that poor toddler that was found chopped up in a rubbish bag. Who could have done such a thing? At least it wasn't Darragh. My poor boy, where are you?* Jules looked down at Juliet and was becoming concerned. *Why are you still asleep?*

Seth came into the barn and held the door open for Granny. She smiled broadly when she saw Jules and then looked concerned. "What's the matter? You look like you've swallowed a lemon."

"Do I? I didn't mean to look so sour. I am worried about Juliet. She is so pink-looking and has slept for two hours."

Seth came over to the pram. "She looks ok to me. It's good to see her so peaceful."

"That will be the spring air filling her lungs," Granny said as she took off her coat. "Let her sleep. She is growing and needs to be left to it. Seth, put the kettle on, and let's all have a cup of tea before I put dinner on. I have lots to tell you about my day, and this is going to explain a lot about what has been going on in the spirit world."

"Do you think she is too hot? Is that why she is so pink?" Jules asked Granny.

"Leave her outside in the fresh air, and she will sleep for another hour. All the Hearn babies thrive when they are left outside."

"Oh, I don't think I could do that. It's nearly dark, and anyone could take her. I will leave her in the bedroom and take a blanket off her."

Seth put on the kettle and lined three cups up. His granny had chosen a small teacup as her own, and Seth realised that she had become part of their family unit. It was like she had been with them forever.

Granny sat at the kitchen table and chatted away about her trip to Cork and how the city had changed. When Jules came back and sat down, she went quiet for a moment which surprised Seth. He sensed a tension in the air. He smiled as he watched Jules spoon three sugars into her tea. She was in need of some comfort, and a pang of guilt ran through his body as he watched her sip the sweet liquid. "I do love you," he announced and then he smiled as he realised he had said this out loud.

"If you two lovebirds want to go off and fuck, then I will understand. You haven't had the chance to since Juliet came into this world, have you?"

"Granny, you are shocking me!" Seth exclaimed. "I... we will have plenty of time for that in future, but at the moment, we can't settle and live a normal life until we find Darragh. I was thinking, I can't be sitting down doing nothing waiting for the spirits to sort out their connection channels...."

"You don't need to do anything. The spirit world has been overwhelmed with newcomers, and their sudden departure from this world has caused a clog in the system. Covid has a lot to answer for. When I was giving my reading this afternoon, Pam asked me to see if her husband was suffering after the bug took him. She didn't have a chance to say goodbye to him and wanted him to know he was loved. The poor man was sitting right next to her on the bench in the park, and he didn't even know that he was dead. Gemma whispered to me that he was in limbo and was in a queue to join the spirit world. So what I am saying is that we have to be patient, and we will get news. Just as soon as the spirits have sorted out their backlog."

"That's just it, Granny, it has nearly been a year since our wee boy went missing, and I can't wait any longer. I was out with Moss yesterday, and I had this idea. Jules, you might not like this, but I think we should invite the local traveller communities to stay on our land. It keeps going through my head that there is a connection, and the person that took Darragh must have a vendetta with the travellers. Why would someone go out of their way to copy a number plate on a van that belonged to a traveller unless they wanted to cause them a problem? I don't know why, but there is a voice in my head that keeps telling me to do this."

"Why do you think that would upset me, Seth?"

"Jules… You have kind of cut yourself off from humanity. You didn't want to come on our trip to Cork. When we went to get Granny, you were anxious about leaving home. Having so many people on our land that you don't know might worry you."

"Yes, you are right, and it does freak me out to think of there being so many strangers so close to us. What if you are inviting the person that snatched Darragh onto our land? What if they take Juliet too? I don't know, Seth. I don't think it is a good idea."

"I was thinking they could stay in the clearing behind Waterfall West. I am quite sure they won't come near us unless there is a problem. I've heard that the travellers are having a hard time because of Covid. If they see that we are trying to help them, then I am hoping that they might open up to one of us and help us find out why Darragh was taken. In the past, children were sold to work at fairs. Granny, you must remember stories about these children."

"There were stories, but the travelling community I belonged to were just decent Irish families who worked hard for a living. Some new travellers have given us all a bad name. You will have to be careful who you invite. Travellers have no morals these days and will have the shirt off your back if you let them."

"You know their ways. Some of them might know of you. Lucy said that the travellers that owned the van that was written off are Irish travellers and they have been in Cork for years."

"So you want me to talk to them, do you?"

"I do, Granny. They will accept you and let you in because you were a traveller once. It would be harder for me to talk to them. You will have to be subtle, though, and tread carefully."

DARRAGH

"Once they see me on TikTok, they will know I am one of them. I hope they don't shun me because I have lived in a house for so long. I wonder if there is anyone left that remembers me."

"I think we should let them stay," Jules announced. "If they know what happened to Darragh and we don't try to speak to them, we will kick ourselves. Just make sure that they know they are not allowed to wander all over the estate."

"I know it is a long shot, and having them stay is going to be a headache, but I just know it is the right thing to do. I just hope Sinead agrees to it. Some of the kids might want pony lessons too."

"I am sure she will agree. Seth, Sinead and I had an idea earlier. We need to create a song about Darragh and release that rather than doing covers on TikTok all the time. We have all the equipment ready to record a song, so we don't need Sonar Cell this time to help us. Do you think Shawn will mind us releasing a single without them?"

"I don't think he will mind. Their music career is going well. We really should keep ours going, too, and we could do with some more sales money coming in. I must give Shawn a ring. He is having a hard time at the moment. I don't think things with him and Jane are going so well."

"Really? I guess I haven't heard from Jane in a while. Oh, I feel bad now. I have been a bad friend," Jules said as she looked into her cup at the last of her tea.

"To be fair, we haven't had much time. I think this is the first time we've actually been able to sit down and talk in weeks. I never knew how much hard work it was to look after a baby. She has us wrapped around her little finger," Seth said, stretching.

Juliet started to cry. "She must have heard us," Jules said, laughing and looked over her shoulder towards the bedroom and then at Granny, who was frowning.

"You want me to leave her for a bit, don't you?"

"I said nothing," Granny said. "Count to a hundred before you go and see if she settles."

Jules managed to count to fifty and then stood up, the sound of Juliet's cries too disturbing to ignore. She ran across the room and then stopped and turned around. "Seth, will you write a song about finding Darragh tonight? We need to get this single out this week."

"I will try, but I need to think of some catchy lyrics so our song gets noticed. I might go and see my horse for inspiration. I get my best ideas when I am with him. You don't mind me going out, do you?"

"No, Seth, that's fine. I'll feed Juliet, and then I will make a shepherd's pie. Is that ok with you, Granny? I will make a meat one for you."

"I will cook, I have nothing against your cooking, but I do like to cook things my way."

"Ok then," Jules didn't have the strength to argue. "The mince is in a Tupperware box in the freezer." Juliet was now crying hard, and she couldn't bear to stay away any longer. *I wonder if Granny will realise that the mince is vegetable based. Should I say anything? No, I had better not. I don't want another run-in with her.*

When Jules got to the bedroom, she heard her phone ping and taking it out of her jeans pocket, she noticed that Shawn had messaged her via Facebook. *That is odd. He hasn't messaged me before. Perhaps his account has been hacked.* She clicked on his face to look at the message.

DARRAGH

'Hi.'

Should I reply? If he has been hacked and whoever asks me for money, I will know it is not him. She rubbed Juliet's tummy to reassure her that she was there and then quickly messaged him back.

'Hi, how are you doing? We've not heard from you for a while.'

Jules picked Juliet up, sat on the bed, and pulled up her t-shirt and bra so Juliet could feed. Shawn messaged her back.

'Did Jane tell you that we have split up?'

She lay the phone next to her and, with difficulty, typed.

'No, she didn't. Are you ok?'

'No, not really. Are you alone?'

Alarm bells were beginning to ring. *Why would he want to talk to me alone? I am not liking where this is going.*

'Seth is here with me,' she lied.

'Will you message me later when you are alone? I need to tell you something.'

Jules sighed, and then a whole range of scenarios went through her head. *Perhaps he is embarrassed to tell his best friend, Seth, he has a failed marriage. Perhaps he is in a bad place and*

51

just needs someone to talk to. Perhaps he is on the edge of suicide, and if I reject his request, he will harm himself. She had a flashback of her Dad hanging from the rafters and then typed.

'Seth is in the other room. I am worried about you. You wouldn't harm yourself, would you?'

A few minutes passed, and Jules's heart was starting to pound. She decided that if he didn't reply, she would call Seth and get him to go 'round to see Shawn. Feeling relieved, she spotted three dots waving in the comment box, so she knew he was typing a long message. The phone pinged again, and she held the phone up to read his reply.

'We broke up three days ago. Jane went through my phone and thinks I have been talking to other women. I have a lot of fans now, both men and women, and somehow they have managed to message me. I haven't been unfaithful. I might have flirted a little with some, but it meant nothing. I have been sleeping in my car. The nights have been cold. Could I come and stay with you for a bit until I get things sorted with Jane. She has not been the same since she had Jack.'

Jules sighed and shook her head. She couldn't understand why Shawn had not called Seth.

'Look, Shawn, you can't be spending a night in the car again. Please can you ring Seth? He will let you stay here tonight and help you to sort things out with Jane. Please don't say you messaged me. It is a little odd that you did.'

She pressed the send button and waited. Juliet had finished feeding, so she sat her up and tried to wind her, hoping she wouldn't vomit. Jules was feeling very uncomfortable about the whole thing and she was feeling guilty that she was keeping his messages secret. *I like Shawn but only as a friend. He has crossed a boundary, and it is freaking me out.* "Are you ok, my baby? Shall we go and see the others and wait for Shawn to call Seth. I should have rung Jane to see how she was getting on with her Jack. You have kept me so busy and your brother has been on my mind all the time. You will like having a brother. He is the sweetest little thing ever and will look after you." Jules was welling up, and as she reached the bedroom door, she could hear Seth's phone ringing. She walked into the living area and realised that Seth had gone out, leaving his phone on the coffee table. With a sinking feeling in her stomach, Jules carried Juliet over to the phone and, feeling a little sick, took the call. "Hi Shawn, Seth has gone down to see Moss."

"Is it alright if I come over then?"

"I guess so. You can spend the night on the sofa if that is ok."

"I'd like that."

"Do you want me to ring Jane to let her know you are here?" Jules saw Granny give her an enquiring look.

"I want to talk to you first. Don't ring her until later. Do you mind?"

"No, I don't mind. WE'LL see you soon." She emphasised the 'we'll' to make it quite clear that it wasn't just her he would be talking to. "See you soon, then." Jules ended the call and looked over at Granny, who had an odd look on her face.

"Boyfriend troubles?" she asked, winking.

"Hell no! That's Seth's friend Shawn. He's just had a row with his wife and is coming over to talk things over. Hopefully, we can get things sorted for them and send him home tonight. They've got a new baby, and I think Jane might have postnatal depression by the sounds of it."

"You've gone red, Jules. I will never forgive you if you break my Seth's heart."

"I am just shocked that you would say such a thing. Please don't say anything to Seth about this. I really am not interested in that man."

"Mmm... I won't. He has been through enough."

"Granny, please, there is nothing to say."

***

With his long black mane and tail flying behind him, Moss galloped across the lower field towards Seth. Seth grinned as he watched his beautiful horse charge over to him, eager to be near him. He had never seen an animal so devoted. Seth climbed through the post and rail fence and waited for Moss to arrive. He had a few pieces of apples and carrots in his fist to treat him. Moss stopped short of Seth, danced about on the spot for a moment, and was clearly overjoyed to be by him. "Calm down, you daft thing. Have you missed me, my boy? Come here and let me hug you. I have a treat for you first." Seth opened his hand and revealed the carrot and apple. It never ceased to amaze Seth how happy Moss was to see him.

Moss pawed the ground with impatience, and Seth laughed. "So you are going to make me come to you. He walked towards his horse and held his hand flat, allowing him to eat. Moss' soft lips picked out the apple. "You fussy thing. Do you not like carrots anymore?" Seth dropped the carrot on the floor, put his arms around Moss's strong neck, and patted him firmly. "There you go, my beauty. I came to see you before it got dark and to think up a song to help find Darragh. Have you got any ideas, my boy? The song looking for Linda keeps going through my head. We will have to come up with something a bit more modern. Everyone is loving Blinding Lights and Times Like These at the moment, so we will have to come up with a good tune... I think we should make it more of an upbeat song for Darragh. We don't want to depress everyone. What do you think?" Moss snorted. "So you agree. Now the words. I will type them in an email and send it to myself. I am having trouble thinking of any words. This is tough. It is easy to write about love and life but not loss. Where's my phone?" Seth felt in his back pocket, but it wasn't there. "Damn, I left it at home. Never mind, I can't think of a single word at the moment."

The muscles in Moss' neck tightened, and his head lifted. He snorted and seemed agitated. "What's the matter? What are you looking at?" Seth followed Moss' gaze and then gasped. He saw Gemma standing in the doorway of the barn in the distance. Her white dress was stained with blood. He blinked, not believing his eyes and then shut them tightly. When he opened his eyes, she was gone. "Jesus! Did you see her, Moss? You did, didn't you? I am not going mad, am I?" Seth shivered and shook his head. *It could be stress or dusk playing tricks on me. Stress can do things to your mind. I don't believe in ghosts. Did I see a ghost? Christ! She was covered in blood. Was it Sinead being an eejit? No, it wasn't. She wouldn't do that to me. Granny said that Gemma wants to help me. Why would she want to do that when I was mean to her when she was alive?* He shivered again.

55

Seth patted Moss's neck again for reassurance. "I'll come back tomorrow and take you out, I promise. You don't worry about her, will you? She is not after you. Just me, and this foolishness needs to stop. It is freaking me out."

Chapter Eight

With the vision of Gemma still in his head, Seth picked up the pace, eager to get home. He had the distinct feeling that she was following him. It did not sit well with him that he had perhaps seen his first ghost. He opened the front door and then shut it firmly behind him, relieved to have made it back in one piece. Jules was sitting on the sofa feeding Juliet and watching the television.

She looked up when he came over and noticed that he looked pale and tired. "Are you ok, Seth? You look like you have seen a ghost."

Seth was taken aback by her words. He shook his head. "I got a bit spooked when I was in the field with Moss. All this talk about spirits dwelling at Waterfall West has got to me. You look tired, my sweet girl. Shall I put on the dinner? What are we having?"

"I don't know yet. Look in the freezer and see if you can find anything worth eating. I need to order some more food, but I haven't had a chance this week. I think there are some eggs in the fridge and chips in the freezer. Granny said she would cook, but I think she has gone to do a TikTok tarot reading. She's in her bedroom and keeps laughing."

"She laughed a lot in the park too. I think doing a reading for people gives her a buzz."

Seeing Seth's phone laying on the coffee table jogged her memory. "Seth, you left your phone here, and Shawn rang. I answered it. Is that ok?"

"Yes, of course. I'll cook us something first and then give him a call back?" he said, looking in the fridge. "Was it urgent?"

"Kind of. Is there enough for Shawn too? He is coming over. He is actually staying over. He has had a row with Jane."

"Yes, there's enough. A row, you say? Did he say what it was about?"

Jules stopped to think for a moment, trying to remember. I don't know exactly. I'm sure he will tell you. He…" The doorbell rang. "That will be Shawn. He will have to sleep on the sofa."

"I am sure he won't have to stay over. He just needs to talk to Jane and settle things."

Seth opened the door and was surprised to see the state Shawn was in. He had thick stubble on his chin and looked like he had slept in his clothes."

"Thanks for letting me stay, Seth. It's a cold night, and I didn't fancy sleeping in my car again."

Seth frowned. "No, we can't have you sleeping in your car. Come in and warm yourself. I am sorry to hear that you are having difficulties with Jane. Sit down, and I will get you a cup of tea and something to eat. I don't like to see you like this, mate."

Shawn sat at the kitchen table, put his head in his hand, and started sobbing. Jules and Seth stared at each other with wide eyes, alarmed by what they saw.

"Are you ok there, Shawn? It can't be that bad," Seth said soothingly. "Jane will come around, I am sure."

Shawn shook his head. "She called me a bastard and threw me out. I haven't been unfaithful, I swear."

"I believe you. You adore Jane," Seth said, sitting next to him.

"She went through my phone, and the girls I messaged want nothing more to do with me. I just want to be with Jane. Things haven't been too good since Jack was born, and we haven't had sex since because she is so tired and depressed. These girls meant nothing to me; it was just a little harmless flirting. I miss Jane so much. It is hurting me inside. I don't think we have ever been apart this long."

Seth was puzzled by his friend and was doing his best to understand what Shawn was telling him. He was also surprised to discover that his friend was a cheat. In his book, messaging other women was cheating. "Have you tried ringing or messaging her?"

"I have, but she is not replying. She has washed her hands of me."

"You mustn't give up so easily," Jules said as she winded Juliet. "I will give her a ring in a minute and talk to her. Like I said…." She stopped, not wanting Seth to think she had already had a detailed conversation with him. She was glad that Granny wasn't around. *Why am I feeling so weird about this?*

"You are doing a grand job coping with a new baby," Shawn said, looking directly at Jules. "Why are we finding it so hard?"

His gaze was making her feel uncomfortable. "It is not easy, and it takes teamwork. That's why Seth is cooking tonight, and I am doing my best to keep this one happy. Having children is hard work. Do you think you were doing your share with Jack?"

Shawn sighed. "No, I don't help enough. I am not good with babies and I don't know what to do. Jane kept saying that I should hold him more."

"When you go back, you are going to have to help more. Jane is probably worn out, and you messing about has not helped," Jules said firmly as she got up. "Seth, I'll cook if that is ok. Last time you cooked egg and chips, it came out an odd colour."

"I think I burnt the oil, but it tasted ok. Shawn, Jules is right. I thought working on the farm was hard work, but looking after a baby is twice as hard. Jane can't do it all on her own." Seth stood up. "I will hold this little one," he said as he took Juliet. "We are both finding this baby thing hard, but it is not going to be hard forever, and I am sure it will get easier. Darragh was easier...." Seth couldn't finish the sentence. "Shawn, you have been an eejit."

"I'm so sorry, mate. I know you have more than enough on your plate at the moment and my being a nuisance isn't helping. Is there any news about your boy?"

"No, we will write and release a song to help remind people to look for him. I think we should do a cover of a recent song and add some 'find Darragh' words to it. What do you think, Jules?" he asked.

Jules smiled. "I like that idea, but we will have to think of a good song. I know! I have just the one. We could sing Ed Sheeran's Castle on the Hill. You can hear the words clearly in that one."

"I will write a song for you," Shawn said. "I used to be good at doing that," he said, looking at them both sadly.

"You are a good songwriter. That's really kind of you," Jules said, trying not to cry. "Sometimes the pain of being parted from Darragh hurts so much."

"I am sorry. I feel really stupid now," Shawn said, shaking his head.

"I want to get a song out straight away, so for speed, we will use Ed's song. Do you think we will have to ask him first?"

"No, you don't have to ask permission to cover a song or produce your own version of a song. What if he sang the song with you? I am sure he would be delighted to help. I can send a message to him if you like."

"Do you have his contact details, then?" Seth asked.

"I don't, but my guitarist does. Gus is Ed's cousin. You know that Ed has family around here, don't you?"

"Oh, this is so exciting. If he sang with me, then that would make one of my dreams come true."

"Are you a fan then?" Shawn asked.

"I am perhaps his number one fan," Jules said, smiling, and then she felt uncomfortable, and she started to wonder why Shawn was trying to be so helpful. *Is he interested in me? Please no.*

Granny appeared with a pile of bedding and then raised her eyebrows when she saw Shawn. "I'll make a bed up for you, dear. You mustn't worry yourself about Jane. I've just done a card reading for her, and I think you will find she is at a crossroads in her life, and you just have to make sure you are waiting at the end of the right path for her."

Shawn looked surprised. Seth felt the need to explain. "Shawn, this is my granny. She is staying with us and helping us out for a bit. She reads cards to people. Granny, you should have let me get the bedding down for you. It is in the top cupboard, and I don't want you falling off anything."

"The day I stop doing things for myself will be the day I lay down in my grave... Thank you anyway."

"Nice to meet you," Shawn replied. "I have to be honest, I am not really into card readings, but I appreciate your concern. I just need to speak to my wife and tell her I am sorry. Seth is right. I have been a proper eejit."

"You also need to stop your shenanigans. Men like you are trouble. Look at your father, Seth. He couldn't keep his dick in his trousers."

"Granny! I don't think Shawn is a ladies' man. You are not, are you?"

"Christ, no!" he gasped, throwing a quick glance at Jules. "I just want to be with Jane and Jane only."

"So before I cook," Jules said, picking up her phone, "I am going to ring Jane and then I will explain that you are here and you need to talk to her."

"Can it wait until morning? I am not sure I know what to say to her."

"No, you need to get this sorted. You must tell her you are sorry and that you love her and only her."

"I have already said I am sorry. She just laughed in my face."

"Did you tell her that you love her?"

"She already knows that."

"When did you last tell her that you love her?"

"I don't remember. She knows that it is hard for me to say those words."

"Shawn, she is tired and depressed after having your child, and she needs to hear that you love and appreciate her."

"Can't this wait until morning? I am not good with this stuff."

"No, you will have to do this, and I promise she will have you back. You can stay the night, and then in the morning, you need to freshen up, man up and go home and be the man she deserves. Seth, help me here."

"Jules is right."

DARRAGH

"Jane? It's Jules. I've been meaning to call you. How are you doing? Is now a good time to talk?"

Chapter Nine

Tom Stone was angry. He glared at his lawyer with disgust and folded his arms. "Are you mad? I am not going to say I am guilty. I thought we agreed that I would get the charges dropped if we say my mind is unsound."

"Look, Mr Stone, when they brought you in, you were naked and clearly distressed. You could have passed then as being mentally unstable but your current condition indicates to me that you are of sound mind, coherent and your mood high. You could reduce a life sentence to fifteen years if you plead guilty to murder."

"YOU are out of your mind," Tom spat, staring at his balding lawyer squarely. "I am no more a murderer than you are. I didn't kill Gemma Day. The evidence found is circumstantial, and it is your job to dismiss this in court. That is what I am paying you for. Or you will be paid once my assets have been released. Have you any word on that, Mr Borden. I don't know how you expect me to survive on nothing. I am in need of some money for personal items. I am tired of borrowing from others, and I now owe well over three hundred pounds to my cellmate."

"I have contacted the Australian courts, and I will let you know as soon as they get back to me."

"This is simply not good enough. Have you spoken to Julia yet? I did ask you to contact her. I need to speak to her. She will not be happy knowing I am suffering in this Hell hole. You do know she agreed to marry me, don't you?"

"I don't know what planet you are on, but she is the one that has filed charges against you for rape, attempted murder and kidnapping."

"She is just upset. Now she has had time to calm down, I am sure she will see the error of her ways and drop these silly charges. She loves me, really."

"It would help things if you could tell us who abducted her child."

"I don't know how many times I have to tell you this, but I got that number on the dark web, and these sites are only live for 24 hours or something like that."

"Yes, you have told the police this, but you must have been given a link to get that number. Who gave you that link, Mr Stone?"

"Hmm…? You'd like me to tell you that, wouldn't you? Perhaps we can do a deal. I need to speak to Julia, and then and only then, I might be able to help you."

"This is not a game, Mr Stone. Julia does not want to speak to you."

"Oh my, that is a disappointment. I think you should talk to her and tell her that I forgive her and will be there for her when I am released."

"I don't think that will be possible…."

"You are not being very helpful. I will need your assistance with another matter. I will need you to get me some Viagra for Mr Steel."

"I'm sorry, I don't follow."

"I am having terrible trouble with my mind, and without Viagra, I can't satisfy my mind or Mr Steel. I told you that I have a sex addiction, and like any addiction, I need help controlling my cravings. When I asked to see the prison doctor, I was met with abuse and laughter."

"You are joking? You honestly don't expect me to ask them to prescribe you Viagra, do you?" he said, laughing.

Tom slammed his hand down on the table and roared. "HOW DARE YOU LAUGH AT ME! This is no laughing matter. You can say goodbye to that Hearn brat if you can't help me."

"There is no negotiation to be done, Mr Stone. If you cannot help, you will find that you will spend a very long time in prison. Life perhaps."

"You are a useless lump of shit. I want another lawyer."

"I am all you can afford, and if you don't respect what I have to say, then I am quite happy to drop this case and move on. You are lucky to have me. You do know that you are facing paedophilic and pornography charges in Australia, don't you?"

"You know, that is rubbish, I have no idea how those pictures got on my computer, and I had no idea that my girlfriends were underage. If you talk to them, they will say they lied about their age and worshipped Mr Steel."

"I don't think the courts will see it like that. There is a small matter of your murder charge too. You are being trialled separately for the murder of Gemma Day. The trial starts on Tuesday, 27 April, and a date has yet to be set for the abduction and rape of the minor Sandra James."

"This is an outrage. I am innocent. As I said, Gemma was a sweet girl but so clumsy. Her death was accidental, so they can't pin that one on me. Sandra James came to me. I didn't abduct or rape her."

"Again, I think you will find that the courts will disagree. Look, Mr Stone, you need to think about this seriously and change your plea to guilty due to an unsound mind. After talking to you this afternoon, I think you should be assessed by a psychiatrist, and then we can present to the court a report showing the state of your mind. There is a good chance you will not end your life in prison."

"I have no objection to talking to a psychiatrist. I think we finally understand each other."

***

Darragh covered himself with his blanket and slipped the cover over his head, doing his best to keep warm. He pulled his knees up under his chin and, beneath his woollen cover, listened to the sounds of the night. He couldn't be sure, but sometimes he thought he could hear water running outside his window. Not a shower but a large amount of water rushing past his room. The past few nights, he had been really cold and shivered until he discovered that it was warmer to cover himself completely. His teeth chattered together, and he shivered.

Tonight, he could hear someone crying in the room next to his. It wasn't the lady that fed him, but someone younger. The girl sounded like she was in pain, and he found tears expelling from his own eyes as he listened. He didn't like to hear her cry and wondered if she felt cold like he was. The crying stopped, and he sighed, pleased that she wasn't hurting anymore. He could hear the woman that gave him food singing to her, and he tried to make out the words. He recognised some of the words but it was not the rockabye baby song that he knew. He remembered his Da singing him the song when he was in the front of a lorry with him. Tears ran down his cheeks as he tried to remember his Da's face. He could see dark eyes, dark hair and a big smile on his face. How he longed to hear his voice again. Darragh felt sad for himself. He wanted the ginger-haired lady to sing to him and smile at him. He wondered why she didn't like him as much as she liked the crying girl. He needed to find out and then wondered how he would get out of the room.

Darragh sat up, but he was shivering too much, so he lay back down and covered himself up again. He decided that in the morning when there was enough light in the room and after he had been given his breakfast, he would attempt to climb out of his cot. The thought of standing on the floor away from all that was familiar to him scared him a little. He could feel himself drifting off to sleep. The sweet voice of the ginger-haired lady was lulling him to sleep. He would dream of finding his Mam and Da waiting for him with open arms on the other side of the door. With this happy thought in his head, he fell into a troubled sleep.

Chapter Ten

The old wooden gate, green with algae, took a lot of effort to open, and Seth feared that the hinges might break. He finally pushed it back against the fence and looped the string onto the hook to keep it from closing. The woodlands were now open to the Irish travellers that Lucy had initially thought had abducted Darragh. The woodlands smelt fresh and spring-like, and he hoped the travellers would like their new home.

The day before, he had dropped Granny off quite near to offices where he had found Jules and lost Darragh. The travellers had been staying in the fields around the office. Granny's eyes had lit up when she had seen the caravans and she looked almost childlike. Her days as a traveller were so obviously dear to her. He asked if she wanted him to go with her to see Brian Smith and to see if they would welcome their proposal. She had laughed and said that it wouldn't take much convincing and not to worry about her. She knew Brian's father and Grandfather well; they would accept their offer if they were still alive.

It hadn't been easy getting Lucy to tell him where the travellers had been staying and even harder to convince her that his idea to let them stay on his land until the pandemic was over was a good idea. She had mentioned that he would need planning permission if he was running a campsite, but he had laughed and said it would be just a coincidence that they had settled on his land.

Seth rested his back on the gate as he waited for the group of travellers to arrive. The wind was up and his dark hair, now a little too long, blew everywhere. He ran his fingers through it and vowed to get Sinead to cut it that afternoon.

He hadn't liked leaving Granny with the travellers and wanted to wait for her, but she pointed at her phone and said that she would call him if she needed him and not to worry if she didn't come home that night. She said that she had a lot of catching up to do, and the Poutine was bound to come out, and all ghosts would be laid to rest. Seth hadn't understood what she meant, but he guessed there would be much talking about the past. She had not called him that night, and he had gone to bed fretting. Jules had laughed and said that perhaps they had stolen her too. Her comment had not made things any easier. He had fallen asleep dreaming that wolves were in the woods and he had woken up several times to check if Granny had phoned. Her call finally came just after eight, and she laughed and said she had been quite safe and really enjoyed her night with the Smiths.

The agreement was that the travellers would be happy to stay as long as electricity, clean water and a Wi-Fi signal were made available to them. Seth had run a power cable down from the annexe of the Manor House through the garden and had left the Wi-Fi code in an envelope for them to use. There was a well in the garden which would provide them with water. He had wound up the bucket and was pleased to see it full to the brim with clean water. He had thought of opening the annexe to them so they could use the washroom but Sinead thought it better not to, as most of the caravans had working showers and chemical toilets.

Seth could hear cars coming up the gravel drive, and he stepped out onto the drive to direct the travellers to the open gate. As they approached, he saw his granny sitting between two burley men in the first van. He felt slightly anxious and waved when he saw her smiling broadly at him. The white van was pulling behind it a large caravan. They were being followed by others. Alarmed, Seth looked at the entrance into the woodland and wondered if the caravans would fit through. He needn't have worried. With only millimetres to spare, the driver slid the caravan through the entrance, and Seth smiled. They were quite used to driving large vehicles. He counted eighteen caravans and was sure there were a few more than he remembered seeing when he'd dropped Granny off.

"So they all got here safely?" Jules asked as she arrived.

"Bejesus! Where did you come from?" Seth gasped.

"Sorry, I should have whistled or sung. You were miles away."

"I didn't hear you coming. I was just thinking how crazy this idea is. We could be heading to shed loads of trouble. Already we are supplying and paying the electricity for them all, and then what if they don't want to leave!"

"I am glad they have come. I just know there is a connection between them and Darragh. Seth, do you see that girl over there with long black hair?" Jules asked as she watched the girl climb out of a Discovery. "Do you think she looks like a Hearn?"

"Perhaps, but I think her hair is dyed."

Jules watched her for a minute, then her attention turned to Granny, walking towards them. "Your Granny looks happy. I think she wants to stay with them."

"Why do you say that? She is far too old to be staying in a caravan."

"I don't think she is happy staying with us. She seems uneasy."

"Do you think so?"

"Seth, we need to go and get my belongings. I'm moving in with Joan Taylor," Granny called out.

"Oh, you were right," Seth whispered.

"Are you sure, Granny? Do you think you will be ok? I don't want you to get cold. It's not warm in a caravan at night."

"I will be fine. It will be like old times. I miss being with my family. These caravans have heating now, although we will have to get some gas bottles delivered. Their usual supplier went out of business.

"Seth!" Jules exclaimed. "Do you see the girl with the black hair? I think she is holding Darragh. Oh my God, she has our boy!"

Jules started to run, but Seth grabbed her arm. "No, Jules. It isn't him. I thought that at first when she lifted him out of the car, but it's not him."

Jules stopped and then let out a sob. "I really thought it was."

Granny sighed. "He is Darragh's cousin. I don't want you two going anywhere near them. His name is Marley Hearn. Let me talk to Jess," Granny said, looking anxiously at Jules. "Promise me you won't be talking to any of them about Darragh. I know there are some that know something, and you two standing on the edge staring at them are making them all nervous. I had a hard enough job getting them to stay here. You two go back home and let me handle this. Yes, there are questions to be asked, which need to be done delicately. I need to win their trust first and then..."

"Oy you! Why are you staring at my Marley?" Jess called out, and with Marley on her hip, she made her way to them, her cheeks red and her forehead furrowed.

"Christ, Granny! You were right. We have upset them. Jess is coming over to us."

"Let me handle this," Granny said as she walked over to Jess and Marley. "Don't upset yourself. Seth and Jules just wanted to make sure you have everything you need. They are going now, so there is no need for you to worry."

Jules couldn't keep her eyes off Marley, and she scrutinised every feature on his face, comparing him to Darragh. All she could remember was her little boy as a baby, and she tried to imagine what he would look like now. She yearned to hold Marley and see how it felt to carry a toddler. Darragh was probably the same age as Marley, and the likeness was uncanny.

Granny was unable to stop Jess from approaching them both. Jess's mouth dropped when she got near Seth. "Fuck me, you look just like Jon Hearn. Are you two brothers or something?" Jess exclaimed, staring directly at Seth.

"No, I don't have a brother called Jon, but I am a Hearn. Are you a Hearn too?" Seth asked gently, not wanting to sound like he was interrogating her.

"Only by marriage. Jon is my husband. He is away at the moment."

"So, do you need a hand setting up your caravan? I can help you if you like." Seth feared that he might have offended her as he felt she was very independent.

"I usually manage by myself, but this one is being a pain in the ass at the moment and is driving me crazy. If you have nothing better to do, then I would be thankful if you could unhitch my van and put it under that tree over there. I would do it myself..."

"That's no problem," Seth said. "Jules, if Juliet lets you, would you mind helping Granny load all her things into the car."

Jules wanted to stay and see more of Marley but knew that Granny wanted them to keep away from the travellers. She wondered if Granny was cross with Seth for helping Jess. "Ok, I'll see you in a bit." She watched them walk over to Jess's caravan and sighed.

"You don't like him being with other women, do you?" Granny whispered.

"No, it's not that. I trust Seth with my life. It's Jess I don't trust. There is something about her that worries me. I can't say what exactly. I think she is hiding something."

Chapter Eleven

The ground was full of roots and leaf litter, making manoeuvring the caravan difficult. By the time Seth had got it into position, underneath an elm tree, drops of sweat were running down his face. Jess was standing close by and directed Seth, but she got him to move the caravan several times until she was happy. Marley watched the proceedings with fascination, and Seth was quite sure that he had heard him say Da once or twice.

"There you go! Are you happy now?" Seth asked, hoping she wouldn't ask him to move the caravan again.

Jess smiled. "You know you could have used the automatic mover to do that? That's what I use to move the caravan."

"Now you tell me!" Seth said, shaking his head.

"I am such a pea brain sometimes. Thanks for your help. Will you do me another favour?"

"Another? I might need to sit down for a minute and get my breath back."

"Will you get away with yourself," she said, laughing. "A man your age with all those muscles shouldn't be puffing just pulling a caravan into place. Jon would have done it without sweating."

"Would he now? I'd like to meet this Jon and see him try and drag a caravan over tree roots."

Jess frowned. "I'd prefer it if you didn't tell Jon you helped me."

"Why's that, then?"

Jess looked a bit uncomfortable. "He doesn't like me talking to outsiders."

"I am not an outsider. We are likely cousins or brothers. I am also your landlord."

Jess still looked awkward. "Please don't say anything."

"I won't, but others here might say that I helped you."

"No, they won't say anything. Nobody talks to him. I am all he has in the world."

"Why is that, then?"

"He has a flat in Cork and is not really one of us. He says his family were once travellers, but he was born in a house, so he can't stay here."

"So why aren't you and Marley living with him in his flat?"

"You ask a lot of questions! You are so nosy. Just like your grandmother."

"I'm sorry. I just think it is pretty mean that he leaves you here on your own to cope with everything. Doesn't he miss Darr... no, sorry, Marley."

Jess put her head on one side. "Your granny says that you've lost your son. I'm sorry about that."

"Yes, he is missing, but we didn't lose him. He was taken. Your wee boy reminds me of him so much. Jules and I are doing everything we can to find him. He has been gone nearly a year now. This afternoon we are going to release a record to remind the public that he is still missing."

"Is that why your wife was staring at us so hard, then? She looked like she wanted to take Marley off me. She hasn't gone mad, has she?"

"She hasn't gone mad and won't take Marley off you. She...We just need to find Darragh. The police have had no luck finding him, so that's why we are going to record another song."

"Oh, I see. I'm sorry, I don't know how I'd cope if Marley was taken. Do you two sing, then?" Jess asked as she hugged Marley close to her and rocked him.

"Yes, we do! Do you know the song Waterfall Way? It went to number one last spring. It became a number one hit on the day that Darragh was taken."

"No, I don't know that song. So are you famous then? Are you in a group?"

"Have you heard of S&J or Sonar Cell?"

Jess shook her head. "I don't listen to pop music. Jon doesn't like me to. He says I need to concentrate on keeping the house clean and learn to care for Marley properly."

"Oh, I see." Seth was beginning to see red flags. "He sounds like he is a bit of a control freak."

Jess looked a bit shocked. *I wish I hadn't said she is bound to clam up now.*

"He doesn't control me. I am free to do as I please," her eyes narrowed a little, and her tone was defensive.

"I'm sorry. I didn't mean to offend you. Is there anything else you need before I go?"

Jess frowned again. "I can manage. Where's the water? I need to fill up."

"You have to go through that gate into the house's garden, and you will find a well."

"A what?"

"A well."

"Fuck that! Don't you have a standpipe?"

"We do. I turned the water off in the house over the winter, and it is a long walk up to the house to get to the tap."

"It's not winter now. Can't you run a hose from the pipe down to us? My Mam has arthritis, and she won't be able to manage it. Or your nosy Granny."

"No, I suppose not. Ok, I will run a hose down from the house. Do you want me to fill up your water holder for you?"

"I can do it," she said as she placed Marley on the floor. The toddler began to cry. "You stop your noise, Marley Hearn. You will be fine playing here while I get us water."

"You can't leave him here alone."

"He won't be alone. Mam will keep an eye on him. MAM?" she called. "MAM?"

A woman with long curly grey hair looked out of a caravan on the other side of the plot.

"Will you come and mind Marley for me while I get us some water?" Jess called.

"I can't, pet, I am cooking, and I have my friend arriving soon."

"I forgot your granny was going to stay with her." Jess huffed. "Will you mind Marley for me? I won't be ten minutes."

"Look, I'll get you some water. It is no bother. He will probably cry, and I doubt Jon will approve of me holding him."

"You are right there. Watch Marley for a minute, and I will go and get the water box."

Before Seth could say anything more, Jess hurried off and left Marley standing alone. He watched the little boy with fascination. Marley looked up at Seth and then watched his face contort with anguish as he realised he had been left with a stranger.

Marley started to cry. "Aww, no, please don't cry. Your Mam will be back in a minute." Marley continued to bawl and picked him up, fearing that he would have a fit. "Now then, don't you cry. Shall we go and find your Mam? I don't know what is taking her so long, but she is right here, I promise." Seth carried Marley around the back of the caravan to where he thought he had seen her go and was surprised to see her smoking. "Hey! I thought you were going to get the water holder."

"I was, but I just needed a quick cigarette first."

"Oh, I see. Marley was crying. Didn't you hear him?"

"I did. He cries all the time." Jess took a puff of her cigarette and then put her arms out to take Marley.

"You'd better put out your fag first. You don't want to get smoke in his face or get him burned. He has stopped crying now he has seen you."

"I won't burn him. Are you saying I am a bad mother?"

"No, not at all. Darragh used to reach out for everything. I took a sip of tea once, and he nearly had the whole cup over him. I just remember babies being too curious for their own good."

Jess's face softened, and she exhaled the smoke away from them. "You'll get him back. He's all right. I just know he is."

"I don't doubt it, but Jules is starting to lose hope. I promised her that I would get him back and I just have to before April 19, which is his second birthday. That is just a month away. Jess, I want to ask you something?"

"What's that then?"

"Do you know why the people who kidnapped him would try to pin it on the travellers? The number plates they were using were duped using ones from a white van owned by one of your community."

"So that's why you've brought us here! You just want to interrogate us all. Well, fuck you! I think that you'd better leave."

"No, that's not true," he lied. "Seriously, I really wanted to help you all. I know it has been hard for you during Covid and Granny used to travel with you when she was young. She is so much happier now that she is with her travelling family."

"You are lying."

"I do want to help but I also want to know who the van that was written off belonged to. I keep offending you. I really don't mean to do that."

Jess shook her head. "I am really mad at you! I know you are desperate to get your baby back. So I will tell you what I know, but you must swear that you won't tell Jon. He will beat me if he hears I have told you this."

"Beat you? Nobody should beat anyone."

"Well, some of us fucking deserve it, so don't go all sentimental on me. I can be a bitch so let's leave it at that, shall we. Brian's van got written off, and he was really pissed when the cops came to see him. Jon laughed when he found out. They don't get on. Jon will be pissed off when he finds out we are staying at your place."

"Seriously. Why is that?"

"Look, you are obviously related, and it is freaking me out how much you look like him. If you had shorter hair and were smaller, you would be identical. He got all fired up when the police mentioned your name, and I know he will kick up a fuss when I tell him that we have moved here."

"You don't have to tell him you are here. I am not being funny, Jess, but you really don't need a man like that in your life. Bitch or not, nobody deserves to be beaten. Usually, people keep domestic violence a secret. The fact that you told me just shows that you need help."

"Fuck off! I don't need help. You are just like the rest of them. You think if you show me a little kindness, you can get into my knickers."

"Um, no! I meant what I said. You deserve better. I don't sleep around."

"Pity."

"What?"

"Look, I can't help wondering if you are better in bed than Jon."

"I am a married man. I think that we need to forget about this conversation. Here, take your boy and let me get you some water..."

"JESS?... JESS?"

"Oh fuck! It's Jon." She looked terrified. "How the fuck did he know we had moved here?" she whispered. "He can't find you here. Stay here and don't move until I give you the all-clear. I have to go to him."

Before Seth could speak, Jess took Marley and disappeared, leaving Seth alone behind the caravan. He felt foolish hiding but didn't want Jess to get beaten for talking to him. *This is a really crazy situation. I should speak to him and explain that I am just trying to help. I am curious to know how much he looks like me. It is going to look very dodgy now if I suddenly appear. Oh fuck, I just don't know what to do now.*

Seth waited for a few minutes, and he could feel his heart pounding in his chest. He gazed out at the woodland ahead and made a snap decision to walk into the woods using the caravan as cover. Being careful not to be detected, Seth began to walk. With each tree he passed, the fear of being discovered became less.

When he was sure that he was far enough away from Jess and Marley's caravan, he stopped as a thought came into his head. *If I walk away now, I will lose the opportunity to find out if Jon knows anything more about Darragh. Walking away is not the solution. I will have to loop around, enter the campsite by the gate, and make out that I haven't spoken to Jess. I will pretend that I am going to see Granny. I wonder how he will react when he sees me?*

As Seth walked, he noticed the wild daffodils were starting to bloom, and that spring had arrived without him even noticing. A wave of guilt swept over him as he remembered that his seeds had arrived a few weeks ago and were crying out to be buried in soil. All he could think about was finding Darragh, which alone gave him a reason to get up each day. *This is not a good way to feel. I have my lovely Jules to wake up to each morning. I mustn't forget that. Why do I feel like crying? Come on, Seth, pull yourself together. The Hearn men don't cry. Come high or Hell water, I will find our boy before the month is out and then think about living again.*

Seth saw someone ahead and stopped walking. The sun was dazzling him, and he found it hard to see. He shielded his eyes from the light and squinted, fearing that his eyes were deceiving him. Gemma was standing a few yards away and was just staring at him. Her white dress was covered in blood, and her fair hair was wet and plastered around her face. Her eyes held his gaze for a moment, and she seemed almost as shocked as he was. "No, this cannot be happening!" He gasped and then looked behind him, with the distinct feeling that he was being followed. When he turned back, he was relieved to find she had gone. He ran to where he had seen her and finding nobody there he yelled out. "Will you leave me alone! I don't need your help!" Exasperated, he thumped a tree with his fist and held his head with his hands. "Am I going crazy? There's nobody here. Just trees and leaves and..." he could smell sickly perfume or perhaps roses. He wasn't sure which.

Chapter Twelve

"WILL YOU KEEP STILL? I'm sorry... Are you having trouble sleeping, Mr Steel? I can hear you tossing and turning, and the bed is making such a noise and is keeping me awake. If you like, I can swap with you. I don't mind sleeping on the top bunk... I've got a book you could read if you have a torch. You could use my torch if you want, Mr Steel?"

"Oh, for goodness sake! Will you shut up, Jasper? And it is Tom, not Mr Steel. I was asleep. I don't know how. These mattresses are too thin and hard."

"But I've heard you say the name Steel in the night when you are talking to yourself. I didn't sleep when I first came here. It takes some time getting used to the routine. I used to stay awake at night for hours on that top bunk. My old roommate used to say that it was because hot air rises, and he was a big man, and he said that I could feel the heat from his body rising up."

"You are talking bullshit. Do you ever shut up? Why they have put me in here with you, I will never know. I have asked for my own room with an ensuite, but I don't think they took me seriously. It is inhumane to expect two people to share a room and sit on a toilet in full view of each other. I am tossing and turning because this mattress is not fit for even a dog to lie on. It's no good. I am going to sleep on the floor and put in a formal complaint in the morning," he grumbled as he climbed down the ladder.

"You will get in trouble."

"There's no one watching us. How do they know I am not going for a shit? There are no cameras in here, are there?"

"All I know is that I wanked off one night, and one of the guards said he saw me doing it. I think there is a camera in the light."

"Don't be so stupid. Everyone has to have a wank, and they only have to look through the spy hole to get their kicks."

"Do you think they are watching us now?"

"Probably. They are sick bastards. AREN'T YOU?" he yelled towards the door. "They are violating our right to privacy."

"We have no rights in prison. We are treated like dogs. It is not fair."

"We'll see about that. They haven't had to deal with Tom Stone before."

"So if we want to wank, we should do it under the covers facing the wall."

"What makes you think I want to wank?"

"I've seen you touching yourself. You do it all the time."

"Look, I'll be frank with you, Mr Steel has not been himself lately. When I am at home, I have to satisfy him at least five times a day. I need to have sex. Mr Steel demands it. You couldn't give him a blow job, could you?"

"I am not gay."

"It doesn't matter. Mr Steel has needs and I can't 'wank' as you put it. He needs a bit of excitement and is hardening just thinking of you sucking me off. It won't take long. You could shut your eyes and imagine you are pleasuring your girlfriend. How horny is this? Mr Steel is ready for you. See how hard and firm he is," Tom pulled down his shorts and hoped Jasper could see his erection. He longed for Jasper to reach out and touch Mr Steel. Pleased that he had hardened without medication, he moved a little closer to Jasper. "Take him in your mouth, Jasper. I need this so badly. I will look after you if you do."

"How will you look after me?"

"You do know that I am a millionaire, don't you? I have enough money to buy you a new house."

"You are crazy. Who would give someone a house for a blow job?"

"I think you would have to satisfy me more than once to earn a house. The offer is on the table.

"Can you see how magnificent Mr Steel is? You can touch him if you like and watch him grow. I am well endowed." Tom was becoming desperate and needed Jasper to act there and then. His erection was becoming painful. The desire to satisfy his sexual need was too much to bear. He wondered if he would be able to stop himself from raping Jasper. "Please, I beg you. Will you just touch him and feel how strong he is?"

"I am good. I can't really see. It is too dark, and I think you should be careful. You are standing under the light, and the camera might see us."

"So you are considering helping Mr Steel?"

"I was living in temporary accommodation before I came in here. I would like a new house to live in."

"So what did you do to get yourself put in prison?" Tom asked, knowing full well that he had done something terrible. He suspected that he was a paedophile.

"I don't like to talk about it."

"Tell me, I won't tell anyone," Tom whispered, pushing his erection closer to Jasper's face. He could feel his hot breath on his tip and knew that he would explode as soon as Jasper took Mr Steel into his mouth. He didn't want to hear what Jasper had to say.

"I invited this kid to my flat and all I did was show him my train set. I like steam trains, you see. I knew he did, too, because he had a Thomas the Tank backpack."

"You touched him, didn't you? You don't want kids, Jasper. You want a real man that can give you the world. Just feel how hard you are making Mr Steel. He wants you to suck him off and make him happy."

"The cameras will see us."

"It is too dark, and my back will shield you. You know you want to."

Tom gasped as he felt Jasper's hand push him away hard in the groin. "Just fuck off! I told you I am not gay and didn't touch that kid. He told lies because I wouldn't give him my train."

"That's not very nice. Look what you've done. You have upset Mr Steel, and he doesn't want to play anymore."

"Good. Just leave me alone. I want to sleep. I am going to report you in the morning."

"I'm sorry, Jasper. I didn't mean to upset you. I will make it up to you. You can have my breakfast in the morning."

"I don't want your breakfast. I don't want anything from you. Do you hear me?"

"You sleep, Jasper, and I will be right here next to you on the floor should you change your mind. I can see you in a new town starting a new life. I know you are innocent, and you will be released from here and lead the best life.

"I am innocent. I shouldn't be in prison," Tom whispered. "Please don't report me, Jasper. I am sick. Take pity on me. I am right here for you. I will always be by your side."

***

Darragh pulled himself up and over the side of his cot and slithered down the rails and onto the floor. He held the cot's edge to steady himself and get used to standing on the floor. He looked down at his bare feet on the dirty carpet. The floor felt hard and alien. It was going to be difficult to walk on this new surface. He let one of his hands go from the rail and shuffled around to face the door. The bucket of wee and poo had not been changed for days, and the smell filled his nostrils, making him gag.

Darragh focused on the door handle and played out in his mind how the woman with the ginger hair had opened the door. He wasn't sure if he would be able to reach. Cautiously, he let go of the rail and then, losing his balance, he sat heavily on the floor. He quickly got back on his feet, and then, angry with himself for falling, he walked towards the door and smiled as he thought of seeing what was on the other side. He felt excited at the thought of seeing his Mam and Da or finding out who it was that he heard crying in the next room.

The door handle felt cold to touch, he could just reach it, and he wrapped the tops of his fingers around the lever and pulled it down. The door clicked open, and a shaft of light appeared in the crack of the door, almost blinding him. He shielded his eyes with his hand and let the door swing open, determined to see what was beyond his prison. Feeling pleased with himself, he stepped into a brightly lit hallway and looked up at a bare lightbulb above through his fingers. It reminded him of the sun. Perhaps it was. He didn't know. He looked away and was puzzled by the images of lightbulbs that still appeared in his eyes, preventing him from seeing what was around him. He shut his eyes, trying to make them go away. He then listened to see if he could hear anyone. The house was silent.

With the lightbulbs fading, he looked down the hall and saw rows of closed doors. But the door at the far end of the hall was wide open, calling him to find out what was beyond. His legs were feeling stronger, and eager to get to the end of the hall, he ran, enjoying the sensation of being able to use his legs. Laughing at himself for going so fast, he reached the end door and gripped the door jamb to stop himself from falling downstairs. His heart was beating hard in his chest, and he put his hand on it, feeling it knocking on his rib cage. He sat on the first step and slid down to the next. He could hear people talking and laughing below. He didn't recognise their voices, but he was sure these happy people would help him find his parents.

Holding the handrail, Darragh made his way down the stairs. They led down to another brightly lit room which smelt strange. He didn't like the smell very much. He remembered his Mam feeding a white cat. He couldn't remember the cat's name but the smell in the room reminded him of the cat's food. He could smell meat, and it was what he pulled out of his sandwiches if he was given that instead of cheese. He was scared to enter the room. He hadn't seen other people for so long and thought they might be angry with him. Standing on the last step and keeping as close to the wall as he could, he peeped around the door frame, and his eyes widened as he processed the scene in front of him. A large man with no hair and a white coat was feeding red meat into a strange machine. At the side of the machine, a long snake wriggled out of a tube and into a crate.

The radio was playing music, and the man whistled along to the song. Unaware that Darragh was watching him, the scary man stopped feeding the machine, pulled the snake out of the crate, and started to twist its body. Darragh's mouth opened in wonder. The snake didn't mind being so roughly treated and did not try to escape.

On the other side of the room was a chunky wooden table, and he could see Peppa Pig lying on her side on it. Her eyes were wide open, and she stared off into the distance. He missed watching Peppa Pig on TV and wondered what she was doing in this room with a snake. He suddenly became aware of the sound of people talking in the next room, and he hoped his Mam and Da would be there, ready to take him home. Not wanting to be seen by the man that had tortured the snake, he waited until he was looking away from him and then walked slowly and carefully towards the open door on the far side of the room, avoiding lumps of meat on the floor. The tiled floor felt cool on the soles of his feet which were starting to stick to the dirty floor.

Carefully, Darragh pushed the door open and slipped into the next room. A queue of people was standing in front of a glass cabinet full of horrible lumps of red meat and small snakes. He shuddered and knew he would not find his Mam and Da in such a horrid place. Nobody noticed him walking past them, and then he saw a glass door open and heard a bell. He looked around him to see where the sound had come from. As the door opened, he felt the cool air wash over him and smiled as he realised he could go outside. He watched a woman come into the room. She was pushing a big chair on wheels with a girl inside. The girl had long dark hair and big brown eyes. She was bigger than him, and it puzzled him why such a large girl was sitting in a pushchair. Fascinated, he watched the wheels rotate and then, smiling at this wonder, he looked up at the woman pushing the girl. He grinned broadly when he realised that it was his new Mam. Her hair was covered by a hood, but he could see wisps of ginger hair stuck to her wet cheeks. He ran up to her, hoping she would hold him and tell him he was safe. Instead, she screamed, and a look of horror spread across her face.

"Where did you come from?" the woman yelled.

"For God's sake, Mary! Take the boy upstairs and get him dressed," growled a man from behind the glass, meat-filled counter.

Darragh spun around to see who had spoken to Mary so sharply. The man turned away, not meeting his gaze. There was something familiar about his voice. He had heard him arguing with his Mary in the flat and feared him. "Fuck off," he yelled at him. He didn't like him talking to Mary like that. He knew he should not go near him or something bad might happen. "MARY," he called out to her, letting her know he would protect her.

"I'm sorry,'" she said, parking the wheelchair to the side. She held her hands out to pick him up, but something felt wrong. He could see it in her face. She didn't want to touch him, and he wondered if he had done something bad.

The door opened behind her as another person entered the room. He had to find his parents, and so he started to run towards the door. He could smell the air outside calling him to come and play with the rain. He got to the door and ran outside into a busy street. The rain beat down on him, and he could feel the wet pavement under his feet. Cars whizzed by him, splashing water into his face, and he stopped on the edge of the roadside, not liking being in this new alien world. So many people were walking by, not seeing him. He hoped he would see his Mam with her soft yellow hair and big blue eyes. She was not there, and now he was really scared and couldn't stop himself from crying. Darragh howled, frightened that he would never see those he loved again.

"Aww, my darling, don't cry. What are you doing out here in the rain with hardly anything on? You are too small to be out in the street by yourself. Have you lost your Mam?"

Darragh looked up at the person speaking to him. She was holding an umbrella over them, stopping the rain from beating down on his head, and her pretty face with bright red lips and rosy cheeks made him feel at ease. He knew she would take care of him, so he stopped crying and put his arms out to be held. She let the umbrella handle rest on her shoulder for a moment, quickly picked him up, held him on her hip with one arm, and caught the umbrella handle before a gust of wind took it away.

"There you go, little fellow. Is that better? You are safe now. Do you see your Mam?" she asked, twisting her body this way and that so he could see up the street. "My, you are just skin and bones, and your clothes are too thin. It is a crying shame."

Darragh had never felt so happy. He lay his head on her soft coat and could feel the warmth of her body seeping into his. She held him close, and he never wanted this moment to end.

"What should I do with you? The police station is not far. I should take you there."

"No, there's no need to do that. He's mine."

Shocked, Darragh looked up and saw the man that had told Mary to take him upstairs standing by them. He buried his head into the woman's coat to escape him.

"You should be ashamed of yourself letting a toddler into the street by himself."

"I was busy in the shop and didn't see him go outside. I'm here now."

"This boy is filthy and cold. You should be ashamed of yourself."

"He has been playing in the muddy courtyard out the back. I will take him upstairs and give him a hot bath."

"You should have put a coat and shoes on him."

"He must have taken them off. Look, I've got a shop full of customers and need to get back to work."

"So, how are you going to bathe him?"

"My wife will do it."

The woman shook her head and sighed. "You should take more care of him. He could have gotten run over. It is lucky I found him in time."

"I am grateful you did. Thank you."

Darragh could feel the man's hands around his waist and tried his best to hang onto the kind woman's coat, but he was not strong enough and yelled out in frustration. He pushed the man away from him. He didn't want to be with him. He looked so much like his Da, but the smell of meat on this person's clothes told him he was bad and evil. "Fuck off!" he yelled. The man ignored him, and instead of taking him through the shop, he carried him down a side alley and into a courtyard filled with foul-smelling dustbins. As they entered the house through the back door, the man whispered in his ear. "If you cause me any more trouble, then you will be fucking sorry. You are nothing more than a lab rat, Darragh Hearn."

Chapter Thirteen

Still feeling shaken from seeing Gemma's ghost or wondering if his sighting had just been an intrusive thought in his troubled mind, Seth walked down the drive back towards the gate that led to the traveller encampment. The area had been busy earlier with everyone setting themselves up, but now the site was eerily quiet. A chill wind ripped through the air, making him shiver.

Seth stood by the gate and wondered if he should disturb Jon and Jess. He really didn't want to get Jess in trouble and then beaten. It didn't sit well with him that a man could beat a woman and get away with it. He was still surprised that Jess had shared this with him. He was more surprised that she had suggested sleeping with him.

This has to be done. Right then, what am I going to say when I knock on their door. Maybe I should say that I have been going round to everyone to let them know they can use the hose for water rather than the well. I'd better switch the water on before I go home. Ok... let's knock on this caravan here and tell them about the water situation. He looked over to the caravan where Granny was staying and smiled. It was almost as if she had never left and had always been a traveller. She fitted right in, and he had never seen her happier.

A woman with a pleasant smile opened the door of the first caravan, and Seth was glad that she hadn't been rude. "Hey there. Sorry to bother you, but I just wanted to let you know that soon you can use water from the hose rather than the well. I am going to run a hose to the gate over there," he said, pointing towards it. "Is there anything else you need?"

"This is kind of you. It will be good to settle for a while and not have the police on our backs every five minutes. It's been a hard few years on the road with everything shut up and not many people wanting our business."

"I know, tell me about it. When everyone is vaccinated, we can get back to leading a normal life."

"My poor Mammy has just had the bug. She hasn't been right since. She says the weather is too cold for her, and she keeps chewing my ear off. We all have our crosses to bear."

"Will you shut the door, Janine? I'm freezing to death here."

"Ok, Mammy. It's just Mr Hearn."

"Not that eejit."

"No, it's not Jon, Mammy."

"Good. Feck, Janine! You'll be carrying me out in a box soon if you don't shut the fecking door!"

"I'd better go."

"Ok. Just let me know if you need anything."

The door shut, and Seth smiled as he heard Janine tell off her Mammy for being so rude. He was glad that his Granny was so easy-going.

Seth knocked on each door and then hesitated, unsure if he should knock on Jess and Jon's door. He scowled as he remembered Gemma's eyes with smudged mascara staring hard at him. Cross with himself for letting a dead woman get to him, he knocked hard on the door and stepped back. Jess opened the door, and he could see that she was shocked.

"Hi, I was just letting everyone know…."

A hand pulled Jess back, and she squealed, and a small man with dark hair appeared in the doorway, scowling at Seth. Seth's jaw dropped, and he could not say anything as he looked at Jon, a mirror image of himself. The only difference he could see was his height. Jon was muscular like himself, but he had to be at least a foot shorter.

"You bastard! You keep away from my family. Do you hear?" Jon yelled.

Fearing that he had been seen earlier, Seth immediately began to feel defensive. He could feel a red mist descending over him. He had not felt so angry in a long while.

"You are a disgrace. I have given you all a place to live, and now you bad-mouth me!"

"Jon, come inside. What the fuck has got into you," Jess called.

"You mind your own business. You shouldn't have come here. Not on this wanker's land."

"I had no choice, did I?"

"I'll deal with you later."

"FUCK YOU! If you lay one hand on her, you will have me to answer to," Seth was fuming.

"Are you going to stop me then, you bastard?"

"Don't tempt me. You're a Hearn and should behave like one."

Jon's face went purple and roaring, he leapt off the step and threw himself at Seth, sending him flying.

"WHAT THE FUCK ARE YOU DOING?" A punch to his chin made his legs give way, and he saw stars as his head hit the ground. Jon threw himself onto him, and he could feel Jon's hands around his neck, squeezing hard. Choking, he opened his eyes for a moment and saw his Dad's angry face. He was drowning again; if he didn't fight back, he would surely die. Gritting his teeth and with all his strength, Seth grabbed Jon's wrists and pulled his grasping hands away from his neck. Seeing Jon's red face close to his, he raised his head and head-butted him. Jon screamed in pain and released Seth's neck, allowing him to roll over, bringing Jon below him and straddling him. Seth brought up his fist, ready to punch him hard.

"NO, SETH! Don't hit your brother. You must stop this. Stop this now. Do you hear me, Sebastian Hearn?" He could feel his granny's hand on his shoulder, pulling on his clothing. He looked down at Jon and, knowing he would not stop fighting, stood up and kicked him hard between the legs causing Jon to yell out in pain. Holding his crotch, Jon curled up into a ball.

"I didn't start this, Granny. This maniac attacked me…." He paused for a moment and then turned to face Granny. Jess ran past him, yelled an obscenity at him, and then got on her knees to try and comfort Jon.

"You said brother. Another of Jethro's mistakes, then?" Seth growled.

Granny tutted and then shook her head. "Yes, Seth. He is your brother. I can't believe my eyes. To think that he, of all places, would turn up here. Seth, there are things you should know."

"What do you mean by that?"

"I didn't think it was important, but now that you have met him, there are things you should know. It is time and is only right."

"Granny, you are talking in riddles."

"I'll be plain then. Jon Hearn is your twin!"

Seth laughed, thinking that Granny was joking. "He looks a lot like me…."

Granny frowned at him. "I'll say it again. He is your twin."

"You're serious, aren't you?"

"I am Seth. Bridie had two babies. You first, and then four minutes later, Jon was born. Bridie had no idea that she was carrying twins. Jon was a tiny baby, and we didn't think he would make it through the night."

Seth was speechless for a moment and then angry. "YOU SHOULD HAVE TOLD ME! You should have told me when you told me that Bridie was my mother. FUCK! This family is so fucked up."

Jess was staring at him wide-eyed. "So if he is your brother, why did you hurt him, you bastard?"

"He will live. I don't know why everyone is looking at me. He was the one that started all this." Seth walked up to Jon, who was now sitting up but seemed lost in thought, his face was white with pain. "You knew I was your twin, didn't you? How did you know?"

Jon's eyes narrowed. "I found our birth certificates, brother," he replied sarcastically.

"Oh, so you had the decency to register our births," Seth said angrily at Granny.

"Why didn't you give him to Margaret instead of me?"

"Look, I am not going to apologise for anything. Both of you were taken care of. Can you imagine how Bridie would have been treated if she had pushed two bastards around in a pram? She would have been run out of Dingle."

"So, where did Jon go?"

"To a children's home. Your aunt Margaret couldn't take care of both of you. Too many questions would have been asked."

"DO YOU KNOW what it's like to be brought up in a children's home?" Jon said coldly. "It was shit, ok! You've had it easy living a rock star's life."

"So you think you had a raw deal, do you? You should try living with a family that is so fucked up that it ends up murdering young women, fucking the daughters and killing babies." Seth shook his head. "You are not staying here. Go back to your house in Cork and never set foot on this land. Anyone that beats up women is not welcome here."

Jess shot him an injured glance. "You have a fucking big mouth. He is Marley's father, and he has rights."

"So go and meet him in a park, but he is not staying here."

"Don't worry. You are a lunatic, kicking me in the gonads like that. I wouldn't stay here if you paid me."

"But, Jon, you haven't seen Marley and me for a week. Please stay for a little bit."

"You can fuck off! Telling people that I beat you. Telling that gobshite."

"I didn't tell him anything."

"Like fuck you didn't. I should have listened to my Mrs. She warned me that you were a bitch and to steer clear of you," Jon said, getting to his feet. Still in pain, he got his car keys out of his pocket and staggered off to his white van. As he sped past them all, Seth noticed that the van had the words 'Hearn Family Butchers' written in blue on the side. *So my bastard of a brother is a butcher. A meat lover. The complete opposite to me. He can't be my twin, surely?*

"You have ruined our lives. Why did you have to go and do that?" Jess yelled through angry tears. "Now Marley won't have a father. Do you know how hard it is to raise a child yourself? You have no idea." Jess stormed off, climbed into her caravan and slammed the door shut behind her.

"I'm sorry," Seth called, but it was too late. Jess did not hear.

"You did the right thing," Granny said softly. "That man is not good, and Jess is better off without him. She will realise that one day. Seth, your head is bleeding. Come back to my caravan, and I will clean you up."

"I will be fine," he said, wiping the blood away with his hand. "I need to go and see Jules and tell her what happened. I have a feeling she is cross with me too."

"Why do you say that?"

"I don't think I make her happy anymore. I feel like I have let her down. Granny, I have to get Darragh back before his birthday, and then I know we will be alright again."

"We will find him, Seth. The signs are looking good, and it's just a matter of time, so we must stay positive."

"I am doing my best, but my mind is playing tricks on me. I have seen far too many dead people lately."

"Your mind isn't playing tricks on you. You have always had second sight, but you have never realised it. The trauma of losing Darragh has opened your third eye. You have become open to the spirit world, and they will help you if you only ask them."

Seth shook his head, and a drop of blood from behind his ear dripped onto his shirt, the red liquid spread out on the fabric at an alarming rate, but all he could think about was seeing Gemma.

"That girl that died in the summer field. Gemma. I keep seeing her."

"She just wants to help you. There's another one that wants to help you, too, but I don't think you will want his help."

"His help? Who do you mean?"

100

"Your father. He wants your forgiveness. He is being very guarded, but I think this is what he wants."

"Well, he can go and fuck himself. Sorry, Granny, but no. That is crazy. He tried to rape Jules, and he tried to kill me. How can I forgive him for that?"

"I don't know, Seth, but he is close by and has thorny black vines around his ankles waiting to drag him into the darkness once he has had his say."

"Granny, you are talking crazy. I can't deal with this right now. I am going home to clean up and speak to Jules. Let's stay in reality and concentrate on the living that might know what happened to Darragh. I am pretty sure that Jess knows more than she lets on. Will you speak to her when she has calmed down? Or get her Mam to. She is not too keen on us at the moment."

"I will see what I can do, Seth, but you need to think about what I have said and face your demons soon. Before it is too late."

"Christ, Granny! You are too much sometimes."

When Seth returned, Jules was making a coffee and singing, and she didn't hear him come in. She was singing the tune to 'Never be Alone' and was making up words to fit the song to find Darragh. She was recording her new song on her phone so she didn't forget the words. She wondered what had happened to Seth and hoped he would be back soon. *I think something is bothering him. I wish he would talk to me.*

"Hey, you, that is perfect. You have to record that. Was that Never be Alone?"

Jules turned around and smiled. "Did you like…" and then saw Seth's blood on his shirt. "Oh my God, Seth, did you fall over? No, wait, you haven't been fighting, have you?"

"No, yes. It wasn't my fault. You will not believe this, but I need a hug before I tell you. I am just a little bit broken."

"Of course, but take your shirt off first." Seth took his t-shirt off and, smiling seeing his broad chest, Jules went over to him, laid her head on his strong body, and embraced him.

Seth put his arms around her and sighed. "That feels good. I needed that." Not wanting to leave his embrace, Jules remained attached to him. "Are you making tea? Can I have one?"

"Of course," she said, pulling away. "Tell me what happened. Is it something to do with Jess and Marley?" she asked, pulling out a clean shirt from the drier. "Sit down and let me look at your head. You might need a stitch."

"Yes and no. Let me start from the beginning." As Jules cleaned up his wound, he told his story and watched Jules' face when he revealed that he had an evil twin. He decided not to tell her about Granny saying that his Dad wanted to contact him. This he found too much to bear.

Jules sipped her tea, and her eyes were wide when she realised that Seth's twin was identical, which freaked her out. "Oh, Seth, this is terrible news. I don't believe it. Why didn't Bridie tell you this? He sounds like an evil twin. Have you ever felt like part of you was missing?"

Seth frowned. "If you are saying we have a deep connection, then absolutely not. I told him to clear off and never come back."

"How did Jess take that?"

"Badly. Jon has a house in Cork and works in a butcher's shop. He is not a traveller. I am so cross with Granny for not telling me about him."

"She must have had her reasons. Oh, Seth, do you think we have ruined our chances of finding out where Darragh is?"

"No, I don't think so. I know Jess is angry with me, but I think she quite likes me. I will go and see her tomorrow and apologise again. I think she is struggling to bring up Marley on her own. Maybe we could help her somehow. When I was talking to her earlier, I got the feeling she knew something and wanted to tell me and probably was going to if Jon hadn't turned up."

"You said she liked you."

"I did, but you know I don't feel the same way. You are my gorgeous girl, my one and only, and I want no other."

"You need to sleep with her, and then she will tell you what she knows."

Seth nearly choked on his tea. "You are joking, aren't you?"

"No, I'm not. I am deadly serious."

"I couldn't. I am sure my charm and offering to help out with Marley will bring her 'round eventually."

"We need to find out what she knows about Darragh now. You need to sleep with her."

"Christ, Jules! You are really serious. Hell no! I am shocked that you think that I could."

"Darragh's life may depend on it. Granny thinks that we are running out of time."

"Did she say that to you?"

"No, but I can sense it. She is restless, and… Jess is our only hope. Don't be shocked. It won't be cheating. You can wear a condom. I won't hold it against you. You need to do this for Darragh and for me."

Chapter Fourteen

Lucy put down her crime thriller and checked her phone to see if she had received any messages on WhatsApp. It had been two days since she had heard from Stephan. She scrolled through their last messages to try and detect if there had been anything she had said that might have put him off talking to her. She suspected she was a little needy as her messages were all about how alone she felt. Past relationships had lasted only a couple of months and then fizzled out. This time around, she was determined to show that she was a strong woman, happy with her own company and a joy to be with. So far, she was coming across as a narcissist and not nice to be around.

With each hour that passed, her resolve to be strong crumbled, and she could barely think of anything but him contacting her so she could tell him how miserable she was. Stephan contacted her nearly every day, and if a day went by without her hearing from him, she would find a message waiting for her when she woke up. He always apologised and said that he had been called into work unexpectedly or had been in an area where the internet signal was bad. The apology consoled her for a couple of hours, and then she would start questioning if he was telling the truth. She had interrogated many liars and sometimes wondered if being a detective made her paranoid.

DARRAGH

Trying not to sound like she was investigating him, she had asked him what he did for a living, and he had given her an unsatisfactory answer. He said he was on call and helped out in the community. Lucy had looked on social media for Stephan to see if he was a genuine person, but she had not been able to find him. His profile picture on WhatsApp was just a picture of a dog - a Jack Russell. She had enlarged this picture so she could read the name on the tag on the dog's collar and discovered that his dog's name was Rufus. She couldn't imagine Stephan having a dog as he was always travelling. The name stung a little as she thought of her ex-partner Rufus Parvel.

Lucy preferred to work alone. It was just as well, as her visions were increasing in number. Any partner would have perhaps questioned her sanity. She was beginning to wonder if she was going insane as she was having two or three mini visions a day. Each one gave her snippets of information about her outstanding cases but were not always detailed enough for her to solve a case. She thought back to her vision of Aiden and remembered him talking to someone that knew what had happened to Darragh. A pang of guilt ran through her and her stomach knotted inside. Seth would call her soon, but she had no news once again. She was still looking for Aiden and had been to every pub in Cork looking for him. The landlord in The Poor Relation, his local, had suggested that he might be staying with his sister in Dublin.

Lucy traced his sister to some sheltered accommodation just outside of Cork. Aiden had not stayed with her, and she seemed appalled that Lucy would suggest such a thing. His sister said he had called her a few months back and asked if she would let him stay with her as he had Covid and did not want to be alone if he should die. Lucy was shocked to hear that his sister had refused and told him to stay at home for ten days which was the right course of action, but she had not checked to see if he had survived. She despaired of mankind sometimes.

"Oh, please send me some good news. I could do with a little help," Lucy called to the man upstairs. She hoped God was listening.

Lucy's phone pinged, and she smiled broadly and grabbed the phone, eager to talk to Stephan. Her breath quickened at the thought of messaging him, and then she panicked, not knowing what to say. She didn't want to sound needy again and put him off like she did with all the others. She didn't want to ask him too many questions. However, there were things she needed to know and she told herself to tread carefully. She was angry at herself for mistrusting him, but it was very frustrating not being able to see what he looked like. She smiled at his message, and her heart beat a little harder.

Hi there beautiful, how are you today?

It was no good. She was falling for him.

I am fine but a little bit sad today because I have been missing you.

Don't be sad. I am here now. I have been really busy at work and have slept all day.

Did you work through the night, then? She really wanted to ask what he was doing that night.

Yes, a colleague was sick, so I covered for her.

DARRAGH

A shiver of jealousy ran through her as Lucy realised that Stephan worked with a female colleague. Trying to stay calm, Lucy typed.

You have a cute dog. I like your profile picture. Does Rufus mind you working nights?

Rufus?

Lucy's eyes narrowed as a red flag flashed up in her mind.

Your profile picture has a photo of a dog. The tag says Rufus.

Oh, that dog. No, I just got that photo off the internet.

Don't you have a photo of yourself, then? I would like to see what you look like.

You saw me when I helped you home when you were drunk.

I really can't remember very much about that night.

You were in a bad way. Promise that you won't get like that again. I don't want anything to happen to you.

I promise. I am embarrassed that you saw me like that. I was having a hard time with one of my cases and still am. I don't want you to think I am a drunk and a bad person.

Lucy sighed. Stephan had managed to avoid sending her a photo of himself.

I know you are not a drunk. You are a beautiful person. When I took you home. You kept mentioning a name. Darren, I think. Has your case got something to do with him, or is that your boyfriend's name?

Lucy smiled and wondered if Stephan was getting jealous.

No, not a boyfriend. I think I was trying to say Darragh. That is the little boy that went missing last year. This case has gone cold, and the only person that might know something has gone missing too. Do you live in Cork? Do you know any of the alcoholics that hang around the city?

I travel, so I live all over Ireland. I do spend a lot of time in Cork, though. I know some of the street people. Who are you looking for?

I'm looking for Aiden. He is a well-known character in Cork, but since Covid, he hasn't been around.

Is he the one everyone calls the Cornetto man? He looks Italian and sometimes sings Just One Cornetto on the banks of the Lee?

Maybe. He does look Italian, but I didn't know he sings. He is a lively character and talks to everyone. It could be him.

If it is him, then he died of Covid last year. His bike was tied to a lamppost, and people pinned flowers to it.

DARRAGH

Lucy was cross with herself. She hadn't thought to look to see if he was dead.

Oh, Steph, I feel sad now. Aiden was my last hope. I don't know where else to look for Darragh Hearn. I get a call from Seth Hearn every day asking for news. It is breaking my heart.

You mustn't give up hope. Something will turn up. It always does. In every good crime story, the bad and the ugly always get exposed. You will think of something, and that small thing will ignite a trail, and you will find him.

Lucy's phone showed that she had an incoming call from Seth.

Hey, I have to take this call. It is Seth Hearn. Did I tell you he was my half-brother? Will you message me again later?

I will try. If you don't hear from me then I am covering Julie again. Take care, baby.

Ok, I understand.

She smiled as she took Seth's call. No one had ever called her baby before. She quite liked it and wondered if a thirty-eight-year-old could be called baby.

"Hi, Seth. How are you?"

"I'm fine. Well, no, I'm not great. We are going to release a song this afternoon and hope it encourages everyone to look for Darragh. Jules is going to sing, and I am going to back her. We are going live on TikTok at 4pm. I am keeping my fingers crossed that we will hear something soon. I know you haven't heard anything, or you would have told me. I have some news for you, but not about Darragh. You have another half-brother to add to your family, and you are not going to believe this, but it turns out that your new half-brother, Jon Hearn, is my identical twin. Everyone says he is identical, but I don't see it myself."

"Seth?"

"Yes."

"You didn't draw a breath then. You need to slow down. You say you have a twin. How did you find out?"

"One of the travellers staying on our land has a child that looks just like Darragh. Her husband, who lives in Cork, is my twin brother. I had the unfortunate pleasure of running into him, quite literally. The fucker punched me; he thinks I have had a better deal in life. He should try losing a son and then see how he feels."

Lucy started to feel dizzy, and then she saw Jon hitting Seth with blood on his hands as he cut into flesh with a shard of glass. Her vision cleared, and she could smell a strong odour of fresh blood. She could hear a cat meowing, eager to be fed, and she looked around her flat for a cat. She frowned. She didn't own a cat.

"Are you there, Lucy?"

"I'm sorry, Seth. I just saw him hit you, and I saw him cutting flesh with a knife or something small and sharp."

"Well, he didn't stab me. Although I am sure he would dearly have loved to."

"Then why do I think he likes to cut up flesh?"

"That would be because he's a butcher. I saw him get into a butcher's van."

"But why would I see that?"

"What do you mean see?"

"Lately, I have been getting lots of visions of blood and piles of flesh."

"Christ, no! Do you think Darragh has been hacked up to death?"

"No, I am sorry if I am scaring you. I think you need to be careful. Someone has fantasies about cutting your flesh. Darragh is still alive and well, but I can feel his sadness when I walk through the streets of Cork."

"So you think he is still in Cork, then?"

"I know he is."

"Can't you do door-to-door searches?"

"I wish I could, but I will need evidence that he is being held in Cork. Nobody will commission such an expensive operation going on my gut feeling."

"I am just going crazy. I wish Granny would see something more than just Waterfall West ghosts. You know she has moved in with the travellers? I am not sure if she is willing to help find Darragh anymore. She says she will but she seems to be reliving her youth."

"You must have faith in her. I've never met anyone that was so in tune with the spirit world. I wish I was. I am practically useless in that department at the moment. Anything I see is like a broken jigsaw puzzle and gets in the way of hard facts. Seth, I've got some bad news. Aiden, the man who knows the person holding Darragh, died last year of Covid."

"Oh no, that is bad news. I am sure you will find her without Aiden's help. There can't be many ginger-haired women in Cork with a disabled child."

"I will keep searching. You know I will. This last vision is bothering me. I think I should go and see Jon Hearn."

"I wouldn't waste your time. He is a nasty piece of shite."

"Maybe you are right. I am curious, though. I want to see how much he looks like you. Do you know where his butchery shop is?"

"No, I don't. I am sorry. The van he crawled into when I threw him off my land had 'Hearn Family Butchers' on the side. Be careful, Lucy. Jon Hearn has a screw loose."

Chapter Fifteen

I promise that one day I'll be around.
I promise, Darragh, that I will find you.
I'll keep you safe, I'll hunt you down,
I'll keep you sound. Turn every stone.
Right now, it's pretty crazy,
Life 'round here is pretty crazy,
And I don't know how to stop.
I was mistaken.
Or slow it down.
I know you have been taken.

Hey!
I know there are some things we need to talk about, I
know. You must be missing us.
And I can't stay. And I can't wait.
Just let me hold you for a little longer now.
Just to hold you in my arms again.
Take a piece of my heart. So if you have a heart
And make it all your own.
Please, we are feeling down
So when we are apart.
And losing you is tearing us apart.
You'll never be alone.
But with your help, we're not alone.

You'll never be alone.
We'll never be alone.
You'll never be alone.

When you miss us, close your eyes.
We may be far, but never gone.
We are with you, baby
When you fall asleep tonight.
Even when you sleep tonight
Just remember that we lay under the same stars.
Don't give up hope. We will find you, Darragh.

And hey!
Know there are some things we need to talk about, I know.
You must be missing us.
And I can't stay.
And I can't wait.
Just let me hold you for a little longer now.
Just to hold you in my arms again.
Take a piece of my heart.
So if you have a heart
And make it all your own.
Please, we are feeling down
So when we are apart.
And losing you is tearing us apart.
You'll never be alone.
But with your help, we're not alone.
You'll never be alone.
We'll never be alone.
You'll never be alone.

DARRAGH

And take a piece of my heart.
So if you have a heart
And make it all your own.
Please, we are feeling down
So when we are apart.
And losing you is tearing us apart
You'll never be alone
But with your help, we're not alone.
You'll never be alone.
We'll never be alone…

Jules put down her guitar, and with tears dropping down her cheeks, she stared into the camera and knew she had to say something to the people watching her live on TikTok. She could see names scrolling up on the screen so fast. She could barely see who was joining them. "Thanks for listening," she found herself saying and then sobbing. She inhaled, trying to compose herself. "Please…" she said. "PLEASE… Please help us find our baby. He will be two on April 19, and I want him back for his birthday. I know he is in Cork somewhere, and I hope he remembers who we are. I long to see his smiling face again and hold him. Someone must have seen Darragh. I will show you a photo. The last photo of him, but he will be a year older and walking and saying his first words. If you know anything, please send a private message to our inbox because whoever snatched him might be watching TikTok. If you are watching, please return him to us or just let us know that he is safe and well cared for.

I understand you have taken him because you were desperate for a child. I know you have suffered and been in pain in the past but taking Darragh is not the solution. You will never be happy knowing how much pain and suffering you have caused trying to fill your void. Please.... give him back to me, and I promise we won't press charges."

She looked up at Seth and could see by his startled expression that he wasn't happy with her last comment. *He didn't know I was going to say that.* "Seth, come over here and tell everyone that we won't press charges if the person that has taken Darragh gives him back to us." Seth shook his head and stormed off, leaving Julia to talk to their fans alone.

Tears were really starting to fall now. Not wanting to become a complete mess on TikTok, she said goodbye and ended the live recording. Jules sat back on the sofa and looked towards the bedroom door, the room Seth had fled to. She didn't have the energy to row with him and just wanted to curl up into a ball and hide from life. She didn't like falling out with Seth, but she would do or say anything to get Darragh back. Barney jumped onto her lap and he rubbed her chin with his head, craving attention. She couldn't remember the last time she petted him, and it felt good to stroke his fur. "You understand, don't you?" The cat meowed in agreement. "I thought so."

As she sat there, it suddenly occurred that she hadn't heard Juliet cry for a while. *Oh my God! She has been sleeping for nearly three hours. That is a long time, and not like her at all.* She gently pushed Barney off her lap and walked to the bedroom to check on Juliet. Barney followed her at her heels, hoping that she might be going towards his feeding bowl. She entered the room and saw Seth sitting on the bed with his arms folded. He did not look happy. Ignoring him, she got closer to the cot and peered in, fearing the worst. Juliet sensed her there, twitched and moved a little. Jules sighed with relief and knew that she would be awake soon. She could feel Seth's eyes boring into her back, and then not liking being in the dog house, she couldn't help but let a sob out as the emotional stress of singing and talking about Darragh all became too much. She wanted Seth to hold her in his strong arms and tell her that he forgave her and that everything would be okay. "Do you hate me?" she sobbed.

Seth was shocked. "Christ, no! I am just…."

"You are cross with me, aren't you?"

"No, I am not cross with you. I could never be cross with you. I just wished you hadn't said what you did. Whoever has taken Darragh needs to be punished. You can't go about saying that they will not be penalised. That is just plain crazy."

"I'm sorry. I didn't plan to say that. I just thought it might encourage them to give up Darragh."

"I know you meant well, but you shouldn't say things like that. We have a justice system for a reason. Hey, come here. I don't like to see you cry."

Pleased that Seth forgave her, Jules climbed onto his lap and felt his warm arms go around her, and she could feel his heart beating. She breathed him in, savouring his warm embrace. "Do you think the song went ok?" she whispered, fearing that he might now hate the song too.

"You did a grand job. It was straight from the heart, and you just never know. It might do the trick and bring Darragh back to us."

"Seth, I don't think I can take much more of this waiting. Can we go to Cork and just drive around and see if we can see him? I know it is a long shot, but it will make me feel better and I will actually feel like we are doing something."

"Yes, sure we can. Do you want to leave Juliet with Sinead?"

"No, I will feed her and then she should be good for a few hours. She likes riding in the car. You think that I am crazy, don't you?"

"No, my sweet girl. You are not crazy. You are just doing what any mother would do. Just don't get your hopes up. Whoever has him is probably keeping him out of sight."

"I won't," Jules said, picking up her phone. "Oh my! We've had so many messages on TikTok. I don't believe it. Have a look."

Juliet started to cry. Jules sighed. "She must have heard the word feed. Have a look through the messages, Seth, and see if there is any useful information about Darragh's whereabouts. Look out for @burningdesire666. That name keeps popping up and wishing us well. I just can't help but think that fan is a bit odd. Maybe whoever burning desire is knows something. I swear half our fans are oddballs or fake people. Famous people like Prince Andrew and Elon Musk have started following us. They just have to be scammers, don't they? I was thinking. Later, you need to go and see Jess and be nice to her. She is another one that knows something and isn't telling."

"What do you mean 'be nice to her'? There is no way that I am going to have sex with her."

Jules smiled. "It might not come to that. You could just flirt with her and perhaps send her a picture or two."

"She knows what I look like."

"No, Seth, she might like to see more than your face."

"Hell no, Jules. NO WAY!"

Chapter Sixteen

"There, there, my wee baby girl. Sleep now and let the clouds lift you into the light. Do you feel the warmth of the sun drying up your tears? Do you see the birds flying above soaring? Do you hear their songs?" Mary Price whispered, gently stroking her daughter's head as she slept. Her dark hair framed her pale face. She tucked a stray strand behind her ear, relieved that Lia had fallen asleep and had stopped sobbing. Their trip to the hospital had been difficult. Lia always screamed when the nurses hooked her up to the dialysis machine, and no amount of treats and distraction methods stopped her from pulling at the wires. Four long hours of dialysis three times a week were becoming a living nightmare.

Lia was going to be four soon, and Mary desperately wanted her to be strong and healthy. She was a bright child and was due to start school that year. Mary knew she would do well there. She imagined walking her to school with all the other children, and she could see Lia happily skipping along. She would be wearing a freshly pressed pinafore, white shirt and her long dark hair would be in bunches tied up with pink ribbons. Lia desperately needed a new kidney. Darragh Hearn was Lia's last chance. Mary sat back in the chair, sighed irritably, and tried her best to calm herself. They had kept the boy for nearly a year now, and she had grown tired of waiting.

The wall between Lia's room and the boy's room was paper thin; she could hear him talking to himself or pulling at his chain. They had chained him up for his own good. They couldn't risk him climbing out of his cot again. When he was quiet, it was like he wasn't there. She shuddered at the thought of feeding him. She didn't like the way he smelt. He was revolting, and she didn't like being near him. When she entered the boy's room, she tried her best not to look into his big brown eyes as it was too much to bear. Her Lia was growing weaker every day and he seemed to be thriving. That was good because he would supply Lia with a perfect kidney when he finally had the operation. Mary put her hands together and started to pray for Lia, for herself and that the kidney would be a match and save Lia's life.

Lia mumbled something in her sleep, and realising that she might be disturbing her, Mary stood up and crept out of her room. The hall was dark, but she dared not turn on the light in case she woke Lia up. She needed a drink to steady her nerves, and then when the warm liquid calmed her, she would talk to Jon about the transplant. As she passed Darragh's room, she felt the hairs lift up on the back of her neck. She could feel him watching her and listening to her as she passed by.

Their untidy lounge was dark and was lit only by the TV. Jon was not lying on the sofa; she guessed he had gone to the toilet. As she poured herself a gin and tonic, she listened to a news reporter talking about how well the vaccination program was going. She didn't like the thought of being injected but knew she would have to when her age group was called. She wondered when thirty-five-year-olds would be notified.

Mary sat on the chair next to the sofa and practised in her head what she was going to say. These days, the word transplant triggered an aggravated response and the last time she had mentioned it, Jon had ignored her for three days. Things were not great between them. The sex was good, but something was missing. He didn't talk to her like he used to. She suspected that he was having an affair. When she washed his clothes, occasionally she smelt expensive perfume on his shirts. She had never said anything about her suspicions, as Jon was bound to lose his temper and lash out.

The smell of stew wafted into the lounge, and losing her nerve to talk to him about the transplant, she got up and walked down the hall towards the kitchen. She turned on the kitchen light and was met with a meow. Their cat was sitting next to the stewing pot with an expectant look on his face. He had pushed the crockpot lid partially off, and it teetered on the edge of the pot. Mary ran over and rescued the lid before it crashed to the floor.

"Hamish! Get down from the side, will you? I know you are hungry. Do you want some of that nice minced leftovers from the shop? You do know that you are the most spoiled cat in the whole of Ireland? Your Daddy may be a lot of things, but he is not mean to you." Mary opened the fridge, and the cat jumped down and began winding himself through her legs. Will you stop that, you daft thing? You know I am allergic to your hair."

"It's a good job I'm not a cat, then."

She felt strong arms around her and his hot breath in her ear. "I am hungry for you, Mary. Save feeding the cat and come and give me a quickie."

Mary giggled. "You said that last night, and look where that got us. We went to bed too tired to eat."

"It is your fault for having such a hot pussy."

"Will you stop that? You know I don't like it when you talk dirty. I can't, not now. I have too much to do, and you know who needs feeding. She felt his warm embrace slip away from her, and then she suddenly felt bad for rejecting his advances. She was tired and hungry for food, not sex. He would be mad at her, but her body could not keep up with his sexual needs. "I have made us a stew. You need to eat to keep your strength up because I have a little surprise for you later," she said, thinking of the maid's outfit she had just bought. She got out a Tupperware box full of mince, took the lid off and then started spooning it into the cat's bowl. Hamish, eager to eat, meowed impatiently as he waited for his bowl to be filled.

"There you go. You like that, don't you?"

"How much of the cat's mince is left in the freezer?"

"Quite a bit." She was relieved that she hadn't been chastised for not being available for sex.

"We need to use it up. Do you know of any stray cats that need feeding?"

Finding this an odd question, she frowned and then thought of a skinny cat she had seen in the alleyway next to their butcher's shop. "The neighbour's cat is a skinny wee thing. Is the mince going to go off soon?"

"No, I just don't like meat to be frozen for too long. You know what I am like. I only like the best for our family."

"Ok, I'll give Mrs Mullens a bag of mince tomorrow."

"No, I'd rather you left a plate out in the courtyard for the stray cats to help themselves."

"I don't think that is a good idea. That will attract the foxes and rats. I don't want foxes and rats in the house. Not with Lia being so poorly."

"What are you talking about, woman? Rats, indeed!"

Alarmed, Mary saw his expression change, and a stony look spread over his face. His eyes were dark and cold.

"So if you are not going to give me sex, then I will have my meal alone. I seem to spend much of my life on my own these days."

"Our daughter is sick and needs me."

"You spend too much time with Lia. You are mollycoddling her, and it is not good for her."

His comment cut deep. "You should spend time with her too. When was the last time you spoke to her?" she spat.

"I don't get a look in. You are always with her."

Trying to hold her temper, she said very calmly. "You need to see how poorly she is. Dialysis is not working as well as it did. You know what I am going to say, don't you? Please don't get cross with me, but she needs proper treatment. You know what I mean." She had nothing to lose, she was being ostracised for not giving him a quickie, and she sensed that he hated her.

"Will you give it a rest, woman! You know I have been busy at work. The shop has been crazy these past few weeks. Now Bernard is back at work, I will have more time to practise carrying out the operation on the piglets."

Jon had bought two piglets, and they lived in the old coal shed behind the shop. Any scraps they had were taken down each morning and mixed in the pigs' feed. It was Mary's job to look after them and make sure they were clean and quiet. It was a thankless task, and she dreaded going near them as they frightened her. They were not quiet, and she hoped that the neighbours wouldn't report them to the council.

Jon was a skilled butcher, and he was good with his hands. She was sure that he would be able to remove Lia's bad kidneys and replace them with the boy's. Still, she suspected there was another reason that was stopping him from practising on the piglets. Seth Hearn was the reason. Jon had always wondered who his parents were and had traced his family back for three generations. She would never forget the night he discovered he was a twin, and seeing Seth Hearn doing so well for himself did not make him happy. She was quite sure that Jon had lost his mind.

Mary sighed. "It's not just work getting in the way, is it, Jon? You are enjoying watching your brother suffer. Why do you hate Seth so much?"

"Don't mention his name in this house."

"No, Jon, this needs to be said. I think you are delaying the operation because you enjoy torturing him. You need to take that boy's kidney out and transplant it into Lia. Then give the boy back to your brother. This foolishness has gone on too long."

Mary felt his fist hit her square on the jaw, and then for a moment she saw the kitchen light bright in her eyes and stars before darkness enveloped her.

Muttering to himself, Jon helped himself to a plate of stew and then, stepping over Mary, he headed off to the lounge to relax. As he walked past Darragh's door, he smiled to himself and hoped Seth felt the same pain he had felt when he was in the children's home.

Chapter Seventeen

The taxi was unbearably hot, and Jules tore off her scarf and stuffed it into her bag. The mask she wore made her feel as if she was suffocating. Her white cotton shirt was sticking to her hot body, and she wished she had worn a t-shirt. Her stomach was cramping up, too, as it always did when she was nervous. Today she would be going into court to answer questions about her and Darragh's abduction. She wasn't sure if she would see Tom Stone in court. She imagined him in a cage in the corner of the courtroom, wearing orange overalls with a muzzle over his mouth. She wondered if he would be wearing cuffs and chains around his ankles.

The buildings and cars whizzing by were making her feel dizzy. Not wanting to get car sick, Jules picked up her coat from the seat next to her and started to search at the bottom of each pocket for her emergency mints. As she looked, she became aware that Seth was staring at her.

"Are you feeling ok, my beautiful girl? You are looking flushed."

"I'm just hot. I wish I had worn something less formal. The skirt is pinching my waist and making it hurt. And this shirt is sticking to me." She felt a cool hand on her forehead.

"You are burning up. Do you think you might be coming down with something? Covid, perhaps?" he whispered.

"I don't think so. We both tested this morning, and we were negative. I feel ok, apart from feeling like I am on fire." Seth pulled his hand away, but Jules clung onto his cool hand and placed it on one of her hot cheeks. "Your hand is so cold, and it is cooling me down. Can I have your other one, please, on the other cheek?"

Seth swivelled 'round on his seat, loosed the seat belt and hoping that the driver wouldn't notice, he cupped her cheeks with his hands. "How does that feel?"

"Oh, so good. You do realise that you are going to have to sit next to me in the dock and keep me cool."

Seth looked sad. "I wish I could. I will be with you in your mind. You will be able to see me in the public gallery. Only I have been allowed to sit there with my mask on, and Lucy too, if she can make it. I will be right there cheering you on. You mustn't worry about giving evidence. Just relax and tell them everything you remember."

"Seth, I am feeling sick. My stomach really hurts. It is just nerves. It will pass."

"You should have eaten something before you came out. I know that would have helped you."

"I just couldn't." She could feel herself tearing up.

Seth slid over to her and held her tight. "Everything is going to be ok."

She could smell his warm body next to hers and tried not to cry, but the tears were streaming down her cheeks. "I just want this day to be over with, and I want that bastard locked up and the key thrown away. What if he gets off?"

"He won't, sweetheart. He won't."

"For the love of God, Mr Hearn! Will you do up your seat belt before I get fined?" the taxi driver called.

"I'm sorry, I will."

"We need to pull over," Jules called out. "I am going to be sick."

The cab driver pulled over, and Jules managed to open the door, pull back her mask, and was sick in the gutter. Seth rubbed her back. "You'll feel better now."

"You young people are all the same. Drinking too much and then paying for it the next day."

"She's not well. She has a fever. She needs air."

"If she's got the bug, I don't want her in my cab. That's the last thing I need today."

"No, it's not Covid. Our tests are clear. If it is ok with you, we'll walk the rest of the way. I don't need a refund on the fare," Seth said.

"Jules, are you ok to get out of the taxi? You need some fresh air. The courts are just around the corner."

She nodded, and they got out of the cab, avoiding the pile of vomit. "How are you feeling?"

"A little better. It's so good to breathe in fresh air."

"You don't think you have Covid, do you? You might show up as being positive later."

"No, it's just nerves. We haven't been out all week or had any contact with anyone."

A cold breeze hit her flushed cheeks, and she breathed it in, trying her best to stay calm. *I don't want to embarrass myself and have a full-blown panic attack in the court or in the street, for that matter.*

The morning was bright and breezy, and it was good to be in the fresh air walking along the streets of Cork. Only a handful of people were on the streets, and all were wearing masks, fearing they might contract the virus.

Jules decided not to wear her mask until they got into the courtrooms. "Will I have to wear a mask in court?"

"I guess you will have to wear it walking through the building, but then I expect you will be able to take it off in the courtroom."

"Good, I hate wearing it."

Jules had no idea what awaited her, and she tried her best to distract her thoughts. Juliet popped into her head, and she hoped that Sinead was coping with her. Jules had pumped enough milk to feed at least ten babies. She felt in her coat pocket for her phone and then realised it wasn't there and tried the other one. "I haven't got my phone. I don't believe it. I must have left it in the taxi."

"No, I don't remember seeing you with it in the taxi. I checked our seats when we got out. I thought that you might have a bag with you, but there was nothing."

"Oh, thank goodness! I put my phone in a small bag but then decided not to bring it because I didn't know where to leave it when I was being questioned. I am getting so forgetful these days. I've still got baby brain. What if Sinead wants to ring me? What if there is something wrong with Juliet."

"Sinead will message me if anything is wrong, so don't worry. I will ring Sinead in a minute to put your mind at rest. Juliet will be fine. You mustn't worry."

As they approached the courts, Seth noticed reporters and a small crowd had gathered by the doors of the court. Instinctively, he knew that the crowd was there to greet them. By the horrified look on Jules' face, he could see that she had noticed them too.

"Oh my God! Seth! The world and his wife are waiting for us."

"Well, it is not every day that a beautiful pop star is abducted and tortured."

"I don't think they are here for me."

"They are, my beautiful girl. The reporters will want you to comment. Just say you are sorry, you can't stop. Put your mask on. We don't want that crowd giving us Covid."

As they walked into the courtroom, they were met with a flurry of questions. Keeping their heads down, Jules and Seth managed to escape them and stepped into a quiet reception area. Fearing they would be chased, Jules looked around nervously for an escape route. "Where do we go?"

Seth frowned. "With him, I guess," he whispered.

Rufus Parvel appeared from nowhere and wore a mask and a clear visor. He beckoned Jules over to him.

"What a dickhead,'" Seth whispered again. "This shouldn't take long. Just say your bit, and then we will go and get you something to eat from your favourite takeaway."

Rufus beckoned Jules again, turning his back on him. Seth hugged Jules and kissed her on the top of her head. "If you don't feel well again. You must tell him. Promise me."

"I promise."

Reluctantly, Jules pulled away and walked towards Rufus who asked her to follow him.

Feeling slightly overwhelmed, she followed Rufus and looked back at Seth for reassurance. His big brown eyes were filled with tears. *Why is he crying? Have I done something wrong?*

Chapter Eighteen

Rufus Parvel led Jules to a waiting room. She expected the corridors to be busy with people, convicts being led by prison officers to court and barristers and judges in black gowns and wigs walking with purpose to court. Instead, the corridors were empty, cold and a little claustrophobic.

Jules could feel her stomach turning over with anxiety. *I hope I don't have to be sick again. I wonder why Rufus is here. I am sure Lucy said he was going to be suspended. I hope he is not representing me. No, calm down, you silly woman. He is in charge of the Gemma Day murder case and not mine. Lucy said she was in court yesterday when they read out a summary of my case. I wonder what the jury is thinking? I wonder if I will have to wear a mask in court. Oh, Goodness, Tom Stone will be there too. Why did I decide to face him? This is madness. I should have asked if I could sit in another room and talk to the court remotely. Oh no! I am going to be sick again!*

Feeling queasy, Jules looked around her for the ladies' toilets. "Mr Parvel, I need the toilet?"

Rufus Parvel turned round and shrugged his shoulders. "You should have said that before we came down here."

She didn't have time to apologise and threw up into her hands. Feeling sorry for herself and with a handful of sick, she looked up at him for help. She could see that he was repulsed. His eyes were cold and grey. "Do you have any tissues?" she asked in a shaky voice.

"This is most inconvenient. Do you have Covid? You should have rung in if you have Covid. That's why I am acting as an usher today. Most of the staff here have it. The walls must be saturated in the stuff. They shouldn't have asked me to help. They know my immune system is compromised," he raged.

Jules was getting angry. "No, it's not Covid. I am just nervous. Look, I don't think I can hold this sick for much longer."

"We will have to go back. Don't you get that vomit near me! The toilets are not far."

Rufus led her back to the toilets, and then putting his hand over his mouth and mask, he held the ladies' door open for her. She decided not to thank him, he was being less than gracious.

After sloping the vomit into the toilet and flushing, she washed her hands thoroughly and then washed her face. The cold water felt good on her hot face, and as she patted it dry with a paper towel, she looked into the mirror above the sink and decided that she was going to have to get a grip. In a few hours' time, she would have given her evidence and then be free to go home, forget about that chapter in her life, and concentrate all her energy on finding Darragh. In her mind, she could see his sweet face smiling at her, and she took a deep breath and steadied her nerves. *I've got to get that bastard, Tom Stone, locked away for life, don't I, Darragh?*

"Are you all done in there? You are due in court in ten minutes."

Jules sighed. *Rufus Parvel is a nasty piece of work and will get his comeuppance soon. Lucy will see to that.* "I'm on my way. I'm feeling better now."

***

Taking a deep breath, Jules made her way to the witness box, trying her best not to look around the court. *I mustn't look in Tom Stone's direction. I mustn't.* The wooden witness box was just how she imagined it to be; shiny brown wood, battered at the edges and in need of a little care. The judge's desk was to her right, but she dared not look at him. She preferred to imagine him to be a Santa-like character, with a big heart and a dislike of men that tried to take advantage of young women.

As she waited in the witness box, the jury caught her eye, and she noticed with some amusement that each member was sitting over a metre apart. All wore various-coloured masks, and all eyes were upon her. *How funny they look, like clowns in a way. They expect me to tell them the truth, and then they will judge me. They are not clowns. They could be assassins just waiting for the right moment to exterminate me. I wonder whose side they are on.*

Do I have to swear to Almighty God that I would tell the whole truth? Feeling anxious again, she looked down for a bible to swear on but saw none. She was confused.

"Can you confirm that you are Julia Hearn (nee Bridgewater) of Waterfall West, The Old Barn, Waterfall, Cork?"

Still looking down for the bible, she heard a faint voice but wasn't sure if she should pay attention to what was being said. A man with a booming voice repeated the same words; this time, they were louder and seemed more real. "Yes, I am Julia Hearn," she replied, looking up and then realised that it was her lawyer, Sidney Armstrong that had addressed her. *Such a powerful name and so young to be a lawyer.* They had met only once. Lucy recommended him and said he was the best lawyer in Cork. Expensive but the best.

DARRAGH

"Are you well, Mrs Hearn? Would you like a glass of water?"

"No, thank you. I am fine to continue," Jules heard herself say and then she focused on Sidney's face, trying her best to understand what he was asking. She was not thirsty, but her nerves played havoc on her hearing. She needed reassurance, and she searched the courtroom, looking for Seth. It was then that she noticed Tom Stone staring directly at her. He was sitting next to a prison officer and was leaning back in his chair with his arms folded. His black suit looked too large for him and his body was old and his skin shrivelled. His grey hair was cropped short, and she could only see the odd patch of blond hair dye. He reminded her of a tortoise, and she almost laughed out loud. *I was right to come and face him. He is just a sick old man that needs to know the truth and take responsibility for his actions.*

"So, Mrs Hearn, I will read out your statement and ask questions along the way. Is that ok with you?"

"Yes, that will be fine," she replied in a hoarse voice and wished that she had accepted the glass of water she had been offered.

Sidney Armstrong read out the statement to the court.

"At the beginning of August 2018, I started work at Waterfall West Manor House, and Tom Stone was staying there to help his sister as she recovered from a stroke. I became aware that Mr Stone was becoming keen on me as he would keep appearing as I worked and was always complimentary. I sensed that he was becoming infatuated with me. I did not give him any reason to believe that the feeling was mutual. On 1st October 2018, a day after I became engaged to Sebastian Hearn, Tom Stone told me that he loved me. I told him that I was not interested and that I intended on marrying my fiancé, Sebastian Hearn. Tom

Stone didn't take any notice of my words, and he kept bothering me. After several weeks of harassment, it all became too much for me. So I told Sebastian Hearn that I was too upset and ill to go to work because Tom Stone had been harassing me."

"When you say harassing, can you explain what Tom Stone was doing to harass you?"

Jules had been listening to her statement and was surprised at how well she had reported his advances. However, she was pretty sure she was not conveying how stressful his pestering had been. *Oh my God! I am making it sound like he had a crush on me and was just being a nuisance.* "So, he just kept appearing and always stood too close to me when he talked. He was freaking me out. He tried to kiss me once." She could feel her cheeks going red with embarrassment. "I do remember him saying that if I complied, he would give me a good life and that I would thank him one day." She wasn't sure if this was helping explain how he had harassed her. She was starting to feel nauseous.

"I'll read on," Sidney said, looking towards the jury. "When Sebastian Hearn went to see Tom Stone, he recorded the conversation, and if you listen to the recording, then you will hear that his sister, May O'Sullivan (deceased), stated that she had noticed that he was bringing underage girls back to his room at Waterfall West Manor House and because of this she asked him to leave. Later that afternoon, I think that it was around 4pm, my fever had gone, and I got out of bed to go to the toilet. I noticed that it was snowing. Tom Stone appeared in my kitchen and said he had my passport and we would go to Australia together. When I told him to go, he pulled out of his pocket a tranquillizer gun. Frightened, I started to run to the bathroom. He shot a dart into my back, and then I passed out."

"We have the dart that Tom Stone used," Sidney said, holding up a plastic bag with a small dart within. "We can confirm that the defendant's fingerprints have been found on this piece of evidence."

Jules looked at the dart in amazement. She knew that Seth had hidden it in a Tupperware box in the bushes near the summer field, but she didn't realise that he had retrieved it. *I wonder if the used condom that was also placed in the box has his fingerprints or DNA. I wonder if there is any proof that he had used it when he raped me?* She shuddered, thinking of him on her, then looked for Seth and held her breath, eager to find him. She found him, and her heart skipped a beat as it always did when she saw his smiling face. She exhaled, so pleased that he was there and not cross with her. She had never told Seth that Tom had tried to kiss her. His big brown eyes were smouldering, and she wasn't sure if he was crying. *Please don't cry. I really am ok.*

"You may sit down, Mrs Hearn, while I read out the next statements from Ms Sinead Bally and Sebastian Hearn."

Feeling a little light-headed, Jules sat down and saw a woman wearing a mask with white spots approach with a glass of water for her. She really did feel thirsty and was so grateful. "Thank you,'" she whispered. As she drank, she listened to the story of how Sinead and Seth had found her in the boot of Tom Stone's car and how Tom had confessed to raping her. She listened to all the gruesome details and still could not remember anything about what had happened after passing out.

Occasionally, in dreams, she remembered feeling someone over her and panting as he orgasmed and violated her but she never saw a face and was glad of that. Seth finding a used condom was mentioned, but it had not become evidence as her lawyer did not hold it up in a plastic bag like he had shown the

135

jury the dart. *That's a shame. Like Dad and Seth said, the evidence is too old to take DNA samples.*

Jules was starting to feel hungry, and her nerves had subsided. She couldn't work out if time was passing quickly or slowly. Without her phone to look at, she was lost. She hoped Juliet was being good for Sinead and wondered if Seth had remembered to ring her to check.

"Julia, please stand. We are going to read out the next part of your statement."

Jules stood up and noticed that Tom Stone had his head in his hands. *Is he remorseful, or is he just playing the room? The latter, I think.*

"At around 1pm, I had just cleaned Waterfall West Manor House with Sebastian Hearn, and we had brought Darragh, our son, with us while we cleaned. Darragh needed to have his lunch, so I took him to our car, parked outside the Manor House and strapped him in his baby carrier on the back seat. I left Sebastian Hearn to lock up the house. When I sat in the passenger seat, I realised that Tom Stone was sitting in the driver's seat. He demanded that I give him the key, or he would tell the police where to find a murder weapon with Sebastian Hearn's fingerprints confirming that he had killed Gemma Day. I panicked and gave him the key. As he drove away, I called out to Sebastian Hearn for help and saw him running towards the car.

"Tom Stone did not stop and abducted Darragh and me. As we drove to Cork, Tom Stone said that he needed my help with his girlfriend Hannah Honeypot and that he would bring me back home after I had helped him."

"Unfortunately, Hannah Honeypot has since passed away," Sidney announced to the courtroom.

DARRAGH

Jules gasped. She had been relying on Hannah to back up her story. *Is that why Tom is looking sad? No, he is just behaving like a cold-blooded murderer. Did he kill Hannah too? No, he was in custody when she died. I think I know what happened. It must have been a drug overdose. I bet that's why she died.*

Jules looked towards Seth for answers, and then she saw that Lucy was sitting next to him, and she could tell by the look on their faces that this news was a shock to them both.

Jules listened to the remainder of her statement with her eyes now fixed on Tom Stone. He kept putting his head in his hands and shaking it as the final details of her kidnapping were read out to the court. She dared not look at the jury, too scared to see if they were on his side or hers. *Is he trying to pretend that he is sorry, sorry that he tried to kill my unborn baby with tablets and remorseful that he sold my poor Darragh to some depraved people on the internet? Why hasn't Sandra James' abduction been mentioned? Then they will know what a sick bastard he is. For the love of God, the bastard is playing the crowd. Please don't feel sorry for him. Oh, Seth, I wish you were here to hold me.*

Chapter Nineteen

From the court's reception, Jules and Seth could see reporters outside and knew that it would be almost impossible to go out and get lunch without being followed. They had picked a spot that gave them some cover, but they were still in view. The cameras flashed whenever they looked at them. Lucy had volunteered to get them something to eat, and she had slipped through the news-hungry reporters without being questioned.

"I don't like all the attention this case is getting," Jules said, taking a quick look at the cameras pointed towards them.

"Don't you worry about them, my sweet girl. You do know that you did a marvellous job in there? You must promise you will eat everything Lucy brings back because the defence lawyers will not be so nice. Shit, I shouldn't have said that." He could see how distressed she was looking.

"Mmm... I will just stick to my story. Oh, Seth, it is so sad about Hannah. She was too young to die. It has to be drugs that killed her. I thought the authorities would have looked after her. I feel so bad that we didn't keep in contact. She tried her best to save Darragh and me too. I was relying on her to back up my statement."

"Yes, it is a shame. I thought they would have taken a statement from her straight after Darragh was taken."

"I don't think they got to her in time. She was just living for Heroin. She had a child in care too. Oh, Seth, my heart bleeds for her."

"I didn't know that."

"I am surprised they didn't call you or Sinead in as a witness. I am sure the jury would want to know what you saw in more detail."

"I've been thinking about the whole thing. It pains me to say this, but he is going to get off on the rape charge. There is not enough evidence. That condom I found could have been anybody's, and you have no memory of what happened to you."

"So all this is just one big waste of time!"

"No, my poor girl, it has damaged his character and credibility. He will get time for kidnapping you and Darragh. He will go down for that. He will get a few years at least for what he has done to us."

"A few years!"

"I know it is tough, but he will get life for the murder of Gemma Day. They will throw away the key for sure."

"Christ, Seth! So do you think the prosecution will rubbish everything I have said? Do abduction and attempted murder of an unborn child and child trafficking count for nothing?"

"It does. Don't get upset. All I am saying is that you have to be prepared for the worst."

Jules could feel her cheeks colouring up with anger. She was not angry with Seth but angry with the judicial system. She felt her stomach cramping. "Oh, Seth, I feel sick again. I don't think I can go back into court and watch that bastard pretend that he is sorry for everything he has done and hear him say it has all been a big misunderstanding."

"You have to, but I will be there for you. Don't look at the toad. Just look at me, and I will keep you strong."

"You promise?"

"I promise."

Lucy appeared, holding some boxed-up sandwiches and three coffees. "These are all I could find. Every sandwich I looked at had meat in them, and I wasn't sure if you ate fish. I got cheese and onion. Will that be alright?" She could see that they were both looking a bit worn out and worried.

"That's grand, thank you. I'm just off to find the toilet," Seth said. "I won't be gone long. I will be right back. So you mustn't worry," he said, looking a little guilty for leaving Jules.

Lucy sat down next to Jules and took a sip of her coffee. "Oh, that is so good. I needed that. You don't mind if I pull my mask down to drink, do you?"

"Oh God, no, I can't bear wearing the thing. I am sure we are all fit and healthy here. I will have to do the same to eat this," she said, eyeing up her sandwich suspiciously.

"Does it not look good?"

"No, it is fine. I just keep throwing up. I'm sorry, I can't eat it now. Coffee will soothe me."

"You're not pregnant, are you?"

Jules laughed. "No, thank goodness. We haven't had time to do you know what since Juliet was born. She is keeping us up day and night. I wonder if there is something wrong with her."

"How old is she now?"

"Just over three months."

"I don't know much about babies, but I think that is what they do at that age. Keep you up all night. I am sure she will settle one of these fine days. When Seth spoke to Sinead, Juliet was sleeping."

"Really? So he did ring her then. Sleeping! Now that is a surprise. She keeps sleeping! I hope she's not ill."

"No, she is fine, perhaps Sinead has the golden touch."

"I am not very good at being a mother."

Lucy gasped. She hadn't meant to insinuate that Jules was a bad mother. "No, sweetie, you are an excellent mother, and you must never think differently. You are brave too. How did it feel seeing Tom Stone in court?"

"I am glad I did. All I see is a sad old man who will spend the rest of his life in prison. Not for what he did to me but for what he did to Gemma," Jules sighed. "I have to appear in court for that trial too. I hope I don't get ripped to shreds when I tell the court what he told me."

"No, you won't. I won't let them. You know they will be pretty hard on you this afternoon, but you mustn't let them get to you." Lucy took the sandwich back from Jules, and as she touched the packet, she felt an electric current run up her arm. Wondering if the plastic on the front of the packaging had caused this, she realised that she was about to have a vision.

"Lucy, are you ok?"

"No... I... Jules, I can see someone looking at the sandwiches. She is sad, and she is buying sandwiches, lots of sandwiches - cheese sandwiches. For Darragh. I can feel her sorrow, feel her pain. She is torn inside. She must keep him alive for Laura. No, Lara. For Lara." Lucy saw Darragh's face lit up by a small ray of light coming in through drawn curtains. She then saw Jules looking at her with wide eyes, and Lucy smiled at her. "I saw him, Jules. He is alive and well and being fed on cheese sandwiches."

Jules was shocked. "Who is Lara? Why is she keeping him alive for her? Lucy, I know he is alive. I always have. We have to find him. There can't be many people with the name Lara, can there?"

"I will look this afternoon. I think Lara is a child, so that will narrow things down. We are getting close, Jules. The woman that is looking after him uses the same supermarket where I bought the sandwiches. At last, my visions are starting to make sense."

"Oh, Lucy, I hope you are right. I am going crazy with all this waiting."

Be patient, Jules. After court, I will go to the office and run some searches. I will ring you as soon as I get some matches." Taking the corner of the packet, Lucy dropped the cheese sandwich into a plastic bag she had found in her handbag. There was a chance the woman's fingerprints might be on the plastic wrapping. When she looked at Jules again, she noticed that she was crying. "Oh, don't cry," she said, hugging her. "We will find him, I promise."

Chapter Twenty

"How did it go, Tom?" Jasper asked as he watched a spider climbing up his lifeline towards the web that stretched across the cell window. The web fascinated him. The spider was a miracle worker, and he had produced this magnificent feat of engineering using nothing more than his own body. The spider gave him hope and promised him freedom.

"Did what go?" Tom asked, throwing his suit in a heap on the floor.

Jasper watched the spider settle in the centre of his web, knowing the spider was lying to him. His future was bleak, and a wave of anger swept over Jasper, furious with the spider's optimism. The spider was laughing at him, so he pinched his body and felt its body juices wet upon his fingers. It felt good to be in control again.

"The trial." Jasper turned to see his cell mate and noticed that he was naked.

"Are you hot?"

"No, I am not hot. I just like to feel the air on my body. The trial is nothing but a formality. I will be out of here in a few weeks."

"You say that, but you have a murder trial to face next week. That won't be so easy. They have a way of making you say things that you regret. I don't trust those lawyers. They like to trick you and make you look bad."

"Do they? I trust my lawyer. He ran rings round that slut, Julia. He made her cry, and everyone saw that she willingly came with me and disowned her child."

"The other day, you said you loved her and would do anything to be with her."

"That was the other day. In court today, I saw her for what she was. Just a lying slut. That sick bastard's breeding machine. Popping out children like there is no tomorrow. I did her a favour getting rid of her unwanted demon child."

"So, do you think you will win then?"

"The jury could see that I was a good man and shouldn't be in this Hell hole. They could see that I was broken, too, and was being stitched up. A little play-acting never hurt anyone. I should be out of here soon."

"What about the murder case?" Jasper asked, licking the spider's blood off his finger.

"I am not worried about the murder enquiry. Gemma deserved to die. All she wanted was that bastard Seth Hearn. I didn't know that she was still alive when I cut her wrists. She should have said. It was all a big mistake. I will miss her pussy, though. She was a good fuck...."

"So you are not queer then?"

"Of course not. All this talk of sex is waking up Mr Steel. This trial has been so stressful; without his medicine and fresh air, he has been useless to me. Do you think he looks magnificent when he is erect?"

"You are sick in the head."

"I need you to suck me off. I will make it worth your while".

"I told you before that I don't do blow jobs. You can wank yourself off, and then we will all be happy."

"So watching me wank will make you happy?"

"No, I didn't say that."

"I can see it in your face. Let me wank here and now, and I want you to watch. I will still reward you. Look how hard and swollen I am. It has been a long time since I jerked myself off. Perhaps Mr Steel will be satisfied with just you watching him." Keeping his eyes firmly on Jasper, he started to masturbate in front of him. Jasper held his gaze, not wanting to look away. He could hear voices in his head. His mother's voice, the dead spider's voice, calling out to him, telling him that he was a dirty shite.

***

It was late into the night, and everyone in the office had gone home. With bleary eyes and a coffee in her hand, Lucy continued her search to find a child that was born in Cork with the name Lara. The name Laura kept appearing in her searches. The search engine was having trouble finding the name Lara. She cursed the computer but was not willing to give up. She hoped that Laura or Lara had been registered at birth. Unfortunately, many of the travelling community didn't bother.

She sighed, looked at her phone, and noticed that Stephan was online. Eager to talk to him and perhaps get some comforting words, she clicked on Messenger and could see the familiar green dot showing on his profile picture. She longed to see his face and not a picture of a dog. Her heart sank when she saw she was the last to leave a message a couple of days ago. This man was doing crazy things to her normally organised brain. She was finding it harder and harder to concentrate on living if she had not heard from him on a daily basis. She wondered if she was now too dependent on him. Seeing him online and not talking to her ignited some very negative thoughts. She wondered if he was talking to someone else or didn't care about her as much as she did him. Silently, she prayed that he would leave a message and then all would be forgiven. She had to be strong and not message him. If she did, then she might come across as being too forward. That would never do. He was doing her head in. Perhaps she would just leave a little message. '*Missing you,*' she typed. Her finger hovered over the send button. She put the phone down and decided to make some more coffee and think about her needy message.

The kettle boiled violently, and Lucy clutched her cup as she waited for the switch on the kettle to click. She had decided not to press send and would wait it out until Stephan messaged her. She wasn't going to chase him. He surely would have asked to meet up with her if he was interested in her. She had no idea where he was in the country; for all she knew, he could be a catfish. She wondered if catfish helped drunk women home and put them to bed. She was cross with herself for thinking he might not be real, and walking back to her desk, she pressed the send button and waited for him to reply. Within seconds, a message came back saying he missed her too and would get back to her as soon as possible. He sent her lots of hearts, hugs and kisses. She smiled but then wondered why he couldn't talk to her there and then. The negative thoughts began to surface again.

Feeling a little lost, she returned to her search for Lara and did her best to dispel the fears that she was being love bombed. If he asked her for money or naughty photos of herself then she would know.

Chapter Twenty-one

Darragh opened his eyes, and he screamed. A large black cat was in the cot with him. The cat's eyes narrowed, and it hissed at him, showing him its sharp teeth. Darragh sat up and quickly crawled to the far end of the cot and hugged his knees so that he became as small as possible. The cat eyed him suspiciously and lowered himself, ready to pounce and strike out. This was not the first time this had happened, and he knew he would be clawed. The chain around his wrist attached to the leg of the cot rattled and had frightened the cat before. Darragh grabbed the chain, yelled at the cat, and shook the chain angrily. The cat let out a deep-throated meow and stayed put. Surprised that the cat had not gone away, he watched the cat's hindquarters wriggle downwards, and he screamed as it leapt through the air and landed on him, its claws digging deep into his hands and knees. Darragh cried out in pain and kicked the cat hard in its stomach, making it shriek and then, relieved, watched it jump over the side of the cot and run off towards the door. The door was ajar, so it squeezed through easily and disappeared.

Keeping one eye on the door, fearing the cat would return, Darragh watched the red liquid drip out of his hands and onto his blanket. Fascinated, he ran a finger through the blood and then, not liking the feel of it, he wiped his finger on his trousers.

His attention turned towards the door, and he longed to go through it and find his way out again. He pulled at the chain, hoping it would break and allow him to leave his cot. When Mary brought his breakfast, he would show her the chain and hoped she might take pity on him and take it off.

He sighed. Mary needed to look at him, and then she would see that the horrible man that looked a bit like his Da had done this to him. She brought him food, so it must mean that she cared about him.

The morning light was about right for him to be having food. He hoped she would come soon because he longed to see her. Mary. He had heard the bad man call her that. "Mary," he said out loud. He would surprise her and say Mary when he saw her. He hoped she would look at him and perhaps say something or sing to him. He smiled, thinking of her being pleased that he knew her name.

Darragh could hear his food being prepared. He knew the routine and today because the door was open he could hear every movement she made. Darragh stood up and held the side of his cot. His legs were feeling a little wobbly today, but he wanted to be ready to surprise Mary.

After what felt like a lifetime of waiting, the door opened. Mary appeared holding a cheese sandwich, a carton of apple juice and a banana.

"MARY," he yelled at the top of his voice.

Horrified, she looked directly at him, and her mouth fell open. Pleased with himself and jubilant that she had looked directly at him, he called out her name again. "MARY!"

"Oh, for the love of God. You cannot be calling out my name. Do you understand?" she was wagging her finger at him and scowling. This was not the greeting he had hoped for, and he cried, putting his arms out to be held.

"No, no, no! You bad boy. Here, take your food and stop being a baby."

Mary dropped his breakfast into his cot and then swiftly left the room. "Mary," he repeated between sobs.

Mary paced up and down outside his door with her hands over her ears. She could not bear this burden any longer. If Jon was not willing to carry out the operation, she would find someone who could. Lia couldn't wait any longer.

She knew someone who could help her but was unsure if she could trust him. Her brother had been a surgeon until his painkiller addiction had taken its toll. He had been dismissed and now delivered medical supplies to hospitals. He also adored Lia, but she couldn't have him round to see them as Jon had fallen out with him over the silliest of arguments. She wasn't sure if her brother would approve of her borrowing Darragh's kidney. It wasn't as if they were going to kill the boy. They would make sure he was sewn up properly and then send him home. The thought of not having to care for him any longer filled her heart with joy.

As well as having a painkiller addiction, her brother had a gambling habit and was always in debt. He had messaged her for money many times or suggested putting the family home up for sale. Each time, she replied that she had no spare money and said their parents would turn in their graves if they knew what he had been up to. She was certain that if she offered him money to carry out the operation, he was sure to do it with no questions. She didn't have money; Jon did. This he kept in a plastic bag in the toilet cistern. He had thousands hidden away in there to avoid paying tax. Without him knowing, she had taken money to buy Lia treats. It would be quite easy to steal it all and leave the flat with Lia and the boy. The thought of having to touch him revolted her but if it meant saving Lia's life then she would have to find a way to cope.

After checking the money bag was still in the toilet cistern, Mary decided to ring her brother. She shut her eyes and imagined Lia playing out in the garden, running through fields of flowers and laughing. She longed to hear her daughter laugh again.

"Mam?"

Lia was awake, and it was going to be a chore to get her to eat and then go out in her wheelchair to the hospital. She knew she would scream when they hooked her up to the machine. Although the waste was being expelled from her body, the pain she suffered each time was too much to bear. "I'm just coming, Lia. I just have to make a phone call."

Mary went to the top of the stairs to see if she could hear Jon working in the shop downstairs. She could hear him talking to a customer, and she was thankful that he would be busy for a few minutes. She didn't fancy getting hit again. If he knew what she was doing, he would surely kill her. Her sister had warned her about the Hearns years ago, and then seeing all the news reports about the shooting of the registrar in Waterfall by Margaret Hearn had confirmed that the Hearns were not to be trusted. Mary shivered. She was quite sure that she was living with a child killer.

Mary looked at her hand, shaking as the thought of Jon brutally murdering a child bulldozed its way through her mind. She had no evidence to back her theory, but she had seen something in Jon's black eyes when they saw the news that a child's mutilated body had been found at the tip. She saw him sneering, and an uncompassionate indifference had swept over his face leaving her feeling icy cold.

She shook her head and knew that she had to get away from him. The only way to escape Jon was for her and Lia to start a new life in another country and change their names. Frustrated, she sighed as she realised they wouldn't be able to leave Ireland as neither she nor Lia had a passport. Her mind raced as she tried to think of a place to hide. She was thankful that she had never married Jon, but Lia was his, and he would not give her up easily.

"Mammy! I don't want to go to the hospital today."

"Now then, what is all this nonsense? You know, the kind doctors are just trying to make you better. Please be a good girl for me," she said, getting out her phone. She scrolled through the names on her contact list and then paused for a moment over the name Steph. All her male contacts had been given girls' names in case Jon went through her phone. She hadn't spoken to Stephan for a while, but she had been kept up to date with what was going on in his life via their aunt. Despite Stephan having a few issues, he was a kind person, and he didn't like to see anyone suffer. Especially family. She pressed the dial icon and ran into the kitchen in case Jon came up the stairs and overheard her.

"Steph, it's me. I hope I'm not disturbing you at work. I need a favour from you. I am sorry I haven't been in contact recently, but you know how Jon is."

.

Chapter Twenty-two

"EIGHT YEARS! You are fucking joking!"

"No, I'm not, Jules. Calm down! Stone will get more for Gemma Day's murder and the abduction and rape of Sandra James. He will spend the rest of his miserable life in prison where he belongs."

Jules sat heavily on a kitchen chair and tried to take in what Lucy told her. She hadn't expected Tom to get life, but she thought he would get at least twenty-five years. She looked over at Seth, who was feeding Juliet and could see he was upset too. "Did you hear that, Seth? Lucy said that the bastard only got eight years!"

"So, what did he get eight years for?"

Lucy wasn't sure how to continue. She knew Jules would be upset, but she hadn't expected her to be so angry.

"He got eight years for abducting a child."

"What did he get for selling Darragh to God knows who?"

"The transaction was done on Hannah's phone, and he is claiming that he had nothing to do with it and Hannah did it in a jealous rage. Things might have been different if she had been alive to defend herself."

"What about the abortion pills he gave me. He nearly took Juliet's life. Surely, they didn't throw that out in court."

"Oh, Jules, I am so sorry. There was insufficient evidence to prove that you didn't take the pills yourself."

DARRAGH

"THIS IS COMPLETE BULLSHIT!"

"I know, sweetie. I am so sorry. When you are in court next week, you just need to tell the court what happened to Gemma Day, and then…."

Jules could feel herself shaking, and the thought of returning to court terrified her. "I don't know if I can face that trial. They will pick holes in my sorry tale like they did before. He is going to get off with murdering her too. I just know it, and he will probably get community service and counselling. The judicial system is just… shit!"

"Look, I know it is tough, but the system works, and people are treated fairly. Although they don't always get the sentence they deserve, they will be locked up and unable to hurt anyone again."

"BULLSHIT!… I'm sorry, Lucy, I am just so cross. I know that creep will not be able to bother me again for a good few years, but he won't die in prison, will he? Oh, Lucy, it is just so infuriating. At least now I can concentrate on finding Darragh. Did you find any children with the name Lara living in Cork?"

"Just a handful. This afternoon I am going to see if I can find any connections on social media. I will let you know. I have a feeling, like Seth has, that Lara has a connection to the travelling community. It is a gut feeling, but if that is the case, then it is possible that Lara's birth was never registered."

Well, that's settled. Then I am going down to see what Jess knows about Lara. She's had long enough to get over being deserted by Seth's evil twin. I have a gut feeling that she knows something. I will let you know if I get a lead. We will catch up later. Lucy, I am sorry if I yelled at you. I just can't get over the toad getting away with so much."

"Don't worry, I've heard far worse. You just rest and try not to worry about the trial next week. I will be in court and won't let them get away with anything."

Jules ended the call and then looked over at Seth. His eyes flashed dangerously, and she knew he was upset too. *Is he upset that I am going to see Jess, or is he upset about the toad's sentence?*

"Seth? Are you angry with me?"

Seth shook his head, took the bottle out of Juliet's mouth and sat her up to wind her. "No, my sweet girl. I will never be angry with you. I am just furious about the toad. I bet he is sitting in his cell, congratulating himself. You know he will only serve half his sentence. I want to swear, but I won't. Not in front of the kitten. She is milk drunk now and so sleepy. I will see if I can wrap her up and get her to sleep it off. Then I am going down to see Granny. She will be able to ask everyone staying on the campsite if they know of a disabled child named Lara. If you go and see Jess then you will be poking the fire. Please don't do that."

"Oh, Seth, this is so frustrating. I need to be doing something to find Darragh. I keep telling you this. You know what I am like. I can't just sit around doing nothing. Can I at least go and see Granny with you. She has been keeping herself to herself and hasn't come up with anything useful. All I hear her talking about is that a pink moon on April 26 will reveal all. If she says that again, I think I will scream."

"You know she is right, don't you. All I know is that great things happen when there is a pink moon. I married you, and our Darragh was born when there was a pink moon."

"It is Darragh's second birthday on the nineteen and I so wanted him to be home for that."

Seth sighed. "We have to be patient…."

154

DARRAGH

Jules' phone pinged, and she looked to see who was messaging her. It was Shawn. Puzzled, she clicked on the message.

Do you want to play?

Her phone pinged again, and she saw a picture of Shawn's penis attached to a second message. A third message came through.

I am lonely.

Her eyes widened with surprise, and she quickly turned her phone off so Seth couldn't see.

"Who was that?"

"Nobody… Just a spam email," she lied, hoping Seth couldn't see her colouring up. *What a shit Shawn is! Should I reply? No, I will just ignore him, and hopefully, he will get the message. Lonely indeed!*

She stood up, put her phone in her back pocket, and did her best to get rid of the image she had just seen. *Shawn needs help. What is wrong with that man?* "Will you put Juliet in the pram, and we will wheel her down to see Granny?"

Juliet burped, sick flew across the floor, and she started to cry. Seth jumped up, held Juliet at arm's length, and looked down at himself to see if he had vomit on him.

"That's just great," Jules said, picking up the kitchen roll and a bottle of spray disinfectant. "It is all down her front and on you too."

"My jeans are a mess."

"I think there are some clean ones on the rack drying. Do you think she is ill?"

"No, she is not ill. She just drank the milk too quickly or had too much. It's not the first time she's done this."

***

It was good to feel the sun on her face. Jules had decided to put Juliet in the baby carrier, hoping her body's warmth would help her sleep. Juliet was wide awake and moaned now and again, not liking being confined.

As Jules and Seth made their way down to the campsite, they both wondered if Granny would be pleased to see them.

"Do you think Granny has been acting a little odd these past few weeks?" Seth asked.

"Like I said, she is keeping to herself. She came all the way from Dingle to help us, and she hasn't really, has she? Do you think she is sulking because Lucy has second sight too and is helping us more?"

"No, I don't think it is that. Since she has gone to live with her people, she has lost herself to them."

"Do you mean she has become part of a cult?"

Seth laughed. "No, she's not been brainwashed. I think she is detaching herself from the outside world. She is quite old. Perhaps she is just giving in to the inevitable."

"What do you mean? Do you think she is going to die soon?"

"No, not die. She has allowed herself to become old and now just lives with her memories."

"I doubt it, Seth. Look, she is playing with the kids in the woods over there."

DARRAGH

Seth followed Jules' gaze and saw his Granny playing hide and seek with a band of small children who were shrieking with laughter when she found them hiding behind a tree or in a bush.

"If anything," Jules remarked, looking at Granny running towards a little girl with pigtails. "I would say that she looks ten years younger since she came here. It's a shame we have to stop her playing. Do you think that we should go back home?"

"I want to talk to her. I have a feeling there is something she needs to get off her chest."

Granny saw him looking at her, and her face changed from glee to despair. "It is not going to be good news. I can feel the air turning icy. Do you feel the malice and evil hanging over this campsite?"

Jules shivered. "Yes, you are right. I can feel it, and I wish we hadn't come."

"GRANNY!" Seth called. "Do you want a cup of tea? Or are you busy?"

Granny approached them and forced a smile, but they could both see her discomfort. "A cup of tea is just what the doctor ordered. Be quick now. Best not to hang about here and get cold." She led them to the caravan and opened the door. As they went in, Jules was sure she had seen curtains being twitched in other caravans. She could feel eyes boring into their backs as they climbed up the steps.

"Is your friend here?" Seth asked as he sat down.

"No, she has gone shopping with Jess. That child Marley is growing so fast, and he needs some new clothes. Now then, what is this about?"

"We've just come down to see you. I haven't seen you for over a week," he replied.

"Well, you've had your hands full with court and everything. Have the jury made their decision yet?"

"They have. The toad only got eight years. We are not happy about that," Seth said as he sat down.

"He will get what is coming to him. I am sure of that. Perhaps not in this life, though."

Jules looked at the side seat with the table in front and knew she would not fit with Juliet strapped to her. She started to remove the carrier without disturbing Juliet, who had finally gone to sleep. With this task completed and her sleeping baby in her arms, Jules sat next to Seth opposite Granny and could see that she wasn't buying into their story. There was an odd atmosphere in the air, and Jules could bear it no longer. "We wanted to ask you to do something for us."

"I knew you wanted something. You know I am doing everything I can to find out about Darragh. It might look like I was out there enjoying myself with the kiddies but I am having to work very hard to win their parents' trust. They have a name for people like me that left this way of life to marry and live with an outsider in a house."

"What's that then?" Seth asked.

"Never you mind. So, what are you hoping I can do for you?"

"Lucy thinks... In a vision, she saw that Darragh was with another child called Lara, or it could be Laura, but she was pretty sure her name was Lara. The girl is in a wheelchair. We want you to ask everyone if they know a disabled child with that name. We want you to ask Jess."

"Jess. Mmm... She is a hard nut to crack. Oh, for the love of God!" Granny shrieked. She jumped up and started to draw all the curtains.

"What's the matter, Granny? What's going on?"

"That man will be the death of me."

"What man?" they both asked in unison.

"Your father, Seth! He is more trouble dead than when he was alive."

Seth was confused. "What are you talking about? My Dad is here? He can't be."

"Yes, he is dead, but he is not gone. Jethro is driving me nuts. He keeps popping up all the time and giving me that mournful look ghosts have when they have been wronged. It wasn't me that killed him, but you would think it was me that had my hands around his neck and squeezed his life out."

Jules gasped and then shot a glance at Seth. *Oh my God, Seth has gone white.* His dark brown eyes were lost, and she knew he was remembering fighting to the death in the Silent Pool at Farm End.

"You've gone very quiet, Seth. Is there something you want to tell me?" Granny asked, pouring hot water into a teapot.

"I killed him, Granny. I killed my Dad. That is why he is here."

Jules gasped and shook her head. "That is just rubbish, and you know it. If you hadn't, then he would have killed you. That was a trick, wasn't it? Why did you trick Seth into confessing?"

"It was no trick. That man keeps bothering me, and now I know why. He needs to get something off his chest first and then he will slide back down into his watery grave."

"I don't know if I believe in ghosts. Are you sure it wasn't someone that looks like Jethro out there?" Jules shuddered as she said his name.

"No. It is him. He is around us now. Listening into our conversation. WHY DON'T YOU SHOW YOURSELF TO US, YOU ALL...YOU COWARD!" she shrieked.

"I don't want anything to do with him. He was going to kill Jules, and he had to be stopped," Seth said, getting up.

"Sit down and listen to me,'" Granny said calmly.

"If you want to find your boy then you are going to have to listen to what he has to say. It might be something, or it might be nothing. The dead can't hurt you. Gemma, do you hear me? You think we should do this, don't you?"

"What's Gemma got to do with it?" Seth asked.

"She wants to help you and thinks you should listen to him."

Seth felt the hairs on his arms and a cool breeze on his neck, and he shivered. "She's here too, isn't she?"

"Oh, for God's Sake!" Jules exclaimed. "Listen to you both. I have never heard such bullshit."

"You've said that a lot today," Seth said. "I didn't believe in spooks until I saw Gemma's ghost. I've seen her a few times now."

"Why didn't you tell me?" Jules asked quietly.

"Because I didn't want to worry you. You've had enough on your plate to deal with. Me going mad and seeing things was not going to help you."

Granny poured tea into their cups. "So that's settled, then. When it is dark we will go to the Manor House and see what he wants."

"BANG!" A loud knock on the side of the caravan made both Jules and Seth jump."

"Is that him?" Jules asked, her eyes wide with fear.

"No, you daft apeth. It's a branch. When the wind is up, it hits the caravan."

"I don't know if we should do this, Granny," Seth said with his head in his hands. "I have a bad feeling about this. What if he comes after Jules again?"

"I won't let anything happen to Jules. If he has any sense, he will not mess with the living. Tonight it is, Jethro Hearn. Be ready for us."

Chapter Twenty-three

Darragh couldn't contain his excitement and called out to Mary as he watched trees, cars, and people whizz past him. He remembered being in a car, and he had seen all this before. This time it was different - he was bursting with happiness. The images he saw were brighter and more colourful, making him feel happy inside. Every time the big car stopped to let more people in, he watched each man, woman or child with a deep fascination. He could not see his Mam and Da, but the people he saw all had kind eyes and smiled at him when they saw him watching.

That morning Mary had come into his dark room with his breakfast, she had stayed by the cot side, and for the first time ever, she had watched him eat, impatient for him to finish. She had laid a pile of clothes down for him. She told him to put them on. Not understanding what she was talking about, he had looked at the clothes and wondered if they might be something to play with. Mary had tutted when she saw that the clothes had been left alone and then returned wearing a pair of yellow gloves and proceeded to dress him. He complied with her wishes and tried to help her, but she kept tutting and told him to hold still. He guessed from the tone of her voice that she was angry with him, which upset him.

It was strange wearing new clothes, and he pulled at the waistband of his trousers and at the neck of his jumper, not liking the feeling of the scratchy clothes on his skin. Despite this discomfort, it had been good to have spent the time with Mary, and he wondered what the day would bring.

A short while later, Mary returned with a coat, hat and a variety of shoes in her arms. After dressing him in these and finding a pair of shoes that fit, she had lifted him out of the cot and pointed to the bucket. He nodded and peed into the bucket, watching the liquid fizz and froth up. When he was done, he was swept off his feet and carried out of the darkroom that smelt so bad. Darragh lay his head on Mary's shoulder, loving being in her arms. She gasped and then adjusted his body so he couldn't get close to her.

He remembered the corridor and the stairs that led down to a place where the snakes were made, and he was taken out of a side door and into an alleyway. Mary kept looking over her shoulder and seemed worried. He looked back at the way they had come but couldn't see what was troubling her.

The sunshine streaming into the alley was bright, making his eyes water. Waiting for them, he saw the girl in the big pushchair he had seen before. Her dark hair was tied into a ponytail, making him think of the horse he had patted. She scowled at him when she saw him and asked Mary why he was wearing her old coat and hat. Mary had scolded her and told her they must be good and quiet, or the wolf would get them. The girl that cried a lot looked scared and did not argue.

Mary had set him down on the floor and told him to hold onto the side of the pushchair and to walk. He didn't understand what she wanted him to do. She moved forward and pushed the chair forward, and he stood where he was and let the chair go. She had sighed and told him to hold on by placing his hand on the chair and clasping her hand around his for a few seconds. She told him not to let go. He understood.

The alleyway led into the busy street, and he watched all types of cars drive by him. His legs were tired, and the shiny black shoes felt odd and slightly hurt. Wanting to please Mary, he kept walking, and they finally came to a place where others were waiting for something. The people were looking up the road, and he looked too, wondering what was about to arrive. Finally, a huge car with two floors came along, and he could not believe his eyes. The driver came out and laid a ramp down so Mary could wheel the pushchair and the girl that cried a lot onto it. He had been so excited to climb in, too and laughed and forgot that his clothes were uncomfortable and his toes hurt.

He climbed onto the seat, and much to his amazement, his Mary sat next to him. The strange girl who had hair like a horse was in her pushchair on the other side of the big car. "MARY!" he called, pointing to another car with two floors. "MARY!" he yelled, pointing to a little girl walking along the street with her Mam. "MARY...."

"Will you be quiet?" she snapped. "You are upsetting everyone."

"MARY!"

"Shhh, will you!"

Darragh could see that she was getting cross, so he decided that he would focus on his shoes rather than looking out of the window. The shoes were sparkling, and they had flowers imprinted on each side. Mary had tied them onto his feet. He tried to wiggle his toes, and they wouldn't move, so he decided to pull them off.

"Leave them alone," Mary commanded.

She sounded really cross, so he stopped trying to leverage them off with the tip of a shoe on his heel and looked out of the window again.

Outside, there was so much to see, and he really wanted to share what he saw with Mary but thought better of it. Moving along at speed was making him feel tired. He could feel his eyelids getting heavier and heavier. Sleep overtook him, and the streets of Cork were replaced with dreams of ponies and his Mam holding him as she showed him a big black horse. "That's Moss," she said in his dreams, and he smiled, pleased that he had been reminded of the horse's name.

Darragh woke up, and as his eyes grew accustomed to the light, he realised that the big car had stopped. Still feeling sleepy, he watched as a crowd of people queued to get out. He wondered if he should join them. "Mary," he whispered, and then he realised the seat next to him was empty. Fearing Mary would leave him behind, he slid off his seat and pushed his way through the line of men, women and children as he looked for her. He dared not call out her name in case he made her cross again.

With difficulty, he climbed down the steps and wondered where the ramp was. The street was busy, and he looked around, wondering where Mary had gone. He saw a woman with long, blonde, curly hair pushing a pram and wondered what his Mam was doing pushing a different pram. He started to follow her and smiled as he thought of going home and feeling her loving arms around him. His Mam was walking quickly, so he picked up the pace but couldn't catch up with her. For a moment he watched his Mam disappear into the distance and then cried out for her. Tearful and exhausted, he stopped walking and, seeing a wooden seat in the street, climbed onto it to rest.

Darragh frowned and then sighed. He needed Mary to carry him and help him find his Mam. Tears were running down his face as he realised he had lost both of them and was alone. Desperately, he looked around for Mary and saw the big car go past him. Fascinated, he watched all the faces in the window, hoping that he might see her. He wanted to be with her so badly. He smiled as he saw her. She was standing by a window with her hands on her hips. He knew she was looking for him because she was scowling and looking all around. "MARY!" he called out, but she didn't hear or see him. "MARY," he yelled even louder. The bus continued on its way.

Darragh drew his knees up under his chin. The sun was going down, and the streets were quiet. Only the cars and buses were keeping him from crying. They fascinated him. The bright colours and the noise they made continued to delight him. As each bus went by, Darragh scanned the faces in the windows to see if he could see Mary. He was surprised that she had not come for him or brought him his sandwich and drink. His stomach grumbled in agreement, and he laughed out loud when he heard the noise. He ran his hands along the bench, feeling the wood and then discovered a sticky mass had attached itself to his finger. He sniffed it to see if he liked the smell and then, disgusted, tried to shake it off his hand.

"You don't want to be eating that," a man said. Darragh looked up and smiled. "It don't want to come off, do it?" Darragh eyed the man suspiciously, not sure if he liked him or not. He hadn't heard anyone speak like that before. The man had a long beard, and his face was almost covered with it. Nestled in the fur on the man's face, Darragh spotted watery grey eyes with wrinkled skin around them and decided that the man was friendly.

"Ere, let me get it for you," he said, swaying gently in front of him. The man put a can on the bench, and Darragh watched as he fished inside one of his coat pockets for something. He pulled a parcel out of his pocket. The man ripped off a piece of paper from the parcel, gently took Darragh's hand, and pulled off the sticky attachment.

"There you go. You are too small for gum." The man fell onto the bench next to Darragh, righted himself, and laughed. "You don't mind me sitting here with you, do you? Are you waiting for your Mam?"

Darragh understood the word Mam and he had the greatest feeling that this kind man knew where she was.

"Mam," he repeated.

"I'll wait with you, shall I?" he said, opening up his parcel.

Darragh was amazed to see that the parcel was filled with chips. He knew what they were because they had a smell of vinegar, and he had eaten some long ago. "Chip!" he called, laughing out loud, pleased that he knew what they were.

"Do you want one?" the man asked, sipping liquid out of his can.

"We should ask your Mam first. You shouldn't take food from a stranger." Darragh couldn't understand what he was saying. He was hungry and wanted a chip so badly.

"Chip," he said, smiling and then pointed to them.

The man nodded his head. "You eat it quickly, so I don't get in trouble." The old man put the paper full of chips between them.

Darragh could not resist and plunged his hand into the potatoes, drew it back quickly, and squealed.

"They're hot. Take one on the outside," he said gently, showing him what to do. Delicately, the man took one little chip, blew on it, and popped it in his mouth.

Darragh watched him and selected a similar-sized chip and did the same. He spat on it rather than blow and then bit a little of it, hoping that it wouldn't hurt him. He had never eaten anything so good and didn't care that it was a little hot. He had never felt so hungry and smiled at the man and said 'chip' again, knowing he would let him take another.

Darragh leaned back on the bench when the chips were eaten and watched the cars go by. After a while of car-watching, he looked back at the old man and noticed that he was asleep. The can he was drinking from was on the floor. Darragh slid off the bench, picked up the can, and sniffed the liquid inside. It wasn't apple juice, and it smelt odd. He put the can to his lips and sipped the brown liquid. He swallowed a little but didn't like the taste, so he put it back on the floor where he found it.

A car horn made him jump, and Darragh spun around to see where it had come from. A car was speeding along the road towards another. His heart began to beat a little faster as he watched the traffic. He got closer to the edge of the road to get a better look. The speeding car slammed on its brakes and got back in line. He heard another car horn and realised he had recognised the car. It was his Mam and Da's, and he remembered the shiny green car that looked so different from all the other cars. A man with dark hair was driving the car, but he could only see the back of his head. "DA?... DA?" The car continued on its way, and seeing it go, Darragh ran in the road, running along behind but then his ill-fitting shoes hurt so much that he had to stop. He kicked off the shoes and looked up to see if he could see the car, but it had gone. He started to cry, and then he saw a red car draw up next to him through his tears. A man he didn't recognise got out. The man picked him up, opened the car's back door, and put him inside. Darragh cried bitterly, distraught that his Da had not stopped for him. The man put the middle seat belt over his lap and clicked it in so he couldn't move. Darragh didn't like being trapped and pulled at the strap. He heard the man get in the front of the car and start the engine.

"I can't believe you let him get off the bus. It is a wonder that he hasn't been run over."

"I told you, Steph, he is an evil boy and got off the bus to annoy me. What is wrong with you?" she asked, turning her head to chastise Darragh.

He knew her voice and his tears turned to happy tears. "MARY!"

"Don't start that again. Here, be a good boy and eat these," she said, passing him a cheese sandwich and some apple juice.

With skill and dexterity, Darragh inserted the straw into the carton and then sucked at the sweet liquid, drinking the contents until the empty carton contorted and emptied.

"We need to get this over with quickly. You know I am doing this for Lia, don't you? You do realise I could go to prison for carrying out this operation?" Stephan said, breaking the silence.

"That won't happen. I was relying on Jon to carry out the operation, and I prayed and had faith in him, but he has let his daughter down. He has been drinking too much, and although he has been practising on piglets, he doesn't have your skills."

"He is an alcoholic and only a butcher. I can't believe you were thinking of letting him try and carry out an operation on Lia. He knows nothing about surgery."

"At first, I believed he would be able to do the transplant, but lately, he has been distracted with his brother. Did I tell you he had a twin brother? Have you heard of the group S&J?"

"I can't say I have."

"The S stands for Seth Hearn. You must have heard of the song 'Waterfall Way'?"

Stephan went quiet for a moment. "I... I know who you're talking about now. Their son went missing and... Oh, for the love of God! That's not Darragh Hearn sitting in the back there, is it?"

"He is the perfect match for our little Lia. He is bound to have some of Jon's DNA. Did you know twins have the same DNA? Jon told me that."

"Christ, Mary! What have you done? The CCTV cameras are bound to have seen me getting out of the car and stealing him."

"I wouldn't worry. Nobody will sit there watching those tapes. Why would they?"

"I hope you are right. I know they haven't had much luck finding him. I have a contact in the police department. She has been searching for that little boy."

"That's good to know. We've done a good job of hiding him, then."

"This is so wrong, Mary."

"It's wrong to let Lia die. The hospitals have given up on her."

"Why couldn't you or Jon donate a kidney?"

"Jon found Darragh quite by chance on his internet and said that the Lord sent him to us. What good mother allows her child to be sold? She's had another baby, and my heart bleeds for that child."

"Lia will need lots of drugs after the operation, so she doesn't reject the kidney."

"Will she? Will you be able to get them for her? I don't know why I didn't ask you before. You can get me those drugs, can't you? I have thousands of pounds in my bag to buy them."

"I can get her the drugs she needs, but there are risks. You know I am a good surgeon, but even so, if there are complications then I just don't have the equipment to save either of them.

170

Darragh might not do well under anaesthetic. I know nothing about his medical history."

"Please, Steph. It is not as if we are going to kill him. We will transplant the kidney and leave him somewhere. Outside of a hospital, perhaps. I am quite sure you could do with the money too."

The track through the woods was bumpy, and Darragh was bursting to pee. "MARY!" he called, hoping that she would understand.

"Keep the noise down," she called back to him.

"MARY?" he called again, holding his groin to stop the pee from escaping. He caught sight of Steph's eyes in the mirror and called again.

"He needs something," Stephan said. "We should stop. He seems upset."

"He is always moaning. Be quiet, you little brat."

"Mary! He is a baby."

"He is evil and conniving, just like his father."

Stephan shook his head, pulled over, got out and opened the rear door. He saw him holding his crutch, so he unclipped the seat belt.

Darragh smiled and knew Stephan understood him.

"Come and pee."

Darragh walked over to the edge of the path and looked for his bucket. He couldn't see and was about to cry when he noticed Stephan peeing against a tree. He knew that was what he needed to do too, but there was no time. He just managed to pull his trousers down before a torrent of pee shot out and splattered on the grass verge. He felt pleased that he had not wet himself and knew Mary would be pleased with him too.

"Will you hurry up? We need to get back to Lia," Mary called out to Darragh as Stephan strapped him in.

"The poor wee thing was bursting. Lia will be fine. We haven't been gone that long. She has the TV and lots of Disney films to watch."

Stephan parked outside a small cottage covered in green leaves. The front door was framed with white flowers. The roof was made of yellow grass. Darragh had never seen such a pretty house. He held onto Stephan's hand, feeling reassured that this man cared for him. He was beginning to like him more than Mary.

"I don't know where we are going to put you all. We could put the kids in the spare room together. Mary, you can have my room. I don't mind sleeping on the sofa." Darragh looked around the tiny living room and felt immediately at home. Lia was watching a cartoon on the TV, and he ran to the sofa to sit next to her and watch it with her. As he approached, she scowled. "Don't even think about it."

Sensing that he was not wanted, Darragh sat on the floor and watched the TV from there, fascinated by what he saw. A small blue animal with large purple ears was following a girl in a grass skirt. The girl looked a little like Lia and had long black hair. The girl on the TV smiled a lot. He quickly looked up at Lia and noticed that she still looked cross.

Mary tutted, "Lia can sleep with me in your bedroom, and the boy will need to be locked into the spare bedroom."

"You are joking?"

"No, I'm not. He has a habit of wandering off. Anyway, we have to keep Lia away from him. He might have got Covid or a cold out on the street."

DARRAGH

"I need to think about what we are going to do. I need to go out for a few hours. Help yourself to anything in the fridge and for goodness sake, treat Darragh with kindness while I am gone."

"Where are you going? You are not going to the police, are you?"

"No, I am just going down to the pub to have a pint and steady my nerves. I need to make this right in my head."

Mary smiled. "You just can't keep away from them, can you?"

"What do you mean?"

"The fruit machines. You can't help yourself, can you?"

"You are crazy. I will have a pint and might put in a few coins. It relaxes me."

"Mammy used to cry when you went out. She said that the Devil had your soul."

"She understood. Don't bring her into this. I had a problem then, but things are different now. I have someone new in my life and I have turned myself around."

"So, you don't owe any money then?"

"Just a little. All it will take is one big win, and all my debts will be cleared."

Stephan knelt down by Darragh. "You be a good boy and do everything Mary tells you. I will be back in an hour or two." He watched Darragh's bottom lip quiver. Darragh stood up and put his arms in the air to be held. "Take his hand, Mary. He needs comforting."

Reluctantly, Mary took Darragh's hand, and both watched Stephan leave the cottage. He looked back briefly and saw Darragh looking up at Mary, hoping she would pick him up and soothe him. She just stood there looking sour, her heart cold as ice.

Stephan got into the car and rang Lucy's number. The phone finally went to the answerphone, so he left a message and was sad that he couldn't hear her voice for the first time.

"Hi there, sweetheart. I really need to talk to you. I miss you so much. I have some news. That boy you are looking for. I, well... I... Lucy, please pick up. I need to talk to you."

Chapter Twenty-four

"Bingo!" Lucy's mouth dropped open as she looked at the twenty-fourth birth certificate she had ordered. "Lia Hearn - Not Laura or Lara but Lia! Mother- Mary Price - housewife. Father Jonathan Hearn - butcher. Well, I never!" She took a sip of coffee and then looked out of the office window at the angry clouds in the sky, trying to work out what the connection was with Darragh. She remembered feeling Mary's sadness and then shut her eyes, trying to understand what was happening in Mary's head. After a few moments of seeing piglets squealing in her mind with Stephan standing in the middle of them, she shook this thought from her mind and opened her eyes. It was no good. She would have to pay Jon and Mary a visit. She was curious to see Jon and was sure that if she went there then she would understand why she kept seeing Darragh there with them. Feeling excited at the prospect of finding her nephew, she took another sip of coffee and looked up the address of butchers in Cork. She immediately found the address, jumped up, got her coat, and headed out of the station, following Google Maps.

The streets were busy with people enjoying being out shopping again, confident that their vaccination would keep them safe from infection. It was good not to wear a mask and see everyone's smiling faces again.

As Lucy approached the butchers, it suddenly occurred to her that she might need a search warrant. It was very unlikely that they would allow her to look round their premises without one if they held Darragh. Her pace slowed, and she sighed, angry with herself for being so stupid. It then occurred to her that Jon Hearn was a stepbrother and that it wouldn't be right for her to interrogate him. It was not ethical to go there on police business, so she decided to go and visit them as a family member and introduce herself as a step-sister. If she got the opportunity to look around, then she would.

Her life had become so complicated. Stephan was causing her a lot of grief, yet she longed for him to message her. He occupied her brain twenty-four-seven, and she was losing sleep worrying about him. She had gone from being a calm, clear thinker to a lovesick crazy woman. She wondered if this was love or something else; an obsession perhaps. She decided not to allow herself to check for messages until later. Trying not to dwell on him any longer, Lucy entered the butcher's shop and joined a short queue.

A broad-shouldered man wearing a white coat and blue and white apron smeared with blood, smiled at Lucy and asked if he could help her. His blue eyes shone, and his stack of wild blond hair on the top of his head just made her stare at him. Realising that she was being rude, she snapped out of her trance and smiled. "Yes. I'm sorry. Is Jon Hearn around?" The question seemed to trouble him.

"He is," he said slowly. She could see that he was being cautious.

"Can I speak to him privately?"

A knowing grin spread across his chubby face. "He is not well today and he has taken to his bed. Who shall I say called? You're not Jess, are you?"

"No, I'm not. I'm his sister."

"They all say that, but I guess you must be. You do look like him. Go on up and see him. He could do with seeing a friendly face, and then he might get off his lazy ass and help me in the shop. Go through the back room and up the stairs. Mind you, don't slip. I haven't had time to clean the floor this morning. You'll see the stairs ahead of you," he said, pointing a large sausage-like finger towards the back room.

"Thanks," Lucy said, hardly believing her luck. As she walked through to the back room, she saw a black cat trying to eat a pig's ear. She bent down to stroke him, and it hissed at her. Not wanting to get clawed, she continued on her way and climbed the stairs to the flat above. She wondered if Mary Price would be there with Lia. She hadn't thought to ask. The door at the top of the stairs was ajar, and she thought it was only polite to knock and announce her arrival. She waited for a short while and then called out. "Is it ok to come in? The man downstairs said that it was ok to come up."

Feeling a little apprehensive, she made her way along the dimly lit corridor to the room at the end. She could see a television flickering. Lucy had a strange feeling that she had walked down this corridor before. Her heart pace picked up as she realised she had dreamed about this corridor. Sometimes her visions came in dreams. She was tempted to look in each room as she passed them but thought better of it.

Lucy found her stepbrother in the lounge. He was asleep and had a whisky bottle next to him. The curtains were drawn, and the room reeked of alcohol. She drew back the curtains and opened the window and then turned to have a good look at Jon Hearn. She blinked hard, not believing her eyes. The man lying on the sofa was a carbon copy of Seth. Every feature was the same.

Seth had told her about him, but she hadn't imagined them to be so alike.

"Is that you, Mary?" she heard him ask. "Have you come back to me? Have you brought Lia home to me?" he croaked without opening his eyes.

Lucy smiled to herself. He had answered her question about the whereabouts of Mary and Lia. It was obvious to her now that Mary had left him and taken Lia with her. She needed to check the house for Darragh.

"It's not Mary. It's your sister Lucy. I was passing by and I thought that I would say Hello!"

"Is that so?" Jon replied in a sarcastic voice. He groaned as he sat up and opened his eyes. He squinted at her and then held up his hand. The light of the window was too bright for him. "Will you close the fucking curtains? Can't you see I am suffering? Did Mary send you?"

"No, I have been building up my family tree and wondered if you could fill in a few gaps for me? I am going around Ireland visiting all my relatives," she lied.

Jon frowned and shielded his eyes so he could see her. "I have no interest in helping you. You should be on your way. Before you go, you wouldn't mind getting me some aspirin and water from the kitchen. I am a dying man."

"So why are you hanging? Did you have a good night out with the boys last night?" she asked, ignoring his request to leave and hoping he might open up to her.

"No, of course not. I am a broken man. My beautiful Mary has left me and taken my Lia with her. How could she do such a thing? My wee girl is too sick to travel."

"Where do you think they have gone to?"

"If I knew that, then I wouldn't be sitting here now, would I? What did you say your name was?"

"Lucy. We have the same Da, Jethro Hearn. I'll get you some aspirin? Do you want me to put the kettle on?" she asked, walking towards the door.

"Yes, that will be good. I shouldn't drink whisky. It makes me do naughty things."

Lucy left the room, not wanting to hear what those naughty things might be. Making him a cup of tea would give her a chance to look around the flat. With her heart beating hard in her chest, she carefully opened the first door in the corridor. This room was full to the ceiling with junk, and she knew instinctively that it was not where Darragh had been kept. The door clicked as she closed it, and she looked towards the lounge, fearing that Jon might see her.

Moving swiftly on, she came across another door on the right. The door was open a little. A shiver went down her spine as she pushed it open. This was the door she had seen in her dreams. The scratches on the wooden panelling were exactly as she remembered. She slipped into the room and looked around. The curtains were drawn and let a sliver of light in just at the top. As her eyes became accustomed to the dim light, she saw the cot in the middle of the room with a bucket next to it. Lucy walked over to the cot, and as she got closer, she saw a blanket with a small body lying beneath it.

In her vision, she had seen Darragh in this dark room, alone and frightened. She looked at the mound under the blanket and tried to determine if it was the size of a two-year-old. It could be Darragh if he was emaciated. Holding her breath, she carefully lifted the blanket and gasped as the cat she had seen earlier hissed at her. Frightened, she dropped the blanket down and jumped back.

"Did you find what you are looking for, then?" Jon asked, his face red with anger. He began to walk towards her.

"I was looking for the kitchen," she lied, backing away from him, trying her best to sound convincing.

"My ass you were," he growled, picking up the pace.

Horrified and terrified, Lucy grabbed the bucket and hurled the contents towards his face, hoping to blind him for a moment so she could run. Jon yelled and spat out stale toilet waste. Lucy raced to the door and flew out into the corridor, determined to escape him. She swung open the door at the end of the corridor and ran straight into the arms of the butcher that she had spoken to earlier.

He laughed and then looked over at Jon.

"She's not your sister, is she? Do you want me to tie her to the bed for you, Jon?"

Lucy struggled to break free.

"She's a lively one!"

Jon's clothes were saturated with pee and faeces. He cussed as he brushed the muck from his clothes. "She's a fucking shit stirrer and needs to be taught a lesson. Bernard, hold her tight while I tie her wrists up."

"DON'T YOU DARE TIE ME UP," Lucy screamed. "Backup will be here any minute."

She felt Bernard's grip loosen as he realised she was a police officer. "Yes, that's right, Bernard. As well as being Jon's step-sister, I am also a police officer."

She stared into Jon Hearn's eyes, challenging him to carry out his threat.

"Did he send you? That bastard Seth Hearn. Did he send you?"

"No, he didn't! I came because I wanted to see my own brother and to see Mary too."

Jon smirked. "So why did you say backup was coming?"

"Because you were scaring me."

"So nobody's coming then?"

Lucy swallowed hard, realising her mistake and tried her best to think of something to stop him from tying her up. "Nobody is coming, but they do know I am here," she said, but her voice was unsteady, and she knew Jon was not buying it. She pulled her arms away from Bernard and rubbed her shoulder. "I should arrest you for assault," she said, turning round to see Bernard's face. She could see that he was nervous. "Christ, what is going on here? Is that what you do? Tie defenceless women up and have your wicked way with them?" Jon was going red with anger again, and Lucy wondered what he would say.

"We should tie her up anyway. She is trouble," Jon spat.

Lucy frowned. "You touch me, and you will both be sorry. You will go down for sure."

"Just lock her in the bedroom. I need time to think," Jon said, pacing up and down the hall.

"Christ, no! I am not going to be shut in any room. Where's Mary? I need to speak to her. I think she might know where Darragh is."

Jon sneered at her. "So this is what this is about. You are looking for that bastard's boy. Well, you won't find him here."

"But he was here, wasn't he? That was his room I was in, wasn't it? You know forensics will be able to tell me if he was. Has Mary taken him somewhere?"

"You ask way too many questions and need to shut up."

"I'll ask as many questions as I like. What is wrong with you? Do you hate your brother so much that you would take his son? How could you be so heartless? You need to make this right, Jon Hearn, give him back, and then pray to God for forgiveness."

Jon Hearn's face was almost purple now. She knew she had said too much. For a brief moment she saw his eyes narrow and his face contorted with disgust. She didn't see his fist coming towards her, but she felt her nose break as his bare knuckles met flesh. She screamed out in pain, saw stars and then felt Bernard's sausage-like fingers catch her. Then...

Chapter Twenty-five

Enjoying a brief moment to himself, Seth scrolled down all the messages he and Jules had received on TikTok since releasing their new version of Darragh, Never Be Alone. He couldn't quite believe his eyes. There were so many messages of support and possible sightings of Darragh. The post had gone viral, and the number of views was rising by the minute. He wanted to go through every message before he and Jules went to the Manor House to see what his dad wanted. Just thinking about his Dad gave him the shivers. He hoped that Granny was being dramatic and his presence there was just a figment of her imagination. He sighed, trying not to think about it.

Seth looked at a few more messages and then put his phone down as a picture of Gemma's ghostly face with mascara running down her cheeks filled his thoughts. He stretched himself out on the sofa and rearranged the cushion behind his head, trying his best not to think about her. *I don't believe in ghosts. If I hadn't seen her then I would be as sceptical as Jules. I wish Gemma would leave me alone. I don't want her help.*

He could hear Jules singing in the shower. He loved listening to her voice. She had taken Juliet in with her as she liked watching the water spray out of the shower head. He thought about Jules' beautiful body covered in foam and could feel himself harden. *We so need to have sex. I can't remember the last time we did. We are just so busy these days; if we are not looking after*

Juliet, then we are sleeping. And then there is Darragh to think about too. Come on, Seth, I must concentrate on these messages and see if anyone has seen my wee boy. He is out there somewhere.

"Seth, is it ok to come in? I'm a bit early, but I was going stir-crazy and needed some company," Sinead asked as she walked into the barn.

Embarrassed that there was a bulge in his trousers, Seth sat up and, trying to look casual, covered himself with a cushion. "No, I am not busy. Come in. You know you are always welcome." The shock of seeing Sinead appear had the desired effect, and he could feel himself relax. "Are you not liking your new home then?"

"My new home is perfect. I just don't like living there all by myself. Oh, Seth, I am turning into a crazy, old spinster."

Seth laughed. "Well, you can always come back and stay in your old room. I am sure Jules won't mind."

"I'd like that, but when Darragh comes back you will need a room for him."

"I guess you are right, but I don't like you to be unhappy. Why don't you get a lodger or a cat?"

"No, I don't want to be a crazy cat woman either."

"I don't think having one cat would put you in that category. You could borrow Barney if you like. If you feed him on salmon and chicken he won't leave your side."

"I love Barney dearly, but I think Jules will miss him. I have a plan. I've just had a brilliant idea. A business idea. It will keep me busy, and then I won't be on my own every hour of the day."

"What's that then? Do you want a cup of tea?"

"Yes, go on then. So I was thinking of opening up the house again and offering week-long pony care classes for kids.

Each kid could have their own pony to look after, and then we could have a show at the end of the week."

"Do you think it is wise to start a new business when Covid is still around? You will need staff too."

"I think Covid's days are numbered. It can't go on forever, can it? Would you help me? We work well as a team. The kids won't know that you are a famous pop star."

Seth smiled. "Is that what you think I am? A famous popstar."

"You know you are. If it wasn't for Covid, then you would be stalked by thousands of girls all wanting a piece of you."

"Do you think so?"

"I know so. Will you help me before I start pushing a shopping trolley around Cork full of carrier bags and cats?"

"You know I will do anything for you. Why not? It will keep my mind off things."

"That's grand. I will start making plans. So tell me again why I am babysitting. Jules said on the phone that your mad granny wanted to hold a séance tonight. It all sounds a bit creepy to me. Are you sure you want to do this?"

"No, I don't want to do it. I am not happy about it. Did Jules tell you who Granny wants to contact or summon?"

"No, she just said it might help you find Darragh."

"Granny thinks my Dad can help. Apparently, he is hanging around the Manor House with something to say. I don't think that he will be happy to see me. It was me that killed him. Jules said I mustn't think that way, but that is the truth. I guess it was a fight to the death, either him or me. So…"

"Seriously! You have to be kidding me. No way! How in fuck's name do you think a man like that will help you find your boy? He didn't care about you, so why would he care about Darragh being lost?"

"Exactly! That's just my point. So you believe in ghosts, do you?"

"Of course, I do. Why wouldn't I? I don't think you should be messing around with the occult."

"He's not the Devil," Jules announced. Her cheeks were pink from having a hot shower. Her hair was tied up in a blue towel, and she was holding Juliet, who was trying to find her breast through her t-shirt. Jules laughed and turned her around. "Just give me five minutes to dry my hair. You can't be hungry again. I only just fed you."

"Let me take the little darling," Sinead said, limping over to take her. Jules passed Juliet over to her and she immediately started to complain that she was away from her food source.

Sinead laughed and cradled her and stroked her cheek. "Hello, little one. Are you going to be good for me?"

"You are walking so much better now," Jules said, taking off the towel and running her fingers through her tight, wet curls.

"Each day, I seem to be getting a little stronger. Soon I will be able to ride again. I can't wait. So, little miss. Are you up for watching a bit of TV with me and having a glass of wine or two while your Mam and Dad meet the Devil?" she asked playfully.

"Oh, Sinead, I fully expect this all to be a load of codswallop. We will be back before you know it. Do you think we should go, Seth?"

"I guess Granny will never forgive us if we don't. She hasn't been the same since she joined the travellers. Nor have I come to that. I keep seeing Gemma hanging around the place. It is doing my head in."

DARRAGH

"Gemma? Our Gemma? Gemma, who was murdered?" Sinead asked,

"Yes, the very same girl. I think I might need to talk to someone about it."

***

Hand in hand, Jules and Seth walked up the path towards the front door of the Manor House, and they could see Granny waiting for them. She was wearing a knitted shawl over her shoulders, and her grey hair looked almost white under the light. Jules was surprised to see that she wasn't wearing a headscarf too.

"You don't think she is wearing huge hoop earrings, do you?" whispered Jules.

"No. Why do you say that?"

"She looks like a fortune teller. You know, like in the movies."

Seth laughed. "No, she is just cold. You should have worn more too. It is going to be cold and damp in the house.

"Hi, Granny. Have you been waiting long?"

"Long enough. I've got something to say before we go in. Look, I know you are, well, non-believers, so I need you to keep an open mind and not be laughing and joking. Do you hear me? The spirits will not help if they are being mocked. We are seeking a truth, and we all... all have to be on board," she said, looking directly at Jules.

Oh God, she thinks I am going to be laughing at her. She does look so funny, though. Crap! I hope she isn't a mind reader, either. "If this helps us find Darragh, then I will do anything. Look, I know you think I am sceptical about all this. I am finding it hard to believe in ghosts. If there are spirits, then I am sure they will understand. I will keep an open mind like you ask."

"Good. Now we need to go to the heart of the house. That is where I will find it."

"Find what?" Seth asked.

"We will know when we get there... What's that, Gemma? Oh, I see. She says she will take us to the master bedroom."

"Is she here too?" Seth asked, looking around to see if he could see her.

"She and another are close by, but the other is just watching us, and I feel her pain. I feel her loss too. May, I will be with you soon, dear. I know you couldn't say goodbye. I will say it for you."

"May!" Jules whispered in an astonished voice.

"Seth, there is no time to lose. Open the door. Gemma is waiting for us."

Seth got his key out and opened the door. Feeling goosebumps and the hairs go up on the back of his neck, he tried to find the light switch.

"No lights," Granny instructed. "Just a torch light," she said, turning one on.

Jules squeezed Seth's hand to reassure him. She could sense that he was feeling nervous. She dared not speak in case she upset Granny or the other spirits. It was hard not to feel afraid. In the darkness, the shadows seemed to linger just that bit longer, and the floorboards creaked a little louder than they used to. She held a picture of Darragh in her mind and imagined herself holding him. She needed to give the spirits a clear image of him. If need be, she had a picture of Darragh in her pocket to show them if they existed.

As they walked up the stairs, Seth was sure that he could see Gemma's silhouette in the torchlight. He looked harder and then realised that he was seeing just a piece of furniture. He tried concentrating only on the torch light and where he was treading and not look into the shadows.

The master bedroom was on the first floor at the back of the house. Seth was sure that Granny had mentioned that they were looking for a room or a piece of furniture located in the centre of the building. He found this puzzling. *Is Gemma taking us on a wild goose chase?*

The master bedroom was lit only by the moon outside. The furnishing smelt of mould, and there was a faint smell of something more disturbing. For a moment, Seth could smell his Dad's cheap aftershave. He held his breath, hoping the smell would go away.

Granny looked around the room as if she was searching for something. "I thought it would be a chair. Gemma, do you want me to sit in it, dear?" she asked, looking at an old rocking chair in the corner. "Seth, be a dear and put that rocker in the middle of the room for me to sit on. You two will have to stand on either side of me and hold my hands. First, I need to light this candle." She pulled out a tea light and a box of matches from her pocket and placed them on a small table next to the four-poster bed. She lit the candle and then adjusted the chair's position, and happy with where it was placed, she sat down facing the flickering light of the candle. "Come and hold my hands, and for goodness sake, don't let go whatever happens."

Jules and Seth looked at each other and were starting to become concerned. Feeling uneasy, they each held her hand and immediately felt a strange warmth coming from her fingertips.

"Now concentrate on the candle. The light and warmth will guide the spirits to us. They need to be welcomed. I know you are here already, Gemma. We need you here. Please stay with us. Are there any spirits out there that would like to come and join us? I know there are some that need to communicate with us. I can see you in the shadows and feel you coming closer. Please make yourself known. The rocking chair started to rock slowly, and Granny was just sitting still and was not making it rock.

Jules gasped silently. The flame on the candle began to flicker. The rocking chair stopped.

Granny sighed. "Jethro, you have come to us. I know you want to share something with us. Do you know where Darragh Hearn is? Is that what you want to tell us? Please rock me again if that is a yes." The rocking chair remained stationary. "Jethro, is Darragh alive?"

The chair started to rock again. Jules didn't know whether to laugh or cry. *How can I trust someone that tried to rape me and allowed so many children to die?*

"The spirits do not lie. Darragh is alive. Jethro, why have you brought us here?" Granny asked. "We know Darragh is alive, but we need more from you. You owe it to your son." The flame flickered angrily. "I know you feel you have been wronged, but what is done is done. You must forgive and forget and move on to the other side. Why do I see the name Ann in my head? Who is Ann?" she whispered.

"Ann Bridgewater is Jules' aunt. The one Margaret killed," Seth whispered back.

"Oh yes, I remember. Do you seek Ann, Jethro? She had passed to the other side peacefully. We cannot help you. He thinks Ann is in the room too. Do you think Ann is here, Jethro?"

190

DARRAGH

The rocking chair started to rock a bit more frantically, and Seth and Jules could feel her hands tighten.

"Don't let go," she whispered.

Jules was dumbfounded and couldn't believe what she was hearing. Jethro had always thought she was Ann, and it sickened her to know that he still believed this. "NO, I WON'T HAVE THIS! I AM NOT ANN," she roared, breaking the chain. The candle flame flickered angrily, and then a huge spark spiralled upwards towards the ceiling.

"JETHRO HEARN!" Granny yelled. "I have been decent enough with you. You came to me as a lost soul needing direction. I am telling you now that you are not welcome here if you mean to bring this poor girl trouble. If you know where your grandson Darragh is, you must declare this and show me where you saw him. Do you hear me, Jethro?" she asked in a firm voice, taking Jules' hand again.

Seth felt an icy chill around him, and he could feel his Dad standing right by him. For a moment he could smell pond water and he remembered the night he and Jules had spent in the silent pool, trying to stay alive until help came. He did not welcome these memories, and the thought of his Dad standing next to him was freaking him out. "What do you want with me? Be off with you. I have no time to entertain you," Seth said. "Just tell me where my son is and leave us in peace." In his mind, he could hear his Dad laughing at him, which made him furious.

"We're losing him," Granny exclaimed. "Jethro Hearn, this is your last chance to redeem yourself, or you know where you will go. If that is the end you choose, then so be it. Is the boy in Cork?" The rocking chair moved forward and stopped as if held with an invisible hand. "I'll take that as a yes," Granny said, trying not to slide onto the floor. "Is Darragh safe?" The chair flew back and smashed against the wall, and both Seth and Jules held Granny's arms and held her up so she didn't fall on the floor.

"I've had enough of your Tomfoolery. We have no use for you here. Leave us be, and do not return. You are not welcome here. Seth, please go and turn on the light. He has gone. It is as I thought. He had no interest in helping us. It's ok, Gemma, you can come out now. He has gone. He lied to you. I am not angry with you, Gemma, dear."

Seth shook his head and found his way to the light switch. He flicked it on, but nothing happened. "The bulb must have blown. Let's go home. I'll change the bulb in the morning." He tried to open the door, but it was locked. "Did someone lock the door? The key isn't here." There was a strange smell in the air. "Does anyone smell burning?" he asked. He looked back at his granny and could see her in the torchlight shaking her head. "It is probably the candle."

"No, it isn't," Jules said. "Seth, the drapes of the bed are on fire. That spark must have caught some of the fabric."

Seth ran over, picked up a mat by the bed, and started beating the flames with it. After a frantic five minutes, the flames subsided and exhausted, he sat down on the bed.

"Well, that wasn't quite what I expected. Are you sure he has gone?"

"I don't know, I did my best, but he is a malevolent spirit, and you can never be too sure about their whereabouts," Granny said, inspecting the smoking drapes with her torch. "He is not here now. He has probably gone off to sulk. Well, at least we know Darragh is in Cork, and he is alive and well."

"We knew that already. He told us nothing new," Seth said, feeling downcast.

"Now that's where you are wrong. While he was playing with us, Gemma was able to probe a little deeper into his mind while his back was turned, so to speak, and she says that Darragh was with family."

"Really?" Jules said. "Why do you say 'was'?"

"Do we have family in Cork? If he is not with family, then where is he now?" Jules was starting to panic.

"He was with Jon? I just know he was," Seth said. "Well, that settles it. I am going to that butcher shop and I am going to have a few words with him. He hates my guts, and he has taken my wee boy to settle some kind of vendetta he has against me. I see that now." Seth stood up and walked back to the locked door. "I can't wait another minute. Stand back. I am going to have to break through the door. This is just some kind of witchery and the door is only made of wood."

"You won't need to do that. I have the key," Granny said. "Didn't you see me lock it when we came in? I wanted to make sure we were not interrupted."

"Seth, you can't go," Jules said, almost crying. "If you do, then you will only fight with him. Look, I know you won't like this, but I think I should go and see him myself. I know Darragh isn't with him anymore, but he might take pity on me and tell me where he is."

"I don't think that is a good idea. He is not going to tell you anything. I should go. If he knows where Darragh is, then I will make him tell me. It is something I need to do," Seth opened the door with the key and felt relieved that he was free of the smoky room.

"Neither of you should go. I will talk to him," Granny announced. "He won't hurt an old woman, and I will know if he is hiding something or someone."

"That might be an idea. I know I will just lose my temper. Perhaps it is better if you go," Seth said. "Ok then, but if he starts to get nasty, come straight out of the shop, and we will be in the car outside, ready to call the police."

"Perhaps we should tell Lucy. Tell her what we know," Jules suggested. *I don't think Seth wants to tell her. Oh my God! He wants to handle this the Hearn way.*

"I know Lucy is in tune with this whole spirit thing, but I don't think she will be able to get a warrant and search his flat just on what my bastard of a father might have insinuated. What we really need to do is our own search and get some real evidence."

As they headed home, they didn't notice that the candle had reignited. The flame on the small tea light candle shot into the air and caught the smouldering drapes as it had done before. The curtain fibres screamed out in agony and began to glow a deep red, angry that their wounds had been reopened.

Chapter Twenty-six

The air in the bathroom was cold, too cold to be standing there just in boxer shorts. Seth flushed the toilet, washed his hands, and returned to the bedroom. He shivered as he walked through the darkness and longed to get under the covers with Jules and snuggle up against her. He wanted to feel her soft skin against his and her mass of curls in his face. He nudged the bedroom door, trying not to let it creak and tiptoed past Juliet's cot. He knew if he even looked at his sleeping daughter, she would wake and cry out. He climbed into bed holding his breath, afraid that even the sound of his breathing would cause the night to yell out and wake those lucky enough to sleep.

Jules was lost under the covers, and he could hear her deep breaths as she slept. He wanted to hold her, kiss her neck, tell her how much he loved her and make love to her. It had been too long, and he yearned for their bodies to become one again. He lay his head on the pillow and did his best to try and sleep.

After a few minutes, Seth opened his eyes, unable to think about anything other than having sex. Carefully, he opened his bedside drawer to find a condom, but the sound of him sifting through the mountain of odds and ends was making a noise and would wake the baby. He silently sighed and lay back down, willing his erection to calm. Settling just for a cuddle and a kiss, he slid his body over to Jules and embracing her, he pulled her to him and cupped her breasts. She murmured something but didn't seem to mind him being affectionate. Her breasts were round and full, and her nipples hard. She hadn't fed Juliet in hours, and now her breasts were engorged with milk. When he squeezed gently on her nipples, warm milk leaked out and felt a little sticky. A crazy thought ran through his head, and he almost shocked himself as he imagined himself sucking on her nipple. *Christ, I am getting perverted in my old age.* Embarrassed, he pushed that thought away and then tried to think of something to stop this idea, making him harden, even hornier. He moved his hand down to her waist and then laid his hand on her hip.

"Don't stop," she murmured in a sleepy voice. "I need to feel you inside me."

He hadn't expected her to say that, and he hoped she was not just dreaming.

Feeling encouraged, he slipped his fingers through her soft pubic hair and gently rubbed her. She gasped and didn't push him away. Seth smiled. She wanted him as much as he wanted her. Feeling her slippery wet, he slid into her and knew he would not be able to stop himself from orgasming early. She was moaning as he moved inside her, and as he got closer to the edge, he could see the tops of trees flying past him below. His breath quickened, and he gritted his teeth together, knowing he must be silent when the moment came.

A loud rapping at the front door tore him away from the edge of oblivion. He froze and looked towards the bedroom door, wondering if it really was someone knocking on it. A series of knocking made him sit up. Jules was awake too.

"Someone's at the door," she said, pulling the covers from over her head. "What time is it? Something must be wrong."

The rapping noise continued, and Seth sighed and jumped out of bed. He pulled on a pair of joggers. "I'll go. It's probably

Sinead. She might have locked herself out of the piggery again when she went out for a smoke. She needs the spare key."

Juliet began to cry. "Oh no," Jules said, pulling the covers over her head again. "Will you make me a cup of tea when you've given Sinead the key?"

Seth ran to the door and then opened it to find Jess standing there with Granny by her side. His smile faded when he realised it was not Sinead. "What's the matter? Is everything ok?"

"Seth, the house is on FIRE!" Jess announced.

"What do you mean? Christ, no!"

"The Manor House is on fire," Jess said again. "I wanted to tell you myself, but she wanted to come too. Look, I'm sorry if I've been a bit off with you. It's been hard without Jon."

"I think Jethro started it," Granny announced.

Seth looked from one startled face to another as their words started to sink in. "The Manor House. The Manor House is on fire? Why didn't you ring me? Has a fire engine been called?"

"I tried, but I couldn't get through. A fire engine pulled up just as we left the campsite," Granny replied, staring hard at Jess. "Go back to Marley. You shouldn't have left him alone in the caravan." Granny folded her arms angrily.

"Don't you tell me what to do, you interfering old biddy!"

Seth looked back at the bedroom door and thought he had better tell Jules the bad news. He left Jess and Granny squabbling on the doorstep.

"Jules, the Manor House is on fire," he called as he approached the bedroom.

"I gathered that," Jules said as she came out of the bedroom wearing her dressing gown. In her arms, she held Juliet wrapped in a blanket.

"Everyone has been ferrying water from the well to the bedroom we were in," Granny said, appearing behind Seth. "We tried to put it out, but the fire got out of control. It's all my fault."

Seth took a deep breath. "The fire service will stop it. I'll stop it. Jules, stay here. I don't want Juliet getting smoke in her lungs. I won't be long." Juliet howled, adding to the tension in the room

"Oh, Seth, I can't stay here. I want to see the house. If you park in the car park, I will stay in the car. If it is too smoky, then I will drive home. Does Sinead know? I should ring her."

Seth threw on some clothes, and they all jumped into the car and sped along the bumpy track towards the Manor House, hoping the building would still be standing when they arrived. They saw a fiery glow above the treetops as they approached, with smoke cascading high into the black sky. They passed Jess as they neared the house, and she turned for a moment to watch their descent down the gravel drive. A shower of stones sprayed her as they passed, and Seth caught a quick look in the rear-view mirror of her standing there with her finger in the air.

"I never liked that girl," Granny said. "I wouldn't be surprised if she had a hand in this."

"Granny!" Jules said, annoyed with her. "We all saw the drapes catch alight. Perhaps they were still smouldering when we left them. We should have checked before we left. Jess may be many things, but she is not an arsonist."

"Then why does she have a black aura? There is no good in that child."

As they approached the Manor House, they allowed a second fire engine to drive at speed into the carpark. When the siren stopped, the sound of wood and furniture crackling in the blaze filled the air.

"We need to stay calm. Granny, will you look after Juliet while we go and see what's happening?" Seth asked, not giving her a chance to continue with her witch hunt. Jules handed Juliet to her and then got out of the car. She could feel the heat of the blaze on her cheeks. "We won't be long. Oh, Seth, this is really scary. I can't bear to look," she said, unable to stop herself from looking towards the house. Seth grabbed her hand, and they ran onto the front lawn, their mouths falling open as they saw the chaos ahead. The house was just a fiery mass, and the urgent cries from the firemen confirmed that the fate of the house was sealed.

"I own the house," Seth called out, but the firemen were too busy to stop and chat.

As Jules and Seth watched the water from the hoses dousing the house, they were joined by the travellers. One of the men was covered in soot and sweat. Seth walked over to him.

"Thank you for trying to save my house," he called.

"We tried to stop the fire, but there was nothing we could do. I am sorry." The traveller was old, and his face worn with time. He shifted uncomfortably on the spot, distressed at having to tell Seth this news.

"You did your best. At least nobody was hurt. At the end of the day, the house is just wood and bricks," he said, trying to comfort the old man. Still, deep down, there was a great sadness inside him as he realised that centuries of memories, art, and May's hard work were going up in smoke. Seth walked back to Jules, and she hugged him, sensing that he was sad. "May, poor May. She would be so sad to see her house in flames," he said, almost crying.

"I know. Seth, we need to tell Sinead. She will be heartbroken too."

Transfixed, Jules and Seth watched the firemen douse the blaze with water. They watched brick walls crash in on themselves and glass crack and fall to the ground. The house was an inferno, leaving parts just a glowing shell. The firemen were fighting a losing battle, and the house could not be saved. The smoke stung their eyes, and the flames called them all to come closer.

"MY GOD!" Jules gasped, pointing to the roof.

Seth followed her finger and saw the outline of a cat on a small section of roof not yet claimed by the fire.

Jules shook her head and blinked hard, thinking her eyes were playing tricks on her. She dared not believe what she was seeing. "Seth," she said slowly. "I can see Barney on the roof. Do you see him? On the bit that hasn't fallen in yet. How did he get up there? What is he doing up there?"

"He must have followed us when we came down here earlier." She ran towards a fireman and pleaded with him to rescue Barney. At first, the fireman didn't understand. She pointed, and he shrugged his shoulders. When she got back to Seth, he had gone from where they had been standing. She looked across, and she could see him running towards the flames.

"NOOOO!" she yelled. "THE HOUSE COULD COLLAPSE. SETH, PLEASE!" She wondered what he hoped to achieve. *There is no saving, Barney. The fireman said he was sorry.* She watched Seth calling Barney and holding his arms out. *He is asking him to jump. Barney is so far up he will never hear him. What is he thinking of? I am going to lose them both. Please no.*

Seth continued to call their cat, and then she watched in horror as a wall fell towards the garden. Seth dodged a piece of burning timber and stayed where he was. A fireman ran over to Seth, and Jules saw that he was begging him to go to safety.

DARRAGH

Barney was now on a chimney pot but looked down as if he was considering jumping. *Surely not. He wouldn't take a leap that far.*

"JUMP," the old man called out. "JUMP. YOU KNOW YOU HAVE TO. ARE YOU A MAN OR A MOUSE?"

Jules' eyes widened, and then to her horror, she saw Barney leap into the air, his legs pawing the air as he fell and then, to her amazement, he landed on all four feet. Frightened, Barney tore off into the woods. The travellers cheered, and all Jules could do was sob with happiness. *He shouldn't have survived that jump. He must have hurt himself. I hope he doesn't end up dying in the woods, his body broken.*

"I reckon your cat has used up one of its lives," the old man said, chuckling.

"I can't believe he just did that. Do you think he is injured?"

"Cats always land on their feet. Was it your cat?"

"Yes, but he might be hurt. I am so worried about him."

"He will be fine," the old man said, turning to go back to the campsite. "He is a white cat, and he has been blessed."

"I thought black cats were the lucky ones."

"No, just white cats. Black cats are the ones to look out for. I cross myself many times if a black cat crosses my path. I am sorry about your house. It is a crying shame."

Seth came over to Jules, smiling. "Did you see our Barney leap? I nearly caught him."

"Oh, Seth, he might be hurt. We need to look for him. We might have to take him to the vet. You shouldn't have gone so close to the house. You could have been killed."

"I thought I could catch him. I couldn't just stand by and watch him get burnt to a crisp. I will go and look for him."

"I'd better go and see if Juliet is ok. I can't watch this fire any longer. It is like watching the Titanic going down. Seth, will you go and look for Barney? There is a torch in the boot."

Seth looked over at the woods and then sighed. "I will try and find him, but he is probably hiding. I will do my best."

As they walked back to the car they found Granny walking up and down with Juliet on her shoulder. Juliet was crying hysterically.

"I'm sorry we were so long," Jules said, taking Juliet from her. "The house is lost. It is nothing but burning rubble now."

"DO YOU SEE WHAT YOU HAVE DONE, JETHRO HEARN? YOU HAVE BROKEN HEARTS AND SEALED YOUR FATE. SOON THEY WILL COME FOR YOU, AND YOU WILL BURN IN HELL," Granny screamed out to the night and then got into the car and slammed the door.

Jules sighed. *That woman needs her head examined!*

Chapter Twenty-seven

Feeling exhausted, Jules slipped Juliet into her bouncy chair and covered her with a warm blanket. She watched her baby's little pink face crumple up in disgust as she realised she was no longer in her mother's arms. Juliet began to cry, so she rocked the chair with her foot and sighed. "I can't be holding you twenty-four-seven; you need to give me a break. There! Look at you. You are not crying now. Life is not so bad, is it?"

It was just starting to get light, but Jules couldn't see further than the end of the path because a thick blanket of smoke had settled malignantly over Waterfall West and wept silently in the fields around the smouldering Manor House. Jules could smell smoke on her clothes, and her hair felt greasy and damp with soot. Every so often she looked up at the door, hoping Seth would return with Barney in his arms.

Earlier, when Jules had driven Granny back to the campsite, she had been strangely quiet. Jules hadn't had the energy to ask if she was ok. She had said goodnight to her and made sure she got inside her caravan before driving home. Jules suspected that Granny might be angry with her. She had no idea why. A little voice in her head whispered that losing Darragh was her own fault and she had brought bad luck to the Hearn family. *Perhaps the Bridgewaters and the Hearns will never get along.*

A scratching sound coming from outside caught her attention and smiling, she ran over to the door and flung it open, fully expecting to see Barney there waiting to come in. She hoped and prayed that her cat had not been injured from falling from the roof. She waited for Barney to appear from the fog, but he was not there. *It was just my imagination. He is probably dying under a bridge somewhere. Why did I think of a bridge? There are no bridges on the estate. I really hope he is ok.*

"Have you seen how thick this fog is?" Seth asked, appearing from nowhere. Jules snapped out of her musings and then looked at Seth's hands. They were empty, and her heart sank with disappointment.

He shook his head. "No luck. He will come home, I'm…"

"WHEN WERE YOU GOING TO TELL ME MY HOUSE HAS BURNT DOWN?" Sinead yelled at them both.

Seth spun around. "I am so sorry, Sinead. I was going to ring you, but then it went a bit crazy. It all happened so fast. I swear I was just going to come over and tell you. Barney fell off the roof and ran off. I've spent hours looking for him. Shit, Sinead, we've all lost our lovely house. How did you find out?"

Sinead looked troubled. "I heard it on the news. They are saying that Waterfall West is cursed," she replied quietly. Her anger was waning. "Fuck, Seth! You should have told me. You said Barney fell off the roof. You don't mean the Manor House, do you?"

"Yes, he had to jump. It was that or burn to death."

"Oh my God! That's awful. Where did he go? Did you find him?"

"No, I didn't. He is probably lying in a ditch somewhere licking his wounds."

"Aww, no, I can't bear it. I'll help you look."

"I've been out all night looking for him. I just need to eat something and have a cup of tea. Come in and have a cup of tea with us. This shitty fog needs to lift. It's almost impossible to see further than your hand out there."

"Ok then, sure. I... I... don't want to see the house - not yet. I can't bear to see it in such a terrible state. At least we have insurance. We do have insurance, don't we?"

Seth frowned. "I was getting quotes, and then Juliet came along. So, no, the insurance has expired."

"For Christ's sake! The house has been burnt to the ground, and we haven't got building insurance!"

"I'm sorry. I've been a right eejit. I don't know what to say."

Sinead sat heavily on a kitchen chair and put her head in her hands.

"I'm really sorry. I'll pay for the rebuild. Our song will pay for the rebuild.

"No, you don't have to do that," Jules said. "Perhaps it is best to leave the house as it is. If it is cursed, then it will probably burn down again. That house was like a millstone around our necks. We are better off without it."

Sinead looked up, her eyes blazing. "That's easy for you to say. I was depending on that house to bring in some revenue. I don't know if you have noticed, but I haven't had any money coming in for a few years now.

Jules felt bad for speaking her mind. "I'm sorry, I was being selfish. I know how much effort you and May put into that house. At least you will be able to still have weddings in the Orangery when things get back to normal." Jules hugged her, feeling really sorry for what she had said. "Seth, you need to rest. I want to go and look for Barney myself. I know where he likes to go when he is wandering around the estate. I need to be doing something. Later I want to go for a drive around Cork. I had a dream last night that I would find him there. I know it sounds crazy, but I just want to look. Juliet has been fed, so she should be good for an hour. She might need her nappy changed."

"Ok, I am shattered, but you won't see much in this fog. Maybe you should wait until later."

"I will go now while Juliet is quiet and reasonably happy. Sinead, do you want to come too?"

"I think Seth is right. I will look later when the fog is cleared if you don't find him. I'm sorry."

"Sorry for what?"

"Sorry that I snapped at you. It is just so hard to take this all in."

"It's ok. I understand."

Jules walked through the fog towards the woodland behind the Manor House, the last place she remembered seeing Barney. As she passed through the stable's courtyard, she noticed that all the horses had lined themselves up along the fence and were watching her. She could just see their heads drifting in and out of the mist. She smiled and wondered why they were all there. Her old horse Connor whinnied when he saw her, and so feeling a little guilty that she hadn't seen him for a while, she walked down the muddy track to greet him.

Jules stroked his damp nose. "I'm sorry I haven't been there for you. You have all your horsey friends now. Have you missed me?" Connor snorted, replying yes, he had missed her. "When you have babies, they tend to take over your life. I promise we will go out soon. I'm surprised that you are all here. Did you know there was a fire last night? I thought you would be in the next field, keeping your distance from the ruins." Connor ignored her and laid his head on her shoulder. She hugged his neck. "You haven't seen Barney, have you? I will bring you a little apple later.

I need to find Barney." Jules patted him one more time and continued on her way towards the woods.

The daffodils were in full bloom and free of mist. As she walked through them, she looked on either side for white fur. The woodland flowers showed no signs of being trampled on. Ahead was an old wood shed on the edge of the woodland near to the traveller's encampment. She stopped a few metres away from the shed and shivered. It was old, and the wooden planks holding it together were black with age. The door was warped, and was ajar, the corner caught in mud. *This would be the ideal place for a cat to hide.* With her heart beating in her chest, Jules squeezed in through the gap and pushed cobwebs away. There was a pile of old logs in the corner. She felt a little ashamed that they were buying logs for the house rather than utilising the trees that needed felling on the estate. *The house isn't going to need logs now, is it? What an airhead I am.*

Jules walked over to the logs and noticed a large gap behind the pile, so she crouched down to see if she could see Barney laying there. It was too dark to see, so she got her phone out and turned on the torch. "Aww, I thought you would be there."

"Are you looking for a cat?"

Jules screamed, not realising that someone had entered the shed. She jumped up, spun around and saw Jess standing there. Her hands were on her hips, and she was frowning.

"Jess! You scared the living daylights out of me. Did you see Barney fall off the roof last night? He ran into the woods. Have you seen him?"

"He's in my caravan. Do you want to come and get him? He is making the place filthy."

"Is he bleeding?"

"No, he's not bleeding. He is limping, but he can walk. It's his fur. He is spreading it all over the place."

"Oh my God, Jess! I can't believe it. Yes, I'll come and get him. You are an angel."

Jess smiled a crooked smile. "Believe me, I am no angel. I nearly kicked him out, but then Marley started to play with him, and it kept him quiet, so I let him stay a while."

Jules and Jess walked down to the caravan. The campsite was surrounded in fog, its whispery fingers lacing their way through the trees. The central area was clear, and sunlight streamed onto the roofs of the caravans.

"I am sorry about your house. There is not much left of it. There is talk that it didn't start naturally."

"What do you mean?"

"Your granny, that crazy old biddy, has been spreading rumours that Jon's father started the blaze. I didn't know dead men could light matches."

"No, you're right. That is a crazy idea. When we summoned Jethro yesterday, a candle caught the bed drapes alight. I don't think Seth put the fire out properly."

"So why would you be summoning the dead?"

"Granny keeps seeing Jethro's ghost. We thought he wanted to help us find Darragh. But it turns out he was only interested in me."

"Did you and he have a thing going then?"

"CHRIST, NO! It's a long story, but he thinks I am my aunt, and yes, they did have a thing going. Margaret, your mother-in-law's sister, killed her. She and hundreds of illegitimate Hearn babies. I don't know why I even entertained the idea that he could help us."

DARRAGH

Jess went quiet for a while. "The Hearns aren't very good to their women, are they? Does Seth play around?"

"NO! Seth is loyal and true. I trust him completely."

Jess opened the door of her caravan and caught Marley standing on top of the cooker top, reaching up for a jar full of biscuits in a rack above. "You get down from there, you little rascal. You've had enough biscuits this morning."

Jules watched as Jess lifted him down and could do nothing but stare at Marley. His soft brown, almost black curls framed his face, and his eyes were big and brown, just like Seth and Darragh's. She couldn't help but let out a deep sob. The pain of losing Darragh was unbearable.

"Are you ok?" Jess asked softly. "Are you upset about the house?"

"I couldn't give a fuck about the house. Houses can be rebuilt, but you can't rebuild a child. Oh, Jess, Marley looks just like my little Darragh," she sobbed.

"I shouldn't have brought you here. Do you want to sit down?"

Jules nodded and sat down on the bed. The tears were rolling down her face. As she wept, Barney limped over to her and started to rub his body against her leg and purred, waiting to be stroked.

"Don't cry. You will find your wee boy again. I am sure he is safe," she said, handing her a piece of kitchen towel to wipe away her tears.

"I know he is alive, but I don't think he is safe. I believe Granny and Lucy when they say he's alive but deep down I know time is running out. I just have the feeling that someone is going to hurt him. I can't bear to think of him being in pain or neglected. I have Juliet now, but it is not the same. I need my Darragh back.

209

I just need to be with him so badly. Jess, if you know anything, however small, please tell me. I promise I won't let anyone know that it was you that told me. When Darragh was taken, we thought that travellers had taken him. Now I am not so sure."

Jess's face changed, and she looked so lost for a moment. She got a biscuit out of the jar and gave it to Marley. "You go and eat this like a good boy and let your Mammy have a chat with your aunt."

Jules heard the word aunt, and it suddenly dawned on her that Jess and Marley were family.

"Look, Jules," she said, sitting down next to her. "I don't want to give you false hope, but on the day that Darragh was snatched, well I heard something. Now I am not going to say who it was, but I overheard a conversation."

"It was Jon, wasn't it?"

Jess looked startled, and Jules wished she hadn't said anything. "Don't answer that. What did you hear? Any little thing might help." Barny jumped onto Jules' lap and she hugged and stroked him but continued to look at Jess, knowing that she had something important to say.

Jess sighed, "I heard someone talking to a woman I don't like very much. He says she means nothing to him, but I know different. He has a child by her, and you would think the sun shines out of that kid's ass. The night before, I heard him tell this woman that he had found what they had been looking for, and God had sent him to them. He said that his bastard brother owed this to him. So, you can take what you will from that. It might be something, it might be nothing."

Jules stared out the window, trying to make sense of her words. There was no doubt in her mind now that Jon had taken Darragh. "Thanks for trying to help me," she said, wiping her tears away with the paper towel. "I know it was hard for you to tell me this. I promise I won't say a word to anyone."

Chapter Twenty-eight

Lucy shivered and winced as a sharp pain reverberated from her broken nose down through her body. She almost threw up as congealed blood was stuck in her throat. She had never felt such pain. Feeling dizzy, she tried to move, but her ankles and wrists were bound. The ground she was on was cold, and the grit beneath her body irritated her. Trying not to move her head too much, she looked around her and could see a small dusty window. It was still light, and she wondered how long she had been unconscious.

Lucy could see new garden tools hanging along a concrete wall, and an old rusty lawnmower was next to her. She realised she was in an outbuilding and guessed she was still at the butcher's shop because she could hear the familiar sound of traffic passing by. A pig grunting nearby confused her for a moment, and she wondered if Jon bought live pigs to butcher in the shop. Nothing surprised her anymore.

The last thing she remembered was Jon hitting her; she was unsure why he would do such a thing. Hitting her was a desperate act, and it just confirmed in her mind that he had kidnapped Darragh. Her mind was racing now as she started to piece the evidence together. For some reason, Jon Hearn hated Seth, and his taking Darragh was not just a wicked act to mentally destroy his brother. There was something more to this case, and it had something to do with Lia. She shut her eyes and focused on the little girl with long black hair. For some reason, she had the feeling that it was this child that had been the catalyst. Lucy could see Lia looking out of the window of a bus. Her dark hollow eyes were lost, and her soul mournful and bitter. Lucy shook her head as she tried to shake this image away. The pain of her broken nose brought her out of her vision. She opened her eyes, thankful to be away from this sickly child. A child near to death whose only chance is for someone to donate... *To donate what? Money? No, not money, something more vital like a heart or a...* Her phone started to buzz in her coat, and she smiled.

Jon Hearn had not noticed that she had her phone with her. She tried to work her hands out of the rope that bound her wrists and cursed when the phone stopped ringing. The string cut into her wrists; if anything, she had made her bindings tighter. She laughed at herself for thinking she could work her way out of her constraints like Houdini. The knots had been tied by butchers who were skilled at tying up meat for Sunday roasts. Lucy's phone stopped ringing. She looked around the shed for a sharp edge that she could use to slice the rope apart. The lawnmower was a possible tool; she hoped it had blades, not a plastic wire, to cut the grass. Lucy slid towards the mower and tried to tip it on its side using her feet. The mower was heavy and difficult to manoeuvre. She could lift it so far, but the handle was getting caught on some boxes. She had to let it go and rethink how she could move it to the middle of the shed before attempting to turn it over again.

The sound of someone approaching startled her, and she lay back down on her side and made out she was still unconscious. She wanted to cry out in pain, but she gritted her teeth and did her best not to move. She heard a bolt slide across quietly as if the person was being careful not to be heard. A large man trod heavy, clumsy steps as he came towards her, and she suspected it was Bernard. She was thankful that it was not Jon. Bernard was only inches away from her, and she could smell a sickly scent of dried blood and chicken guts on his clothing, confirming that it was him. A large hand with fingers like sausages stroked her cheek. His rough fingers ran through her hair and then down her back. She gritted her teeth as she felt his fingers slide under her jumper and then up to her bra hooks. His touch revolted her. "You undo that, and I swear to God you will go to Hell!" She opened her eyes and saw him stand up. His legs were apart on either side of her body. He grinned, and she frowned as she watched him unbutton his blood-stained white coat and then unfasten his flies. A defiant rage filled her body. She rolled onto her back, pulled her knees up and then forced her bound feet into his crotch with all her might.

"FECKING GOD!" he yelled out, holding his crotch and cursing some more. "What the feck did you do that for?"

Lucy sat up and managed to push herself back into the corner of the shed. Her knuckles grated on the hard floor, but she didn't care. She needed to get as much space as possible between them and assess her options. There would not be much she could do to stop him from attacking her. She would have to talk her way out of the corner she was in. Her eyes focused on a St. Christopher he was wearing around his neck.

"Do you think Our Father would approve of your shenanigans?"

He looked confused. "Do you mean Jon?"

"No, you silly boy. Our Father in Heaven. Nowhere in the Bible does it say that a man should take a woman before wedlock. You will go to Hell if you touch me, and your mother will spit on your grave." She stared at him coldly and hard and then at his St. Christopher. Slowly, his fingers went up to his necklace, and he caressed the pendant and looked frightened.

"I am sorry if I scared you. I shouldn't have done it. I couldn't help myself. You reminded me of my Mammy. Your face is a mess. There is blood everywhere."

Lucy didn't know what to think. He was obviously sick in the head, and she suspected that he had educational needs. He would be easy to manipulate. "So, if your Mammy was here now, she would want you to do the right thing, wouldn't she?"

Bernard nodded.

"You've seen my badge, you know I am a police officer, and if you don't want to go to prison, you need to untie me. Jon shouldn't have hit me. He will be punished, but you will be pardoned. Do you understand?"

"He will sack me, and then I won't be able to feed my family."

Bernard having a family took her by surprise. "For the love of God, Bernard! Untie me and go home to your wife and family, a free man."

He shook his head. "No, I can't. My wife is sick, and we need the money."

"Look, Jon doesn't have to know you were here. I could have just untied myself and escaped. Where is he?"

"He's serving in the shop."

"That is good. He won't know that you have been out here. I will just make it look like I got out myself. Is there a way out into the alley?"

"Yes, but he might see you. The shop only had one customer and he said he wanted a smoke. He will be wondering where I am and…."

"So this is where you are. I thought as much."

Bernard spun around, startled by Jon's sudden appearance, and Lucy's heart sank as her escape plan dissipated.

"I was just... just seeing if she was ok. You shouldn't have hit your sister."

This declaration surprised Lucy.

"She is no sister of mine. She is police. She was lying."

"Then why do we have the same father? Jethro Hearn. Does his name ring any bells? I have had a DNA test done. Seth will confirm this too." She watched Jon's face turn red and wished she hadn't mentioned his brother.

"That shitty bastard will say anything to make himself look big. Bernard, gag her, dump the bitch in the wheelie bin, and let the garbage truck take care of her in the morning. Don't let anyone see you. You nearly got caught last time. Wheel the bin out with the others. The bin men will be here in the morning."

Lucy's mind began to race as she realised that this would not be the first time he had left a body in a bin. The image of the child's butchered body they had found at the dump flashed before her eyes, and she could see her bones in the bin with shop rubbish being wheeled up a side alley next to a butcher's shop. A black cat wound through Bernard's legs as he pulled the bin along. A neighbour pulling their bin out waved to Bernard, and she felt his anxiety rise as the neighbour chatted to him about the weather.

"Don't you want me to make cat mince of her first?"

"No, not this time. I don't want to poison Hamish."

Lucy snapped out of her daydream. "You are both going to go to Hell. You sick bastards! Bernard, you don't have to listen to him. You have a chance to save your soul. If you want Our Father to forgive you, you must untie me and do what is right."

Jon sneered. "I don't think that is going to happen. Dead cops don't squeal."

Chapter Twenty-nine

As Tom Stoned headed back to the prison, the morning's events ran through his mind. Being forced into a prison van disgusted and humiliated him. Having to go to court when he was clearly innocent made him feel physically sick. The sound of the barrister reading out the heinous crimes he was being charged with was insulting too. The handcuffs around his wrists were laughing at him, and he dared not look at his wrists. He had been given a sentence already for kidnapping Julia and her brat. He thought it ridiculous that he had to go back to court. He didn't know Gemma Day had been alive when he cut her wrists. How could he have known?

The thought of Gemma's firm breasts and tight hole sent shivers down his body. He smiled as he realised Mr Steel was stirring, which pleased him. As soon as he got back into his cell, he would jerk off and think of himself inside her limp body. He remembered doing the same to Julia. He looked down at himself and admired his erection. It had been a while since he had felt so hard. He was alone in the van, and the thought of jerking off there and then would have been sensational if only he hadn't been wearing cuffs. Mr Steel would have to wait but in the meantime he would just stroke his tip to keep him happy.

As he walked through the prison, still erect, he knew other inmates were watching him and admiring the size of his penis. If he could have removed his ill-fitting suit and paraded along naked, he would have. There was no doubt in his mind that those that liked other men were interested in him. This thought alone kept Mr Steel strong, and he almost came just thinking of one of them sucking him off.

Tom was looking forward to seeing Jasper. Although his cellmate had said he wasn't interested in him, he knew it was only a matter of time before he would be begging him to play with Mr Steel. The cell door was locked behind him, and he saw Jasper sitting at the desk, writing. His cheeks were flushed, and he appeared to be annoyed. The pen he was using was not working, so he shook it angrily and threw it down, then realised that Tom was standing by him.

"Do you want to borrow mine? I have plenty of lead in my pencil?" he said suggestively.

"You need to take a cold shower," Jasper replied, trying not to look at his erection. "You are not right."

"Do you want to have one with me? I will be gentle with you and let you wash Mr Steel."

Jasper didn't say no, and this gave Tom new hope. "Mr Steel knows how to please you. He wants to help you."

Jasper gave Mr Steel a sideway glance and shook his head. "I need to write this letter. Do you have a pen?"

"I'll get you one, but I will need paying back later." Mr Steel was begging for attention, but the wait to be pleasured would intensify the experience. It was good to feel his manhood behaving properly without Viagra. He felt powerful and very horny. Tom leant over Jasper and picked up the pen from his shelf, allowing Mr Steel to brush against his cellmate's side. He felt Jasper flinch, and feeling a little disappointed, he pulled away. "Later, Jasper, later," he said, scribbling on a spare paper to see if he could get his pen working. "Who are you writing to?"

"To my mother. I want her to come and visit me. She was very cross with me when the police came. I didn't get the chance to explain. It wasn't my fault what happened."

"I understand. We are like two peas in a pod. We have both been stitched up. We will get through this together."

"How did court go this morning?"

"Just the usual bullshit. The trial starts tomorrow. I suppose all my haters will be there over the next few days, telling lies about me. Julia has let me down, she lied in court, and now I've got eight years in this place to deal with. Of course, I am going to appeal. The jury obviously had it in for me. My lawyer is a complete waste of space. When I release my assets, I will hire the best lawyer in the country."

"I thought you said you had money."

"I do, but it is being held back for unknown reasons. Don't you worry. I will reward you handsomely for any services you provide me with."

"What are assets?"

"Mmm, I wouldn't expect you to understand. You are a bit backward, I guess."

"I am not backward. You are so rude."

"I'm sorry, I didn't mean it like that. What are you supposed to say? That you have special educational needs? I have needs, too," he said. "We all have needs and desires. Mr Steel has needs too. Do you want to see what he can do?"

"No, I'd rather not. I want to write my letter."

"Here's the pen I promised you," he said, handing it to him. "If you need any help with spelling, just let me know. I am a fountain of knowledge. We are here for you, I am holding a torch for you, and Mr Steel is standing to attention."

"Thanks," Jasper said, taking the pen out of his sweaty palm. "I think it's you that needs help. Just keep away from me, alright?"

"Where do you expect us to go then? It's not like we can go for a walk."

"I don't care. I just want to write this letter and need some alone time. I can't think with you going on all the time."

"I'm only trying to help."

"I don't want your help. I just want you to leave me alone. You're a wanker."

"There's no need to be like this. Our lives will be so much better if we become close friends. Do you know what it is like being a sex God? Damn hard." Tom laughed at himself. "No pun intended. We both have needs. I need to have sex once or twice a day, and you will feel so much better when I admit that men or boys make you horny. You are queer, and I can give you what you need."

Jasper roared and leapt up. His chair went flying backwards. He grabbed Tom by the throat. "I am not queer," his hold around his throat tightened.

Tom pulled at Jasper's hands, his face red, and he could not breathe. "I'm sorry," he croaked. "Please, Jasper!"

Jasper released him and pushed him back against the wall. "Just stay out of my face and don't ever call me a queer again. Do you hear?"

Unable to speak, Tom rubbed his throat and nodded.

Chapter Thirty

"Stop the car, Seth. I can't bear to hear Juliet scream a moment longer. I am going to have to go in the back of the car and feed her. Do you think she is in pain? Remember how Darragh screamed when he had an ear infection."

"No, Jules, there is nothing wrong with her. She just has her parent's temper. Granny keeps saying we should let her cry a little and let her soothe herself."

"Is that so!" Jules said, folding her arms in defiance. "Your Granny says a lot of things. I don't have a temper!"

Seth laughed. "Let's give her five minutes more and see if she is tired and falls asleep. She has a fine pair of lungs on her and she will get tired soon."

"We were meant to go to your brother's butcher's shop in stealth mode. I'm glad you will let me go and see Jon rather than Granny. She didn't approve, did she?"

"She just said that we knew best. She was with Jess' mother when I called her. I don't think she wanted to argue in front of her," Seth said as he swerved around a cyclist. The cyclist seemed shocked to see him. "This car is too quiet. I miss our old green car."

"I don't. It was difficult to drive. I am glad we sold it. I wonder if Jon will talk to me. He won't. I just know it. If he is busy serving in the shop, then I will sneak in the back and go and see if I can find Darragh," Jules said.

"No way! You will be putting yourself in danger. If anyone is going to break and enter, it will be me. You put your hood up and take Juliet into the shop and cause a distraction, so I have a chance to look round his flat without getting seen. If you wear a mask and hide your curls, he won't recognise you or Juliet."

"What if I can't think of a distraction? If Juliet keeps crying like this, all his customers will leave, and he will throw me out. Seth, please stop. Juliet is hiccupping. She is so mad. Let me sit with her at least and hold her hand. I can't bear to hear her cry."

"Just five more minutes, and then I will pull over. She has to learn to be patient." The traffic was busy, and there was nowhere to pull over. Seth tutted. "At this rate, the butcher's shop will be shut before we get there."

Lost in thought, Jules looked out of the window at the people passing by. She checked the contents of every pushchair she saw with the hope that she might see her Darragh. The car was crawling along which made it easier for her to see everyone that passed. For a moment, they stopped in a queue of traffic, and Jules saw an old man with a long beard lying on a bench. She couldn't help but stare at him. He was fast asleep and didn't notice people walking past him. A can of lager was on the floor next to him, and as someone walked by, she noticed that the can had been knocked over and was spilling its contents across the floor. *Oh dear, I hope he has money to get another one. I wonder if he is hungry. Perhaps he would like some hot chips.*

It took longer than usual to drive through Cork and their anxiety was building. Seth drew up behind a dustbin lorry, a road away from Jon's butcher's shop. He reversed the car into a space and smiled as he saw Juliet sleeping peacefully. "There, I told you she would sleep once she had complained enough."

"She is probably scarred for life and thinks she has parents that don't care about her," Jules said, almost crying.

"You know that is not true. So, what's our plan then? You have got your phone with you, haven't you?"

"Yes, of course. I will go and see if he is serving in the shop and then give you a ring."

"Let me get the pram out of the boot," Seth said as he got out of the car.

Jules got out, too and opened the back door to get Juliet out. She smiled when she saw how peaceful Juliet was looking. "Look at our baby, Seth. She is sleeping like an angel. You do know that all Hell will break loose when I put her in the pram. She hates being in there."

As Jules waited for Seth to assemble the pram, she watched the evening sunshine dance on the roof of the car. Today, in her head, it was the first day of summer, and she hoped that the sun would stay with them until autumn.

With the pram now ready to deposit their baby in, Jules carefully unstrapped her and with teeth clenched, she transferred Juliet into the pram. Juliet's eyes opened immediately, and her face contorted as she began to cry again. "Damn! I know you don't like it in there, but when we start moving, you can see the sky and the birds. Juliet, my baby, please don't cry," she said, inserting a dummy into an open mouth.

"You are right. She doesn't like the pram, does she? She is doing me a service. If she keeps that noise up, my sick brother won't hear me break in."

"I thought you were joking. No, Seth, you mustn't break in. You will get in trouble if you do that."

"I will wear gloves," he said, pulling some out from his jacket pocket. "Nobody will know it is me. They will think it is

Jon if I try to make myself look a little shorter. We have to know if Darragh is still in that flat. We will kick ourselves if we don't check."

"Wait until I ring you, so you know he is busy. Once you've had a good look around, come straight back to the car. Please, Seth, I don't want you getting into trouble and returning to prison."

Jules wheeled the pram around to the butcher's shop and was pleased to see Jon Hearn was chopping up a rack of ribs for a customer. Staring at Seth's double was a strange feeling, and she shivered. Juliet was still crying, and Jules contemplated returning to the car and aborting the mission. She rocked Juliet's pram as she got her phone out. Jules rang Seth's number and realised she was shaking. "He's in there, and the shop is busy. I am going to buy meat. We can give it to the cat later."

"Ok. I just need ten minutes. I can see you from where I am standing."

Jules looked back the way she had come, but she couldn't see him. "Seth?"

"Yes, my gorgeous girl."

"Be careful."

"I will. Don't you worry? I am just visiting a relative, aren't I? What could go wrong?"

Jules pulled up her hood, tucked her golden curls away and fitted a floral mask over her mouth. She took a deep breath and tried not to think of the things that might go wrong. *What if he comes upstairs with a chopper and attacks Seth. What if someone is guarding Darragh, and he or she has a gun. What if Mary is there with Lia, and she calls the police. What if... Why didn't we check to see if Mary was in? Oh my God!*

DARRAGH

Jules entered the butcher's shop backwards. She pushed her back against the door to open it and began to pull the pram through the doorway. The door was heavy, and then without warning, it was pulled sharply inwards by a customer, sending her tumbling backwards onto the floor. As she fell, she let go of the pram and watched as it started to free wheel out of the shop towards the road. "MY BABY!" she screamed. Jules scrambled onto her feet. Her legs felt like they were lead weights as she pursued the runaway pram. She saw people watching the pram with open mouths and was dumbfounded that nobody was taking action. Jules leapt forward and just managed to catch the handle as the front wheels of the pram hit the curb. Her heart was thumping hard in her chest, and she burst into tears as a scenario played out in her mind of what might have happened had she not stopped the pram. She could sense that everyone was looking at her, and she was sure they were disgusted by what they saw.

Jules turned the pram around and saw that Jon was standing in the doorway with a customer. Jon was scowling and appeared to be annoyed with her. Anger welled up inside her. *He has no right to be annoyed with me. I could have lost a second baby to him*. She had no doubt in her mind now that he had taken Darragh. She pulled off her mask and ripped her hood down to let out her golden curls. Jules pushed the pram over to him. "WHAT HAVE YOU DONE WITH DARRAGH, YOU BASTARD?" she yelled, holding firmly onto the handle of the pram.

Jon was taken aback, and his eyes widened as he realised who she was. "The woman is deranged," he said to the customer standing next to him. "Did you hit your head, darling?"

"You know I didn't hit my fucking head. What have you done with him?"

"Do you want to sit down and rest? You are in shock. I will make you a cup of tea."

He was trying to act all concerned and thoughtful in front of the customer. *If he goes upstairs to make me tea, then he will find Seth.*

"I am fine, thank you. I just want to buy a pound of mince." She had no clue why she had said that, but it was all she could think of.

"Well, I am sorry we are clean out of mince. You will have to try the supermarket."

"Well, sausages then."

"Not one sausage to be had. They are all promised to my loyal customers."

Out of the corner of her eye, she noticed Seth climbing the stairs at the back of the shop. She had imagined that there would be another way to get to the flat upstairs. She needed to give him a chance to search, but she had outstayed her welcome, and now Jon was going back into the shop, shaking his head in disgust. She was beside herself with anger and looked around for a large object she could hurl at the window. The wooden A-frame sign with today's specials was all that she could see to throw. She put the brake on the pram, picked up the sign, and hurled it at the window with every ounce of energy she had. The corner of the sign smacked into it, and the plate glass fractured into a thousand pieces. She felt triumphant and so much better to vent all her anger against the one man that held the key to her finding Darragh. She stared fiercely into Jon Hearn's shifty eyes and knew that the police would not be involved. Too many questions would be asked. Jon's eyes narrowed, and she could sense his evil soul screaming at her. She had never felt so hated.

DARRAGH

A crowd was starting to form around the shop, and not wanting to see Jon Hearn ever again, she unhooked the brake and wheeled Juliet away from the butcher's shop. Jules heard people tutting, and she was sure she heard someone say she was a nutcase and shouldn't have children, but she didn't care. She prayed that Seth would be able to slip out of the shop as Jon cleaned up the glass. She had caused a distraction and given Seth the ten minutes he needed. When she returned to the car, a small voice whispered in her ear that she had perhaps sealed her little Darragh's fate. Tears streamed down her face, and she sobbed hard, hoping Seth would return with their little Darragh in his arms.

From the flat above the butcher's shop, Seth had heard the noise of the window smashing, and he had frozen, frightened that a car had gone into the shop downstairs. He had run around each room in the flat looking for Darragh and, not finding him, had fled downstairs, hoping and praying that his precious Jules and Juliet hadn't been mowed down. Seeing that they were not on the scene and the broken window had not been caused by a car crash, Seth had fled out into the courtyard and trying not to run, he emerged into an alley and then ran out onto the high street and looked about him to see if he could see Jules. He wondered how the window had got broken. He could see Jon and another butcher sweeping up the glass, and he wondered if he should go back upstairs and have another look. One of the bedroom's bothered him. It had a cot in the middle, and the room smelt of pee. If one of Jon's children was being kept in that room, social services needed to be called. He was sure the flat was empty but hadn't checked all the cupboards or the roof space. He hoped Darragh hadn't been shut in a cupboard or left in a cold roof space to die. He had to believe that Darragh was still alive.

Seth looked over his shoulder at the dark alley behind him and noticed it had become misty. It was a dark alley with very little sunlight. He watched the mist rise and then take on a form. He shuddered, knowing that something odd was happening. After a few moments, he was sure he could see Gemma's face in the thick mist, and her eyes were wide with fear. "Noo… Don't do this to me." Her hands came out of the mist and formed a shape. She repeated the action with her hands, and Seth realised that she was showing him the letter 'L'. She then pointed a little to the right of him and then her form sank into the mist again. Disturbed by what he saw, Seth looked out onto the street and saw the dustbin men pulling the bins towards the edge of the road, ready for collection. He looked back towards Gemma, but she had gone, and the mist too.

"The letter 'L'? What is she telling me? I wish she had pointed at the flat and told me to return. I must be going mad. Who do I know that begins with L? I AM going mad. I best go back to Jules, or she will be getting worried about me."

As he walked along, he could heard a phone ringing. He recognised the ringtone. Lucy's phone had their song Waterfall Way as a ringtone, and he thought about ringing her to update her on their progress when they got back home. He could still hear his song playing, and he thought the phone might belong to one of the refuse collectors.

The street was busy, and he managed to slip away from the side alley without his twin seeing him. As he walked along, he wondered why Gemma's spirit had looked so terrified. He stopped and decided to give Lucy a call there and then. Just to check that she was ok. Her name did begin with 'L' after all. The first time he rang, she appeared to be engaged. The second time he called, her phone rang for a while and then went to her voicemail. He left a message asking her to call him. "Are you happy, Gemma? I have done my best to help you," he called out, causing passers-by to stare.

***

Lucy's phone was ringing, and there was nothing she could do about it. She tried to call out, but the tape across her mouth muffled her cries. The bin she was in was being wheeled towards a dustbin lorry and she banged hard on the edge of the bin with her elbow, hoping and praying that she would be found.

Her phone had rung many times through the night, and she was thankful to whoever it was calling her because this was her only chance of being heard.

For a brief moment, the lid of the bin was opened and then quickly closed again as the contents were scrutinised. She had done everything she could to get nearer to the top of the bin, but her wrists had been tied to her ankles to stop her from standing up. She had spent the night upside down and could not right herself. The blood kept rushing to her head and was making her dizzy. She suspected that she might be running out of oxygen too.

Lucy had begged and pleaded with Bernard to let her go, but he would have none of it. The realisation that this was going to be her demise shocked her. She was too young to die. She had called on her spirit guides to help her. They whispered words of encouragement but could do nothing more for her. She kept hearing that Day was there for her too. Gemma wanted to share her untimely death with her. Lucy saw how Tom Stone had beaten her unconscious and left her to die. She saw him dump her in a water trough and cut her wrists. She had found herself trying to comfort Gemma and promised her that he would get his comeuppance.

Lucy gasped silently as she felt her bin being attached to the dustbin lorry. With all her might, she banged the sides of the bin with her elbow and prayed that her phone would ring. Her prayers were answered, her phone started to play Waterfall Way, and then her call went straight to the answerphone. She felt the bin being lifted into the air. She was crying and screamed out as the bin was lifted high. Lucy felt the bin turnover, and the lid flew open, spilling her and its contents into the dustbin lorry. She smiled as she saw daylight, and then her heart froze as she heard the sound of the crusher spring into action. The metal claws embraced her, bones cracked, and she screamed out in pain, her agony ignored by mortals. Lucy knew she was dying.

From above, Lucy looked down at her battered body and realised it was nothing more than an empty shell. Her old eyes stared blankly towards Heaven. A warmth was running through her as she watched. The lifeless body below fascinated her. She couldn't draw her eyes away from it - she had been beautiful, even in death. She felt no pain now and couldn't help but smile, realising that her ordeal was over. Being dead wasn't so bad. She became aware that she was not alone, and as she turned away, a bright light called to her, willing her to come towards it and meet her loved ones. Her spirit guides were waiting for her. They held out their arms and welcomed her back home.

Chapter Thirty-one

"Come with me," Seth said, taking Jules by the hand. "I've got something to show you."

"But Juliet is sleeping. I don't like to leave her on her own."

"We are just going to the barn next door. Juliet will be fine. Sinead will be here in a minute. She just rang me to say she was walking over," Seth said, leading Jules to the door.

"Can't it wait? Have you polished the tractor? Is that what you want to show me?"

"No, silly. I have a surprise for you. Do you know what day it is?"

Jules nodded. "The nineteenth, Darragh's birthday," she said sadly.

Seth stopped and hugged her. "I know you hoped to get him back today, but we must be patient. I have left lots of messages on Lucy's phone. I bet they have Jon down at the station and have the thumb screws on him. We are going to get good news soon. I just know it. As well as being our wee lad's birthday, it is also our second anniversary. I didn't know what to get you. I had to think real hard, and I was pretty stoked when I came up with the perfect gift."

"Oh, Seth, you don't have to buy me gifts. I feel really bad. I just haven't had the time or energy to get you a gift."

"Actually, I didn't buy you anything. I did something far better. Come and see," he said, leading her out of the house and towards the barn. I just hope no one is late."

"You haven't organised a party, have you? I don't think I am up to being merry."

Seth laughed. "No, not a party, something far better. "I am going to blindfold you."

She felt his warm hands cover her eyes and started to feel nervous. *I hope you haven't bought me a car.* Then she remembered that he hadn't bought anything. Her heart was beating hard, and anxiety was building.

"Now step carefully. I didn't realise how uneven the floor was here. I am going to hold your hand in a moment because I don't want you fainting or anything like that."

Her senses were on fire. She could hear strange noises. She could smell perfume, a sweet sickly smell of roses and then she heard someone sneeze. "Seth! Is this a party?"

"No, not a party, I promise. Just a few close friends. Look!" he instructed, taking his hands away from her eyes.

It took Jules a while to focus, and then she smiled as she realised that the group of people in front of her was Sonar Cell. Shawn was looking directly at her, and he smiled at her. He had his electric violin under his chin, and she heard him count the other band members in. They started to sing, and she recognised the words immediately. It was one of the songs Seth had written about her. The melody was different to the one she had written for it. She liked the new music better. It had an uplifting beat and a catchy tune. Her eyes flickered from one band member to another. They were all grinning back at her and enjoying playing. She squeezed Seth's hand. "I love it," she whispered. "I love the new version of Summer Heat so much."

DARRAGH

I've been watching you for a while
I know what makes you smile
Love your pretty face
Makes my heart race
I think you've seen me too
Gonna come and talk to you

Do I make your heart beat?
When you see me in the street
Feel that summer heat
You're a cool breeze
Not going to tease
Blowing in your ear
Heart beat,
Heart beat
Summer treat

Gonna make your Daddy groan
When I take you home
Feel your heart beat
Feel my heart beat
You're a warm breeze
Warm breeze
Puts me on my knees
Do I make your heart beat?

When you see me in the street
Feel that summer heat
You're a cool breeze
Not going to tease
Blowing in your ear

233

Heart beat,
Heart beat
Summer treat

I just wanna see you
Not going to lie to you
Need your hot lovin
I'm cooking like an oven
Feel your heartbeat
Heart beat
Summer treat

You're a cool breeze
Not going to tease
You're a cool breeze
Not going to tease
Blowing in your ear
Heat beat
Heart beat
Summer treat

"My good-for-nothing husband can play a fine tune when it suits him," Jane whispered to her.

The song ended, and Seth, Jane and Jules clapped jubilantly. Jules couldn't help grinning and turned towards Jane. "I am so happy that you are here. They've done an amazing job." She then realised that Jane's baby was strapped to her in a scarf. All she could see of Jack was his tiny hand.

"Seth, we shouldn't leave Juliet any longer."

"Don't worry. Sinead has messaged me to say she is with her." He smiled broadly at Shawn. "You've done a grand job with our song," Seth announced. "Thank you so much for coming over and turning our song into something awesome. Come into the house and have a little lunch with us."

"Oh my God, Seth! The house is a mess, and the fridge is bare."

"I think you will find we have plenty. Earlier, Sinead did a little online shopping."

Shawn came over and hugged Seth. "How are you doing, mate? That was so good. That just has to be another number-one hit. It will be if S&J front the band. I recon Summer Breeze will shoot up the charts. The guys are stoked and eager to record."

"Do you think so?" Seth replied, smiling broadly.

"I know so!"

"We can stay," Jane said. "But the guys have to get back to work. Shawn and I did a test this morning and haven't got Covid.

"We don't worry about Covid here. I am sure it is dying out," Jules said, looking at Seth for reassurance.

Jane sighed. "I wish that was true. There are plenty of Omicron Delta cases coming into the hospitals. The hospitals are still full of critical cases. People aren't seeing on TV how bad things are."

Seth and Shawn walked ahead, and Jules and Jane followed behind. Jules was lost in thought. Seeing Shawn had set her nerves on edge. She was glad that he hadn't hugged her. *I hope Jane hasn't been through his phone again and seen that he sent me that horrid picture. What if she thinks I am interested in him? I have to pretend I know nothing about it if she asks. Please don't ask me anything. Nothing happened. Nothing...*

"How are you doing?" Jane asked.

Jules tried to stay calm and tried her best not to sound like she was about to cry. "Well, I am not doing too bad. I have to stay strong for Darragh's sake. It is his second birthday..." she replied, choking up a little. "I don't think I am going to be much company. It is just so hard being without him." *Come on, Jules, pull yourself together. You have to, for Darragh's sake.* "How about you? How are things going with Shawn?" she stuttered.

"Things are a bit strained at the moment. We are working through our problems. Everyone goes through a rough patch now and again. Mammy thinks I should leave him, but then she didn't want us to marry in the first place. What do you think I should do?"

"Oh my! I guess if you love him, then you have to put what happened behind you. It was probably lockdown madness that caused him to stray. He does love you, you know."

Jane laughed. "So you think that he is just a lovable rogue, then? Luckily for him, I do love him. Did you like the song? He worked night and day on it for you."

For me! Is he obsessed with me? "Like it? I loved it. I am feeling really bad that I haven't done anything for our second anniversary. I should have been more appreciative. I am just feeling a little numb inside at the moment."

"Seth understands. You've had a lot on your mind recently. Seth said you both have to appear at that freak's trial soon. At least you know Stone will get life for killing that poor girl. It is a crying shame. Gemma was such a lovely girl."

"Who knows what sentence that bastard will get. It seems you have to be filmed shooting people down before getting a life sentence. Do you know he only got eight years for what he did to Darragh and me?"

"That's no good. He should have got life for that too. Jules, you are so angry. You should talk to someone. I... I had to admit defeat in coping with Shawn's shenanigans, and I now see this really nice lady in Cork. I think it would help you to talk to her. She is trained to deal with all manner of traumas."

"What are you seeing her for? Oh, my, that sounds rude."

"No, it's not rude. Most of us have had mental health issues, and some deal with them better than others. I am seeing her for anxiety and fear of abandonment, and we are working through some childhood issues."

Jules nodded as tears wound their way down her cheeks. *Why am I crying? Jane must think I am deranged.* "It might help," she said quietly. "I keep thinking the crying feeling inside will go away. I am not sure if she will be able to help me. I am so confused at the moment."

"I'm so sorry. I didn't mean to make you cry. It is good to cry and let all the bad stuff out. I will give you her number. We are all worried about you. You have lost so much weight."

"I am finding it difficult to eat." *Christ that stung! I thought I was getting fat with all the biscuits I've been eating.*

As they walked up the path to the barn, Jules could see Seth and Shawn talking to someone. She recognised him immediately and scowled. Detective Rufus Parvel was there, and his long overcoat was flapping in the wind. The breeze had come from nowhere. It was an ill wind, and her heart sank. "Oh no! My poor Darragh," she cried, running up the path. "Have you found him? Have you found Darragh? Please tell me he is ok."

Seth shook his head. "He is not here about Darragh. He is here about Lucy," Seth said, looking puzzled.

"Has something happened to her?" he asked Rufus. *Something has happened to her. I just know it. I just wish he would take off that stupid mask so I could see his face and know the truth.*

Rufus sighed and looked up to Heaven, searching for the right words. "No, she hasn't found your son. Can we go inside so I can put on the lunchtime news? That will give you all the information you need."

"I'd rather you just tell me." Flashbacks of being at the butcher's the day before, Gemma's ghost and trying to ring Lucy raced through his mind. *I should have gotten in contact with Lucy. I am such an eejit. Something bad has happened to her.*

"No, I'd rather you watch the news; it will tell you all you need to know."

As they walked in, Sinead appeared from the bedroom holding Juliet. She walked over to them smiling and then noticed Rufus and frowned. "What's he doing here?" she asked.

"Oh, Sinead! Something bad has happened. He wants us to watch the news. I hope another child's body hasn't been found."

Seth looked around for the TV remote, but it was nowhere to be seen. They normally left it on the coffee table. He looked at the clock on the wall. It was nearly one, and the lunchtime news was about to start. "Jules, have you seen the remote?"

"I last saw it on the coffee table." Then she spotted it on the floor next to the sofa. "I see it," she declared, walking over to retrieve it. She turned on the TV, and everyone sat down to watch the news. Only Rufus remained standing. He looked uneasy and folded his arms while waiting for the newsreader to appear. The presenter mentioned that vaccinations were going well and that the spread of Covid was beginning to decline. She quickly moved on to the main news story, and a picture of DI Lucy O'Leary appeared on the screen. Seth shot a worried glance towards Jules, but her eyes were fixed on the screen.

"Detective Inspector Lucy O'Leary's body was found today at Cork's waste plant. The police department will be issuing a statement later on today and will be appealing to anyone that may have seen or heard from Lucy in the past 24 hours. DI O'Leary had been bound and gagged, and it is believed that she had been left overnight in an industrial bin somewhere in Cork yesterday. Lucy died from fatal wounds inflicted by a rubbish lorry crusher.

"We visited her parents this morning, and they had this to say. 'Words cannot convey how we are feeling. We have lost our beautiful daughter. She was the kindest and most thoughtful person and we cannot imagine who would want to hurt her. She will be truly missed.'"

A picture of Lucy's smiling face appeared on the screen. Horrified by what she had seen, Jules turned off the TV and looked at everyone. The room was silent. Seth was staring hard at Rufus.

"So why are you here," he asked angrily. "You could have just called us."

"Well... I could have. I am just trying to collate any information I can. We need to build a timeline. Why did you call her yesterday? Her phone was found in her pocket, and you left a message. You seemed concerned about her."

Seth frowned. "I ring her regularly for an update about Darragh." He remembered hearing her ringtone the day before, and then it hit him. "For the Love of God! I was standing right by her as the bin was being hooked onto the dustbin lorry." He gasped and then shook his head. "I know where she was. I heard her phone ring. She was in Jon Hearn's bin. Why didn't I stop and think and to find her? That bastard Jon Hearn has left her in one of his bins to die. Shit! I can't believe it. I was warned or shown what to do, and I did nothing."

"I see," Rufus said. "Who is Jon Hearn?"

"Jon Hearn is my brother. He runs the butcher shop in Marlboro Street."

"And you were there yesterday."

"Yes, I told you. I was there as the rubbish was being collected. I heard her phone ring. Her ringtone is our song Waterfall Way. I saw Gem... I had the feeling that something was wrong with Lucy, so I rang her to see if she was ok. I should have tried harder. I can't believe she got crushed to death. This is too much to bear."

Jules watched on in horror and amazement as she listened to Rufus interrogating Seth. She could see Rufus sucking in this news. *He is going to arrest Seth. I just know it. He thinks he put her in the bin. I can't have this.*

"I was with Seth. Lots of people have the ringtone Waterfall Way. It could have been anyone's phone that was ringing. You need to go straight to Jon Hearn and arrest him. He murdered Lucy, and he abducted Darragh last year. He is a sick bastard, and he needs locking up."

"And you can prove this?"

"No, of course, I can't prove it, but if you do your job properly and get your sorry arses over there, then I am sure you can get enough evidence from his flat to get your proof. We were just shopping in Cork and happened to be there, so if you think you are going to harass us with any more questions, you will be disappointed."

"I will need a statement from you both."

Jules stood up and put her fists on her hips. She could feel the colour rising in her cheeks, shaking with rage. "There is nothing more to say. Who is in charge of this case? It is not you, that is for sure! Lucy was filing a complaint procedure against you. No, you don't have to tell me! I will ring the police station and find out. I would be grateful if you left. You are not welcome here."

Rufus shook his head. "You can't speak to me like that."

"So sue me. I eat arseholes like you in court for breakfast," Jules said angrily as she walked across the room to open the door. She flung the door wide open and glared at him with angry red cheeks. Rufus stormed out, and Jules slammed the door shut behind him. She turned to see everyone staring at her with their mouths open. "So, does anyone want a cup of tea?" she asked.

Chapter Thirty-two

With a heavy heart, Seth knocked on the door and waited for Granny to answer. The walk down the drive had been difficult as he really did not want to see what was left of the Manor House. The woods shielded his view of the charred ruins, and he was thankful for that. It had been a week since Lucy's passing, and he had not seen or heard from Granny. This puzzled him and annoyed him too. She used to be the life and soul of the party. Since joining the travellers, she had become distant from him and kept herself to herself. *Perhaps this is what happens when you become a traveller, you ostracise yourself from other humans. I don't think it is good for her. I hope she will see me.*

He and Jules were still in shock about what had happened to Lucy, and they had rung the police station every day to ensure they were investigating Jon Hearn. Each time they were assured that everything was in hand. They were not convinced.

Seth knocked again, and not hearing any movement, he walked around the caravan and peered into each window to see if he could see anyone. *I wonder where she is?*

"If you are looking for me, then I am over here," he heard her call. Her voice was coming from Jess's caravan.

He turned around and saw Granny standing in the doorway with Marley on her hip. Feeling relieved that she was not lying dead in the caravan, he walked over to her. "You had me a bit worried. I thought you might be ill."

She smiled and hugged Marley tighter. "No, you eejit! I am as right as rain. Aren't we, my wee love," she said to Marley, pushing his hair out of his eyes. "This boy needs a haircut, and you do too. The Hearn boys all have mops for hair."

Seth laughed. "I've been meaning to get mine cut. Are you minding Marley for Jess, then?"

"Yes, she has gone to see his Da. She needs money for clothes for him."

"I wouldn't have let her go there. You do know that Jon killed Lucy, don't you?" Seth said, smiling at Marley. Marley smiled back and put his arms out to him, hoping he would take him. Seth took him. It was good to hold his nephew. "Do you think I am your Da?" he asked him. Marley ignored him and started to play with the buttons on his shirt.

"Lucy sends her regards and tells you not to worry."

Seth frowned. "Have you spoken to her in Heaven then? Does she know what happened to her?"

Granny smiled. "A lot of spirits talk to me. Lucy saw herself being thrown into the bin, but she put up a fight. She keeps showing me a St. Christopher. I don't know why."

"I wonder if Jon wears one? That bastard needs stringing up. Being crushed to death is a terrible way to die. Does she know who killed her?"

"She didn't say. I think victims see their end played out like a movie. They don't feel the pain, and they don't see the face of their murderer. That is the way it is."

"Oh, really? That's a shame."

"Did you come down to ask me something," Granny asked.

"I was just checking to see if you were ok. You should come up to the barn. We miss you being there. I do, anyway."

"Your wife doesn't, though. I know when I am not welcome."

"You are welcome, I promise. Jules is under so much pressure at the moment. It was Darragh's second birthday on Monday, and now Lucy is gone, and she was our only real hope of finding him. Jules is losing weight. I can't say that to her. She would go mad if I did. Stone's murder trial is on Monday, and we both need to appear in court that week. I am worried about her."

"It's not easy for you both, but it is a pink moon on Monday night, and you must be ready to take the bull by the horns."

Seth sighed. "You really love your pink moons. I hope the wait will be worth it."

"I have great hopes for that day. Seth, will you come in for a moment. I have been trying to get the ring to work so I can cook Marley some lunch, but it has a computer to start it, and it is beyond me."

"Do you think Jess will mind me coming in?"

"She loves you, really. She goes about things arse-faced," she said, laughing.

Seth stepped into the caravan and was impressed by what he saw. Everything was neat and tidy, and Jess had every electronic gadget imaginable. "It's like a little palace in here. She has Bluetooth speakers in every corner."

"Mmm, is that what they are? I thought they were cameras."

The ring Granny had trouble with was an induction hob with digital buttons. Granny sat down, and Seth put Marley on the seat next to her. Marley smacked the table, expecting his food to appear.

Seth remembered Darragh doing the same thing sitting in his highchair. "He does look so much like Darragh. Granny, do you want me to cook?" He saw a packet of noodles on the side. "It won't take me a minute."

"That would be grand, and then I can play with my grandson," she said, smiling.

Seth started to cook and looked out of the window at the woods. He found himself willing Gemma to be there and to give him a clue to where Darragh might be. He was looking at the place in the woods where he had seen her before. He accepted it now that she wanted to help him.

"You are trying too hard. She doesn't know where Darragh is," Granny said, surprising him.

"Can a man not summon up spirits in private," he replied, laughing.

"Nothing goes unnoticed here. Don't give up hope. All the channels will be clear on Monday night, and we will know all."

"I hope you are right. I was sure I would find Darragh when I looked around Jon's flat, but all I found was an old cot in a dark room. My fear is that if he can dispose of a police officer so casually on his premises, then he is capable of darker deeds."

"He is not going to hurt him. He needs him for something important. The spirits whisper to me that he loves his daughter more."

"Is that so? I don't know if I am comforted by that remark. He sounds just like Dad. He didn't care much for his sons, but he doted and fuc... Sorry, Marley, Dad slept with his daughters. Is he still around?"

"He is, but he won't come near us. I have set a hex around the site and your barn too. Just don't go into the woods alone."

"Couldn't you have hexed the woods, too," he said, laughing

"No, you eejit, I'm not a fecking witch!"

Feeling uplifted and reassured that they would find Darragh, Seth walked home, and as it was such a lovely day, he decided to go for a horse ride. He would try and persuade Jules to go with him. *Just being out in the fields will make her feel so much stronger. My beautiful wife is suffering. I feel her pain. I will ask Sinead to babysit. She needs something to keep her mind off the loss of the Manor House. I wish I had renewed the house insurance. We are not having much luck at the moment. Perhaps Granny is right, and things will improve once we have the pink moon.*

***

It didn't take much to get Jules to agree to go for a ride on Connor, and when he looked back at her on her old horse that was way too big for her, he couldn't help but smile. Her pale face was lit up, and her golden curls shone in the warm spring sunlight. His heart was overflowing with happiness at that moment, and he had never loved her more.

Moss plodded along through the new spring grass and did not seem to be his usual energetic self. "Are you getting to be an old boy and just like to hang around with your mates in the lower field? Do I not take you out enough?" he asked, patting his neck. A cloud of black hair filled the air, and Moss's ears turned this way and that as he took in his surroundings and watched clumps of black hair fly by his nose. "Are you up for a little run?" he asked Moss. "I don't think we will get past trotting. I am sorry, my poor boy. I will take you out more, I promise."

"I think Connor is enjoying himself. I can feel him smiling," Jules called.

"I don't think I've ever seen a horse smile before."

"I am glad that he is happy."

They turned off through the fields that used to be his farm. Seth looked at the fields he had ploughed and then left to return to meadowland. The desire to farm the land had left him. It wasn't that he didn't want to be a farmer. It was just that he was putting his business on hold until Darragh returned. He came out of his musing and noticed the big old oak tree in the middle of the field. This was Darragh's tree. Darragh's name meant that he was strong like an oak tree, and it only felt right to go and see the tree and ask it for help. "Do you mind if we stop at the tree?" he asked Jules, turning towards it.

"No, I don't mind, that's fine. I think Connor needs a rest. He keeps coughing."

"Both our horses have gotten fat and lazy. We will have to come out regularly to get them fit again."

"Have I brought you to my tree before?"

"I don't think so. I didn't know you had a special tree," she replied, laughing.

"Don't mock me. This tree and I go back a long way."

Jules jumped down from Connor's back, pulled his reins over his head, and let him crop the new grass around the tree. "Don't you eat any old acorns, though. I don't want you to get colic."

Moss just wandered over to a sunny patch of grass and closed his eyes.

"I think my boy needs a sleep. He is going nowhere, so I will leave him be for a while.

"This tree must be at least a thousand years old. Now, I don't want you to laugh at me, but this tree needs a hug. Will you come and hug it with me?" Seth asked, smiling broadly at her.

"You know I would do anything for you." Jules wrapped her arms around the tree.

Seth did the same and put his ear to the gnarly bark. "Can you hear anything?" he whispered to her.

"No, not a thing," she replied, blowing a fly from her nose.

"The tree is telling you how much I love you."

"Is that so? It is a wise old tree and…." A cold icy breeze whipped over her face, and she could feel the hairs stand up on her neck as she realised that someone was standing close to her. A malignant presence.

"Seth, hold my hand. Your Dad is here, and I can feel him. Don't let go of the tree. He is looking for me," she whispered urgently. She felt Seth's fingers entwine with hers, and she gripped his hand tightly. "Don't let go and say nothing. He doesn't hear my voice, but he will hear yours. I am safe with you holding me. GO AWAY, YOU BASTARD!" she yelled, but she knew her words were useless. She dared not breathe too heavily as she felt Jethro so close now that the hairs on the back of her neck were standing on end. *I can smell him. Cheap aftershave and cigar smoke.* "Please don't hurt me. Please don't hurt me," she whispered, fearing that at any moment, he would grab her by the throat and drag her down to Hell and feed on her soul.

Seth's grip tightened, and then at lightning speed, he pulled her to him and sandwiched her between himself and the tree. She sighed with relief feeling Seth's body enveloping her, saving her from his Dad's evil spirit. She was safe there and knew no harm would come to her. Seth said nothing but she could feel his heart beating hard and smell his earthy fresh lemon scent she loved so much. She was petrified, but her body was crying out for Seth's. Still barely able to breathe, she waited for what seemed like an eternity for Jethro to continue on his way and leave them be. She felt Seth's hot breath on her ear; all she could think about was him making passionate love to her.

"I love you," Seth whispered. "He has gone."

She smiled and then knew this was true as she slid back into reality, hearing the sound of birds singing on the branches above. A robin sang the sweetest tune, and it was then she knew it was safe to come out, and she brought her lips up to his, kissing him, thanking him for saving her. She needed him there and then. Her hands found their way to the button on his trousers.

Seth pulled away a little and looked down at her. "I will never let him hurt you. You know that, don't you?"

"Yes, I do. Seth, I need you now. My body is craving yours. I know you think I am crazy, but I need you to make love to me here and now. Your tree wants this. Press me into the bark and love me. Please, Seth."

Seth picked her up, and Jules wrapped her legs around him. "I love everything about you. I would be lost without you," he whispered, kissing her, his body shaking with anticipation.

The oak tree's gnarled bark stung her back but it only made her desire for Seth stronger. She could feel his heart beating against her. She had dreamed about this moment, and it was almost as if they were playing out a scene from one of her dreams. "I love you too... I think you should kiss me again because...."

"Don't talk, my lovely wife," he whispered, unbuttoning her shirt to reveal her full breasts. "I love you to the pink moon and back."

The oak tree hummed silently to itself, and her spirit seeped through the bark into the star-crossed lovers planting her seed into their bodies. She waited patiently for the next of the Hearns to be spawned.

Whispering to the trees around her, the great oak tree breathed deeply, pleased that her work was done. Jules and Seth lay between her roots, too exhausted to thank her.

DARRAGH

Chapter Thirty-three

TAP, TAP, TAP. Darragh opened his eyes and listened to the strange sound. Along with the tapping noise, and long before he had been fully awake, he had heard a long squeaky scratching noise that irritated him. TAP, TAP, TAP. He was curious to know where the tapping was coming from. He pushed back the duvet cover and slid off the bed. The room he was in was so much brighter than his old room, and although the curtains were drawn, they let in lots of light. He liked his new room and the kind man that had given it to him.

TAP, TAP, TAP... SCREECH... CAW, CAW. Darragh spun around, trying to find where these annoying sounds came from. His eyes fixed on the curtains, and he realised that the noises were coming from there. Feeling a little afraid, he walked over to the curtains, grasped hold of the fabric and then pulled the fabric back. He gasped. A big black crow was sitting on the window ledge outside staring at him. Its shiny black eyes were focused on his eyes. The crow's head turned from side to side to see him better. It tapped more urgently, now making the window vibrate.

"NO!" Darragh screamed. "NO!" He banged on the window ledge with his hand to scare the bird, afraid it would break the glass and come and peck him. "FUCK OFF!" he screamed, banging the window ledge again. The crow's wings spread wide, and the scary bird flew up, cawing as it went. Darragh watched it

251

fly towards the woods ahead, and he waited until it had gone, fearful that it would come back and get him.

After a few moments, satisfied that the crow had gone, he looked back at his warm bed and wondered if he should get back in and wait for his cheese sandwich and apple juice to appear. The door looked easy to open, and it was tempting to go and explore. He didn't want to make Mary cross by coming out of his room, but he wanted to see Stephan again. He hoped he would give him chips like the old man in the street had done.

Feeling anxious that he was disobeying Mary, Darragh opened the bedroom door and made his way downstairs. Stephan had given him a shirt to wear in bed, which was much more comfortable than the clothes Mary had given him. He desperately wanted to pee and needed to find a bucket. Before he had gone to bed, Stephan had taken him by the hand and led him to a small room. He had shown him a strange-looking seat with a furry lid. Stephan had opened the lid, and Darragh had looked at the water at the bottom of it. Stephan had said to pee, pointing to the water, but Darragh had shaken his head and ran out of the strange room back to his new bedroom that smelt of fresh air and flowers. He had slept really well in the bed, despite there being no bars.

As he climbed each stair, Darragh could hear music from the kitchen and was eager to see who was singing. He smiled as he remembered his parents playing and singing in his old house. The music was getting louder, so he started to hurry, his heart full of joy hearing tunes he recognised. He stumbled, slid down the last step, and laughed as he fell onto the soft carpet. Picking himself up, he ran towards the kitchen.

The tiles on the kitchen floor felt cool on his feet, and he looked around to see who was playing. Sunlight streamed in from a window above the sink and danced on the floor. He stepped on the warm patches of light and noticed Stephan eating some toast at the table. Darragh's stomach rumbled, and he pointed at the toast, hoping his new friend would share it with him.

"Are you hungry, little man? Do you want some toast and jam? Hop onto the chair, and I will get you a plate," Stephan said, pointing to the chair opposite.

Not understanding him, Darragh came up to Stephan and pointed to his toast. "Toast! Toast."

Stephan smiled, "Here, let me help you." He got up, lifted Darragh, and sat him on the chair. "You are so little, and you need a cushion." He disappeared into the front room.

Sitting on the hard seat made Darragh realise how desperate he was to pee. He saw a red bucket with a mop standing next to it in the corner, slipped off the chair, and ran over to relieve himself. He saw Stephan return with a cushion and then heard him gasp. Darragh felt scared that he would be angry with him and made sure that he didn't get any pee on the floor. Mary would be cross if he did. He then heard Stephan laugh.

"You are an odd little thing. What is wrong with the toilet?"

"Pee!" Darragh said triumphantly, pointing in the bucket proudly.

"Mmm... I don't think you have used a toilet before, have you? Did Mary keep you in nappies, then? Come and get some toast and let me wash your hands."

"With his hands washed, Darragh sat on the cushion on the chair and watched Stephan butter and spoon jam onto a piece of toast. He surveyed his new friend and looked closely at his hair and face. Stephan reminded him of his Mam. He had the same hair colour as her but was short and curly. He had big blue eyes like she did. His teeth were not the same. When he laughed, he showed his teeth, and he thought they were a bit like Mary's. The toast was cut up and given to him in pieces. Darragh inspected a piece and hoped it would taste good. He hadn't had the red sticky stuff before. He licked it and smiled. His tongue liked it a lot, and he couldn't help licking it again.

"You're a hungry wee dote. I have no idea what my sister has been feeding you, but you look like you haven't had anything nice in a while."

Darragh was hungry and ate the toast quickly. He pointed again at Stephan's plate and smiled at him. "Toast," he said, grinning.

Stephan looked up and shook his head. "You can have another. Do you need a drink too? I don't have beakers. You like apple juice, don't you, but I only have coffee here. I will have to give you water for now in this cup," he said, getting up. "Here, have my toast, and I will get myself some cornflakes. Let me get you a drink." He passed his toast to Darragh. "It's just you and me now. Lia and Mary have gone to a hospital appointment this morning. She's taken my car. It will probably come back with a dent in it. She always bumps into something. When I get everything I need for Lia's recovery, I will have to do a little operation on you. Actually, it is quite a big operation, and I know you don't know what I am talking about. Well, the thing is, Lia needs a kidney desperately, she is not getting on with dialysis, and the toxins build up too quickly in her body. I am going to turn the kitchen into an operating theatre, and all I will do is borrow one of yours. Well, not borrow. Give your cousin one of your kidneys, stitch you up, give you painkillers, and in a couple of days, you will be fine and can go home. I promise that I will take good care of you. I was a top surgeon once. Not so long ago, I had a bit of a breakdown. It happens. You do understand, don't you?"

DARRAGH

Darragh watched Stephan's mouth move and listened but had no idea what he was talking about. It was good to hear a human voice. Nobody had really talked to him like this in a long time.

As Darragh licked off the jam from the large piece of toast, Stephan filled a cup of water up for him and then sat down to read the paper. He flicked through the pages and then exhaled sharply. Darragh looked up and wondered what was wrong. Stephan picked up the newspaper to look more closely.

"No," he said, sitting down again. "My poor Lucy! No! I don't believe it. No wonder she hasn't been taking my messages. My poor sweet Lucy is dead!"

Darragh frowned, realising that something bad had happened, and jumped from his seat. He needed a hug, and he also wanted to see what was making Stephan so upset. He hugged his knee and looked up at him to try and work out why his new friend was crying. Darragh started to cry, too, hoping that he hadn't upset him. He climbed up onto his lap and sat on his knee and clung to him. Stephan sobbed uncontrollably, and so did Darragh. He could feel his pain.

Through his tears, Darragh could see Lucy's face on the newspaper and stopped crying. There was something comforting about seeing her brown eyes staring back at him. She was family. It was almost as if she was standing beside him, telling him not to fret. He heard in his head that she would come and find him. Help him find his parents again. He stared hard at the photo, and for a moment, he was certain he saw her smile widen and her eyes sparkle a little. Darragh got down off of Stephan's knee and stood by him, not sure if he should go back to his room.

Stephan stopped crying and blew his nose on some kitchen towel. Darragh could hear a man speaking, and he looked around the kitchen to see where the man was. The voice was coming out of a box on a shelf above the kitchen table. Music began to play, and he smiled as he recognised the song coming from the box. Waterfall Way was playing, and he could hear his parents' voices loud and clear. All Stephan had to do was open the box, and his parents would be inside. "DA!" he yelled, feeling intense excitement. "DA!"

Stephane smiled. "Yes, you are right. I need to do what is right. I will take you home."

"You will not!" Mary barked. Lia was standing next to her, and Darragh was surprised she could walk.

"We need to do the operation this afternoon. Lia has refused dialysis, and I will not hold the child down to have it, so we have come back home. Have you been crying?"

Anxiously, Darragh clutched Stephan's leg. He didn't like seeing Mary when she was angry.

"Has something happened, Steph? Why have you been crying? Christ, you are turning into a baby. Where's the brother I used to know that was afraid of nothing?"

"I can't do it. I can't operate on him. It is not right. We need to take him home."

"So you will let your own flesh and blood die! You owe this to me, Steph. I am the one that has always got you out of trouble. How many thousands of pounds have I given you to pay off your debts? Please, Steph. This is the first time I have asked you for anything."

"I can't. This is morally wrong. Just leave me alone. Have you not seen the news? Lucy O'Leary, the love of my life, has been murdered. I don't know if I can go on without her."

"You are being wet. She is just another one of your good-for-nothing women. If she meant anything to you, then you would be a couple, and she would be living with you. You've always had commitment problems. Women don't like addicts. Nobody likes a gambling man. You need to make things right with God and the only way to do that is to save Lia's life."

"I can't do it today. I need to get her drugs, so she doesn't reject the kidney."

"So get them. What are you waiting for? If you can't operate today, when can you?"

"Monday, Monday 26th. I have a courier bringing them to me on Sunday night. It is going to cost a lot."

"Money is not a problem. We just hope Lia doesn't get too sick for you to operate. Lia, we are going to have one last dialysis treatment. You have to be a good girl and let the doctors help you."

"No, Mammy!"

"I will get you that doll you always wanted. Uncle Stephan is going to make you better. You'd like that, wouldn't you, sweetie. If you do this one last treatment, I will get you that doll."

"The vet doll with all those cute little animals?" Lia asked.

"The very same."

Darragh listened to the chorus of the Waterfall Way coming from the box and smiled.

'If you're going Waterfall way,
then stay, please stay.
I can't wait another day
Hey, hey, hey, please stay
I want you to stay.'

Soon he would be home. Stephan would take him home.

Chapter Thirty-four

As morning on 26th April 2021 approached, Seth opened his eyes and looked up at the roof window from his bed, checking if it was light. It was still dark. He had woken on numerous occasions that night and each time he had looked at the clock on his phone to see what time it was. He had woken up every half hour. As he tried to sleep, he had let Granny's words run through his mind, promising him that they would be able to talk to the spirits and find Darragh. He hoped that the spirits, or whatever they were, wouldn't talk in riddles like they had done before. All he needed to know was where his son was. He was willing to fight anyone that dared to stand in his way. He was going to bring Darragh home no matter what.

When dawn broke, he drifted off into a troubled sleep and had the most startling dream. He heard himself call out with distress as he felt Gemma's arms wrap around him. He felt her cold breath on his neck, and he could feel her icy cold hands running over his naked body. He was too scared to move in his dreams. "NOOO…" he called out. He heard in his mind her voice telling him to be patient, to stay calm and that she would help him. "No, I don't want you to help!" he called out, opening his eyes.

Feeling peculiar, he shivered, doing his best to get rid of the feeling of being touched by a ghost. He was sure he could still feel her cold hands on him, caressing him intimately. He shivered an icy shiver and then sat up in bed, hoping the feeling of being touched by a ghost would leave him. He needed Jules to wake up and help him. Desperately, he patted on the bump in the duvet that was Jules and heard her mumble something. It was so reassuring to hear her voice, and he smiled for a moment, thinking of them making love. "Are you awake?"

Juliet began to cry, but he didn't mind because the sound of her crying had made Gemma leave him. His body had stopped shivering too. He needed a cup of tea to calm his nerves, so he got out of bed and went to see Juliet. "Do you want your Da?" he whispered. She stopped crying and smiled broadly when she saw him. "There you go, my sweet baby girl. Your Da is here for you. Come with me, and we will see if there is a bottle in the fridge for you. We must let your Mammy sleep. I have to tell her first where we are going."

"It's ok, I am awake," Jules announced, pushing the covers back. "Oh, you're up. Did you have a bad dream? I heard you call out."

"Kind of."

"Will you pass her to me, and I will feed her. Seth, what time is it?"

"Six, just gone six."

"I had such a lovely sleep. Oh goodness! This is the first whole night's sleep I've had since Juliet was born. I can't believe it," she said, sitting up and smiling broadly. "She's made it through the night without needing to feed."

"You are such a good girl," Seth said, passing Juliet to Jules. "Here, let your Mammy feed you." Seth got back into bed. "I think I've probably had the worst night's sleep ever."

"Did you? Were you worried about anything?" Jules pulled up her nightshirt and let Juliet feed.

"A lot is going through my mind. Tomorrow we have that clown's trial to deal with. I dreamt a lot about Darragh. I guess I have been waiting for the 26th to come for a while now." He shuddered again as he remembered Gemma's ghostly arms around him and holding him where she shouldn't. "You know it is the pink moon tonight, don't you?"

"That old chestnut! You mustn't get your hopes up. I know you say Granny got the spirits to help her last time to find us, but you mustn't get carried away. I think it was your determination to find me that led you to me. Today I will ring the police department again to see if they have arrested your twin brother."

"I don't like you calling him that. He is no twin of mine."

"If he hasn't been arrested, then we should go and see him and get him to talk to us."

"Do you mean like in the movies? Are we going to put a hood over his head, tie him to a chair and start to pull out his fingernails until he tells us all he knows?"

"Something like that."

Seth laughed. "You are serious. We can't do that. As much as I'd like to."

"It drives me mad that he knows something, and the police are doing nothing about it. I know he won't talk to us, but he might talk to Jess. She will help us. I know she will," Jules said, stroking Juliet's cheek as she fed.

"So what do you suggest…."

The bedroom door flew open, and Sinead burst into the room. "You need to get up, Seth. Your mad Granny has had a vision. I was in my car going down the drive, and she leapt out in front of me from nowhere and said that you need to come and help her find the virgin, her hair a thatch of bower."

"Christ, Sinead! Have you not heard of knocking? You nearly gave us a heart attack!" Seth said, jumping out of bed.

"She has more to tell you, but she is just waiting for Lucy to come through. I think she wants you to drive her to woodlands around Cork, and she says she will know when we are in the right one."

"That's a bit vague," Jules huffed. "Seth, this is all codswallop. That woman needs locking up."

"So you are not coming to look, then?"

"No, I am not. I will talk to Jess and see if she will talk to Jon."

"I wouldn't do that. She could end up dead like Lucy." Sinead said. "Seth, do you still have those maps we used last time?"

"I do, but I have to agree with Jules. I am not sure I trust the dead. Luck hasn't been on our side lately. There are those out there that mean to harm us. The fire, and then the other day we got spooked by my dead Dad. Gemma has had her moments too."

Sinead shook her head and looked angry. "Seth Hearn! You shock me. This is our first real chance of finding Darragh, and you are going to let a little bit of misfortune get in the way and stop you from getting your boy back."

"I wouldn't call losing a whole house a little misfortune. Anyway, there is quite a lot of woodland around Cork. We could be gone for days, and we need to find him tonight while there is a pink moon."

"So you do believe in fairies," Sinead replied with a hopeful look. "They helped us before, so why wouldn't they help again. It will be so much easier this time. We are clearly looking for a woodland dwelling with a thatched roof. There can't be many houses in the middle of the woods."

"No, you are right. I agree. I think we are looking for a building. Let me shower and get dressed. You have a look at the maps. They are on the bookshelf."

"There's no time for a shower. Granny is waiting in my car outside."

"Ok, just let me fling some clothes on and get some food. I am starving. Jules, my sweet girl, please stay in the house. You are safe in here from you-know-who."

Jules looked at Seth's concerned face and sighed. "I don't like being left alone, but it will be hard to manage in a car all day with Juliet. No, you all go, but you need to keep me updated. I can't help worrying, though. Seth, you have to promise you won't hit whoever has got him. I don't want you ending up in prison too. When you find Darragh, you have to call the police. You can't handle this the Hearn way."

"I promise I will message you. So do you believe in fairies, too, then?"

"No, of course not, but I feel that Lucy is with us now, and she will look after Darragh until we find him. Seth, be careful. If you think you are being led down a dark path then turn and run. Your Dad will be waiting for you, and I.. I... don't want to lose you too."

"I won't let anything happen to him," Sinead said. "Come on, Seth, you need to get a wriggle on. Granny is bouncing off the walls and is eager to get going."

Chapter Thirty-five

Seth, Sinead and Granny had only been gone for half an hour, and Jules found herself pacing up and down with Juliet in her arms. She felt like a caged bird and could not think of anything but finding Darragh. A battle was going on in her mind. She couldn't allow herself to believe in angels or spirits helping them. She felt cross with herself for letting Seth go on a pointless journey. *He is just going to come back tired and disappointed. The whole notion of looking for a house in the woods with bowers on the roof is crazy. And virgins, what was all that about? Stuff and nonsense!*

An image of the rocking chair flying across the room stopped her in her tracks. She had thought about it many times and had done her best to work out how that had happened. The floor was uneven, and the chair shouldn't have been able to slide on the floor unless a great force had been placed on it. She then remembered feeling Jethro's ghostly body so near her that she could smell him and almost feel his breath on her neck. These thoughts sent chills down her body, but she refused to let him get the better of her. *It's no good. I've got to go and see Jess again. I can't just sit here doing nothing.* "Juliet, you must be good and not be so grumpy. If only you could talk and tell me what will make you happy. Darragh was so easy. You, my sweet baby, are a puzzle. I will put you in the car seat in a minute, and then we will drive down to the campsite. I would walk, but I don't want to be open to… well… him."

Juliet's big blue eyes watched her talk, and she thought she saw her smile for a moment. Feeling encouraged that she was finally getting through to her, she hugged her tighter and went to the bedroom to feed her and get her changed.

Not wanting to be outside for a moment longer than she needed, Jules drove into the campsite and parked outside Jess's caravan. She looked back at Juliet and, seeing her eyes closing, decided to leave her to sleep. She looked at the sky to make sure there was no sun to heat the car and then noticed a plume of smoke coming from the back of the caravan. Locking the car door, she walked to the back of the caravan and found Jess smoking there. *I wonder where Marley is.* Jess looked tired, and she gave Jules a weak smile.

"He's been up all night, and now he is finally asleep," she said, nodding her head towards the caravan.

"Is he ill then?"

"No, he doesn't sleep much. He never did. He is asleep now, though. That's what counts."

"Aww Jess, you should have a sleep too. You look exhausted. Juliet is like that. I can't remember the last time I had a good night's sleep." It then dawned on her that she had actually slept for most of the night. She decided to keep that to herself.

"Mammy says that it is a sign of intelligence. He is too curious to sleep. Maybe your Juliet is going to have brains too."

"Maybe. Jess, I need your help. Would you go and ask Jon if he knows what happened to Darragh. I went to his shop the day Lucy died, and I ended up breaking his window. When Seth was in his flat above the shop, he saw an old cot, and I just can't help but think that Darragh was there at some point. I keep trying to tell the police, but they are only interested in finding Lucy's killer. Oh,

Jess, I don't know what to do. I just know he had something to do with it."

"With Lucy's murder?"

"No, not that," she lied. "With Darragh's abduction. You said as much the last time we spoke. Seth, Granny and Sinead have gone off looking for him, but I don't... I don't believe…."

"In all that hocus pocus shit. Mammy told me what your mad granny saw in a vision."

"Exactly, but the police are just not interested in finding Darragh. That was Lucy's case. You went to see Jon the other day, didn't you?"

"I did, but he wasn't pleased to see me at the shop. I need money to bring up his son, but he has been ignoring my messages. He used to give me money for Marley. He bought me that car, but now the shite has gone, I haven't had a penny. I was going to drive over and see him this morning, but I don't have money for fuel. He won't like that in case Mary and his precious daughter Lia sees me."

"Oh, so you know he lives with them then? Or he did. I don't think they are with him anymore."

"I know about them. He doesn't know that, though."

"Wow, Lucy thought Mary had something to do with Darragh's disappearance. When they grabbed Darragh, Mary was in the van that ran over Sinead.

"Oh Jess, I know you are tired, but please help me. I will drive you and Marley over there."

"I do need to speak to him about Marley, but you know what he is like. He has a temper and will get angry if I start questioning him."

Jess put her cigarette to her lips and drew on it. She looked at Jules with sympathetic eyes as she exhaled the smoke. "The only way I can get him to talk is if he comes back here. I could say Marley is really sick. When he comes here, he won't be able to resist fucking me. Only then, after he has had his way with me, will he tell me anything. He tells me a lot of things after sex. It is like he wants to be held like a baby then, and he will lay his head between my breasts, and I will be able to tease anything out of him before he sleeps."

"That is a lot to ask of you. Would you do that for me? No, not for me, for Darragh?"

Jess laughed. "I need a good fuck. Is Seth good in bed? I've heard that the Hearn men are well skilled in pleasing women."

Jules laughed. "I don't know how to answer that. Things are good in that department."

"You've got a keeper there. He only has eyes for you."

"Oh Jess, I don't know what more I can do to find my little Darragh. If we don't find him today, I have this terrible feeling that we will never find him."

"Don't listen to your stupid granny. You will find him. You must never give up hope. Now let me ring the butcher's and see if he picks up. Using the shop number will catch him off guard…." Jess said, stubbing out her cigarette in an ashtray hidden below the caravan. She stood up, took her phone out of her back pocket and rang the shop.

"Jon? Marley is sick. I don't know what to do. He keeps calling for you. Babe, you've got to come to him. He needs you… Yes, I've given him medicine, but he won't eat. He might eat if you come and see him. Is the shop busy? Can Bernard cover? It is all quiet here. Your brother and your granny have gone out for the day. Please, babe. Marley misses you so much… Ok, I can do that. I miss you too. Ok, see you soon."

DARRAGH

Jess cut the call. "There it is done. He will be here in half an hour. I'd better put Marley in the shower. He likes to play with water. It will look like he has been sweating."

"You don't have to do this. I don't want you to get in trouble or hurt. If he gets angry, then just drop the subject."

"I can tell he wants me. He makes me feel so horny."

***

As Seth waited to be served in the petrol station, he looked out the window at Granny and Sinead waiting for him in the car. They were sitting in the back seat together, looking at the map for any woodland that had outlines of buildings showing. They had spent the morning driving up bumpy tracks through woodland towards outdoor pursuit buildings and hydro or electric units. He had lost count of how many tracks they had been down. Granny hadn't said anything, but he sensed she was becoming anxious.

Seth looked back at the queue he was in and wondered what was bothering her. *There has to be something she is not telling me. Shit! I know what it is. Like last time, there is a time limit. We need to find Darragh today. Time is running out. That's why she said she didn't want anything to eat. She wanted me to keep on looking and not waste any time.* He looked down at the pile of sandwiches and drinks in his basket. *We need to eat to keep our strength up.* He had bought Granny a sandwich anyway. *We will all have to eat while we are driving. Sinead and I can take turns behind the steering wheel.* He didn't know why but he had never felt so hungry.

He reached the cash desk, told the cashier what pump they were at and waited for her to tot up his shopping. She smiled at him when she told him how much the bill was.

267

"Are you Seth from S&J," she asked. "You look like him."

"No," Seth replied, swiping his card to pay. He hoped she wouldn't see his name on the card. "That's my brother," he replied, knowing what she would ask next.

"Can we have a photo together? I finish in five minutes. I am your brother's biggest fan. You really look like him. Please," she asked again, seeing him turn to leave.

"I'm really sorry, but we are late for an appointment, and we have to get going. Another time perhaps, but if you contact my brother on TikTok, I will be sure to tell him to say Hi. What's your name?"

"Tara," she replied. "Tara Jones."

Seth shot back to the car, feeling a little bad that he had lied. He jumped in the driving seat and then handed the bag to Sinead. "Here, pass me the keys. I'll drive while you two eat. We have to get going. Have you found any more buildings in the woods?"

"We have found loads," Sinead replied. "This is going to take all day. Do you think there is a better way to do this?"

"We just have to be quicker, don't we, Granny?" he asked, looking at her in the rear-view mirror. Granny looked out the window, and Seth thought she was ignoring him for a moment. "Don't we, Granny?"

"Quiet, Seth, they are whispering something. I can hear Lucy in the background. Yes, it is most urgent that we get going. I can see knives being sharpened and a big pot of water on the stove bubbling away. We have done half of the woods in Cork now, so we only have the other half to do."

"I don't like the sound of that," Sinead said, frowning. "It sounds like... well. Is someone about to cook Darragh?"

"Sinead! That's an awful thing to say," Seth snapped as he started up the car. Christ, Sinead!"

"No, not eaten," Granny said slowly. "He is being prepared for something, but I am not sure what."

"So where are we going next?" Seth asked as he pulled onto the road.

"Keep going for about five miles, and then look for a country park."

"We are going to have to be a bit more choosy. Nobody is going to be holding him in a country park. It would be too public. Where's the next wood?" Seth asked.

"You're right. The next one is just a footpath up to a wooded area."

"Is there a road to it? Do you think we should be looking for dwellings that are accessed by a road?"

"What do you think, Granny?" Sinead asked.

"The spirits say this is where the Virgin Mary dwells, so I don't think she will be wanting to walk up a muddy track."

Seth sighed. "Do you think you could ask the spirits for an address?"

"It's not a fecking telephone exchange. Spirits are there to guide us, not give us directions. Lucy keeps frowning. Her image in my mind is not clear. She is showing me white flowers around the door. Thank you, dear. I can see the house now. It's a pretty cottage, and the roof is covered in white flowers in the summer. I will know it when I see it. We are not looking for a virgin, after all. Virgin Bower is the name of the flowers. So we only go up roads that would lead us to a cottage. Because I see a car in the drive now."

"I guess that is a bit of a help," Seth said, putting his foot down on the accelerator.

"Seth, drive for about ten miles and then there is a forest with a road through it. There are a few buildings along that road. Let's see if there is a house like Lucy has described," Sinead suggested, her finger tracing the route they were taking on the map.

"Lucy is saying something," Granny announced. "She has just been assessed and is with us completely now. I can see her face as clear as day. She seems to think we are on the right path. She is showing me a picture of Mary. The woman has long red hair in ringlets, holding a child with long dark hair and rocking her. She is a bit too big to be rocked like a baby. The child is sleeping and holding a doll in her arms. Mary is crying. I think the child is very sick. I see such sorrow."

"Do you see Darragh?" Seth asked.

"Oh my, I see him standing by her, holding her leg. He is there, but she doesn't see him. Mary does not care for the boy. He is there for a purpose. I can see years of grief rolling out in front of her and see her miserable life playing out. She is a tortured soul, and I see her crying black tears. She should not be near children. Thank you, Lucy, for showing me what you see."

"We will find him. We have to find him today. I see the road you are talking about on the sat nav," Seth said, gripping the steering wheel tighter. "He just has to be in a house down there."

"The spirits say you must hurry, and there is a small chance we will get to him on time."

Chapter Thirty-six

The doll's hair was coming out in clumps. Black woolly hair lay in piles around Lia's feet on the carpet. Hair bands with hair attached were strewn on the sofa between her and her Mammy. Mary watched Lia as she brushed the vet doll's black hair vigorously. "Be gentler," she said softly, trying not to upset her.

"Mammy, it won't stop being curly. I miss my other doll. Her hair was long and shiny. Not like this stupid thing," she said, throwing it down.

"Well, you shouldn't have thrown your other doll in the river, should you?"

"She wanted to swim. Why didn't you fish her out for me?"

"We couldn't reach her, could we? The river was running too fast and took her away. She is ok, though. I do believe she is on a beach somewhere sunning herself."

"I want her back. She doesn't like being in the sun."

"Don't you worry about her," Mary said, sighing. "She has a big umbrella over her."

"Mammy, what is Uncle Steph doing in the kitchen? Is he making lunch? I'm starving. I haven't eaten all day."

"You can eat later if you are still hungry. Steph is getting ready to make you better, and then you will never have to go to that horrid hospital again."

"Is he going to make him better, too?" she asked, pointing towards Darragh, who was on the floor playing with a plastic model horse that Stephan had given to him.

Mary frowned. "No, he has just been allowed to keep us company while we wait. He should be in his room, but Steph thinks he should play down here." Watching Lia's kidney donor play irritated her more than watching Lia destroy her new doll.

"Do you like him more than me?" Lia asked, her eyes filling up with tears.

"No, my wee girl. I could never love him."

"Then why do you keep looking at him and not me."

"I must keep an eye on him in case he decides to take himself off somewhere."

"He likes to run away. He is a little shite, isn't he, Mammy? I heard you tell Da that."

"It is not nice to swear, Lia."

"But you…"

"Right, I am ready for him," Stephan announced, appearing in the kitchen doorway. He wore a mask over his mouth and a plastic apron and gloves. "Did you shower him like I asked you to?"

"No, he wouldn't go in the shower," she lied. The thought of having to undress and wash him revolted her.

"It would have been good if you had. I guess I can cover him with disinfectant. Look, Mary, I can't do this by myself. You will have to hold him while I inject the anaesthetic."

Mary tutted. "If I must, I must. Do you have another apron and gloves? Lia, sweetie, Mammy is going in the kitchen with Darragh for a moment. I have a little something for you while you wait." She pulled a new dress with hair accessories for her doll from her bag and gave her the packet. "This is for my beautiful girl to play with while Mammy is busy."

"Oh my, she is going to look beautiful now," she said, ripping the packaging open. "I can't wait to put this on her."

Darragh looked up at Stephan and laughed. He couldn't understand why he was wearing such funny clothes. He had been so engrossed in playing with his new toy that he hadn't noticed him come into the room. Darragh had walked the toy horse around and talked to him, trying to remember where he had seen a horse like this before. He stroked his nose and then remembered patting a huge black horse like the one he held. "MOSS!" he called out to Stephan, holding the horse in the air. "MOSS!"

"Is that the name of your horse, then?" Stephan asked. Stephan went back into the kitchen and then reappeared with an apron and gloves for Mary. He held them out for her to collect, not wanting to leave the sterile environment he had created in the kitchen. "Mary, will you bring him to the kitchen for me? It will only take me half an hour to extract the kidney, and then I will be ready for Lia. You have showered her, haven't you?"

"Of course, I have," Mary snapped, standing up. Irritated by her brother's mithering, she snatched the apron and gloves from him, put them on, walked over to Darragh, and wondered if she could carry him through the kitchen without touching their bodies. The plastic apron would not protect her from feeling his scrawny body against hers. As she got close to him, she could hear a strange noise coming from the chimney. Puzzled by this, she bypassed Darragh and crouched down by the chimney to listen. She could hear a dragging sound against the walls of the chimney. "I think there is an animal in your chimney, Steph…."

A huge ball of soot shot out of the fireplace and was followed by a black bird that cawed loudly. A cloud of soot filled the room and covered her and Darragh in a fine black dust. Mary screamed hysterically. Unfazed by Mary's screaming, the crow cawed, flew up to the ceiling, and then swooped down onto Darragh's head.

"NOOOO!" he yelled, swiping his hands in the air to try and get the bird off of him. He could feel the crow's claws digging into his scalp, which hurt so much that it made him cry out in pain. His hand struck feathers, and he felt the bird's talons rip the skin on his head as it flew off. Darragh screamed in pain again, and frightened, he started crying. The crow flew up towards the ceiling, glided onto the top of the dresser, and cawed loudly. Through tears, Darragh was sure that he could see the bird's beady black eyes flashing a little red as it looked back at him, and he knew that it wanted to cause him more damage. "NO! BAD BOY!" Darragh yelled out.

"That boy is cursed. He is a demon. Look what you made it do to me," she yelled at Darragh, trying to brush the soot from her clothes.

Lia cried hysterically when she realised that her doll's new dress was covered in soot too. Stephan cursed and ran over to the front door, opened it wide and picked up an umbrella from a pot by the door. Cautiously, he walked over to the crow and poked the bird gently, trying to get it to fly away.

"Will you get out of here, you crazy bird," Stephan called out. Darragh crawled behind an armchair, terrified that the bird would come to get him. From his hiding place, he watched the horrid crow flap its wings as it circled the room. Fearing the worst, Darragh drew himself into a ball on the floor and hid his head in his arms, fully expecting the scary monster to find him. He could feel some wet sticky stuff in his hair. He screamed out when he heard the evil black bird's wings moving in the air above him, and he shouted out 'no' again. He heard Stephan swiping the air with the umbrella. The crow cawed continually and then, annoyed that it could not get near Darragh, flew away through the door.

Stephan slammed the door behind the crow and ran over to Darragh. He picked him up and hugged him. "Don't cry, little man. It is ok. The crow has gone now. Aww, look. Your head is bleeding, but only a little. You will live. Mary, will you take him up and shower him? He can't have the op until he is clean."

"No way. I am not going anywhere near that little shite. He did that on purpose."

"What are you talking about? He is just a baby."

"He is in league with the Devil, and I will have nothing more to do with him."

"So you don't want me to operate on him, then? Is his kidney not good enough for Lia now?"

"Mammy, I don't want his kidney," Lia screamed. "He is the Devil."

"Hush now. His kidney does not belong to him. It has always been yours. He has stolen it from you, and now he will give it back. Yes, Steph, I want you to operate. Take him upstairs and wash him. The operation will go ahead as planned. Lia needs her kidney back."

***

Seeing that Juliet was sleeping deeply, Jules decided that she would go for a drive rather than go home. She didn't want to be around when Jon arrived. She didn't want to see the demonic version of her lovely Seth, and she certainly did not want to speak to him again. As she turned out of the drive onto the lane, she decided to head into Cork and go for a walk along the river. She would strap Juliet to her and not use the pram. Juliet hated being in there and it was a bit of a faff to set it all up. It was a beautiful day, and she was sure Juliet would enjoy a little outing.

As she drove along, she started to think about Jess and hoped that Jon wouldn't notice that she was making a recording. Anxiety was building, and she wished she hadn't asked her to record everything. *When he realises there is nothing wrong with Marley, he is sure to smell a rat. What if he kills her like he killed Lucy? If she does get him to sleep with her, where will they put Marley? Does he watch them while they do it? Christ, this is all wrong. I have to go back and stop this all from happening. I can't let that bastard hurt her. She is so young and naive. This is not a fairy story. He will hurt her. I know he will.*

Jules pulled over into a passing point, decided to do a three-point turn, and waited for the road to clear. A small white van was heading towards her. *I'll wait for that to go by and then turn around.* As the van passed, she realised Jon was driving the butcher's van. The blue lettering on the side of the van flashed past her in a blur. *Oh my! I hope he didn't see me.* She had turned her face away just in the nick of time. She looked to see if she could see the van, but it had disappeared down a bend in the road. *He was driving like a bat out of Hell.* She spun the car around and followed, fearing that she would be too late if she didn't get back quickly.

Jules parked the car in the Manor House car park and leapt out. She got Juliet out of her car seat and strapped her in the carrier. The buckles were being tricky to fasten, and she scolded them for being a pain. She skirted the ruined Manor House and shuddered as she passed it by. The charred walls and broken windows cried out to her, daring her to wander within and dance with danger. She tried her best not to look, and flashbacks of

276

DARRAGH

Barney jumping from the roof taunted her. It was good to leave the house behind, and she couldn't help but notice that the back garden looked picturesque and was a stark contrast to the scene of devastation behind her. *Poor May would be so sad to see her lovely house like this.*

Juliet slept on as Jules crept into the foliage at the end of the garden. The campsite was on the other side of the hedge and wooded copse. She shivered at the thought of seeing Jon again. A twig snapped behind her, and she spun around to see what it was. The path was quiet, but she had a distinct feeling that someone was following her. Jules picked up the pace and almost tripped. Angry with herself, she slowed down. *What if I fell and crushed Juliet. Stay calm. It is just a squirrel or the wind making a noise.*

Another strange noise behind her made her turn to look. A large black crow was following her. Jules laughed inwardly at herself for thinking that it was a man. She watched the crow for a minute and wondered why it was on the floor and so near to her. "Are you injured?" The crow put its head on one side and cawed. The bird seemed healthy enough, but it was freaking her out. She had never been so close to a crow. "SHOO!" she hissed, fearing that she would be heard. The crow hopped closer, and Jules found herself starting to back away. She began to run and held Juliet to her. She looked over her shoulder and saw the crow open its wings, ready to fly. Seeing the clearing ahead, she burst out into the campsite, ran into the centre, and looked back. The crow landed on the edge of the campsite, then turned and flew away, cawing loudly. *That was weird. I swear the crow was going to attack me. There was something evil about that bird. That was not normal. I wonder why it didn't come into the clearing. I guess it was too nervous to get me with everyone watching. I shouldn't have gone in the woods alone. What was I thinking of!*

Her cover blown, she decided that she would just walk up to Jess' caravan and knock on the door. The campsite was busy with travellers tending their caravans and chatting to each other. They didn't seem to mind her being there, so she continued on her way. She could see Jon's van parked next to the caravan. She wondered what he would say to her when he saw her. If he was nasty, then she would call the police. *He is trespassing. Seth told him in no uncertain terms that he should never return to the campsite.*

Feeling a little nervous, Jules knocked on the caravan door and waited for Jess to open it. After a minute, Jess opened the door and was surprised to see her. She was wearing only a dressing gown, and she pulled the gown tighter to stop any bare flesh from showing. "What are you doing here?" she hissed. "I have a guest."

"I think he should leave. He shouldn't be here."

Jon appeared behind Jess, and he was holding Marley. "Has he sent you? I have come to see my sick son," he announced. "You can't deny me that."

"You have seen him, and now you should leave. Seth will be back in a minute, and he will call the police," she lied.

Jess stared at her in disbelief. "What do you think you are playing at?" she said angrily. "I should never have trusted you."

Jules had not expected her to be angry. "I think it is for the best, Jess. He should never have come here. He is a dangerous man."

Jon's face had gone a dark shade of red. "Is that so? I don't think it was me that smashed a window and caused hundreds of pounds of damage."

Jules could feel anger building inside of her. "If you hadn't taken my son, then your window would still be in one piece."

"I have had nothing to do with your son. Mary has him. And my money, too, the bitch!"

Jules' mouth fell open. She hadn't expected him to reveal this to her, and she sensed that he had let his whereabouts slip out accidentally.

"Who the fuck is Mary?" Jess screamed.

"You knew I lived with her and my daughter. I've told you before. She means nothing to me. She is just the mother of my daughter. I am married to you."

"You never mentioned her before, you bastard," she spat. "Get out of here," she screamed, trying to pull Marley out of his arms.

Jon shook his head. "You are an unfit mother and a whore. He is coming with me," he yelled, pushing his way out of the caravan.

Jules jumped out of the way and shouted after him. "You give him back to her. You have no right."

"I have the perfect right," he called, walking towards the van.

"HELP!" Jess called out to anyone that would hear. "HELP ME, PLEASE. HE IS TAKING MARLEY!"

Her second call for help was heard, and two travellers ran over to assist. If Jules hadn't had Juliet, she would have done anything to stop Marley from being taken.

"Don't let that bastard take Marley. He can't take him," Jess called out to her fellow travellers.

"Jon, give the child back," one of the older travellers called. Jules recognised him. He had said that cats always land on their feet.

"He is my son, and his mother does not look after him properly. He will be better off with me."

"I am not going to ask you again, son. Give the child back. We don't want any unpleasantness here."

A crowd of travellers formed around his van.

"She doesn't feed him properly, and now he is sick. She is not a fit mother."

"Jess looks after him the best she can. You should be ashamed of yourself. You don't have time to take care of a child. Leave him with his mother, or we will have to take him from you," the old traveller said, stepping a little closer to him.

Jules' heart was beating hard in her chest, and she wondered how he would respond. She hoped he wouldn't hurt Marley.

Jon shook his head and put Marley down. "Here, have him. I have no time for this carry-on. You've always had it in for me, Brian. I want nothing more to do with thieving gipsies."

Jess ran over to her son and scooped him up. "Now get out of here, Jon, and don't ever come back."

"Don't worry, I'm going to. Don't blame me if Marley dies. His blood will be on your hands." Jon got into the van, and the travellers parted to let him drive through. Jess was crying.

"He is going to take my son and murder him like he did yours," she sobbed.

"No, Jess, we will keep Marley safe."

Jules felt a lump rise in her throat, and tears started to fall. *Why does she think Jon murdered Darragh? For the love of God, please let Darragh still be alive.*

Chapter Thirty-seven

For once, the food Tom had been given smelt good. He carefully lifted the potatoes up with his fork and then each vegetable, inspecting the lukewarm food for any signs of contamination. It was a well-known fact in the prison that some of the guards liked to spit into the food before handing it through the letterbox in his cell. He noted that Jasper always did the same. Not trusting his eyesight, he got closer to the first potato just to be sure there were no foreign objects attached to it. Feeling confident that the first potato hadn't been spat on or rolled across the floor, he took a bite and spat it out. The saltiness was too much for him, and desperately he took his glass of water and gulped down the liquid. He heard Jasper laugh.

"How can you be eating your food when it has been boiled to death in a vat of salt water?" Tom spluttered.

"I don't mind a bit of salt," Jasper said, forking a big mouthful of meat. "You are getting thin. You just have to eat it quickly and not think about what happened to it after it was cooked."

"So you have noticed I am looking a little trimmer these days. Will it be the same when they send me off to the next prison? Will they be serving me contaminated kitchen slops there too?"

"Well, you are not going to the Ritz, are you? I would only ask for food that is in packets. When I get some money, I will stock up on packets of crisps, biscuits and Babybels."

"You can't live on those. I won't have to put up with eating shit for much longer. I will be a free man soon. I am going to appeal my sentence. Getting eight years for a misunderstanding is outrageous. A decent jury or whoever listens to an appeal will see that I have been stitched up."

"Word is that you will get life for killing Gemma Day."

"Who said that?" Tom snapped. "How did you hear that? You hardly ever leave this cell."

"When we go out for exercise, I listen to what the other V.Ps are saying."

"V.P? Don't you mean V.I.P?"

"No," Jasper laughed again. "V.P. means vulnerable person. You really don't get it. We are kept away from the others for our safety."

Tom shook his head. "I need to be with decent people. I can't be kept locked up with a bunch of looneys. You must realise that I am innocent. I shouldn't be here," Tom croaked. "I will lose my mind if I have to stay in this place another day," he sobbed. Tom felt Jasper's hand on him and his delicate fingers rubbing his back, trying to comfort him. It felt good to be cared for and soothed. Tom's eyes narrowed as he realised that if he kept up this charade, then in no time at all, he would be able to slide Mr Steel into Jasper's mouth and release all his pent-up anxiety deep into his throat. The thought of Jasper's delicate, almost girl-like mouth sucking him excited him. He pushed his meal away, lay his head in his arms, and pretended to cry. Jasper's hand continued to caress him, sending shockwaves down his body. Mr Steel would make an appearance again tonight for sure. He deserved this, and the thought of going to his trial the next day floated away.

DARRAGH

***

Stephan placed Darragh on a chair in the corner of the kitchen and told him to stay there and play with his phone. He had put a moving picture on it for him to watch, but this was of no interest to Darragh, so he left the phone on the window ledge. He wondered why the table had been moved to the middle of the kitchen. Watching Stephan clean the table and spray everything with a bottle containing wee was much more interesting than looking at his phone.

Darragh wondered where Mary was. He hadn't seen her since Stephan took him upstairs to shower. He smiled as he remembered the warm water hitting his body and the bath filling up with water. He liked splashing in the water around his feet and didn't mind Stephan washing his hair or body. His hair was still wet and smelt of apples. Memories of the bird on his head returned, and he scowled. "Bad bird!" he called out to Stephan, pointing at his head's top.

Stephan looked up at him. "Did it frighten you? It just got scared from falling down the chimney. You are safe here with me. I will call Mary now, and she will hold you while I give you a little injection. It will only hurt a little, and then you will feel sleepy. I promise that you won't remember a thing." He walked towards the door and called out to Mary. Darragh copied him and called her too.

"For goodness sake!" Mary grumbled. "I am here now."

"Sit Darragh on your lap and hold his arms."

"No, he doesn't like sitting on my lap. Sit him on the table, and I can hold his arms there."

"I just thought it would be more comforting for him. You really don't like being near him, do you? Why's that?"

"He looks too much like Jon's bastard. I saw her with Jon and tried to convince myself that nothing was going on. I almost believed myself, and then I saw that she was holding a baby that had to be Jon's. Darragh is the spitting image of Jon's child. It makes me physically sick being near him."

"But you are not with Jon now. Does it matter that he looks like his child?"

"No, it doesn't matter, but I swear this child is possessed. You saw that crow on his head. That is not normal."

"I suppose not," Stephan said, picking up Darragh and then sitting him on the table. "Are you going to be a good boy for me? There you go, sit here, and Mary will hold you for a moment."

Sighing, Mary held his arms and held her breath too.

"Mammy, I need a drink," Lia called.

"You can have a drink soon, be patient."

"Mammy, I can't wait."

"Can she have a drink, Steph? Nil by mouth is cruel."

"No, not until after the operation."

"Will you be quick then?"

Stephan shook his head. "These things can't be rushed," he replied, injecting Darragh's arm.

Darragh felt a sharp pain in his arm and then started to cry. He couldn't understand why his new friend had hurt him.

"Ouch... Bad boy," he called out. The lid on the big pot of water boiling on the stove began to vibrate, and he watched steam shooting up from the vent. The steam filled the room, and he wondered why everyone was lost in this warm mist. He could hear laughing and thought his Mam was near. "MAM," he called out, but she couldn't hear him. He called again. "Mam…"

Chapter Thirty-eight

Jules listened to Juliet cry for over an hour. She had given her milk, comforted her and changed her nappy, but nothing could console her. Jules lay her between her legs on the sofa, and exhausted, she slumped back in the chair, not knowing what to do for the best. *Should I call a doctor? I wish Seth was here. He would know what to do.*

It was late afternoon, and Jules had messaged both Sinead and Seth, but she had not received any updates or calls. *It's no good. I will have to take this mad baby out for a drive. That is the only way I am going to get any peace. If she doesn't stop crying, then I will go to A&E.* "Where shall we go?" she asked Juliet. Juliet stopped crying as Jules picked her up. "You know we are going out, don't you?" Shall we go and see if we can find your Dad?" Jules looked at her phone for the umpteenth time and saw a call coming in from Sinead. "At last!"

"We haven't forgotten you. The signal has been crap for the past couple of hours." Jules could barely hear because Juliet had started to cry again.

Jules could tell from Sinead's down beat voice that they were not closer to finding Darragh. "So, no luck then?"

"No, we have nearly covered the whole of Cork and just have the last quarter to do."

"So what are you looking for? Another white building?"

"Kind of. Granny keeps seeing white flowers, and I just Googled all flowers blooming in April, and we think it is some kind of... Clematis. We found one called Virgin's Bower, but that doesn't bloom until late June. Hellfire! I see a house with white in the garden... No, it is just some kind of daisy thing. Hold on, Granny is talking... She says that the plant we are looking for is over the door, and it has bloomed early. We are near, Granny says. She also says that Juliet must have the colic. She can tell from the cry."

"I don't know what to do with her. Has she got any suggestions?"

She says that you need to keep off the dairy and give her fennel. Soak some fennel seeds in water and give her the water, then... wrap her up and take her for a car ride. Don't be tempted to take her for a walk around the estate. It is not safe at the moment."

"Ok, I will try that. What does she mean it's not safe? No, she is right. A crow freaked me out. I found something out today. Jon says that Mary has Darragh and …."

"Hello... Jules."

"I'm here… did you hear what I said?"

"Hello…" The call ended. Jules looked at the screen, hoping that Sinead would come back. No call came. *Damn, they have lost the signal. Just a little more woodland to investigate. Darragh has to be out there somewhere. That Jon knows where he is. I just know he does. There must be a way I can get through to him. I don't think he hates me like he hates Seth. He did look genuinely concerned about Marley getting sick. Jess says that he has a softer side. If I take my poor Juliet with me, I am sure he won't hurt her or me.* "Right, my poor baby, I think I have some fennel seeds tucked away." Jules put her on her shoulder as she looked through various jars in a kitchen cupboard. An unopened jar of fennel seeds was tucked at the back, ready for a fish recipe she had found on the internet. She flicked the kettle on and then opened the fridge to see if there was a little something to nibble on before she went out. A tub of grated cheese called out to her, and she reached out to take it and then remembered that Granny had said to avoid dairy. She sighed. She wasn't sure if she would survive without milk or cheese. "It has to be done," she said, closing the fridge door quickly.

It was only when she got to the entrance of the campsite did she realise that Juliet had fallen to sleep. Juliet had taken a little of the fennel water, but it had been a struggle to get her to drink from a bottle. Jules stopped the car and looked at her angelic face as she slept. Nobody would have guessed she had been a screaming mess only minutes earlier. *It is no good. I can't take you with me. I would be using you as a human shield. What was I thinking of?*

Jules backed the car up, turned to the left and drove up to Jess's caravan. She gently pulled Juliet's car seat with her baby asleep and grabbed her changing bag. She found Jess having a cigarette behind the caravan. *Maybe leaving Juliet with her is a bad idea. What if something happens to her while she is having a smoke?*

Jess saw the car draw up, and Jules saw her put out the cigarette. When she stood up, she realised that she had been crying.

"Are you ok?" Jules asked gently.

"I am not great. I am scared that Jon will come back to take Marley away. I know I am not a good mother but I do love my baby. And so does Jon. You saw him with him. He is just not good on the commitment side of things."

"You are an excellent mother. It's not easy bringing up children. This little thing may look all innocent, but she has been a complete nightmare this afternoon. Granny thinks she has colic. I gave her fennel seed water and now look at her. She is sound asleep and looks like an angel. Jess, I don't want you to be mad at me, but I am going to see Jon. I swear there is something he isn't telling me. Seth and company haven't found Darragh yet, and I swear I will lose my mind if I don't do something constructive. Like you say, he does care for Marley and if I try to get him to feel sorry for me... Oh, I don't know exactly... I am sure it will come to me when I am there. Will you look after Juliet for an hour? I am not planning on staying there long. In her bag are a bottle of formula and some more homemade gripe water, if you need it."

"I wouldn't go. He thinks you are a bunny boiler. Perhaps you are. He was so angry earlier. He needs time to cool down, and well, I don't think he will help you... not after today."

"I have to, Jess. Time is running out. Evening is setting in, and if my baby is not found today, then I don't think he ever will be." Jules stifled a sob. "I... have to find him."

"I think you are wasting your time. Promise me you won't go upstairs with him. He is a randy sod and well, you know...."

"He thinks I am a demon. He is not interested in me. Nor me him."

I am just saying he was desperate for a bit earlier. Just be careful, ok?"

***

The sun was starting to set, and the prospect of searching the last of the wooded areas around Cork before it got dark was daunting. Big black clouds were gathering, encouraging the night to flow in undetected.

"The wind is changing," Granny declared. "It is going to pour down soon. We are close, Seth. Evil is building, and the spirits are doing their best to stop those that want us to fail at bay."

"Who wants us to fail?" Sinead asked.

"They know who they are," she said as she gazed out the window at a woodland stretched out as far as the eye could see. "We are in the right area. I can feel it. Seth, stop the car, please. Let's get out here for a moment."

Seth looked at Granny in the rear-view mirror. She was looking tired. "Sure," he said, pulling into a passing point. "Why do you want to stop here? No tracks or paths are leading into the woods."

"I know, but I need to get out and smell the air. When it is about to rain, you can hear and smell and feel a whole lot more."

Granny got out of the car, and Seth and Sinead did too. Seth looked around and ducked as a crow flew over his head. It was so close that he could feel the air from his wings. Instinctively, he held up his arms to protect himself after the bird had gone by. "Christ! Where did that come from? That bird is crazy. Did you see that? It nearly took my head off." The crow settled on a branch and then cawed at them all. "Is that bird laughing at me?" Seth asked.

"He is warning us not to come closer. It has no brains. He has led us straight to Darragh. Get away with yer," Granny yelled. The crow cawed and flew off into the woodland. "I dare say he is going back to whoever to tell them we are coming."

"You are joking," Sinead said. "That was just a wild animal having a bad day."

"That was no wild animal. It is one of Satan's guards."

"I don't know about that. This is Cork, 2021, not some dark fantasy or demonic fairy-tale," Sinead stated, putting on her coat.

"That may be, but things go on in the woods that are never spoken about, 2021 or not. We will have to keep our wits about us if we are going to find Darragh. This way, she said, walking into the woods. Lock the car, and like I say, keep an eye out for that house. It has to be here somewhere."

"It's going to be dark soon. We should bring a torch," Seth said, opening up the boot. "Are you sure about this, Granny? We said we would only go up tracks that would take a car."

"Yes, I am sure, and the spirits are in agreement as well. We need to get there before dark. I think we have a bit of a walk ahead of us."

"Are you going to be ok, Granny? You are…"

"I am not too old to go for a walk. Sinead, will you manage, dear, with your leg. I see you still limp a little. Do you want to wait in the car?"

"I am fine. It only hurts when I sit still for too long," she replied, looking at the map. "Seth, there are lots of paths in this woodland, and some are larger than others. We should head towards a logging track. Cars can go along there."

Granny started to walk quickly. "As long as we head north, we will find what we are looking for, path or not."

The track north was narrow. Only animals and the occasional human had walked along it. The feeling of not knowing exactly where they were going was beginning to freak Seth out. The old pine wood, the trees, and the last of the light filtering through the branches cast twisted shadows. The air cooled as they walked, and the rain began to fall. Large drops hit their heads and shoulders. Their coats were not waterproof, and the material lapped up the droplets as the rain increased.

"Granny, shall we stop under this big old tree and keep out of the rain. I am sure it is just a passing shower," Seth asked.

"No, it is set to pour for a few hours. We do not have the time to wait."

Seth shivered and walked on. He was wet through, and he could see that Sinead was wet and cold too. The map was stowed away in her coat, but he suspected it was now a wet soggy mess. "Sinead," he whispered, so Granny couldn't hear. "This is crazy. Do you think we should go back while we know which way to go? How much longer do you think we have to walk?"

"I don't know. Last time I looked at the map, we were only a quarter of the way into the woods, which was a half-hour walk. So another hour before we reach the logging track, I guess."

"Christ, I think we should go back."

Granny stopped and turned around, and put her fists on her hips. "I hear you whispering. Have a little faith in your old Granny. The spirits are buzzing in my ear and telling us to forge on. We will find what we are looking for, I am in no doubt."

Silently, the three walked on, the rain relentlessly beating down on them. Seth could only admire his Granny for her courage. He wished that he could believe what she was saying. It would be a bitter pill to swallow if Darragh wasn't there waiting for him. He smiled as he thought about his baby boy holding up his arms to be picked up. The rain from the pine needles throwing a torrent of water on him woke him from his daydreams.

"This is the track," Sinead announced as they stepped out onto a wide straight path between the trees. "We need to turn left to keep going northwards," she said, looking up a steep hill. "Cars or log lorries have been up here. Look, you can see tyre marks in the mud here."

Granny started to walk up the hill. "When we get to the top of the hill, we will know we are going in the right direction. Lucy is spurring us on to hurry."

Seth shook his head and walked behind his Granny, hoping and praying he would not be disappointed. The steep track and the rain made climbing the hill difficult. As they reached the hill's crest, Seth saw a car's headlights approaching them. The lights were on full beam, and the glare was blinding. They shielded their eyes and were barely able to see. As the car passed them, Sinead called out.

"I saw him. I saw Darragh in the back seat of the car. He is sleeping, but I would know that sweet little face anywhere."

"Are you sure, Sinead?" Seth called as he began to run down the hill after the car.

The car was driving slowly, trying to avoid potholes. Seth ran as fast as he could, desperate to catch up. He raced along, remembering the number plate number. He called out for the car to stop. The car began to speed up, and Seth pounded along behind the car. He wished he hadn't called out, as he had spooked the driver. The wheels spun as they hit the top gear, and the engine roared in protest. The car hurtled off into the distance, leaving Seth behind, distraught and breathing so hard he thought his lungs might burst. Seth stopped running and leaned forward, holding his thighs, trying to breathe. He was crying and sobbing, and he was feeling defeated. His wee boy had only been a few metres away from him. "If only we had got to the house sooner, then we would have found him. What will we do now? FOR THE LOVE OF GOD!" he yelled out to the universe.

DARRAGH

Seth walked back to Sinead and Granny. He wiped away his tears and was thankful that his son was alive and well.

"You tried," Sinead said. "We've written the number plate down. We need a dry place to ring the police. Seth, we got the number plate. We will find him. The police will find him tonight."

"I should have gotten in front of the car and stopped it. I was that close," he said, holding up his thumb and finger to show an inch. "That close!"

"We should go and see where they have been holding him. There's a light down there," Granny said. "I can see the light coming from a window down the hill. Do you see?"

"What's the point?" Seth said miserably. "We should just go home and let the police deal with it."

"No, we need to see ourselves and find out why the spirits still want us to go there."

Seth shook his head. "Granny, the spirits must be tired of helping us. We have let them down. We were not quick enough."

"The spirits never grow tired, dear. The night is still young, and the pink moon will rise soon. We will know more then. Many channels will be opened to us. That energy brings new life, new hope and new beginnings. They whisper that Darragh will shine tonight. We should go to the house and satisfy our curiosity."

Seth followed behind again with his head hanging low. The rain continued to pelt down on them. He had never felt so miserable in all his life. He felt his friend's hand slip into his.

"You did your best, Seth. Don't be sad. We will find him," Sinead whispered.

Chapter Thirty-nine

The dark night stole through the streets of Cork, seeping into every corner and every doorway. Many of the tiny shops were closing, but the windows were brightly lit, displaying an array of goods and promising shoppers that they would not be disappointed if they ventured inside. Office workers were gone from the streets, and just a few people headed home with carrier bags full of shopping. Recipes and meal plans for that night were forming in their heads as they walked. Worries about their hectic days slipped away, and their pace quickened as they thought about their loved ones waiting for them to return.

Jules pulled the zipper up on her jacket, flipped her hood up, and then tucked her hair away so she wouldn't be recognised. Large splots of rain began to fall, and she could tell by the dark clouds in the sky that there would be a torrent of rain at any moment. She shivered as she approached the butcher's shop and crossed the road as it would be easier to watch the shop from the safety of a covered alleyway that ran alongside the jewellers shop. Thankful for being out of the rain, she stepped back a little into the shadows to watch and wait for the right moment to go and see Jon. The alleyway smelt of pee and moss. The raindrops were increasing, and she wished she had not worn her nice white trainers.

The rain was getting heavier, and she drew tighter the cords around her hood. A clattering noise behind her made her jump, and feeling nervous, she looked over her shoulder to see if anyone was there. *No, nothing. It must have been a cat or a rat. God! I hope it wasn't a rat.*

Her eyes focused on the butcher's shop. She saw a man in a white coat with a blue and white striped apron standing behind the counter. He pulled out trays of meat and took them into a back room. She waited for him to return and realised it was Jon Hearn. His dark hair and how he walked confirmed that it was the poisoned dwarf. She laughed at herself for calling him that. It was an apt name for him.

So what am I going to say to him? Hi, Jon. I am sorry about earlier and for breaking your window. You have had a child taken, so you know what I am going through. Please, if you know where he might be, then tell me? I need your help... He won't help me. I don't know why I am here. Jess says he thinks that I am a bunny boiler. Perhaps I am. What if I smashed his window again and called the police myself? When they come, then I can tell them that he says he knows where Darragh is and won't tell me. They will have to listen to me then.

A cracked paving stone leaning against the wall in the alley caught her attention. *What if I dropped this slab on the floor? Then I might get a lump big enough to throw.* Being careful not to be seen, Jules picked up the slab and then dropped it onto the concrete floor. The slab broke into a thousand pieces, and she shook her head in disbelief. There wasn't a piece big enough to cause any damage.

Her attention turned back to the butcher's shop and she saw a woman with long ginger hair walk in. *Oh my God! That's Mary. I don't think it's a customer.* She watched for a moment, not sure if she should approach. The way Jon spoke to the ginger-haired woman and pointed at her angrily confirmed in Jules's mind that she was definitely not a customer. She could feel anger building inside her. *These two bastards stole my baby and they need to give him back.* She stepped out of the alleyway and looked for a gap in the traffic to cross. From out of nowhere, a hand covered in a plastic glove covered her mouth and pulled her sharply back into the alley. She squealed with fright. *Please don't murder me!*

"Don't scream. We don't want them to see us."

The grip around her mouth loosened, and she whipped herself around to see who her assailant was. She recognised the long mac, and even though he had a black hat on and a mask over his face, she knew who it was. "Parvel! What are you doing here?" she asked, looking back at the shop to see if Mary was still there.

"You nearly spoiled the whole operation," he whispered, wiping his hands down his mac, disgusted that he had physical contact with her.

"What operation is that? Don't tell me that you will finally arrest that bastard for stealing my son?"

"No, that is not my case. When we get word from the lab that the blood found in the shed was O'Leary's, we will arrest him. We have had a tip-off from St Christopher," he laughed. Then he frowned. "I shouldn't have told you all that. Look, I am sorry about your son, but I don't need you flying in there and causing trouble."

"So, who is looking after our case now that Lucy has gone?"

"I don't know. Look, it is a cold case and will stay closed until new evidence turns up."

Jules was livid. "You are fucking joking! All you have to do is go over there now and arrest them both. Sinead saw Mary in the van when Darragh was snatched. Jon told me today that she has him, and that is a fact. What is wrong with you all?"

DARRAGH

Jules looked back and saw Mary leaving the shop. From across the road, Jules could see that her face was red with anger. Her brief meeting with Jon had not gone well. *What is she so upset about?* She got into a car parked outside the shop and started the engine.

Parvel lurched forward and tried to grab Jules' arm, sensing she would make a run for it. She managed to pull her arm away. "I just wanted to talk to her, mother to mother. I have to speak to her." She ran towards Mary's car. A bus slammed on its brakes and narrowly missed crashing into her. Jules held up her hands to apologise to the driver. *Fuck, that was close!*

Mary's car sped away. Although it was dark now, Jules could just make out the top of someone's head sitting in the back seat. She could see dark curly hair, just like Marley's. "DARRAGH!" she yelled, running after the car. The car picked up speed and then slowed down at some red lights up ahead. *I must get my car and follow them.* She felt for the keys in her pocket as she ran. The car was parked in a side street and was not far away. She threw the door open, jumped in the car and fumbled with the key, trying to get it in the ignition. "Oh, for the love of God, go in, will you." The car showed as being on, and she looked at the dashboard to make sure. It was odd not hearing an engine springing into life. She pulled the car out into the main road and noticed that the cars were moving ahead. She prayed that she would not get held up by the lights and managed to get through as they changed. She was about four cars behind Mary's, and seeing her turn right, she did too.

Three more sets of lights were kind to her, and now Jules was only two cars behind Mary's. She felt sure that Mary didn't know that she was being followed.

The rain poured down as they left Cork. Jules followed Mary's car at a safe distance, trying her best not to spook her. *Where is she going, I wonder? If we keep on this road, we will be in Waterfall soon. Wouldn't it be ironic if Darragh was being held in Waterfall?* A fox ran in front of Jules' car and she slammed her foot on the brake so she didn't hit it. *I don't think it heard me coming.* A bus heading into Cork passed her. She remembered travelling into the city before the pandemic when she went busking with Seth. *I miss busking so much. I wish we could do it again. I guess we can't now we are famous. That's a shame.*

Her attention returned to Mary's car, and she scolded herself for taking her eyes off it. The car indicated that it was going left, and she had to wait for a car to pass, which meant that Jules was now right behind her. *I hope she doesn't see me. Oh my God! She is turning onto the road that takes me home. How odd. Why is she coming this way? Is that what she was asking Jon? Was she asking him where we live? Is she taking Darragh home? No, surely not. Why would she do that now, after all this time?* Tears started falling down her face as a tidal wave of emotions swept over her. The small hope that this was the case was fighting to be heard, but all the pain in the past was dragging that hope down. "Please, if there is anyone up there listening, then please, please turn into Waterfall West."

Jules followed Mary, and she couldn't stop the tears from flowing. It was making driving difficult. She wiped her tears on her sleeve and kept driving, her heart beating hard in her chest as they approached the turning to the Manor House. Mary slowed for a minute, and Jules smiled. *She is definitely looking for something. Please just turn in.*

Mary's car crawled along for a few seconds and then started to speed up and Jules' prayers were dashed as she watched

Mary continuing up the lane. *Surely she read the sign.* As she passed the sign herself, she noticed that the lights above the board were not lit, and there was a branch across it covering the lettering. "Nooo... don't go on, please stop." Jules put her foot on the accelerator and sped up until she was right behind Mary's car. She had to stop her. *I will pass her by and block her way with my car as a roadblock.* For a moment, Jules met with Mary's eyes in the mirror, and although she was sure she wouldn't know that it was her because it was dark, the fact that she was now tailgating her had spooked her enough to make her speed up. Jules followed, trying to keep a small distance away, but it was now evident that Mary was really scared as the car's speed continued to increase.

"YOU STUPID BITCH," Jules yelled. "You don't know these roads, and you have my baby on board. You will get him killed." Jules could barely keep the car on the road, the rain poured down, and the road surface was super slippery. "PLEASE DON'T DO THIS TO ME," Jules yelled to the universe, knowing that fingers were being pointed at her for scaring Mary.

The two cars hurtled along, and Jules gritted her teeth, fearing she would hit the grass verge and lose control. "WHY WON'T YOU STOP? PLEASE! DARRAGH IS WITH YOU." Jules flashed her lights angrily at Mary, hoping that she would slow. The road was straight for a small stretch ahead, so Jules put her foot down and was surprised at how quickly the electric car accelerated. With her heart beating hard, she drew up alongside Mary's car and quickly wished she hadn't because Mary was losing control of hers. Mary's car veered off the road and flipped sideways into a ditch. Jules watched in her rear-view mirror as the car turned over onto its roof, slid along, and finally tumbled down into a wooded area.

"NOOO!" Jules screamed as she slammed on the brakes. With tears streaming down her face and the rain beating down on her, she ran to where she had last seen the car and slid down the bank to the wreckage. The car was upside down, and the windows were all smashed. The lights were on, and the engine was still running. Smoke poured out of the crumpled bonnet. Jules crouched down, desperate to see if Darragh had been injured. The car's interior was dark, so Jules pulled out her phone from her pocket and put the torch on. Mary was lying in a heap on the roof of the car. Jules didn't know if she was alive or dead. The back seat was empty. Something black and shiny caught her eye in the glass at her feet, and she picked up a small plastic horse. She had an overwhelming feeling that this belonged to Darragh. She stood up and looked around her, convinced that Darragh had been thrown from the car. The rain made it difficult to see, so she circled the car, holding her phone high, so the light reached deep into the woodland. "DARRAGH? DARRAGH?" she screamed, and then she listened and prayed that she would hear his voice.

There was a lot more smoke coming out of the car, and it occurred to Jules that it could catch alight or, even worse, explode. If Mary was injured, then she shouldn't really pull her out of the wreckage but if she called the emergency services then it would be too late. *This is a matter of life or death. I have to get her out.* Jules kicked the broken glass out of the way the best she could and then grabbed hold of Mary's arm to see if she could straighten her a little. The seatbelt was still on her, and this needed to be unclipped if she stood any chance of rescuing her. Jules got on her hands and knees and felt for the seat belt release button. The car was filling up with smoke, making it hard to breathe. She found the button and released the seat belt. Mary groaned as Jules tried to pull her out. She knew she was in pain, but flames were now coming out of the front of the car; this was bad news. "Mary, the car is on fire. You need to get out of the car. I can help you, but I need you to try too. Mary, do you hear me?"

"It hurts. My head hurts."

This was not a good sign. "Can you move your legs?"

"It hurts."

"Mary, was Darragh with you?"

"Darragh? Yes," she replied, coughing in the smoke.

Jules got her hands under Mary's armpits and hauled her heavy body partway out of the window. "Mary, was Darragh in the car with you?"

"Yes, in the back he…."

"Christ, he must be in there still!"

Mary was heavy to move, and it took all of her strength to drag her out and to safety. She was still groaning but alive, at least. The flames were getting bigger, and it looked like the car would explode at any moment.

"I have to check the car again. I didn't check the passenger seat. He could have been thrown there. I will call you an ambulance in a minute." Jules ran back to the car and shone her torch into every corner, desperate to find her son. The smoke and flame-filled car made it almost impossible for her to see. Blindly she put her hand into the smoke to feel for him. She couldn't find him and anxiously moved her hand into every corner, desperately looking for Darragh. A huge flash and a ball of fire threw her into the air, and an ear-splitting boom filled her ears. In the distance, she saw the car engulfed in flames and watched the fire dancing from the windows. She wanted to go back to make sure Darragh wasn't under a seat, but then all she could see was darkness and someone laughing behind her as she passed out.

A crow cawed out into the night, its black eyes now red as he watched such a terrible tragedy unfold. A fire from Hell was burning brightly again, which pleased him more than anything. Darragh deserved to die.

Chapter Forty

The Heavens opened, torrential rain hit Stephan's cottage, and huge puddles began to form on the footpath. The house's eaves protected a white clematis woven into a trellis around the front door. Willed by the spirits, the Virgin Bower had bloomed early and shimmered in the darkness, the outdoor light enhancing each delicate petal and glossy leaf.

"It's beautiful. May used to have some of this growing next to the front door of the Manor House, do you remember?" Sinead asked Seth, getting a little closer to look at the plant. "It's flowering a little early, though."

Seth shook his head, unable to absorb her words. The thought of being that close to Darragh and unable to rescue him was taunting his troubled mind. "I think it was Mary in the car. Do you think anyone else is in the house?" he asked, walking in front of the window. The curtains were drawn. "Do you think we should go back and find a sheltered place where we can get a signal and ring the police? This rain is getting on my nerves now."

"We should knock," Granny declared, walking up to the front door. "The spirits think we should."

"I doubt anyone will open the door. If I were them, then I would stay quiet." Seth tried the door handle and was surprised to find that the door opened and revealed a dark front room and a door in the far corner with a shaft of light below. "Well, that was a stroke of luck. Do you see the light coming from the door over there? Someone is in and has a few questions to answer," he said angrily, walking in.

"Seth!" Sinead hissed. "For God's sake, don't hurt them. I know you are angry. Promise me."

"I promise you nothing. Whoever helped to take Darragh doesn't deserve mercy."

"There'll be no violence here," Granny announced. "Enough tears have been shed." She turned on the light and called out. "WE NEED TO TALK TO YOU!"

The front room was covered in a black dust, and a pile of thick soot covered the hearth and carpet.

"They've had a fine old time here," Granny tutted, walking over to the kitchen door. "HELLO," she called.

"Mary, where have you been …."

The door opened abruptly, and Stephan appeared holding a pair of scissors. Shocked to see them there, he pulled his mask down with his blood-covered hand. "What are you doing here? Jon, is that you?"

Not believing his eyes and feeling such anger boiling inside him, Seth leapt forward, grabbed Stephan's shoulders, and pushed him back into the kitchen and against a wall. He knocked the scissors from his hand and then grabbed him with both hands around the neck. "It's Seth, actually. WHAT HAVE YOU DONE WITH MY BOY? If you have hurt even one hair on his head, then I swear to God, I will squeeze the air from your lungs and…" Out of the corner of his eye, he noticed Granny and Sinead were standing by the kitchen table and were looking at a girl with long dark hair. She was covered in a blue cover, exposing a patch on her side.

"I haven't... Let me explain," he croaked.

304

DARRAGH

Seth dropped his hand and stood away from Stephan. He looked at the girl and then back at him, confused. "What the fuck are you doing? Are you some kind of sick doctor? Is this how you get your kicks?"

"No... no... Hear me out. We are related. This is Lia, she is your niece. Well, I'm not related. I would have been if Lucy was alive. I would have married her, you know?"

Seth's eyes narrowed. "You are talking bullshit."

Sinead was feeling for Lia's neck. "I can barely feel a pulse, Seth. What is going on? Was Darragh here?"

Stephan looked confused. "My sister said she would sit with him while he recovered. I thought she had taken him out for fresh air. I thought you were her."

"What do you mean, recover? What is wrong with him?" Seth growled, ready to take Stephan by the throat.

Stephan put up his hands to stop Seth from hurting him. "Look, I will say this very quickly, so listen! I need to get back to Lia and stitch her up. I have taken one of Darragh's kidneys and transplanted it into Lia. Your niece was dying, and my sister Mary was desperate. I am a skilled surgeon and have successfully performed this operation on both. I hope..."

Seth had to stop himself from thumping him and put his hands in the air feeling vexed. "What do you mean, hope?" He sighed. "Are you trying to tell me that Darragh's kidney is in this girl?"

Stephan nodded. "Extracting a kidney from him was the easy part. He felt no pain. He just needs to rest for a few days. He will be perfectly fine. We were going to bring him back to you."

"So where is Mary taking him?"

"I don't know. Did you see her?"

"We saw them about half an hour ago. She drove past us with Darragh in the back," Sinead said, looking worried. "We need to get this girl to hospital, she is not breathing right."

"So this is why the spirits have been showing me a man holding a knife. Pink moon or no, it is not right to take these matters into your own hands." Granny was now pacing up and down the kitchen and shaking her head. "This is all wrong."

"She will be fine. She is probably going into shock," Stephan replied weakly.

"Seriously!" Sinead called. "We need to ring for an ambulance. This is fucking crazy. How did you think that operating here, in this shitty kitchen, would be the right thing to do?"

"I am sorry, all right! I was just trying to save a life."

Seth got closer to the makeshift operating table to see how ill Lia was. "Do you have a good signal anywhere?" he asked. "We need to call for the emergency services."

"Do you mean the police or an ambulance?"

"Both!" Seth could see that this news was not going down well, and pre-empting Stephan's next move, Seth grabbed hold of him. Stephan began to struggle, but Seth managed to hold onto him. "Don't even think about running."

Sinead had her phone out and started to ring 999. "I've just remembered. You can ring emergency services without a signal... Yes, please, I need an ambulance and the police here urgently. I have found a girl that has been seriously injured. She is having problems breathing. Please come quickly... What is the address?" she asked Stephan, but he didn't reply.

"WHAT IS THE FUCKING ADDRESS?" Seth yelled out.

DARRAGH

"Virgin Bower Cottage, All Saints Wood, Cork," Stephan stammered.

"I did everything I could," he replied, looking at everyone, hoping they would understand.

***

Barely alive, Lia was loaded into the ambulance, and the blue lights of the police cars lit up the night sky. The rain had stopped, and the clouds were racing over the biggest pink moon Seth had ever seen. The cool night air was a welcome relief compared to the steamy kitchen. As he watched Stephan being pushed into a police car, he did his very best not to think about Darragh bleeding to death somewhere. Stephan's words that he was a skilled surgeon did not comfort him. *He is a complete eejit. Who in their right mind would attempt to carry out a delicate operation at home? What was he thinking of?*

It was getting late, and all three had told the police how they had come to be at Virgin Bower Cottage. Granny had openly said that the spirits had brought them there, and then when the police officer laughed, she had told him off. Seth had said that DI Lucy O'Leary had mentioned that Stephan lived there and that he might have information about Darragh. He told him that he had seen Mary driving Darragh away from the cottage. The police officer stopped laughing when he realised who Seth Hearn was and then began to write everything down with a sorry look on his face. The fact that Darragh had been operated on and his life was in danger had made the search for him more urgent. For the first time in a long time, Seth had hope. Hope that the police will start to search for Darragh in earnest now. They had the registration of the car and with the pink moon so bright he hoped that the police would be able to track Mary and Darragh down that very night.

When the police officer walked away, Seth realised that Sinead and Granny were missing. He found them sitting in the back of a police car with blankets around them to keep them warm. He was shaking, too, his clothes were wet from the rain, and he felt like his body was in shock. *I need to ring Jules. I am dreading telling her all this. Christ! It is nearly midnight. She will be doing her pieces. I bet she has left me a thousand messages.* He pulled his phone out of a soggy pocket and checked to see if she had left a message. There was a weak signal, which pleased him, but he could see no messages from her. *Not one! Oh my, she is going to be so mad at me. That is really odd. I wonder why she hasn't called me.* He rang her and waited, but she didn't reply. "Jules, if you get this, I just wanted to tell you that I'm sorry I haven't called. A lot has happened. I guess you are sleeping. We will get a taxi home, and I will tell you everything. I saw Darragh! He is alive and well, but... I will be back soon."

Chapter Forty-one

The first thing Darragh saw through the treetops when he woke up was a huge pink moon in the sky. He felt woozy and thought he was in his new bed, but his covers had been replaced by thick leaves, and his pillow was wet moss. He continued to stare at the moon, too afraid to move in case Mary or Stephan tried to get him and hurt him again. For a moment, the moon was replaced by a picture of the needle that had hurt him so much. The pink moon returned, and he smiled at it, wondering how it had gotten into his room. Feeling a little stronger, he tried to sit up, but as soon as he tried to move, he winced in pain. Something was hurting his side, and it hurt more than the needle had. He patted his body, trying to locate where the source of the irritation was coming from. Through his shirt, he realised that something was stuck to his side, preventing him from running his fingers over the part that hurt so bad. When he felt less tired, he would try and get whatever it was off of his body. The moon was smiling at him, and this made him feel better. He couldn't take his eyes off of the pink orb and he was sure he could see a face smiling at him.

The pink light made him unsure if it was night or day. Darragh shut his eyes and wondered if he would wake up in his warm bed. Then he remembered that his bed was in the house of his bad friend Steph and Mary. Not wanting to go back there, he opened his eyes again and decided to sit up to see what was around him. He wasn't afraid, just curious to see if he recognised where he was. As he sat up, he felt a sharp pain in his side, and he gasped and held his hand on the sore spot. He was pleased to be sitting up, and the moon gave him enough light to show him that he was in woodlands. There was something strange ahead. He could see a car upside down not far from him. The car had thick smoke rising up from it, and this fascinated him as he watched the smoke spirals twist and turn upwards towards the moon. He wondered why it wasn't on the road and driving along with all the other cars. Darragh wanted a closer look, so holding his side, so it didn't hurt him again, he stood up. He felt a little dizzy and laughed as everything wobbled around him. The ground was covered in leaf litter and was not as nice to walk on as carpet. The leaves were wet, and water squelched up between his toes, but he didn't mind.

As Darragh approached the car, he saw broken glass around it, twinkling in the moonlight. He wondered if it would be fun to play with these sparkling toys. Another object caught his eye. A black horse. Moss was lying just a few feet away from the car. Triumphant, he picked him up and held it to him, so happy that he had found his best friend again. He crouched down in the leaves, and holding the horse's back, he let Moss run around him. This hurt his side quite a lot, but he had to let his horse run because Moss was happy when he did this.

On Moss's third circuit, Darragh stood up quickly as he realised he was not alone. He looked around and saw a person sleeping on the edge of the clearing. Being careful not to wake them, he walked over and stood by them to see who it was. He blinked hard, thinking that he was seeing things. "MAM!" called out. He couldn't believe his eyes. "Mammy," he said again, walking closer. He smiled broadly and kneeled down beside her. His side felt sore, but he didn't care. He stroked her cool arm and ran his fingers through her beautiful, curly blonde hair. He had never felt so happy. He lay across her, hugging her, desperately wanting her to hug him back. He breathed her in, revelling in her sweet smell of flowers and the smell of burnt toast which was odd. It felt good to be with his Mam again. "Good boy," he whispered, hugging her tighter, and he tried to pull one of her arms around him. "Mam," he said, shutting his eyes and stroking her hair again. "Good boy."

***

The taxi bounced down the uneven track that led away from the crime scene. Tired from all the talking they had done with the police, Seth lay his head back against the headrest and looked up at the sky. The rain clouds cleared, and the pink moon looked even bigger than before. The police had kept them talking for ages but answering all their questions had spared them a trip down to the police station. It was nearly two o'clock in the morning, and all he wanted to do was get home to his wife. The taxi driver was chatting away merrily with Sinead and Granny. They had avoided talking to him, too tired to chat. Seth blinked, trying to keep his eyes open and was then cross with himself for nearly falling asleep.

"So what were you all doing out here in the middle of the night?" the taxi driver asked Seth, waking him from his dreams.

"We were just visiting friends," Seth replied lazily.

"I have never been up here before. Are there more houses here?"

"A few, I guess. This is the first time we have been up here too."

"What were the police cars doing at your friend's house? It looked pretty serious. Do you know what was going on?"

"No," Seth lied. "A burglary, perhaps."

311

"Now, here's the thing," the jovial taxi driver continued. "People are leaving their houses unlocked and don't think about the consequences. They need their heads examined. So you said that we are going to Waterfall West. You do know it was burnt to the ground."

"It is a ruin now, we live further up the drive, past the stables in the Old Barn."

"I don't think I can take you past the house. I will have to drop you off at the bottom of the drive."

"Why's that?" Sinead asked angrily.

"Because that place is cursed, and I have heard stories."

"You are being ridiculous," Sinead said, huffing.

"Well, I am sorry if I have offended you, but I am not willing to chance it. I have been warned to keep away from there, and that is what I will do. Especially on a night like this. Do you see that pink moon up there? My old Mam said I should not be out driving under a moon like that."

"Why? Do you turn into a werewolf, then?" Sinead asked sarcastically.

"Your Mam was right," Granny announced. "Some full moons bring dark spirits out from the shadows, and the weak can be... well, influenced."

"I thought you said dark spirits would be distracted, and we would have a chance to find Darragh."

"I did, and they showed us, didn't they. The night is still young, Seth. You must have faith."

"Is Darragh that boy that went missing last year?" the taxi driver asked.

"Yes, he is my son," Seth hadn't meant to say that. *Christ, now everyone in Cork will know where I live.*

312

"Oh, I am sorry to hear that. I lost a son to cancer. I am sorry for your loss."

"He is not dead yet. We will find him." Seth knew he was being insensitive, but he couldn't bear to talk about him any longer.

As they approached Waterfall West, Seth watched the woods go by and started to feel for his wallet to pay the driver.

The driver tutted as he swerved around a car. "It's a good job I have got my wits about me. Somebody has parked their car and left the door open. Some people have no sense."

Seth saw the car and then gasped as he realised it was his. "Oh my God! Stop the car. It's my car. For Christ's sake, stop the car!"

The taxi cab driver slammed on his brakes and pulled over. Seth flung the door open and ran back to his car. He peered inside it, looking for Jules and then noticed the keys were still in the ignition. "JULES? JULES?" he called, looking around him.

Sinead joined him and he threw his arms into the air in frustration. "Sinead, she's not here. Do you think she has been taken again?"

"No, there has to be a reasonable explanation."

Seth got his phone out.

"Are you trying to ring her?"

"No, I am ringing the police. Something has happened to her. I just know it has." His phone was low on charge, and the screen dimmed. "I can't see to call," he said, looking up at Sinead. A shadowy figure caught his eye. For a moment, he saw Gemma standing opposite the taxi back down the road, and he frowned, not wanting to believe what he had seen. Last time he had seen Gemma, it had been in the alley next to the butcher shop. *Last time she warned me about Lucy. Perhaps she is warning me about*

Jules. He had only seen Gemma for a moment, but the vision had been clear enough for him to see her pointing into the woodland.

"What's the matter, Seth? You have gone white," Sinead asked, looking towards the spot where he had seen Gemma. "Have you seen a ghost?"

"I don't like to call it that, but yes, something is telling me to look in the woods over there. If I don't look, then I won't forgive myself," he said, taking the keys out of the ignition and shutting the car door.

"Do you want me to call the police?" Sinead asked.

"Let's go and look, and then, if we don't find her, we will ring them."

As they approached the spot where Seth had seen Gemma, Granny came across to them, and they watched the taxi drive off. "I sent him on his way, he was beginning to annoy me," Granny said with her arms folded.

"But I haven't paid the man yet," Seth said, puzzled.

"He has lost his nerve. I dare say he will send us a bill."

"JULES?" Seth called.

"Do you think she is still here?" Granny asked.

"Perhaps the car broke down, and Jules has walked home," Sinead suggested.

"She would have taken the keys and shut the door. She's not answering...." Seth stopped near the place where he had seen Gemma standing. Something was glowing yellow in the grass, and curious to see what it was, he bent down and pulled out a registration plate.

"Shit, that's from the car we saw earlier!" Sinead exclaimed.

"How come it is here? Why..." He saw skid marks in the grass, and then fearing the worst, he slid down the bank into the woodland and called up to the others, "I found the car. The car Darragh was in and... It's a burnt-out shell. NOOOO!"

Seth could see bodies lying motionless around the car. His heart was pounding with anxiety as he ran towards the smaller of the bodies, and he cried out when he realised that he had found Jules. She was so still, lying flat on her back with her arms and legs wide open. *She looks like she is making leaf angels.* He couldn't get to her soon enough and fell to his knees, knowing something was terribly wrong with her. Her clothes were scorched, and the skin on her face was red and raw, yet her hair was perfect. He held her face; it was cold at the side, but the scorched area was hot. Encouraged by this, he felt her neck for a pulse but was unsure where he was supposed to press. He held her wrist and then breathed a sigh of relief. He could feel her pulse. Crying, he hugged her and stroked her hand. He wanted to cradle her but knew he would hurt her more if anything was broken. "My wee darling, talk to me. Wake up and talk to me. Please, Jules."

"I'll call an ambulance and the police. Don't move her," Sinead said, taking out her phone. "Granny has found Mary over there. Seth, she is dead."

Granny knelt down on the other side of Jules and looked for something in her bag. "This is not meant to be."

"Where's Darragh? For the love of God, I hope he is not in the car."

"No, he's not in there. Sinead looked. He is still alive, I am sure," Granny said in a shaky voice.

"I hope you are right. I don't know how much more bad luck I can take." Seth looked up at Granny and realised how tired she was. She looked pale in the moonlight.

"When the ambulance comes, you must go home to bed. You need to rest, Granny."

"There is plenty of time for rest tomorrow. Tonight there is work to be done."

"You seriously don't think we will find Darragh tonight, do you?"

"Seth, you must have faith." She pulled out a small bottle from her bag, unscrewed the lid and sniffed the contents.

"Better than coffee any day." She held the bottle under Jules' nose and moved the tiny bottle about so she could breathe in the scent. Jules sat up and gasped. Seth's mouth fell open in amazement.

"WHERE'S DARRAGH?" Jules demanded. She looked from Granny to Seth. "Where is he? He was here just a minute ago."

Seth tried to stay calm. He was concerned that Jules might have a concussion. "Lie down, Jules, you might be hurt. You have been in a car crash, and well, Darragh isn't here."

Jules frowned. "I haven't been in a crash. The car exploded a minute ago, and then he was here. Darragh was here! I wanted to hold him so badly, but I couldn't move."

"You must have hit your head. Stay calm, Jules and lie down," Seth said, holding her.

"Help me up, Seth. He is here, I tell you."

Seth shook his head. "Sinead has called an ambulance for you."

"No, there is no time. He is here somewhere. We just need to look. Help me up and help me search for him."

Reluctantly, Seth pulled her up and was ready to catch her. She wasn't in pain, and he wasn't sure why she had been unconscious.

DARRAGH

"Seriously, we have no time to lose, and we need to start searching for him," she said, pulling out her phone from her coat pocket. The torch was still on. "He can't have gone far."

"Lucy agrees," Granny said, getting herself up off the floor.

She smiled. "See, I told you." Jules felt her face. "Oh my, my face is on fire."

"So why didn't he stay here?" Seth asked.

"I don't know, Seth. He is just a toddler. Seth, he speaks. I heard his voice. He called me Mammy. DARRAGH?" she called, looking around her. "DARRAGH, Mammy is here."

Sinead came over to them. "The ambulance will be here in a moment, and the police too. Oh, thank God, you are ok. Why are you calling for Darragh? Was he here?"

"Jules seems to think so, and Lucy too."

"He is nearby, Seth. I promise he is. DARRAGH?" she called again. "Are you coming with me?"

"I can't go yet. Mary is lying dead over there."

"No, she can't be. I pulled her out of the car. She was alive then."

"She didn't make it," Sinead said sadly.

"Oh, Seth. It is all my fault. I followed her back from Cork. I saw Darragh in the car. I scared her, and she drove too fast and went off the road. Please don't say she is dead. I was so stupid. I could have killed Darragh too."

Sinead shook her head. "You did nothing wrong. I saw him in that car, too, and you did what any desperate mother would do. Jules, there is something you should know. I don't know how to say this. Darragh has had one of his kidneys removed. Mary's brother transplanted it into Lia."

317

"NO! My poor Darragh. What a bastard. Why isn't Darragh in the hospital then?"

"Stephan did the operation at home," Granny tutted.

"That is crazy. We need to find him now and get him seen to. That is not right. Oh, my poor baby. Oh, Seth, Juliet is with Jess. I haven't fed her for hours. She has probably had the milk I left her. There is a bottle in the fridge at home. Granny, will you give that bottle to her? You were right. My milk has been making her sick. I have to look for Darragh. We all need to. He might wander onto the road. Or he might have collapsed."

"I will sort her out, she will be fine with Granny, and she might tell me a little more too."

"The police will be here in a few moments, and then they will organise a proper search," Seth said, unsure what to do for the best. "We need help. The light from our phones or the pink moonlight is not enough. If they bring a dog too, then it will be better."

"Is Mary really dead? I promise I did try to save her."

"I know you did."

"We are going to find Darragh tonight. Aren't we, Granny?"

Granny was frowning, and she was looking behind them. "We have company."

Seth followed her gaze, and he sighed. "We do not need this! Not tonight. What is he doing here? How did he know we were here?"

With an angry look on his face, they watched as Jon walked towards them until he realised that there was a body lying next to the burnt-out car. He gave them a pained look and then ran towards Mary's body.

DARRAGH

"Sinead, here are the car keys," he said, passing them to her. "Would you get Juliet's milk and take Granny home. I have no doubt that Jess will be awake, and you will have to deal with a wild baby. I have something I need to do."

Sinead took the keys. "Ok, but promise me that you won't do anything you regret. Killing Jon Hearn will not help matters," she said sternly. "I don't want to be visiting my best friend in prison."

"Please, Seth, be sensible," Jules begged. "Parvel should have arrested him for murdering Lucy."

"Is that so? I just want to talk to him."

Jules watched Seth head over to Jon, and she was feeling anxious. She didn't want to watch what was going to happen. She turned herself so she couldn't see them and noticed that there was a path leading away from the clearing. She was sure that this was the route that Darragh must have taken. Jules could hear Jon wailing with grief and knew she had to step in if Seth lost it. Jon was cradling Mary on the floor, and he appeared to be crying. *Surely Seth won't hit a grieving man?*

She watched Sinead help Granny up the slope that led to the road and knew that every minute that passed was a minute too long. She couldn't wait any longer and had to search for Darragh. She feared walking into the woods alone and hoped the pink moonlight would protect her from those who wanted to harm her. She just had to find him.

Chapter Forty-two

Darragh hadn't wanted to leave his Mam, but she was asleep, and Moss needed to go for a run. He shivered as he walked, missing the warmth of his mother's body. His shivers turned into one large shiver that continued no matter how he tried to stop it. His body was shaking all over. He laughed at himself. He didn't know why he was shaking so much.

The path leading away from his Mam glistened in the moonlight, and he was curious to see where it led. Moss wanted to go that way, too, so he held his horse out so he would show him where to go. The trees on either side of the path were thinly spaced, and he could see for a long way. He was pleased that there was nothing scary to see.

The path came to a fork, and Moss decided to go to the left. As Darragh walked, he started to feel thirsty and tired. He hoped he would find a carton of apple juice along the way. Darragh saw a log on the side of the path and ran over to it to sit down for a few moments while Moss rested. He wished he hadn't run because his side was really hurting now, and he wondered why this was.

Moss liked being on the log, and he trotted along it, happy to be playing with him. When the pain in his side stopped aching, Darragh thought of his Mam and wondered where she was. The path ahead looked dark, and he decided to return the way he came. He was desperately thirsty now, and the thought of apple juice waiting for him ahead spurred him on. Moss thought he should be brave and take the dark path ahead because there would surely be apple juice that way.

After a few minutes of walking and not finding any apple juice, he turned back and told Moss off for telling him to go this way. Darragh looked at his hands and realised that he had left Moss behind on the log. He was feeling really tired, and his body was still shaking. Darragh looked down at his shirt and saw a dark mark on it, right where he had the pain. The stain was getting larger as he watched.

"CAW, CAW…"

Darragh stopped walking, and his eyes widened with fear as he recognised the call of the bird that had attacked him earlier. He spun around, searching for it. The crow swooped down in front of him out of nowhere and narrowly missed his head. "BAD CROW!" he yelled. The crow landed on the path in front of him, barring his way to his Mam and Moss. Darragh ran towards the crow trying to scare it away. The crow remained stationary and tilted its head to one side. Darragh stopped a few steps away from the bird and he was afraid. "NO!" Darragh yelled. "BAD CROW!"

The crow cawed again and flew up in the air. Its wings flapped near his face, so Darragh started to run. He didn't want the bird anywhere near him. He wanted to run back the way he came and not into the dark wood ahead, but he had no choice. The crow was behind him, and somehow Darragh was managing to keep ahead of the scary bird that wanted to hurt him. His side hurt him, but he did not dare to stop in case he was scratched again. He looked over his shoulder at the crow to see if the bird was following and then breathed a sigh of relief. The bad crow had gone.

Darragh started to cry. There was liquid coming out of his side and dribbling down his body. He put his hand on the stain to stop the liquid from coming out of him. The way back was clear; he so desperately wanted to go back but was afraid. Afraid that the bad crow was hiding. Darragh looked around him and listened to every sound. Slowly, he started to walk deeper into the woods and then gasped as a crow twice the size of the one he had seen earlier swooped down onto the path in front of him. He stayed still, hoping that the monster crow had not seen him. His heart was beating hard with fear. He watched the crow's movements and was ready to run but wasn't sure if he could outrun a crow that seemed to be getting bigger every second.

Through his tears, Darragh saw the crow's body begin to change shape. The bird's body was stretching upwards and was taking on a human-like form. Darragh was glad that the crow had almost gone. He was less afraid now and watched with fascination as the man with a crow's face became a face he recognised. "DA!" he exclaimed, walking forward to get a better look. "DA!" He had found his Mam, and now his Da was there too, smiling at him. His Da's hair was as white as snow, and his face older than he remembered. He couldn't help but stare. Beckoning him to come over to him, his Da held out his arms, and Darragh smiled back, eager to be held.

As Darragh got closer to his Da, he turned and started to walk down the track leaving Darragh behind. Darragh followed. Now and again his Da beckoned to him and smiled at him just when he was about to cry again. After a few minutes of walking, his Da pointed towards something off the path and turned towards him, urging him to follow him down a slope. Curious to see where he was taking him, Darragh followed, and after a short steep walk down a hill, he saw a large pool of water ahead. Darragh could see the pink moon reflecting in the water. He looked up at the moon and wondered how the moon had become two. His Da was standing on the water's edge, and Darragh joined him and stood by his side. He could see his Da's hand now; it was smooth and white, and he longed to hold it and feel his father's love again. Darragh held up his hand, but his Da did not see him. He wondered if he had done something wrong.

The water in the pond caught his attention and was so still and such a beautiful pink colour that Darragh could not resist touching it. He looked up at his Da to see if he was allowed to touch the water and saw him nod. He wondered why his Da hadn't spoken to him and longed to hear his voice.

The banks of the pond were steep, and the water was difficult to reach. Darragh got close to the edge. His bare feet slipped a little in the mud, still wet from the rain. Again, Darragh held up his hand for help. He longed to touch the water but couldn't do it alone. Darragh looked back to see why his Da wasn't helping him. His Da had gone, and this saddened him because he so wanted to feel his warm hand on his. "DA?" he called. The night was so quiet and the pond so inviting, but he knew he wouldn't be able to play in the water without help. "MAM," he called, hoping she would come to his aid.

"AGHH…" Darragh screamed as the bad crow slammed into his back and pushed him forward. Losing his balance, he slid down the bank into the water and screamed again as the cold water hit his body. Instinctively, Darragh held his breath as his head went under, and he moved his arms and legs frantically to try and make himself go back up. His head came up, and he breathed in a little pond water. Frightened and confused, he coughed, trying to get the cold pink water out of his mouth. "DA!" he cried out, spluttering. His Da had gone from the edge of the bank. Darragh grabbed hold of a branch hanging over the water and clung to this and cried. He didn't like being in the pink icy water, and he didn't like being alone.

***

"Have you come here to gloat?" Jon asked as Mary was carried up the slope by stretcher to a waiting ambulance.

"No," Seth replied. "I am sorry for your loss. How did you know she was here?"

"She rang me," he replied, holding up her phone. "Her last words were that she loved me and I should be a good father to all my children. I hoped she might still be alive when I got here. What do you care? You will return to your rich and famous life, and I will have to pick up the pieces and do the right thing. I was going to marry Mary until she ran off with my money and my daughter."

"You say that, but you were married to Jess. Did you know that Lia has gone to hospital? I don't think the operation went all that well. What were you thinking of?"

"It's got nothing to do with me. Mary told me earlier that she had found someone to do the transplant and that Lia was being operated on. She should have let me do it. I was nearly ready. She begged me to forgive her."

"Nothing to do with it. My foot! For fuck's sake! You are a butcher. Why does everyone think it is ok to carry out operations themselves? Why didn't you ask the family if you needed a donor that bad? The Hearn family is big enough. I am sure there would have been a match. Now my poor boy is probably bleeding to death in the woods out there. Where the Hell are the police?"

"You called the police?"

"Of course, I did. Are you in cloud cuckoo land?"

DARRAGH

"You shouldn't have done that."

"You shouldn't have snatched my son or put Lucy in a wheelie bin."

"Why would I do that? That was all Mary's doing."

"My ass it is. You don't expect me to believe that, do you? She's not here to defend herself. You are a sick bastard. I don't know why you weren't arrested weeks ago."

Jon smirked. "They have nothing on me. I know they want to talk to me, but I gave them the slip earlier. Thanks to you, I will have to lay low for a while."

"Why, thanks to me? I am not a pile of murderous shite. You should have been left to die in the woods like all the other Hearn bastards."

Jon's eyes narrowed, and he pushed Seth hard in the chest. "Don't you ever call me a bastard again, or I will hurt you so bad, you will wish you were never born. Taking Darragh from you was not enough. I will not be happy until I see you burn in Hell," he spat, bringing his face close.

Seth was furious, and he could feel his blood boiling. He grabbed hold of Jon's shirt and pushed him back. Jon laughed and then charged towards Seth, his shoulder hitting him square in the chest. Seth fell to the floor bringing Jon with him. They wrestled and furiously punched each other, wishing each other to die. Glass from the car's windows stuck in their backs as they rolled near the smouldering wreck. Seth saw Jon grab a long thin shard of glass, and he couldn't stop him hammering it into his arm. Seth yelled out in pain and raised his fist, ready to punch Jon hard. Just one more punch would permanently wipe the smile off this sick bastard's face. The sound of sirens stopped Jon for a moment and seizing his opportunity, Seth roared, punched Jon hard in the jaw, and saw his eyes roll.

Seth straddled and grabbed him by the throat; he knew the next punch could kill his twin. He owed Lucy this. An unwanted memory taunted him. He remembered fighting with his Dad to the death. This time he had a choice. Feeling frustrated, he yelled out, wanting to kill Jon but he wasn't able to carry out the deed. He wasn't a murderer. He heard men shouting and looked up. A group of armed police were sliding down the bank, running towards them. Then he saw Parvel and his heart sank. If he killed Jon, then Parvel would not hesitate to arrest him. Jules and Sinead would never forgive him. "Oh, for the love of God! Not him. That is all I need now." Feeling relieved that he hadn't delivered a fatal blow, Seth jumped up and waved to the police officers, asking them to come over to him.

Jon got onto his knees and, drawing breath, looked back at the men charging towards him. With terror in his eyes, he jumped up and started to run. Smiling and with a certain amount of satisfaction, Seth watched Jon flee for his life. The police tore after his brother, and he knew it would only be minutes before they caught up with him.

As Seth waited for Parvel to reach him, he looked over towards Jules but he couldn't see her. "Oh crap! Where is she?" *I hope she isn't mad at me for fighting with Jon. Oh no, she has gone to look for Darragh. I know she has. She needs to rest. There is no point looking for him without help.*

Parvel ran up to him, and he was breathless from running. It surprised Seth that he was still wearing a mask when he clearly needed more air to breathe. He was gasping for breath. "For God's sake, man! Take off the mask. You can't breathe."

"I'd rather not. Not until Covid is gone," he gasped, pulling at the mask to give him more air.

"Jules says that you are arresting him for murdering Lucy."

"She shouldn't have told you that. Just suspicion of murder. You are innocent until you are found guilty."

"Are you here to help us find Darragh?" Seth asked, suddenly realising that Parvel knew nothing about the case. "No, I'm here just to arrest Jon Hearn. I told your wife that your son's disappearance is not my case."

"So, do I wait for police assistance then?"

"No. There is no point. I cancelled the call. You are lucky I didn't arrest you for wasting police time."

Seth was shocked and angry. "You are joking! My boy was here. He is out there in the woods alone and frightened. What do you mean by wasting police time? That sick bastard you are chasing stole him for his kidney."

"It is not my problem. I will be frank with you." Parvel's breathing was more even now. "It is very unlikely that you will ever see your son again. It has been over a year now. If missing children are not found in the first few weeks, the odds of them being alive is slim."

"I don't believe I am hearing this. Jules saw him not half an hour ago."

"So why didn't she hold on to him?"

"She was unconscious, but she swears he was here."

"There you go, my point exactly. Women who lose their children become delusional. I saw her earlier nearly getting herself killed running after Mary Price's car. Do you not think it is a strange coincidence that your wife is at a crime scene and Mary is dead. I will need to speak to her later."

"No, you have got this all wrong. Jules tried to save Mary. She pulled her out of a burning car to safety. Darragh was in the back of the car, but the car exploded, and my poor sweet girl was knocked unconscious from the blast. She has gone to look for Darragh in the woods alone and that is where I am going now. To look for my son, who is now missing a kidney thanks to Mary's sick brother. If you think I am imagining that, you can go and fuck yourself."

Seth marched towards the path where he had last seen Jules. "Parvel," Seth called back. "Lucy was right. You are a complete wanker!"

***

Tom Stone sat on Jasper's bed with his head in his hands. The cell floor was bathed in pink moonlight and taunted him. Seeing the moon sickened him and reminded him that morning was approaching and the Gemma Day trial would begin. Jasper was standing by the cell window, looking up at the moon.

"It's beautiful, don't you think? There's not a cloud to be seen, and... What is wrong with you? I thought you were going to bed," Jasper asked.

"I am a broken man. I just know that there will be a lot of lies at court tomorrow, and they will throw the book at me. It's not fair. The innocent always get hit the hardest."

"But you are not innocent. You like hurting young women."

"Are you deranged? Of course, I don't like hurting them. I can't help if they are weak and don't know how to handle Mr Steel. I can't spend my life alone in prison," he cried, looking up at Jasper for reassurance. His face was washed in the moonlight, and for a moment, Tom saw a beautiful young woman standing there. There was a connection between him and Jasper that was far deeper than he had realised. "You dream of being outside in the world again. You know I will always be your friend and be there for you."

Jasper looked up at the moon. "No one has ever been friends with me. You do not want to be my friend. My mother always said that I was a stray and unlikeable. The moon is my only companion."

"I really do want to be friends with you. I know I am only a man, but I think you are a beautiful soul. If I go to prison, I pray we will find ourselves as cell mates again. I know I drive you mad, but I can change," he lied.

"I don't expect that will happen. My trial is coming up in a couple of weeks, and I am guilty... Guilty of many things. The jury will not be so kind to me. I am not innocent."

Sensing that Jasper was opening up to him, Tom got up and joined him by the window. He didn't seem to mind. "Do you mind if I hug you?" Tom asked gently. "Just a quick hug. I am so afraid of tomorrow."

Jasper nodded, so Tom put his arms out, hoping Jasper would reciprocate. Jasper looked at him warily. "I don't know how to hug."

"Just hug me like you hug your mother. You can pretend I am your mother."

Jasper looked alarmed. "She used to hug me, but then she always wanted me to fuck her afterwards."

Tom stepped back in horror. "You didn't, did you?"

"I had no choice. She said she would tell the police about me."

"What was there to tell?"

"Plenty, but then after a while, she stopped asking."

"That is good. It is not right to fuck your mother."

"I missed doing it, so I looked for others."

"Men or women?"

"Both. I am not gay, though. I just like fucking. I eat little boys for tea."

"So why won't you help me with Mr Steel. You know he wants you badly. I am no little boy. You have seen him many times."

"I just don't want to hurt you."

Tom could feel himself hardening, noticing that Jasper was erect too. If Mr Steel was going to see any action, it would be now. All he needed was a quick blow job, and then he could sleep. Tom reached out and grabbed hold of Jasper, and although it sickened him to do so, he began to pleasure him. Jasper didn't resist. He groaned in ecstasy and came in minutes. Disgusted, Tom wiped his hand on Jasper's trousers and looked into his eyes. "I need you to give Mr Steel some love. He wants to feel your sweet mouth." Jasper was crying, but he guessed that this was because of the sexual tension between them. Still crying, Jasper got on his knees and took Mr Steel in his mouth. Tom smiled and felt electricity running through his body. Mr Steel loved being in Jasper's wet mouth, and Tom tried to remember what it was like to be inside the women he had been with. One by one, young girls' faces flashed before his eyes as Jasper worked his magic on Mr Steel. Tom screamed out, knowing that he was about to explode. He held the face of his most treasured fuck in his mind - Julia, his Julia. He could hold back no longer. Mr Steel was screaming out in sexual agony...

A sickening crunch made his blood run cold, and then he felt a searing pain so bad surge through his body that he thought he might faint as Mr Steel, his pride and joy, was ripped savagely away from his body. Tom fell onto his knees and screamed like a baby, over and over, as the enormity of what had just happened hit him. Mr Steel lay on the floor, between him and Jasper, in a pool of blood.

"WHAT HAVE YOU DONE?" Tom screamed, trying to hold back the blood that was coming from a gaping wound between his legs. "What have you done?" he sobbed.

Chapter Forty-three

Jules ran up the moonlit path looking out for Darragh. She called out his name and didn't need her torch to find her way. The moon cast a light that was nearly as good as daylight. She stopped when she saw a fallen tree or a large bush to see if Darragh had wandered off the path to investigate. When she reached a fork in the path, she had taken the right turn but had returned because there was a fallen tree blocking the way. She wondered if Darragh might have climbed over the tree, but it was huge and not easy for a toddler to tackle.

As she ran back, she searched the path for clues. She didn't know what she was looking for. The path was muddy, but she couldn't see any footprints. *He hasn't come this way.* When she reached the fork again, she saw Seth running towards her. She had never been so glad to see him. Seth hugged Jules, relieved that he had found her safe and well. "You shouldn't have gone off on your own. We should have waited for help."

"I couldn't wait. Darragh is here somewhere. Are the police coming to help us search?"

"No, that bastard Parvel put pay to that. They should have Jon in custody now, so that is one less thing to worry about. Have you been up this path?" he asked, pointing to the path on the left.

"Not yet. I should have gone up that way first. I was trying to think which path he would take. It couldn't be the one I just came from. It is completely blocked by a tree."

"Jules, you need to slow down. You are sweating and should be in the hospital."

"I am fine. I am really cross that the police aren't here. What is wrong with Parvel? Does he think we are making the whole thing up?"

"Parvel is an eejit. We will find Darragh ourselves." He didn't have the heart to tell her what he had said about them finding Darragh alive.

Together they walked hand in hand, checking every inch of the path or shrubbery for signs of their son.

"If you feel faint or strange, then let me know, and I will carry you. I nearly lost you to sepsis once. I am not going to let that happen again."

"I am fine, Seth, don't fuss. I just want to find him." A small dark object sitting on a log ahead caught her eye. "Do you see that log ahead? I think there is something sitting on it. A rat, perhaps."

"I don't think it is a rat," Seth replied, trying his best to work out what they were seeing. "It would have run away by now."

"No, it's not. I think I know what it is," Jules called as she ran towards the log. Seth followed.

As they got closer, they saw a small black horse standing on the log.

"What is this doing here?" Seth asked, picking up the horse to look at it.

"It's Darragh's. I found it near the car earlier."

"How did it get here then?"

"Seth, you can be such an eejit sometimes. Don't you see? Darragh brought it here. We are so close. DARRAGH?" she called. A crow cawed from a tree nearby.

"You are waking the crows up. I think the crow agrees and is going to help us to find him."

The crow started to swoop over their heads, cawing loudly and then swooped down and tried to steal the horse from Seth's hand. "Get away with yourself. This is not for you to take," Seth yelled. The crow dive-bombed him and scratched his ear as it passed him. "Get off, you bastard!"

"SETH!" Jules screamed as the crow landed on her head, and she felt its sharp beak peck her eyelid. *It wants my eye.* "NO!" She grabbed hold of its wing, pulled it off her head, and threw the bird onto the floor.

Seth ran over to her. "Are you ok?"

Jules nodded and backed away from the crow now walking towards her.

"This is not right. We are dealing with darkness. Run, Jules, before it comes back for us."

They started to run, and as the crow attacked them, they swiped it away with their arms. Seth saw a branch, picked it up, pulled Jules behind him, and was ready for the next attack. The crow came for them again, and this time Seth hit the crow full-on with the branch and hoped he had broken its neck. The crow lay on its side and then started to change shape. Seth blinked, thinking that he was seeing things. "RUN! This is no ordinary crow."

They started to run again and didn't look back.

"It's him, isn't it? It's your Dad again. He came after me earlier. We don't need to run. The dead can't hurt us. If we run, we might miss something."

"I am not so sure about that. The crow is real enough, and we are both bleeding."

"Just surface wounds. We need to concentrate. I think your Dad was trying to stop us from coming this way. We might have missed Darragh when we were running. Do you think a two-year-old would walk this far? It is the middle of the night. Do you think Darragh stopped to sleep? Where do you think he was going?"

"Perhaps he was trying to find his way home. If he kept walking this way, he would finally meet up with the Waterfall West Estate just by the traveller site."

"Oh my! You don't think he is back at home looking for us, do you?"

"No, he might have made it to the campsite."

"I'll ring Jess. I'll ask her to look out for him."

"Ring in a bit. I think my Dad wants us to keep walking. I think we should go back. If he goes for us again, then that is where we need to look for Darragh."

Feeling frightened of what lay ahead, Jules and Seth started to walk back the way they had come.

"When we find Darragh, do you think he will remember me?" Seth asked. "A child will always know who his mother is, but I am not so sure about the father. Do you think he will be afraid of me?"

"No, Seth. I don't know why you would think that. Of course, he will know you," Jules said, inspecting a bush along the path for any signs of Darragh.

"I hope so. So, spirits, if you can hear me, you need to show us where our boy is. This is all I ask. I will never ask you for anything again. Send me a sign."

"You are sounding like Granny now. If anyone is going to find him then it will be you and me."

"Maybe, but it wouldn't hurt to have a little help along the way, now, would it?"

335

"No, but I think I have had enough of spirits for one night. We have to stay positive," she said, looking around for the crow. A firefly ahead of them caught her attention. It was flying by the tree where Seth had picked up the branch. "Look, fireflies." The solitary firefly was joined by others, and she couldn't keep her eyes off them. "I've never seen fireflies before."

"No, nor have I. Perhaps they are a sign."

They walked back to the tree and saw the fireflies move into the woodland behind. "Do you think they want us to follow?"

"We will ask the tree."

"Seth, don't be crazy. Trees don't talk."

"Just humour me."

Feeling irritated by Seth's childish behaviour, Jules watched as he put his arms around the tree trunk. He put his ear against the bark and listened. After a minute had passed, he pulled away and shook his head. "The tree is sleeping," he said, leaning back against it. "I could hear it snoring."

Jules was getting angry. "Seth! This is no time to be funny."

"Maybe it will wake up and talk if you are here too."

"Seriously! I think we should keep walking and look for Darragh near the campsite. I will ring Jess."

Seth sighed, put his hands back on the trunk behind him, and shut his eyes. Willing the tree to help him. A white light in his eyes made him gasp.

"Seth, what's the matter? Is the crow coming back?" she asked, looking behind her and praying they would not be attacked.

As clear as day, Seth could see hundreds of years pass by in the woodland. He saw huntsmen out in the woods and deer running by the tree. He willed the deer to outrun the huntsmen. Fearing for their lives, the deer ran down the hill and stopped by a pond. For a second, Seth thought they might fall into the water. The frightened animals looked up and then seeing that they were still being followed and darted off, narrowly missing a spear. The pond the tree was showing him looked familiar. The shape and plants around it reminded him of the silent pool he and his siblings had visited on Farm End.

"Well, here's a thing. The tree is showing me a pond."

"Not the Silent Pool, for Christ's sake!"

"Almost, but not the same. A kindred pond. I think Darragh is there."

Jules was starting to worry. "Our baby can't be in the Silent Pool. That's in Findon in England."

Seth opened his eyes and stepped away from the tree. "It's not the same pond, but a deep pool nonetheless. Do you have enough power on your phone or a signal to bring up maps? We need to find a pond in this woodland, and that is where we will find Darragh."

***

Darragh was feeling cold and sleepy. His hands were aching, holding onto the branch, and he couldn't stop shaking. He had let go once, but then his head had gone under the water, and he had coughed the water out as his hands had scrambled to find the branch. Determined not to let go of the bough again, he had to stop his eyes from closing by singing to himself. He didn't know the words to Rockabye, but he knew the tune. When he stopped humming, his eyes shut, his hands loosened, and he could feel himself sinking. Each time he woke himself up by calling out Moss's name. He wished Moss was with him and wondered where he had left his friend.

He wanted to get out of the horrid pink water and climb onto the bank, and he looked around him for a way out. All he could see was a steep bank around him. Feeling disillusioned, he started to hum again, hoping that someone would come and help him. As he hummed, he saw small golden, sparkling lights coming towards him. Mesmerised by this spectacle, he watched the lights fly up and down the bank until finally they flew above his head. He smiled and wanted so much to touch them. The little lights danced around him, and he laughed out loud. They started to sing his song in soft little voices that sounded so much like his Mam and Da singing, and they comforted him, giving him hope. He watched them fly higher and higher and then disappear over the lip of the pond.

The woodland became silent again, and he called out Moss's name, hoping he would appear. He was scared to call out his Da's name in case the bad crow man came back. He realised now that although the crow man looked like his Da, it wasn't him at all.

Working his way along the branch, he pulled himself closer to the bank to see if he could follow the fireflies. The sound of footsteps made him stop still, and he watched and waited to see who was coming to the pond. He hoped it wasn't the crow man. Darragh was surprised to see a huge brown animal appear. It was too small to be a horse. The creature hadn't seen him, and he watched its front feet slip a little in the mud as it stretched its long neck down so it could drink from the pond.

Darragh was afraid. "BAD BOY!" he called out. The deer jumped back in fright and disappeared. Darragh started to cry. He was sorry that he had startled the animal and wished it would return. He wanted the dancing lights to come back too. He called out for help, but his cries were lost in the wilderness.

DARRAGH

On the tree above, Jethro in crow form, waited patiently for another Hearn bastard to die. It wouldn't be long before Darragh joined the others.

Chapter Forty-four

"PLEASE, HELP ME. I AM BLEEDING TO DEATH!" Tom cried out, pounding on the cell door and holding a blood-soaked blanket between his legs to try and stop the bleeding. Jasper was sitting in the corner, rocking and talking to himself. Fearing for his life, Tom kept beating on the door, desperate to be saved. He was growing weaker by the minute.

"PLEASE, HELP ME!" He called out to the guards. "I HAVE BEEN ATTACKED."

"I told you I would hurt you."

"What are you? Some kind of monster?"

"You promised me that you would always be there for me. It's not kind to call someone a monster."

"HELP ME! FOR GOD'S SAKE, HELP ME! I AM GOING TO DIE. THIS IS AN EMERGENCY."

"They won't come. They never do," Jasper whispered and started to talk to himself again. "I am not a monster. I am not a monster. I am sorry, mother. I am not a monster...."

In a frenzy, Tom beat the door with both fists and yelled out for help. Each time his cries became fainter and fainter. Then too weak to stand, he slid down to the floor and prayed that someone would help him. With each minute that passed, he knew that he was a minute closer to death. He was losing too much blood. The blood rushing from his body had formed a pool around him. Mr Steel had withered to the size of a finger and lay discarded in the blood next to him. Any hope that his penis could be stitched back onto his body had long gone. Tom laughed to himself as he remembered himself as a child back at Waterfall West Manor House and the local priest visiting him to give him bible lessons. He hadn't thought of Father O'Hara for years. That sick man had liked to punish him if he wasn't paying attention. The priest had been very fond of Mr Steel. He wondered if Father O'Hara would be waiting for him in Heaven.

The pink moonlight was making the ever-expanding pool of blood glisten, and he imagined himself in a boat sailing to his home in Sydney. He wondered how long it would take him to get there. A tear rolled down his cheek as he thought about Mr Steel. He was going to miss him. Tom's eyes closed and whispered as he drifted into a never-ending sleep. "I am innocent, I am innocent." He heard Jasper laugh…

***

"Seth, there is no signal here. Google maps is not connecting. I wonder if I can get through to Jess." She scrolled through her contact list but stopped. "I shouldn't call. Jess is probably asleep, and I don't want to wake Marley. Oh, look! Sinead has left a message. Thank God! Juliet has been fed and is asleep. Do you think she is asleep, or do you think Sinead is just saying that so we don't worry?"

"Juliet is asleep, I am sure of it. Perhaps she just needed to understand that we can't be with her twenty-four-seven. We should keep walking. Darragh could be right under our noses. I just know he is close."

"Wouldn't it be funny if he was sitting near the pond you were talking about and was just waiting for us?"

"I don't think it is going to be that easy. Somehow, I think my Dad has had a hand in this. Why can't he just leave us alone?"

"Because he will not rest until he is with his beloved Ann. I guess he blames you for his death too."

"Great! So we are stuck with him forever."

"Pretty much. We need to keep moving and look for a pond. Do you think we should go home, in case Darragh has made it back to the campsite? Seth, it is so frustrating knowing he is somewhere here and not knowing where to go."

Seth sighed and looked around him. A cold breeze rustled the leaves on the trees. "We shouldn't stay here. If we are going towards him, we will know because that crow will return. I know we are being watched. Dad is here and just waiting for us. Let's start walking and see what happens."

"Ok, but first, let's follow those fireflies. They've come back. Do you see, Seth?" she asked, pointing towards the sparkling lights.

"I guess it wouldn't hurt to try."

The fireflies hovered in one spot and then started to move down the slope through the woodland, and their golden fiery bodies were bright and seemed to glow more brightly as they followed them. Jules smiled, feeling their joy and warmth. Instinctively, she knew that they were helping them. She hoped Seth wouldn't think she was crazy and change his mind. He held her hand and squeezed it.

"They are taking us to him. We are going to find our boy," he whispered.

Jules smiled with relief. "He is close. So close..."

A bullet-like ball of feathers with talons hit her hard in the back of the head. Jules screamed out in pain, and she fell on her knees and screamed again as she felt sharp claws tearing into the skin on her head. She tried to pull the evil crow from her head but couldn't pull it free. "SETH…" She felt Seth's hands over hers, trying to pull the bird off her head. Her skin was tearing, and she cried out in pain as he tugged. The pain was like nothing she had felt before. She felt faint and dizzy, and then a mist began to swirl up around her. She was crying, begging Seth to stop because she was sure she was being scalped.

"You shouldn't have left me, Ann. I am here for you now. I don't like hurting you, but if that is the only way you will listen to me, then so be it."

The mist cleared, and she found herself standing by the silent pool at Farm End. The pain was not as intense now, but her scalp was on fire, and she thought she might be hallucinating.

"Jethro?"

"I am here, my love. It is so good to see you here with me."

"Look, I don't know what you are playing at, but I am not here for you, and I never was. Ann was my aunt. I am not her. Do you hear?" she yelled. Jules felt a sharp pain in her head, and she wondered if the talons had reached through to her brain. She put her hands up but couldn't feel the bird on her head.

"What witchery is this?" she roared. "If you love me, why do you stop me from finding my son and torture me?"

"The Hearn bastard is not yours. I have taken care of him for you."

Jules was fuming. Despite the pain, she was lucid enough to give him a piece of her mind. "You are delusional. I don't care who you think I am. I will never love you and I will do everything I can to save my son and live happily with Seth Hearn, the man who killed you. You have no right to interfere in our lives, and I know you cannot hurt us. You play games and tear my skin, but I will never let you win. I will never let you hurt my children, and I will never let you hurt anyone again."

She heard him laugh, and this made her more furious. She remembered him trying to rape her and seeing his evil face as he tried to drown Seth. She hated him with all her heart and soul. There must be others that despised Jethro as much as she did, and she could feel the pain and sorrow of all those that had died at his hands. Lucy was in her mind, too, and she could feel her close by, willing her to destroy him. This battle was not hers alone to fight. She felt a tingling run through her body. A feeling of peace washed over her, and then she watched in amazement as the light of souls passed rose up from the pool and the shadows around her. Jules could feel the pain in her head intensify, but she would not let Jethro win.

"I call on the spirits that share my pain to tear your evil spirit from your body and drag it down to Hell, where it belongs. I will not stand for this foolishness. Do you hear, Jethro Hearn? I have condemned you to Hell!"

Jules looked to her right and saw Lucy standing there smiling. She looked to her left, and the shadowy figure of her mother and aunt appeared. She gasped, not expecting to see her mother. Her mother and aunt's pale skin, blue eyes and golden curls were bathed in white light. Jules sensed that Ivy was there, along with the spirits of all the children Jethro had murdered. Fifteen orbs of light appeared, each one the soul of the babies he and Margaret had killed appeared and darted frantically skimming the water in the pond.

"See, you bastard? I am not alone. You are no match for those that you murdered. You are going to Hell, and you will leave my kin alone. Do you hear me? We all wish this, and we are free of you! You are condemned to burn forever more in Hell. BE

GONE WITH YOU!" she yelled, holding onto her scalp lest it be ripped off. White light exploded over the pond, and she heard him scream a blood-curdling scream so loud that she had to put her hands over her ears. *He has gone to Hell. He has gone to Hell. He cannot hurt us anymore.*

Jules fell back onto the floor, and the crow released its grip and flew away, cawing as it flew. She opened her eyes and saw Seth on his knees next to her. "He's gone, Seth. Jethro has been taken to Hell."

Seth was crying. "I heard everything. My poor wee dote, he nearly killed you."

"No, Seth, he could never hurt Darragh or us. I told you. The dead cannot hurt the living."

"But you are bleeding. I am going to carry you home."

Jules sat up. "Just give me a moment. I will be ok. Seth, I don't know what happened there, but I saw Lucy, my Mum and all the spirits he and Margaret killed. Seth, it was kind of beautiful. We all worked together, and then he was gone. I..."

"MOSS?"

"Did you hear that?" Seth asked, standing up. "Someone is calling for my horse."

"It's Darragh! It is his voice. I can't believe it. Where is he calling from?"

"DARRAGH? DARRAGH?" Seth called.

"MOSS! MOSS! MOSS!"

Seth pulled Jules onto her feet, and they listened for him to call again.

"DARRAGH, WHERE ARE YOU?" Jules called.

They heard him call out Mam and followed his voice down the hill towards him.

"Why doesn't he come running to us?" Seth whispered.

345

"It's too dark. It is better that he stays where he is, and we find him."

A cloud covering the pink moon cleared, revealing a pond with the moon's reflection within, like a broken jigsaw. Seth ran towards the pond, stood on the edge and then called out, fearing that he was in trouble. He was met with silence.

Darragh looked up at the man standing on the side of the pond, trying to work out if it was the crow man or his Da. He had heard him calling, and the voice sounded like he remembered, but he was scared. Scared that the crow man was going to hurt him.

From his watery hiding place in the darkness, Darragh watched the man and waited.

"He's here somewhere," Jules said as she joined Seth at the edge of the pond.

Darragh gasped when he saw his Mam standing there too. He knew he was looking at his parents and longed to be with them.

"MAM!...MAM!" he called. He had never felt so happy. He held his arms up to be lifted out of the pond.

"SETH! There he is. NOOO! He is going under."

Seth tore off his jacket, dived into the pond, and swam over to where they had seen Darragh. Darragh was underwater. Trying not to panic, he dived, searching furiously for his baby. The pond water was too murky to see, so he felt in the water for his body.

Jules screamed for them and would have jumped in too, but she noticed that the pool sides would be difficult to climb. She remembered seeing Seth and Jethro fighting in the water and then waiting for what seemed like an eternity for the victor to break through the water. She whispered to herself and asked the spirits to help her and Seth.

DARRAGH

Answering her prayers, Seth came up for air, but he was not holding Darragh. He dived down again. She held her breath, waiting again for him to resurface, and her patience and prayers were rewarded. Seth reappeared with Darragh in his arms. He swam over to her and passed him up to her. She took him up in her arms, and Darragh coughed water all over her. She didn't care. He was alive. She hugged him and wrapped him in Seth's jacket to try and warm him up.

Seth climbed out of the pool using the branch Darragh had been clinging to. The pool banks were not as steep as those at Farm End. Seth looked to Heaven and thanked all that was good for helping him find their son.

Darragh lay his head on his Mam's shoulder, feeling her warm body and her arms around him. He was smiling ear to ear. Being back with his parents was the best feeling in the world.

"Seth, we have our son back. The spirits were right," Jules sobbed. "I can't believe he is here in my arms. He is alive, and he feels just like I imagined. We are here, my sweet boy. Your Mam and Dad are here for you. Thank you, spirits, for helping us. Thank you!"

"We have a lot to be thankful for. I am the happiest man that ever lived." Seth looked up at the pink moon and thanked it for shining its magnificent light on them all and for helping them find Darragh.

I hope you enjoyed Darragh. If you did then please head over to Amazon here https://www.amazon.co.uk/Natasha-Murray/e/B006MHISOU click on Darragh and scroll down to find the review link. Please leave me a short review and help me to get the Waterfall Way series noticed.

You might be interested in reading Chanctonbury, a dark and twisted tale set at the Chanctonbury Ring in Findon.

Would you like the Devil to grant you your dearest wish? If you could change the past or your future – would you? Six troubled souls meet at the Chanctonbury Ring and are forced to fight their demons!

One autumn day, six people with troubled pasts meet at the Chanctonbury Ring, a circle of beech trees on top of an Iron Age hill fort on the northern edge of the South Downs. The Devil, believed to lurk within the hill, rather than offering them a bowl of soup, takes it upon himself to grant them their dearest wishes. Sadly, there are consequences for such kindness!

"I couldn't put this book down, each character is believable, and the author demonstrates her understanding of human nature and endurance. Many twists and turns in the plot present each character with new dilemmas and decisions and keep the reader guessing until the very end!"

Sarah – after being held hostage in Afghanistan, is traumatised and finding it difficult to cope with daily life.
Evie has for sixty years carried the ashes of her lover with her.
Tom - a widower, has had to live with his guilty conscience for far too long.

Michael - an ex-soldier on the run, has not been well and is sure his mind is playing the cruellest of tricks on him.

Amy - a shell of what she was- finally summoned the courage to stand up to her manipulative boyfriend, Ted.

Nabeel - after fleeing from Afghanistan, meets Sarah again and believes she owes him her life.

Natasha Murray is an award-winning West Sussex author. She is a diverse writer and produces books for all ages. During the She says, "I enjoy writing, and it is both a pleasure and a compulsion. There is nothing better in life than creating parallel universes."

Get your copy of Chanctonbury here getbook.at/Chanctonbury

- For more information about Natasha and her books, then please visit her website at https://cutt.ly/5fR483w

- Or her Facebook page
- https://www.facebook.com/NatashaMurray3004 or

- Twitter https://twitter.com/NatashaM_Author

- Instagram @authornatashamurray3004

- Goodreads
  https://www.goodreads.com/book/show/55983155

- TikTok @authornatashamurray16

Printed in Great Britain
by Amazon